Blue Note

This book is a work of fiction. Names, characters, places and incidents are products of the author's imagination or are used fictitiously. Any resemblance to actual events or locales or persons, living or dead, is entirely coincidental.

ISBN-13:9780692105078

Edited by Junior

Technical support by Randi

Cover design by jack and Randi

Blue Note

I ran as fast as my idiot cowboy boots would allow. As I turned the corner, Ivy passed me by.

"Can you see him?" I hollered at his back.

"No Jack, I'm just running in this direction for the hell of it."

"Smart-ass!" I wheezed.

"Yes, I can see him. Shut up and run!"

Felt to me like we'd run a couple of miles, it had only been a few blocks. *I can't take another step, I gotta quit smoking.* I stopped and put my hands on my knees and gasped for air. Ivy was a good fifty yards ahead of me now and getting smaller by the second. He turned down the alley that runs parallel to Broadway in our little coastal town of Blue Note. I stood and took one full breath before I felt the tingle. The terror that surrounded me was immediate, panic wasting no time as it bullied its way deep into my soul. I had to try and stop the expletives before they flew from my mouth. I knew it was hopeless.

"Nickel, dime, quarter, nickel, dime, quarter, nickel, dime, quarter! ^&**%%^**^&)()))$#@#@!"

I slapped myself so hard the smack echoed off the windows next to me. I thrust both hands over my mouth with vice-grip intensity; it did no good as the obscenities railed through my fingers. My right foot began stomping before I threw the first punch. Right, right, right, left, left, left. I was in the mix now and my head began to violently tick up and down at jackhammer speed. The spots before my eyes ignited in Fourth of July fashion; I couldn't blink them away. Exhausted but still thrashing about, I collapsed to my knees. I shuddered, twitched, and convulsed before I finally slumped onto my right side and drooled.

When I woke, I counted to ten as I slowed my breathing down to a crawl. I looked around me. *Ok, why am I out here in the street? I was chasing Ivy, but when was that and where'd he go?*

I stood up and, bit by bit, ambled from the middle of the street to the sidewalk. I went down the alley, all was pitch black. I kept going a block and a half before I heard the first faint guttural scream. No, it wasn't a scream, it was more like soprano gargling. I continued towards the sound as my eyes reluctantly adjusted to the midnight hour. I saw a shadowy figure bent over by a dumpster

1

about thirty yards further up the alley. I stopped. *I don't have my gun.*

"Jack, where have you been?"

I recognized the voice long before I saw Ivy looking up at me. I said nothing as he turned his head away. I was now close enough to sense the terror and see the wriggling legs and stocking feet of the person Ivy held in his arms. I peered over Ivy's shoulder and then involuntarily backed up a step. The young man's frantic eyes looked up at me as his mouth flew open and formed a perfect O, followed by a surge of blood. The young man flailed his fists at Ivy as he retched from side to side. Panic was the last thing I saw in the poor boy's eyes when he leaped to his feet. Hell bent, he lunged forward for all of five steps when his arms reached out and valiantly grasped at the nothingness in front of him. It appeared to me as if he was trying to embrace someone. He wailed the only word I was able to understand just before he crashed and burned.

"What did he say?" Ivy asked.

"Pretty sure he said Mommy."

Ivy turned the boy over; scraps of ribbon and yarn clung to the blood on his face. "He thought he'd be safe behind the dumpster, someone was waiting for him. He ran straight into a trap," Ivy exclaimed.

"Jesus Ivy, what is that?"

"Not sure, but it looks like a letter opener or maybe a fancy butter knife."

The butt end of the presumed murder weapon stuck out the front of his neck, right about where his Adam's apple should have been. Ivy reached out to inspect the handle. I grabbed his arm.

"Don't touch it!"

"I wasn't going to touch it; I just want to get a better look. There's a modish R on the end of it."

"Yeah well, leave it alone. Ivy, what is that in his hand?"

The young boy had something tightly held in his clinched fist. Ivy turned the boy's hand over a bit before he bent down and put his eyes right next to the object. Ivy sat back and reached in the front pocket of his slacks and pulled out a silver pocket knife. He opened up one of the blades before he bent down and pushed the point of the blade into the cavity formed by the young mans fist. I started to tell him to stop when I heard the click. A stream of light leaped forth between the boy's right thumb and index finger. Ivy gently held the boys sleeve as he turned the light up illuminating my face. Ivy slowly let the boy's hand down. He stood and flicked a dead spider off my shirt before he reached into a back pocket and took out his handkerchief. He winced as he wiped away the spittle and froth that clung to the corners of my mouth.

"You had another episode, didn't you?"

I didn't answer him, there was no point.

"Jack, where's your hat?"

I reached up and set my hand on my head. Don't know why people do that.

"It was going to fly off so I took it off."

"I understand that, but, where is it?"

I started to answer him when a light from an upstairs window came on. I backed into the shadows and watched as the window flew open.

"What's going on down there!" a silhouette yelled. "I called the police on you hoodlums."

"Jack, I'll stay here. You'd better go get your hat. Won't look good if the police search around and find your hat near the scene of the crime."

I hesitated.

"Go on, please Jack. Just go!" Ivy ordered.

I did my best to retrace the same path I had run earlier. I walked halfway back to the tavern and there atop a parking meter sat my black Stetson hat. I secured it on my head and tipped the brim down in the front before I peered up at the Redwood Tavern Marquee. The sax squealed in the middle of the song, "Running Bear". Made me think about running, but I knew I had to go back and help Ivy. I heard a lone siren as it bounced off the walls and then trailed into the night. I stood stone still in the shadows next to the front door of Fullers' Hardware store. Another siren and then another. *You can't leave Ivy there all by his lonesome, but I'll probably just get in the way.*

I took the long way around the block into the alley. I sat in the dark behind a dumpster and listened to Ivy as he tried to explain to the hulking policeman what had happened.

"Sergeant, I've already told you twice."

"Ivy, sometimes I'm slow to understand, so tell me again."

"Ok, but this is the last time. Jack and I were standing in the parking lot having a smoke when this kid runs by on the other side of the street."

"I thought you said you didn't smoke? Ivy you're getting your stories mixed up again."

"I don't smoke, but the guys in the band do," Ivy insisted.

"Where's the rest of the guys. Don't tell me they didn't care," the sergeant barked.

"I already told you, Mr. Hurtwood came out and yelled at them. He said they were taking too long on their break. They filed back in the tavern and then the kid runs by," Ivy said as the sergeant reached up and put his left hand on his unshaven chin and his right on the back of his head and wrenched. Even from where I was I heard the bones in his neck crack. Sergeant Ronald Klavinski has never been known for his subtleties.

I peered around the dumpster at the sergeant. He started to ask Ivy another question when one of his men shined the penlight in his face. The sergeant put his arms up in front of his eyes and then wiggled his hands. He looked just like a grimacing bridge troll before he yelled, "Get that damn light out of my face! Ok Ivy, keep going," Sergeant Klavinski urged.

"Well, I take off running after the kid but he was too fast for me."

"Why was the kid running? Was he afraid of his own shadow?"

"I told you there was a guy wearing a black hooded sweatshirt running after the kid. I chased both of them for maybe two blocks and then the guy wearing the hoodie looks back at me and turns away from the kid. I chased the hoodie for a bit before I headed back for the kid. Well, then I hear someone screaming in the alley. When I got to the kid, he was slumped over against the back of the hobby shop. As I walked up, he collapsed to the ground and clutched at his throat. I held the kid and over and over, asked him who did it, but he just couldn't answer me. Then he leaped to his feet and gave it the full Monty, made it all of maybe six wholesale steps before collapsing. That's when he yelled Mommy."

Caught up in emotion Ivy's voice trembled as he spoke to Sergeant Klavinski. I suppose holding a young man as he dies would do that to a person.

The sergeant asked, "What does full Monty mean?" Ivy frowned. "Never mind, did he have that penlight in his hand when you were chasing him?"

"I don't believe so. My guess is he grabbed it away from the person that attacked him."

"Maybe he grabbed the penlight from you?" Sergeant Klavinski asserted.

"No sergeant, he did not grab it from me, but I'd say there is a better than average chance you will find fingerprints on the light, and I guarantee you, they won't be mine," Ivy said with resolve.

The sergeant backed away at that point. Ivy's suggestion caused a logical pause in the conversation.

"Ivy, did you happen to notice what time it was when the kid did the Monty thing?"

"Yes, it was straight-up midnight."

"Officer Daily, make sure you put gloves on before you touch that penlight. The fingerprints on it could lead us to the murderer."

"Gotcha sergeant," Officer Daily said as he pried the boy's hand open and removed the penlight. "Hey Kennedy, come over here, shine your flashlight on this," Officer Daily said as he held up the penlight for his fellow officer.

The only thing I could see on the policemen was their tan shoulder straps. I watched two shoulder straps walk over and when the light came on, the officer with the flashlight said, "Fuller Hardware, I'll bet every guy in town has one of these. This will lead us to everybody and to nobody."

"Careful, there might be fingerprints on the damn penlight. Bag it!" Sergeant Klavinski ordered in an elevated weary voice.

"Sergeant, what about this thing stuck in his throat?" Daily asked.

"Don't touch it. From here on out everything will be handled by our detective. Speaking of which, the bloodhound will be here as soon as she gets her sweet ass out of bed."

"Did someone call my name?" flew from the shadows.

Sergeant Klavinski jerked his head around before mumbling, "Oh, hello detective."

I recognized Detective Knox's voice. She eased past Klavinski and stood frozen over the boy. She had her own penlight piercing down on him. A harlequin's mask of blood and debris covered the boy's face. She knelt and gently rolled him from one side to the other as she searched his pockets.

"He has no ID, any of you recognize him?" Detective Knox asked.

All three policemen peered down at the boy. In unison they shook their heads no.

"He looks familiar, but with all that shit stuck to his face I just don't know," Officer Kennedy said.

"Ivy, how'd that cut-up yarn and ribbon get on his face?" Detective Knox asked.

"My guess is it happened during the initial struggle. I think you'll find a lot of debris around the dumpster; remember that is Robson's Hobby Shop," Ivy said as he pointed at the block letters painted on the back of the store.

Detective Knox looked over at the dumpster where I was hiding. "*I gotta get outta here,*" I said to myself.

Brooding, she stood erect like a palace guard, threw her shoulders back and stuck out her chest. Her shoulders weren't that impressive. She slowly turned and glared at the police officers.

"If I hear about any of this information being leaked, as sure as hell is hot I'll find out which one of you did the leaking," the detective warned as the ambulance pulled into the alley.

The bearded driver exited the ambulance, cleared his throat, and spit then dragged the back of his hand across his mouth. He was wiping his hand on his pant leg when Detective Knox shadowed him like a cheap suit.

"What?" the driver said as he backed up.

"Christ, the county must really be hard up. Bag the kid and I mean now!" she ordered.

Ivy tried to slink away.

"Not so fast Ivy," Detective Knox said as she wiggled her index finger at him.

Ivy continued to back away.

"Ivy, I take it you witnessed some or all of what took place this evening."

Ivy nodded his head just a little. She took a small notebook out of an inside pocket of her jacket and licked the lead on the pencil, twice.

"From the beginning, tell me everything that happened here tonight."

Ivy's shoulders slumped lower as he started all over again.

2

Ten minutes later the boy was in the bag and on his way to the morgue. I watched as Detective Knox took notes. She stopped now and then and told Ivy to back up and repeat what he'd just told her. When he was done with the detailed explanation, she ordered, "Don't you dare move; I'll be back in a few."

She walked the same path Ivy and the kid had run. After her second trip, she told Klavinski that he and his guys could go but Ivy had to stay put. I watched Ivy's shoulders slump again.

"Ivy, now that we're all alone. You and Jack are always thick as thieves, so where is he?"

"I don't know, really I don't," Ivy said in his, you can trust me, voice.

"Ivy, you said all the guys in the band went back inside the tavern. I just looked in the Redwood and Jack isn't there. Where is he?"

Ivy didn't say a word.

"Where's Jack!" Detective Knox shouted.

"Detective, I really don't know. But yes, Jack did follow me, he just couldn't keep up. My guess is he went back home or something along those lines. Honest, I really don't know where he is."

By the time Ivy uttered the last few syllables, I had already backed out of the alley and was hiding behind a Rambler parked across the street from the alley. I took my hat off and set it on the front tire. It's a good thing I moved because Detective Knox wasn't done, not by a long shot. She walked back and circled the dumpster twice before heading straight for me. I slid under the car; my nose tight against the dangling tail-pipe. She was just whispering distance from me when she stopped and looked around. I kept one eye on her as she strolled back to where Ivy sat. I guess he didn't see the need in standing any longer.

Detective Knox started to say something to him when the light from the window above came on again. Even from a distance I could see that the detective was just as tall and lean as the last time I'd had the pleasure. I've heard her compared to a demon by some and a goddess by others. If she weren't so damn hard-headed, I think I could learn to like her. Suffice it to say, we've had a disagreeable past.

"I've called the police on you hoodlums. They'll be here any minute now!"

"I am the police," Detective Knox yelled up at the silhouette that had morphed into an old woman.

"Why, what in the world would a woman be doing on the police force? If I was you I'd get out of here before the real police show up."

"Come on Ivy, let's get out of here before the real police show up," the detective said.

Ivy slowly got to his feet and the two of them walked out of my eyesight. I stayed put. Ten minutes later I saw Ivy creeping around. He was bent over at the waist and whispering for me to come out.

"Jack, it's all clear. It's safe now. Come out! Jack, I know you're here somewhere."

"Over here," I said in a hoarse whisper.

Ivy walked up to me and before he could say another word, I asked if he'd been in the bar.

"Yes, I went in to explain to Whitey what happened. He said you're fired, Stuttering John is going to take your place in the band."

"Ah hell, that isn't fair. Geez, what was I supposed to do?"

"Wait, after I explained everything that had happened, I think he changed his mind. Whitey said for you to be sure and go to rehearsal Tuesday night at six."

"Oh man, I can't thank you enough. Ivy is the coast clear now?"

"Yes, you can go on home now. Take your hat that you hid in plain sight." I grabbed my hat off the wheel and put it on. "I'll talk at you later," he said and then hesitated. "If I were you, I'd stay clear of Detective Knox. She has a bone to pick with you."

"So I heard. Ok, guess I'll see you Tuesday, say five thirty," I said hoping Ivy would say yes.

"I'll be working at the university, but I'll probably make it here by five or so. Jack, how are you fixed for cash?"

"You need some money?" I asked.

"Funny. No Jack, I wasn't talking about me."

"Oh, well I've got a couple dollars, but thanks for asking."

"Jack, I asked because I know you're not taking your Tetra. Your illness is serious and very real. Please Jack, you have to take your medicine. I can loan you enough to refill your prescription," he said as he casually stared at me with those dark eyes that belie his true self. Dr. Ivy Fin is fair haired and moves about and speaks like the scholar that he is, but those damn eyes of his just don't fit.

"I still have some," I said as I gazed at the ground in front of me. I was searching for a way around the subject. There was no way, not with Ivy staring at me. "Ivy, I hate the medicine. It makes me so sad inside, like I want to jump off a cliff."

"Jack! Don't you ever mention jumping off a cliff again, you hear me!"

"Sorry, I didn't mean that. I just, ah screw it. I don't like being depressed, after I take the medicine, people look at me like I'm some kind of slow talking, dimwitted, moron, I hate it."

"Jack, are you trying to tell me that there are intelligent morons?"

"What are you talking about?"

"I'm talking about your pension for and need to exaggerate all the time. Stop it! I never know when you're being serious."

"Yeah, ok I'll stop it," I said as I stared at the ground again.

"I'm sorry to be the mean nurse, but you have to take your meds," Ivy demanded as I peeked at him from the ground in front of me. "Jack, we can talk about this on Tuesday. I'll see you then."

Blue Note

I thanked him and patted him on the shoulder before he strode away. I walked back to the Redwood all hurt and in an untoward mood; that's a term Ivy frequently uses. I slunk through the parking lot to the back of the building and crept up the stairs to my apartment. I turned on the light in my little kitchen and looked into a pair of beautiful blue eyes.

Blue eyes said, "Hi Jackie, I heard you were part of a murder tonight. Did you do the murderin'?"

"No Sugar, I just happened to be in the right place at the wrong time is all."

"I didn't think so. I saved a beer for you. You want a beer? It's in the fridge."

"No Sugar, I just want to go to bed. I'm very tired."

"Ok, hope you don't mind, but I changed the bedding for you. The sheets were pretty rank. Ok, if I stay?" she said in that sweet tone at which she alone is so skilled.

"Of course you can. Did you bring your toothbrush?"

"Yep, got it right here in my back pocket," she said as she turned to show me.

I like her pockets.

3

I opened my eyes and reached beside me for Sugar, she wasn't there. I sat up in bed as the pain shot from my eyeballs to my toes. I turned and softly set my bare feet on the frosty floor. The day after one of my episodes is always the same. Pain in places I didn't know existed. I guess it's from the violent moves I make. I heard someone tapping on the little window over my kitchen sink. I moaned and groaned all at the same time as I walked out to see who it was.

"Hi Cat, how you been?"

He didn't answer me. I eased over to the door and opened it enough so he could mosey over to my kitchen sink. Before I could get the door shut he was up and yowling at me for something to eat. He's an alley cat that has seen better days. I say that every time I see him, thinking it might be the last but he just keeps coming back. I opened the fridge believing I had nothing but the one beer Sugar had brought over the night before. I was wrong.

There wasn't much, but there was a lot more than there had been. I took a quart of milk out and peeled off the tinfoil cap. That must be music to the cat's ears, because he always swooshes against my arm a couple times before I bend down and let him head-butt me. I've heard lots of cats purr before, but this guy's purr sounds like a rollercoaster coming off its tracks. I reached in the sink and took out a bowl that Sugar washed for me. I had to hold the cat back with one hand while I tried to pour with the other. He wiggled his broken tail as he lapped at the milk. Then he sat tall and poised like some cultured, high-society feline before going to work. I like him.

I sat at my little square kitchen table and had a look at the calendar I leave for quick reference. It serves as a scheduling reminder, a doodle-pad, and a phone book. I glance at Sunday, the 6th of September. Sugar left me one of her sweet messages.

"Li'l John came by erly to help me with my rouns. I lef sum milk, sum tuna, a apple, a banana, and a fresh bagle from Hobson's.

Luv u, Sugar."

Didn't feel like having any fruit, so I opened the can of tuna and spread some over half the bagel. There was enough tuna for two, so I shared with Cat. After we ate, Cat curled up on my bed and licked his lips while he slept. I eased into my tiny bathroom, opened the medicine cabinet, and stared at my bottle of pills. I took two of them out and stuck 'em in my mouth and swallowed. I remembered to drink a glass of water. I knew that regardless of how hard I tried not to, I was destined for zombieville. I think the fear of going there is worse than actually being there.

I wandered out and sat on my steps, they face dead east. I let the sun beat down on my face. I think I stayed out there for an hour or so, but it could have been ten minutes, I'm just not sure. I don't remember getting back into bed so when I woke up and saw Detective Knox staring at me, I was a bit startled. She was sitting at the foot of my bed petting Cat.

"Jack, you really should lock your door. This guy may look mean, but he's really just a pussy-cat."

I gazed at her while I yelled at myself from the inside out. *Say something!*

"Sugar says he's a brown and tan tabby but being that I'm color blind I know for a fact that he's black and gray." *Why'd I say that?*

Detective Knox smiled at me.

"Ok, whatever you say. Listen Jack, I can come back another time, you don't look so great."

I tried to wipe the idiot off of my face, but it was no use. She saw right through me. So I trudged forward.

"How, how can I help you?" I slurred.

"Jack, are you on some kind of medication?"

I was gonna try and answer her, but decided to give up. I just pointed at the bathroom. She slowly stood up, turned her back to me and walked in the bathroom. Even in my stupor from where I was, she sure did look good. She walked out with the bottle in her hand.

"Jack, did you write this on the label?" she didn't give me time to answer. "Somebody printed Vertigo in big block letters. Doesn't look to me like something from a pharmacist."

"No, I, I didn't."

I wrote Vertigo on the bottle to cover up the name of the prescription and the truth. I mean I had only just been diagnosed a few short months before. Maybe the quack was wrong, maybe… She took the bottle back in the bathroom and came out and sat by Cat again.

"Jack, it says on the label, take one pill after breakfast. Did you take a pill this morning?"

"I took a pill," came out in slow motion as I set my feet on the floor.

"Jack, where do you think you're going?" she asked.

"Back out on the steps. That's where I was when you came in, right?"

"No Jack, you were here in bed asleep when I got here."

"You sure?" I muttered.

"Yes Jack, I'm positive. Listen Jack, I don't think you should go out there right now. It's hotter than the Devil's breath."

I didn't hear a word she said or did I? She pushed me back onto the bed. "Are we gonna play a little hanky-panky?" I babbled.

"You'd like that, wouldn't ya," she said as she stood up over me.

I couldn't say what was on my mind, wasn't because I was afraid of being vulgar or forward, I just couldn't get the words to come out. She was starting to wiggle around. I must have asked her two or three times to hold still, but she just wouldn't listen to me. I felt like a mouse looking up at a big Hawk. I was getting dizzy, so I made up my mind I was going to shut one eye. She kept staring at me.

"What?" I slurred.

"Jack, I'll come back later. We can talk then. I need to find out what you know about the boy that was murdered last night. I'd tell you not to leave town, but you're not going anywhere. Jack, if you can hear me go back to sleep," was the last thing she said. At least it's the last thing I heard.

4

I woke up that evening at about six o'clock; the bar was busy for a Sunday. Felt like my mouth was full of cotton. I walked over to the fridge and took out the bottle of Lucky Lager Sugar had left for me. I got lucky, it was a 32 ouncer. I sat at my table and drank straight from the bottle as I studied the only picture in my apartment. It's an oil painting of John Wayne and Maureen O'Hara done on velvet. Sugar gave it to me. The frame's a little beat up, but I like it. For whatever reason I wasn't feeling the overload of angst and ire Ivy is always talking about. As a matter of fact I felt very calm; maybe it was the bottle in my hand.

I went back in my bedroom and grabbed my old huaraches from under my bed. I retrieved the beer and climbed the stairs up to the rooftop, so I could watch the sunset. There's a long couch on the roof inside of what I'd call a duck-blind. In my opinion, other than standing on the cliffs over the inlet our town is named after, there is no finer ocean view.

I took a big swig and watched a seagull race west right over my head. He flew straight into the ball of fire, which made me think of the poor kid that flew too close to the sun. Then I watched a mass of thin lazy clouds blow over the horizon. I don't really know what the colors are that I look at, but it doesn't matter, they're still bitchen to me. I stood up and walked to the west edge of the roof, so I could listen for the Blue Note, I couldn't hear it. I leaned way over the edge of the roof and looked down at the sidewalk. There were several cracks in the concrete next to the front door of the bar. *I wonder if those cracks were made by someone that leaned over the roof too far. Nah, that'd hurt like the dickens, besides, why would anyone do such a stupid thing?* Looking down made me dizzy, so I backed all the way to the couch and sat down.

For some odd reason the beer didn't last very long. I thought about going downstairs and having a beer but decided not to. Bar beer is too expensive for someone in my present financial state. The avenues going north and south in the town of Blue Note are numbers; that is except for Broadway. All the streets heading east to west are words in alphabetical order from Alpine to Yodel; I guess the town wasn't big enough for a Z word. I traipsed up to the 7-Eleven on Broadway and Key Street and paid a whole $1.35 for a six-pack of Olympia bottles, a bit steep, but to me there is no finer beer. As I neared the Redwood, I realized how incredibly hot the air around me was. When I walked into the parking lot, I saw a marked car that made me hotter still. I began feeling some of the angst and ire I fear so much.

Shit, this is going to ruin my evening.

I thought about turning around and walking to the park, but I didn't for fear that someone might think I'm a hobo. I decided to sneak by the stairs that lead to my apartment and go in the back door of the tavern and up to the roof. Once on the roof I looked around. I smiled, the coast was clear. I walked around the duck-blind and nearly sat on Detective Knox. She was cleverer than I thought.

"Hello Jack, did I surprise you?"

"No, not at all," I lied as I looked at the bag containing the beer. I said the first thing that popped into my head. "You want a beer?"

"Well, it is my day off. Sure, why not?"

I set the bag down and pulled out two beers. I keep a church-key on a shoestring nailed to the duck blind. "You want me to go get you a glass?"

"No thanks, I'm thirsty and I don't want to wait," she said just before she took a long pull from the bottle. "Ahh, that sure is good. Jack, I like your sandals, but those fuchsia Capri's have gotta go."

Jack Hawkins

I looked down. "They're not Capri's, they're beach-combers. And they're nice on a night like this. It's too hot for Levi's."

She couldn't hold back the smile followed by a warm giggle. "I was just razzing you, are you always so defensive?"

I sat down and cranked the top off my beer.   "No, sorry, didn't mean to sound so pitiful. The truth is, at the moment they're the only clean pants I've got," I said as I gazed at her profile. She sure was a beautiful woman. She knew I was staring at her, I think she liked the attention.

She had her auburn hair cut in a professional pixie, at least that's the way I'd describe it. She wore only enough makeup to flatter her brown eyes and her more than ample lips. She had a square jaw-line that accented her sculpted face. I'd say we're about the same age, but I'd never tell her that.

"Jack, I talked to Whitey last night, and he says you didn't come back after the midnight break. So where were you? And don't tell me you were up here."

"I followed Ivy for as long as I could, but he left me in the dust. I need to quit smoking, have you got a cigarette?"

She turned away from me and opened one of those cigarette cases women carry. You know the kind that look like a coin purse with squiggly metal bar snaps at the top. She handed me one of those long cigarettes I hate. I was desperate, so I kept my big mouth shut. Her blue jeans were so tight she had to lean back to get her fingers in her front pocket. She pulled out a red Zippo, and immediately after she lit my cigarette, she said, "Ok Jack, playtime is over. Where were you last night?"

"I just told you, I tried to follow Ivy, but I couldn't keep up."

"Then where'd you go?"

I looked at her just before I thought I felt one of the tingles. The look on my face must have been a good one because she reached out and held my hand in hers. She asked if I was ok. I set the beer down and closed my eyes. Didn't start the coin thing, just tried to relax and slow my breathing down. She held on to me with both hands. Her hands sure were warm.

I took about five slow deep breaths before the coast was clear. Detective Knox was still holding on to me when I opened my eyes and gave her a small smile. I was ok and she must have felt it because she let go of me.

"I'm sorry detective, but I followed Ivy all the way to where he ran into the alley. I stopped so I could catch my breath when, when." I just couldn't finish the sentence.

"Jack, did something happen along the way?"

"Yes, I... I had one of my episodes. I got very dizzy. When I woke up I was in the middle of the street. And then I heard the sirens. I couldn't just leave Ivy there all alone, so I stayed and hid in the shadows."

"Before you hid, did you see the boy?"

"Yes, I saw him jump up and try to run. And I heard him call out for his mother. Miss Knox, don't tell anyone about my episodes, please?"

"Jack, I don't like Miss, it sounds so juvenile. My name is Jolene, but I prefer Jo. Remember, I said this was my day off. Well, I think it'd be nice on my day off if you used my first name, ok?"

"You know something, I like the name Jo. I like it because it fits you so well. Ok, Jo it is."

She was getting better looking by the second.

"Jack, is that everything?" she asked as she bore a hole thru me searching for the truth.

"No, I guess not. I was behind the dumpster, but I moved and hid behind a car. Then you came back from the bar. That's all I know, really."

"I knew it! If I'd kept going, I would have found you. Shoot, that would have been fun."

"Fun for who... m, I think that's when you're supposed to say whom."

"You're a funny guy, you know that."

"So I've heard. Jo, can I ask you a question?"

"Sure, shoot."

"First of all, I noticed the kid's shoes weren't on his feet. How do you think that happened?"

"That's a strange question, but a good one. I don't know how that happens, but it's very common to find a dead or dying person with their shoes off. I think the fright or desperation of the moment is so overwhelming they run right out of their shoes. Go to the library and look at pictures from the Civil War or any other war for that matter. It's amazing how many of the young men lying dead out on the battlefield are missing a boot and sometimes both boots.

"I didn't know that, sounds like one of those strange but true unexplained phenomenon. Don't go to the library that often, but next time I do, I'm going to check," I said as I wondered how much she would actually tell me. "Ok, that answers one question, next question. Who is the boy?"

"Some of the information is private, but I can tell you his name is Timmy Allen. He does odd jobs for Senator Rose during the day and he works at the bowling alley at night. He was seen arguing with a bearded man an hour or so before he got off work. We have no idea who the bearded man is."

"Say, was the bearded guy wearing a black hooded sweatshirt?"

"No, not when he was arguing with Timmy."

"Ok, can you tell me what was stuck in Timmy's throat?"

"I can't divulge that information right now."

"I can't divulge that information right now," I mimicked. "Well, you sure as hell divulged some of the information, because when I got home, someone asked me if I was part of the murder that took place. How did that information get leaked?" I made a point of narrowing my eyes at her when I said it. I didn't really care, but by her reaction she sure did.

She shouted, "Who told you that!"

"I can't divulge that information right now," I said like the smartass I harbor. I was hoping she'd drop the subject.

She was swearing something fierce under her breath. I had struck a nerve. "I'm going to start up the fires of hell," she said to the wind before she did all she could to calm herself.

"You have any more questions?" she hissed.

"As a matter of fact, yes I do. How about the senator, have you talked to him?"

"No! His butler or aide, whatever the hell he is told me Senator Rose had an emergency meeting in Sacramento. A little too convenient if you ask me," she said as I nodded yes in agreement. She stopped talking for a moment. "Jack, now that we're being so up-front with each other, there's something I need to ask you. Ok, if I ask you a personal question?"

"I suppose, is this off the record?"

"Yes Jack, this is just between the two of us. Why was your license taken away?"

"It wasn't, I can still drive legally."

"Jack, not that license."

"Oh, my P.I. license, I couldn't come up with the renewal money is all; and maybe a couple other minor infractions."

"How minor?" she asked as she shifted on the couch, tilted her head to the side and studied me.

"Some security guard over in Creston has claimed that I broke into one of the ranches there. Once I get that cleared up, the state is going to give my license back."

"Whose ranch was it?"

"That's private, and at the present time I can't divulge that information. Ok, so please don't ask, ok?"

"Touché, I won't ask right now, but that doesn't mean I won't ask you some other time," she said as she looked at her empty beer bottle. "Jack, I'd better get going. Thanks for the beer." She stood up real erect before she tilted her head sideways at me. An uncomfortable moment or two passed.

"Jack, does the State of California know about your illness?"

"No, why?"

"Where'd you get the medicine?"

"A doctor in Montana, why?"

"Well... never mind," she said as she walked over to the stairs. She took a step down and stopped. "Oh, something I forgot to tell you. When I first got here, there was a young girl sitting in your apartment. Jack, can you spell statutory?" she said with what I would call a shit-eating grin.

"She's older than she looks," I declared in a desperate voice. "I've seen her I.D."

"I'll bet you have, yes, I'll just bet you have. Jack, be careful and take care of yourself. Um, maybe you should see a doctor, and I don't mean Ivy Fin, he's the wrong kind of doctor.

"What kind of doctor are you talking about, a witch-doctor?"

Jack Hawkins

She didn't answer me; she just turned and swooshed down the stairs.

5

I went down and peeked in my door at Sugar, she was busy sweeping the floor. "Hi Sugar, you know you don't have to do that," I said as she bent over and swept about a week's worth of dirt and sand into the dust pan. She heard me but didn't say a word.

"You want to come up and sit with me. I know you don't like beer; I could run up to the corner and get you some wine. That sound good to you?"

"Jack, who was that pretty lady, is she your girlfriend?" Sugar asked with the first cheerless look I'd ever seen on her face.

"Sugar first off, she is most definitely not my girlfriend, you are," I said as the wonderful smile she is so famous for returned. "That was Detective Knox and she asked me a whole lot of questions about the young man that was murdered. Which reminds me, how did you know about the murder?"

"Li'l John told me. He hears lots of things, says he has connections, whatever that means."

"Li'l John hah, I gotta meet this guy. Ok, do you want me to go to the store for you?"

"No, I brought some Bali Hai. Sometimes I have it for dinner."

"What? Sugar, you say the darndest things. Why would you say something like that?"

"It says on the label that it's good enough to eat."

"Sugar, that's just a marketing tool, geez. Ok, enough of that. Grab your dinner and come on up with me," I said as she took

23

the bottle out of the fridge. Then she ran over to her bag of tricks, as I call it. She pulled out a small transistor radio.

"I don't know where you got that, but I think some music would be great."

She followed me up and set the bottle down in front of me. "Jack, since I can't have the wine for dinner, ok if I go get something to eat?"

"Yeah, ok, but where are you going?"

"Just going down to get the ham sandwich I put in your fridge. Are you hungry?"

"Well, now that you mentioned it, yes I'm starving."

She brought the sandwich up, in halves.

"Sugar what would I do without you. You think of everything. You know what?" She shook her head no. "I love you more than all the grains of sand on every beach in the world, and that's a lot."

"Jack, I love it when you tell me things like that. Tell me another, please."

"Sugar, I love you more than all the laughter and all the smiles on every happy face in the whole wide world, and that's a lot."

She smiled to beat the band as she handed me my half of the sandwich and, of course, a beer. We ate and drank in absolute peace. We both swayed as the Drifters song, "Up on the Roof" played. After we ate, Sugar went down and took a quick shower. Don't remember when I've had a nicer night.

Blue Note

6

Sunday was gone, and Monday meant it was time for me to get a job. Of course when I woke, Sugar was already up and out the door. She left a note for me on the calendar.

"Jack, dont wery bout a thing, I kin take care a u.

Luv u, Sugar"

Geez, she's such a wonderful creature, I sure am lucky, I said to myself. Maybe ten seconds later I heard someone tap on my kitchen window. I turned to smile at the cat; it was my hawk-faced landlord, Mr. Hurtwood. He came around to the kitchen door and let himself in. He's one of those real tall guys that bend over so they can stare you right in the face while they're talking.

"Jack, you're a week late paying your rent. Normally I could ask Whitey to give me your pay, but since you got fired, I can't even do that," he said as he pointed a purple veined finger at me.

"I'll have the money by the end of the day."

"You better, I have several people interested in your apartment. Have the money by tonight, or I'm going to have to ask you to move out. I'll give you 'til six o'clock. Here, sign this," he ordered as he handed me an eviction notice. I stared in disbelief.

"It's legal," he said as he handed me a pen.

I read it; he'd already included an additional $8.75 as a late fee. The total was $133.75. *How am I going to come up with that much money?*

"Jack, just sign it."

I signed it. He folded it up right in front of me, didn't even say goodbye. I got dressed; had to wear my dirty Levis. I ran west on Friendly Street thru the park. When I reached the man-made tunnel, I skipped my way down the stairs 'til I was inside the tourist section of the Blue Note cave and tore north along the cliffs for at least five hundred yards before I entered what locals call the 'hobo cave'. I flew into the darkness without warning the men sitting around the campfire. A nightmare full of sallow, ravenous, unshaven faces with blood in their eyes jumped up. I stopped dead in my tracks.

"I'm sorry; I didn't mean to scare you guys. I'm looking for Sugar and Li'l John. Do any of you know where they are, please?" I said as the closest guy to me stepped forward.

"Who the fuck're you, I oughta kick your ass just for being a jerk. Believe it or not we got rules in this here little shanty town. And rule number one is, no jerks get to run in unannounced and spook my ass, especially jerks I don't know," he said as he and his thin-lipped hobo buddies surrounded me.

"*I can handle this guy, but not all of them. Shit, I don't have my gun with me,*" I said to myself.

"Tuck, back off and let the guy explain. We may be many things, but deaf ain't one of 'em," a little man of maybe fifty wearing a tattered red plaid Pendleton jacket said as he walked up to me.

"Thanks," I said in relief.

"Don't thank me yet. There's still plenty of time and maybe good reason for us to kick your ass up around your shoulders. Who did y'all say you was lookin' fer?"

"I'm looking for Sugar and Li'l John. You all must know them," I said to the little man.

He put both hands on his shiny bald pate and rubbed back and forth several times before he stuck his right hand out. I thought he wanted to shake my hand, but he said he needed to see some I.D. or I'd have to leave. I gave him my license, he looked at it and mumbled, "Jack Hawkins, 6'2", eyes're blue," as he looked me up and down. He gave back my license.

"I'm Friar Tuck and the rest of the men go by the same. We've had some guy coming by every other week lookin' fer Maid Marian, says he works fer the county. She don't wanna meet him, and we're not gonna help the guy out; if ya know what I mean. So state yer business and then maybe I'll be able ta help ya."

I thought as fast as my little brain could go, nothing came to mind. *I can't tell them I'm looking for her, so I can borrow some money. They'll laugh me right out of the cave.* I'm not an accomplished liar or a fast thinker, so I had to tell them the truth. They laughed harder than was fair, at least I thought so.

I suppose they could see or maybe feel the desperation running pell-mell thru my brain because one of the Tuck men finally said, "I believe they've gone over ta th'other camp. You know where it is?"

I started to answer him, but the frustration along with the reality seemed to all come home at the same time. My shoulders slagged and my heart raced to a new desperate beat. I turned to the guy that said they'd gone and as I asked him where the other camp was, I felt the tingle. The panic was immediate, and I guess the look on my face was too. Every Friar Tuck in the cave backed off.

"Nickel, dime, quarter, nickel, dime, quarter, nickel, dime, quarter, N(%(*)#()$(*%%W@**!!"

My right foot started to stomp as my head ticked up and down. Left, right, left, right, I punched. I guess I ordered a double, because I started all over again. As I fell to the sandy floor of the cave, the bald-headed man caught me. He laid me down and held on just tight enough so that I wouldn't hurt myself as I convulsed.

I believe I was awake, but my eyes were still closed. I heard the Blue Note playing just as sweet as if it had come straight from the Sirens of Anthemusa. Legend has it that before the tourist tunnel was dug, the air forced out of the inlet cave produced a note that was such a perfect middle C, you could tune a piano to it. After the tourist tunnel was dug the note changed from C to a horn player's dream, a laid-back B flat. Then the tourists came, and our quiet little beach town was no more. And when all was said and done, the County of San Luis Obispo left the workers high and dry, nameless, jobless, and homeless.

Some straggled back to whence they came, but most had no place to return to. Abandoned, they walked the streets, slept on park benches, or huddled in the hobo cave. That's what I call real progress.

Jack Hawkins

When I finally woke, I had a large piece of burnt driftwood stuck sideways between my clinched teeth. I did the confusion thing before the, who, what, where, when, and why started. As I spit the twig out of my mouth, I looked around me. All the guys were still hunkered down; as far from me as the cave would allow. That is, all except the bald-headed guy, he was still holding on to me.

"Dad and baby sister had the 'Grandees' too. I used ta find whatever I could ta jab in their mouths ta keep 'em from swallowin' their tongues. Actually, old Doc Henderson says ya cain't really swallow yer tongue, but ya can choke on it, how ya feelin'?"

"Like an idiot," I slurred as Mr. Tuck helped me sit up.

"I heard tell there's medicine y'all can take ta keep the shudders from startin' up. I guess you ain't got none," he said as I said, "*Doh!*" to myself.

Took a minute or so before I got a fix on why I was in the hobo cave. I looked at Friar Tuck as he called out to Larry. A young man with lost eyes and a scruffy beard slunk up from the shadows and stood stoop shouldered waiting for a cause.

"Yeah," Larry answered.

"Larry, take this gentleman to th'other camp. Make sure he don't fall down or nothin'. If he does, hold him still, but do not put yer hand near his mouth. He just might bite, and I don't believe you want what he's got. Ok get," Mr. Tuck ordered.

I followed Larry out of the hobo cave back to the man-made tunnel and up the stairs. When we were back up on top of the cliffs I told Larry we were going to take a detour before we went to the other camp. He balked something fierce, so I promised him a cold beer. Then it was he following me. We got to the steps leading up to my apartment and I told Larry to stay put. I leaped up the stairs thru the kitchen door and into my bathroom. I shoved one of my pills in my mouth and swallowed. I ran out to the fridge and grabbed the one bottle of Olympia I had left from the night before. I closed the door and stared at Cat as he walked along my kitchen counter. He purred so loud I could not deny him. I threw a saucer on the counter and filled it with milk. "See ya Cat."

Blue Note

I raced down to Larry and after I handed him the beer, I asked if I could have a drink. He gave me the strangest damn look before he finally spoke.

"I've had fellers ask me for a sip and they ended up guzzling down the whole damn bottle. Now are you gonna let me have this here beer or not?" he said as he wrapped his hands tight around the bottle.

"You must be Larry Tuck, is that right?" I said. Guess he didn't see the humor. "Look Larry, I just took a pill with no water. I need to wash it down. Tell you what, you hold the bottle and pour however much you think you want to in my mouth. Ok?" I asked in good faith.

He cranked the top off with a knife and held the open end over my mouth. I tilted my head back and patiently waited for him to pour. He let about a thimble-full fall into my mouth. I gave him my very best version of incredulous eyes.

"Larry, you stingy mooch. You cadge my last damn beer from me and then you don't even have the decency to give me one itty-bitty drink."

"A stingy mooch, I gotta remember that one. Ok, tip your gullet back and I'll give you a bit more," he said while he laughed to himself. I was amazed he found something funny and knew how to laugh.

I tipped my head back and he poured a little in. He gave me a look that told me he was expecting a response of some kind.

"Thanks for being so generous, Larry."

He didn't acknowledge me; he just stuck the open end of the bottle between his waiting lips and gulped. About ten seconds later he wiped his mouth with his shirt sleeve and handed me the empty bottle. I set it on the steps and when I turned around, Larry had his back to me walking out of the parking lot.

"Larry, where are we going?" I asked as I ran to catch up.

"We're goin' to the canyon, where else?"

"What canyon?" I asked totally confused.

"The canyon behind Hobson's Bakery," he said with some attitude.

I thought *geez, give a guy a little beer and he's ready to rule the world.* Then I thought *there's no canyon behind the bakery. What's this guy up to?*

We walked at what anyone would call a brisk pace. Larry didn't look back to see if I was keeping up with him, he just put his head down and trudged along the way a plow-horse might. So I followed suit and matched his strides with my own. We had a long ways to go and, in my mind, a short time to get there. At some point restlessness gave way to the Tetra.

After I had crossed into the netherworld and entered zombieville, I stumbled. Not just once, but several times. Larry stopped and gave me a shake of the head and a look from the real world down into the chasm that held me captive.

"Geez Louis, tell me you ain't gonna start up with the swearin' heebie-jeebie-epo-shit again."

He stood there glaring at me waiting for an answer. I thought *say something you witless imp.*

"No Larry, I'm not," fell from my mouth at about the same speed lava flows across a flat road.

"You better not or I'm leavin' your ass right here where we stand," he said as he backed away.

"Larry, Friar Tuck was wrong 'bout that. I don't ever bite, and you can't get what I got."

He studied me for a long time.

"For some reason I believe you. You wanna sit down for a minute?"

I couldn't answer him. So he pulled me over to the curb and sat me down.

"Your name is Jack, right?" I didn't answer. "Ok well, Jack, are you aware of the nasty things you say before you start ta twitchin'?" I didn't answer. "Well, I think you oughta know that there are some folks in this world that would take exception to your vulgarities. The lady I called gramma used to say that men that make a habit of cussin' are just covering up their true selves. She said most of 'em're as evil and wicked as a snake with hands."

"A snake with hands, I gotta remember that one," I said to Larry. Don't think he understood me.

"Ok, maybe I oughta go get Li'l John. He could carry you to wherever it is you gotta go."

I heard everything he said, and although his intentions were good, the thought of sitting there on the curb bothered me.

Funny thing is, even though I was bothered, I still didn't answer him or get up.

"Then it's settled, you wait here. I'll be right back," Larry said as he started walking away.

"Larry, wait… please?" I said like a drunk.

I made a valiant attempt to stand up. He ran back and helped me. I started walking down the road in the exact same direction we had been walking and so he followed behind. The more I walked the better I began feeling. At some point I exited zombieville and reconnected with the world around me.

"Thanks for helping me. I'm better now. This happens every time I take one of my pills. There is a period of time after the onset of the drug I take that is difficult to describe. It's like I fall in a dark hole and I can't get out. I hope you will try to understand?"

"Understand? Hell, I know exactly what you mean, I've been livin' it. You go to the place where us guys in the cave are all the time. Ain't no fun a'tall is it?"

"No, it's not. Thanks for understanding."

"You have no idea how much I wish I didn't understand," he said as he passed me by.

I was beginning to like this guy. This time as I followed, I noticed the soles on both of his boots were flapping with every step he took. And his pants were worn so thin they shined. And his shirt was so small his long sleeves barely made it past his elbows. I need to remember this so the next time I get down and start feeling sorry for myself I can put things into a more proper perspective.

"Were you talkin' to me?" Larry asked.

"No, well, I guess maybe I was. Listen Larry, I noticed your boots are ready to slide off your feet. What size shoe do you wear?"

"I can fit into an 11, but I will wear anything up to a size 13 and maybe even bigger, why?"

"I have a few pairs of shoes that I don't ever wear. Would you wear a pair if I gave them to you?"

"If you're asking how I feel about receiving handouts. Well, fact is that's all I ever get, handouts that is."

"Ok well, when we get back to my apartment remind me to give you a pair."

"Can I have all the pairs you don't wear?" he asked.

I must have given him a strange look because he said, "They're not for me. I was thinking on givin' 'em to the guys at the cave. I'm not a stingy mooch all the time," he said with a much-needed grin.

"No you're not. Sure, you can have them all. Say Larry, why do Sugar and Li'l John hang out by the bakery?"

"My guess is for the free food Mrs. Hobson gives 'em. And since Maid Marian does her rounds up here and not down there, she gets to it quicker."

"Gets to what?"

"Why to work, what'd you think I meant?"

"Rounds, you mean her rounds at work?"

"I guess you could say that. She don't have to show up at no certain time, but she goes about her rounds the same way a person with a real job would."

"What? I don't understand. I've asked her to tell me what she does at work, but she won't say. Why do you think that is?"

"Jack, if you walked around town looking for handouts and diving in dumpsters and trash cans all day, my guess is you wouldn't tell nobody either."

My mouth was hanging open. I felt like a big fool and a heel, all at the same goddamn time. We walked up to the front of the bakery right about the time I finished berating myself. Didn't want to admit it but I was starting to feel some of the angst and ire the medicine is supposed to prevent. I'd never had two episodes in one day, but there was no reason I couldn't. Leastwise, none I could think of. I told Larry I had to sit down for a spell.

"Wait here, and don't worry. I promise I'll be right back," he said before he walked away.

I stared into space for a while before I asked myself what exactly it is that I thought Sugar did all day. *She told me she worked at the thrift store on the edge of town. She also told me that if I ever had an emergency that I should go to the hobo cave. She said someone there would be able to find her in a hurry.*

I stopped myself at that point and let the ugly truth raise its uglier head. *Jack, you are an arrogant, smug, no count jerk. The truth is you didn't care what she did or where she worked or lived as long as she slept with you. You should be ashamed of yourself, but you have no shame, do you?*

"Hello Jack," Sugar softly said as I looked up into her wet eyes. All I could see was the hurt I had caused by finding her out.

Larry stood beside Sugar and by his posture I believe he felt her pain.

"Jack, none of us set out to be hobos, it just happens, we just are," Larry said in Sugar's defense.

Sugar's nose crinkled, her shoulders drooped, as the life plummeted from her eyes. She fell to the ground right where she was, buried her face in her hands, and softly sobbed.

"Jack, we shouldn't have come here," Larry said just before the bass drum fell from the sky.

"You bad Sheriff, you hurt Maid Marian! Go now or Li'l John make you go!" roiled from a dark cloud that hung over me. It sounded as if it had come from Zeus himself.

The voice inside my head said *back up*, and then my instincts hollered, *"Run as fast as you can!"*

I was looking at two huge knees coming my way and before I could take even one step, I was in the clutches of a colossal man-child. He squeezed for just a moment to let me know he could easily grind my bones to make his bread. Then up I went over his shoulder. With his arm airtight around my waist, he began carrying me away as if I were a mere feather in the wind, or an old load of rubbish.

"Li'l John, please stop," Maid Marian said.

He came to an instant halt.

"Li'l John, please put him down."

The giant did as he was told.

"Now step back and take a good look at him. I think you're going to like what you see. Go on, he won't mind, you know it's rude to stare but you can do it just this one time," Maid Marian said.

The giant gracefully stepped back and looked at me from on high. I felt just like a chap in a movie looking up at the largest face in the entire world. And the face was shifting its focus from left to right and back again.

"Ahh, ha-ha-haaaa. He is the Robin you told me about, right?

"You're so smart Li'l John. See, I knew we couldn't fool you. Yes, he is the Robin Hood that I told you about," Maid Marian coddled.

"Ahh, ha-ha-haaaa, I like Robin. We fight with sticks now. Larry, get me stick," the giant said.

"No fighting right now, first you have to be nice and introduce yourself," Maid Marian said as the giant smiled. "Do it the way we practiced, ok?"

The giant doffed his cap, dropped down to one knee, and bowed his head. A large scar ran the length of his scalp. I put my hand on his shoulder, felt like I had just put my hand on an ox, a great big one. "Li'l John, you are now and will from this day forth be in the service of the King. And you must always obey Maid Marian and help me, Robin Hood that is, when you can. Do you agree?" I asked.

"Ahh, ha-ha-haaaa yes," the giant said still respectfully facing the ground at my feet.

"Then rise and join my band of merry-men as one of our own," I proclaimed.

The giant rose to a height of what looked like seven feet. His cheeks rolled forth like two crimson cannonballs beneath a pair of playful puppy eyes; they waxed a brilliant crystalline blue. His golden hair was just long and shaggy enough to cover some of the great satellite disks that also served as ears.

Is this real or am I dreaming?

His enormous lips were the color of a raw porterhouse. And when he suddenly smiled at me, one pillow sized slab of marble was thrust forward. I did my best to fix my eyes on his patchwork clothing, but the tooth and the laugh took center stage; the rest of the stage too.

"Ahhh-hhhuh, hhuhhuh-hhuh," he blubbered as the air was forced out and around his single offset front tooth. I felt as if I was in a wind tunnel and the skin on my face was rippling.

Maid Marian, now standing, was graciously smiling through the intense heartache which I had caused. I had to make things right. Although I was still experiencing an ample amount of angst and ire, I stumbled forward. I dropped to a knee, head down and reached up for Maid Marian's hand.

34

Blue Note

Dear lady, please forgive my faults and my frailties. I have caused you great pain, which was not my desire. You are the will-o'-the-wisp I have been searching for my entire life, please allow this sylvan fool a second chance to serve thee," I said in the most awful English accent I could come up with.

"Rise Sir Robin, you are forgiven. Now tell me of your concerns," Maid Marian requested in a most gracious voice.

I stood and then stumbled a bit.

"He took some kind a medicine to keep him from startin' up the swearin' heebie-jeebie-epo-shit," Larry Tuck graciously explained to Maid Marian.

"Jackie, what's wrong? Is this about those pills in your cabinet?" Sugar asked in her real voice.

"I'm ok, and it's such a long story. Hey, you know about the pills! Anyways, I guess I don't care if Li'l John or Larry hears me. Sugar, my landlord came by this morning and told me I would be evicted if I don't pay him the rent money by six o'clock. I know it's probably rude and terrible of me to ask, but do you have a hundred and thirty some odd dollars I could borrow? I'll pay you back," I begged.

"Jack, I said I could take care of you. Yes, I have that much and then some. I never keep it on me, so we'll have to go get it, is that ok?" she asked in a soft voice.

"Ok my fair lady, lead the way," I said as I lowered my right hand and swept it in a westerly direction.

Sugar started to walk but stopped and looked back at Li'l John. "Come on Li'l John, you too," she said with a heartwarming nod. Li'l John's tooth lit up as he featured an enormous smile.

Larry hung his head just before he turned to walk away. Sugar looked at me with a pouty face. I guess she was hoping for my approval. I nodded my head yes.

"You too Larry," Sugar said to Larry's back.

He turned and shined a smile he must have stolen as a little boy. And then there were four. Sugar held my hand as we walked. Not sure if it was to hold me up or because she felt the need to be affectionate. Either way I liked it.

"Sugar, I really am sorry for-"

She put her finger to my mouth as she softly shushed me.

"Sugar, does Li'l John know the difference between the real world and Sherwood Forest?"

"I don't know, maybe not. Truth is I don't care. He's the gentlest, kindest, most well-meaning and subservient person I have ever met. Besides you that is," she said with a tiny wink.

"Subservient, my, my, that's a big word. You sure do surprise me sometimes. I'm impressed and I like it," I said.

"Thank you. Jack, what was that will-o-the thing you said to me back there?"

"To be honest I'm not sure." She gave me a strange look. "It's something Ivy says now and then. I believe will-o'-the-wisp is an elusive and wonderful place where I dream of living. Does that make sense to you?"

"It sure does. Even hoboettes have dreams. My dream is to live in a place where people are kind and help one another. You could say I'm a dreamer, but I'm not the only one. Am I?"

"No Sugar, I'm sure you're not."

She smiled back at me. "Jack, can I ask a big favor of you?"

"Of course you can, what is it?" I asked eager to help her in any way I could.

"Other than a warm meal, companionship, and a soft place to lay their heads, the men that live in the cave like to be clean. I don't know if you smelled Larry, but he needs a bath something fierce. Would it be ok if he cleaned up at your place?"

"No."

"No?" she asked in a sad voice.

"Sugar I meant no, I haven't smelled him. Yes, of course he can clean up at my place. We'll go there right after we get the money."

"Ok, then to your apartment we go."

"Sugar, I really do need to get the money as soon as I can. You understand, don't you?"

"Yes, and we're going to your apartment cuz that's where I hid the money."

"What?"

"I couldn't leave the money in the cave or the canyon. Somebody would a took it for sure."

"Would have taken."

"What?"

"Never mind, that was a smart choice you made; leaving it at my place. But weren't you afraid I'd take it?" I asked in jest.

"Yes, I was afraid you'd take it, but that's ok, cuz I know where you live," she said and giggled.

"Sugar, you kill me. You know that?"

"I hope you mean I kill you in a nice way?" she asked.

"Yes, you kill me in a nice way."

We'd made it back to the empty parking lot in nothing flat. After we climbed the stairs, I stopped and stared. There was a note pinned to my front door. *Gosh, Hurtwood said I had 'til six o'clock. Please don't be a get out note.*

Jack Hawkins

7

I opened the note, it was written on very expensive bordered paper. Had a strange smell to it that I think is supposed to be impressive. Fancy Dan handwriting said, *"I have a job for you and I know you need the money. Meet me at the Blue Note; I'll be standing by the flag pole next to the scenic area. Twelve noon. I'll wait until exactly a quarter after, no later. Bring the note or no job."*

"What's it say?" Sugar asked before Larry could.

"I'll tell you in a minute," I said as I ran into the kitchen and looked at my black cat clock. The tail wagged from left to right as the panic ran thru me. *"It's nearly twelve now!"* I yelled at myself.

I ran down the stairs and told Sugar and the guys that they could follow if they wanted, but that I had to run to the Blue Note. Then I hauled ass.

I raced up Broadway and out Friendly Street and wound through the trees in the park by the cliffs. Nearly ran over a woman pushing a baby carriage. Before I was through the trees, I could hear the metal grommets as they banged off the flag pole. A man wearing a blue suit got in a silver XKE and drove away. I figured he had to be the guy. I yelled as loud as I could and waved my arms like a crazy man as he disappeared. Dejected, I turned and with head down trudged back towards the park.

Blue Note

"Hey asshole, over here!" someone yelled.

I looked back as a bony man and his shadow slunk out from behind the flag pole. Just the sight of him made my blood boil. I walked up to him and looked hard in his face. His name is Bobby Johnson, but he's better know as Rat. Rat had that same damn repulsive sneer on his face he did the last time I had the pleasure. I believe the sneer is a reflection of the doctor's face that delivered him. I don't think of him as human, to me he's a stoop-shouldered weasel with the face of a rat, and an ugly one at that.

"You should have been euthanized at birth, you ugly-ass rat!" I said in a raised voice.

"Eat some shit asshole," Rat hissed at me.

"Now gentlemen, nothing is ever gained thru name calling," was softly spoken from behind me.

I turned and looked over at the Suit that had driven away in the XKE. He smiled at me just before he asked for the note. I debated whether or not I should give it to him. *Maybe he didn't write it.*

"How would I know about the note?" Suit said in a casual way. He had a point, so I handed over the note. He tore it up and put it in his pocket.

"Ok, what's this job you have for me?"

"It's simple, I want you to use the talents I've heard so much about and find the person that killed Timmy Allen."

"You mean the kid from the other night?"

He nodded yes just before he looked past me and started backing up. I turned and looked at Sugar, and directly behind her stood Larry and Li'l John.

"I understand why you might be concerned, they're my friends, and they won't harm you. I give you my word on that."

"Nice, so you brought the filthy farm animals with you, and that goddamn gorilla!" Rat shouted.

Larry stepped forward. "I know you, you're the guy that stole that little old lady's purse and then blamed it on Friar Tuck, you're a stinking, no good lyin' thief!"

"Mr. Hawkins, please control your friends. At least until we are finished with our business."

"I'll do that as soon as you do," I said as I looked in Rat's direction.

"Mr. Johnson, if you want the finder's fee we agreed upon, you're going to have to control your emotional outbursts. Are we clear on that?" Suit said.

"Yeah, I guess so," Rat gave in to Suit.

"Now, Mr. Hawkins do we have a deal or do I need to look elsewhere?" Suit asked.

"You do understand that at the moment I don't have my P.I. license?" I asked. I really didn't care about that, but I wanted to be upfront about it.

"Yes, we know. That's why the note had to be destroyed. There will be no written record of your employment. Do we have a deal?" Suit asked again.

"Yeah, I suppose we do. However, there is a problem. If there isn't a contract, how am I supposed to get paid? And who is doing the paying?"

"I'll let you know all of that after you get started. As far as being paid, there is an envelope in your refrigerator. It contains what I believe to be a handsome amount of money. As the information you glean from your investigation mounts, so shall the compensation. Do you understand?"

"Yes, can I ask you a question?"

"If your question is who I am, the answer is no. Anything else you want to know?"

"Yes, who do you work for?"

"Mr. Hawkins, I or an associate will check in on you from time to time. We'll be monitoring your progress. Goodnight," Suit said as he walked away.

"Hey, what about my money?" Rat yelled at Suit's back. Suit stopped.

"Mr. Johnson, we will no longer require your services, you're terminated," Suit said as he got in his car. As he pulled away he dropped an envelope out the window.

Suit was long gone before Rat raced over and picked up the envelope. Sugar, Larry, Li'l John, and I started back for my apartment. We'd walked maybe twenty feet heading into the park when Rat hollered, "I'll see you shit stains later!"

"That does it!" Larry yelled, just before he put his flapping soles in motion.

Rat screamed like a little girl as he headed for the man-made tunnel. He would have made it, but for the fact that Friar Tuck was waiting for him. Rat panicked as his head swiveled from side to side.

"You little rat-ass liar, I'm gonna kill you," Friar Tuck bellowed as he and Larry circled Rat.

I stepped between the combatants. "Li'l John you hold Larry back and I'll do the same with Tuck."

"Let me at him," Friar Tuck insisted.

"No! Damnit, not 'til you explain why you're so angry at Rat," I said. I was beginning to believe I really was in Sherwood Forest.

Friar Tuck looked like he was going to blow a gasket trying to calm down.

"Take a deep breath," I urged.

Friar Tuck took a couple of breaths and then in a soft yell began explaining. "I was up behind the bakery and this rat-ass comes by with a lady's purse, an empty one. He says, 'You know anybody needs a purse?'"

"Well, of course I was thinkin' Maid Marian might need a purse. So I says, 'Yeah sure, what's the catch?' And rat-ass says, 'No catch, here, you can have it.'" I grab the purse and head fer the cave, but only make it half a block or so before the cops see me and jump out of their patrol car. They ask where I got the purse and I tell 'em the same story I just told you. One cop stays with me and the other drives away with the purse. The cop I'm standing with tells me the purse was stolen from an old lady's shopping cart at the supermarket. I put two and two together and I realize I've been bamboozled by this rat-ass. Well, wasn't long and the other cop comes back. He looks at me and says, 'Where's the wallet and checkbook that were in the purse?'" I tell him, 'God's truth, I don't know.'" They took me to jail, kept me there for two whole weeks!" Friar Tuck yelled at Rat.

I look over at Rat and he's shaking his head no. He starts pleading, "He's a damn liar. You can't believe him, he's nothin' but a fucking hobo!"

Larry and Friar Tuck were chomping at the bit to get at Rat. Li'l John and I kept them at bay.

"Only reason they let me out of jail was this dumb-shit rat-ass forges a couple of the old lady's checks and gets caught. Ain't that right, you Rat!"

Rat tried to slither away, but I stopped him.

"It all makes sense now. I haven't seen you since you were caught stealing tips off the bar at the Redwood. I thought that was why you disappeared, but it's not, is it? No, you've been in county jail all this time. Haven't you, you Rat!" I yelled, just before I felt the first small tingle.

"No, it ain't true. That old lady owed me for work I done at her house, so I just paid myself," Rat professed as he looked at Li'l John. "What're you looking at you big dumb ape?" Rat hissed.

"Rat, stop it!" I yelled. "Can't you see he's trying to help you?"

"Screw him, he's nothing but a big baboon," Rat said as he scrunched his face at Li'l John.

"Robin, is Rat making fun of me?" Li'l John asked in a hurt voice.

I started to answer Li'l John when Rat took a step forward and mimicked, "Robin - is Rat making fun of me? What a dumb fuck!"

I felt another tingle and tensed as I waited for the nickel, dime, quarter. Rat wouldn't give it a break and looked over at Sugar. "Don't look at me like that you filthy, dirty faced hobo bitch." I backhanded Rat and watched the inkblots fly; still no epo-shit.

Rat covered his mouth as he blinked nonstop before he turned and look at me, shock jacketing his face. I could see him debating what to do before he pulled a knife from an ankle sheath. I didn't give the little jerk time to move and hit him square in the nose. His knees buckled and he sat down right where he was. Blood splattered across his face and neck. His head wobbled as he tried to gain his sensibilities. Then as if charged by an electric pulse, he wiped his face, smearing the blood up into his hair and across his teeth. Droplets of blood hung from his ears.

I was glaring down at him waiting for the nickel, dime, quarter to start, it didn't. Rat slowly got to his feet before he gave me a pair of injured eyes. I thought about hitting him again, but Friar Tuck beat me to it. He gave Rat a roundhouse kick to the side

Blue Note

of the leg. Rat howled like a wounded animal as he went down again. This time when he stood he hopped on one leg before limping away. When he was what he believed to be a safe distance from us, he screamed, "You asshole Jack, I'll get you for this! You just wait and see, I'm gonna get you!"

"I see you anywhere near the Redwood or my apartment and I will break your neck. That's not a threat, that's a goddamn promise. You hear me!" I roared as Rat limped south along the cliff-line.

I picked the knife up and turned towards Sugar; her eyes said a mouthful before she actually spoke. "Jack, the look on that guy's face and the tone of his voice scare me. You need to keep an eye out, he's going to do anything and everything he can to pay you back," she warned. I knew she was right, we all knew she was right.

It was nearly one in the afternoon. We were all hot from the verbal and physical mêlée' that had just taken place, and just to add a little fuel to the fire a Santa Ana heat wave was in the wind. Friar Tuck and Larry were still fuming when they said goodbye. Sugar tugged at my shirt and mouthed, "*Larry.*"

"Larry, remember what we talked about this afternoon," I asked. Larry turned a little and shrugged his shoulders at me. "*The shoes,*" I mouthed.

"*Oh yeah, the shoes,*" he mouthed back.

From my vantage point I could tell Larry did not want to leave Friar Tuck. Friar Tuck knew too.

"Larry, y'all go ahead on. I'm fine and I have somethin' I need ta take care of."

Still Larry did not move.

"I'm fine. Go on, get," Friar Tuck softly said.

Larry waved before he reluctantly turned and headed back with us to the Redwood. He stopped just one time and watched Friar Tuck disappear down the man-made tunnel.

8

When we got back to my apartment, Sugar led Larry and Li'l John up to the duck blind. I hustled into my kitchen and flung the door to the fridge open, sure as heck there was an envelope sitting on the top empty tray. I grabbed it and sat down at my little table. I think I might have said a prayer, but I'm not going to admit to it. Anywho, I opened the envelope, actually I ripped it open. There was a bunch of twenties and some hundred-dollar bills. I was in poor-boy heaven as I sat and stared.

When I came out of my trance, I grabbed two twenty-dollar bills before stuffing the torn envelope down the front of my Levi's. I walked out the kitchen door and yelled at the guys to come back down.

"Sugar, will you take Li'l John to the corner 7-Eleven and buy whatever he wants to eat and drink. I'm going to keep Larry here and show him the shoes he and I talked about this morning," I said as I gave Sugar a wink and the twenties. She frowned.

"Go on, I'll explain later." She didn't move.

"Sugar, you have to trust me on this, please?" I said.

She turned to Li'l John and grabbed his big paw and yanked just a little. He heard what had been said and smiled from one great ear to the other. Of course Larry was hungry and thirsty too, and he objected.

"Larry, you have to stay here. Please, just tell her what you want," I urged.

Blue Note

He frowned at me before he said, "I want a ham sandwich; you know the big ones in the cooler. And I want one a them Texas sized dill pickles and the largest cherry coke slurpee they sell, ok?"

Sugar started walking down the steps when I asked her if she could buy beer. "Yes, I suppose so but I never buy beer, I only buy that wine you said can't be my dinner."

"Ok then, can you buy two six packs, bottles, and a Bali Hai, please."

She smiled before she and Li'l John strode down the stairs and disappeared thru the parking lot.

"Ok Larry, about those shoes I promised you. I think it'd be a good idea if you took a long shower before you try the shoes on."

He looked at me with a thousand-mile stare.

"You're going to let me take a shower, here? Oh man, I can't wait," he said as he pushed me aside and headed for the bathroom.

"There's plenty of soap and shampoo. Stay in as long as you like," I said as I grabbed the envelope out of my Levi's. I started counting and when I got to the last bill, I heard the shower turn on.

"Two thousand dollars, man oh man. Wow," I whispered to myself.

I rolled the bills up the way you see gangsters do in the movies. Just seemed like the right thing to do. Then I shoved the roll as deep in my front pocket as I could. I started thinking that it'd be a good idea if Levi's came with zippers on the pockets. That way nobody could just stick their hand in and steal your money. I shook my head back and forth a few times, *geez, zippers on pockets, that'd look crazy ridiculous.* I smiled. *Only a guy with lots of money would think of something that nutty.*

A reality check came in the form of a mirror. As I walked over to my closet to get the shoes for Larry, I looked in the full-length mirror on the door. I had a bulge in my front pocket that could not be denied. *Hey, maybe? Nah, you look like an idiot, everybody that sees you is going to stare at the pocket. You can't walk around like that; you have to put the money in a safe place, like maybe a bank.*

Jack Hawkins

I heard Larry sing, "I was born by the river - in a little tent - oh and just like the river, I've been runnin' ever since. It's been a long, long time comin', but I know-uh-oh – a change gon' come."

Made me think real hard on the money and what the right thing was that I should do with it. Only took a few seconds and I knew exactly what that right thing was. I walked out to the kitchen and looked in the little waste basket I keep under the sink. There was a brown paper bag that I'd put a beer in a week before. I put the money in the bag, opened the fridge then my tiny freezer door. I was going to hide the bag behind some frozen French-fries and string-beans.

I stopped. There was another bag hidden in the freezer. I opened it and it held mostly dollar bills, a few coins too. *Funny how great minds think alike*, I said to myself. Then I thought of Mr. Hurtwood. I'll talk to him this evening, hope he'll work with me. Now I need to get Larry up and running. Being that Larry and I are nearly the same size made things easy. I opened my closet and took out a pair of my best slacks. No, they're not real expensive or dressy, but they're nice pants. Then I did the same with my shirts. Found a button-up that would go with almost anything. Thankfully, I had a pair of clean underwear and socks. I took out all three pairs of the shoes that I hardly ever wear. *I guess I'll let Larry decide which pair he likes.*

"We're back," I heard Sugar call out.

I laid out the clothes and shoes for Larry on my bed, then I opened the bathroom door and yelled, "Larry, I set some clothes out for you on my bed. Just put 'em on, ok?"

"Ok," rang out between verses.

I walked out and closed the door behind me.

"Gosh Jack, I heard you when I was coming up the stairs. I think that's the best I've ever heard you sing," Sugar said with a smile.

"Thanks a lot!"

"What's wrong?"

"That was Larry you heard," I said in a pouty voice.

Sugar giggled, "Oh sorry."

"Yeah, right."

"I hope you're hungry, I got you a surprise," she quickly said, which was in my opinion an attempt at changing the subject.

"Sugar, I'm just kidding about the singing, I like to hear you laugh; even if it's at me."

She smiled, "Thanks for being so nice."

"Sugar."

"Yeah, what is it Jack."

"Don't push your luck," I said as I gave her a hug and a small kiss.

"Lookie here what I got you," she said as she opened a white bag. "Six tamales, they're authentic. I bought 'em from that old Mexican couple that have the little heated push cart."

I looked in the bag. "Sugar, there's only three tamales in here. Didn't you just say you bought six?"

"Well, Li'l John ate two on the way back and I had one. I was so hungry, hope you don't mind?" she said, with that wonderful shy look in her eyes.

"Of course I don't mind. We can get more if you want?"

"Jack, why the good mood?" Did you forget about your landlord? I can get the money for you whenever you want. But, you'll have to stand outside and close your eyes."

"Sugar, that's why the good mood. The suit that wants me to help him paid me enough so that I don't have to borrow any money. I want you to know how much it meant to me that you would do that for me. You keep the money hidden and when we get a chance, I'll take you to the bank so you can open up a savings account, how's that sound?" I said with a big smile.

"No, no, I have to keep the money hidden. I can't open a savings account. They'll want to know my name and where I live and see my identification, and I don't want them to know who I am or where I live. Please Jack, no banks," she said as she backed away from me in a panic. She crossed her arms over her chest as if my suggestion made her cold.

"Ok, ok, we don't have to go to a bank. You can keep your money here, all right? I don't like seeing you like this. You're safe here with me, ok?"

"Ok," she softly said.

I had to brighten up the mood. "What kind of beer did you buy? Remember, this is a celebration?"

"I bought you the Olympic beer you like so much. That ok?"

"Yes, perfect. Thank you. Sugar, what'd you get for you and Li'l John?"

"I bought us some grape Kool-Aid. I saw you had a big pitcher in the cupboard. I'll have it done in a jiffy. Grape is Li'l John's favorite, I like it too."

"What about the Bali Hai? Don't you want to have some of that for dinner?"

"No, it gives me a headache the next day. I don't think I should have wine for dinner anymore. That ok with you?"

"Yes, of course that's ok with me. Geez, you make me feel like a pusher or something. Now that you mentioned Li'l John, where is he?"

"He loves being on your roof, says he wants to live there. Jack, is it ok if he's up there? What I mean is, I don't want you to get in trouble with your landlord."

"Yes, he's fine up there. For now that is."

I was heading up to see Li'l John when Larry opened my bedroom door and stuck his head out. "Jack, would it be ok if I shaved?"

"You mean is it ok if you use my razor?"

"Yes, that's what I mean, hi Maid Marian." He closed the door. "Jack, I'm gonna use the scissors I found too. Um, I always take a shower after I shave, is that ok?" he said from the other side of the door.

"Yes, take another shower."

"Say, I like the clothes you put out for me. Are you sure about this?"

"Yes, I'm positive. Larry, I forgot to tell you. Put your clothes in the hamper. I'll see about washing them, but I might end up throwing them away."

"That's ok with me, I hate 'em."

"Jack, can I have the shirt Larry was wearing. It used to be mine and I like plaid shirts, especially green ones," Sugar informed.

It's green I thought. *Could've fooled me. It's so dirty I would have sworn it was black.*

"Yes Sugar, you can have it."

"Jackie, you want a beer now?" Sugar asked.

"No, Larry and I are going to go to the Coke plant to see about a job. I know a guy that works there and he told me that if I ever needed a job, he could put in a good word for me."

"Jack, you already have a job. Didn't you get hired today?"

"Yes, I'm not thinking of me. I was thinking of Larry and Li'l John, thought they'd like a job."

"Yes, I think Larry would love a job, but not Li'l John," she said in a matter of fact way.

"Why not Li'l John?" I asked, confused.

"He can't be anywhere at a certain time; not sure he can even tell time. He likes being his own boss and going where he wants to when he wants to. That's what happens to a person when you live on the streets for a while. That's how I feel too," she said with a bashful smile.

"Sugar, I understand, I suppose. But you do understand you can't go on living like this forever, don't you?" She wouldn't answer me. "Sugar, try to remember I'm on your side." Still no answer. "Sugar, you told me you worked at the thrift store, did you make that up so I wouldn't know, about…"

"What you really mean is, did I lie to you?" I didn't say anything. "Jack, I didn't lie. I do work at the thrift store, but only when they have work for me. Sometimes I work five maybe six days in a row. And sometimes I don't work for five or six days. I go by every day and ask. When they get behind with the donations and need clothes sorted, put on hangers, and hung up, I work. Otherwise I don't."

"Sugar, I didn't mean that you lied to me, I'm sorry you thought that. All I really want is for you to be happy." She didn't say anything back.

I sat and watched her make the Kool-Aid and pour herself a glass. She took the rest of the pitcher up to Li'l John. I followed after her with two of the tamales, figured I only needed one. Li'l John was lying down with his head on one arm rest and his feet hanging over the other. He looked happy, and by the way he jumped up, I'd say he was very thirsty. He devoured the tamales while I watched. I noticed that when he ate his eyes darted from side to side. As if he thought someone might try to steal his food.

"I'm going to go down and check on Larry."   Li'l John looked up at me. "Robin, thank you for tamales and Kool-Aid, you give to the poor and that is why you are good. Are you coming back up?" he asked as he tipped the pitcher back.

"I'll come up and sit with you when Larry and I get back."

"Robin, where you going?" Li'l John asked.

"To look for a job," I answered.

He withdrew from me as if I had mentioned poison or the Sheriff of Nottingham. I smiled at Sugar and went down to see how Larry was doing. I walked in the door and Larry was standing with the Texas sized dill pickle in one hand and half of the sandwich in the other. I did a double take.

"Geez, you don't look like the same guy."

"Why not?" he asked with his mouth full."

"Well for one, I thought your hair was black, but it's brown. And you are standing up tall and not stooped over. Funny thing is, with my clothes on you look kind of like someone I know. Just can't put my finger on who that is. Oh well."

He just shrugged his shoulders. "Guess my hair was kinda dirty, feels clean now. Thank you, Jack."

I looked down at the shoes he'd picked out to wear. I thought for sure he'd take the dress shoes or the desert boots but he had on my black high-top Converse. I would have never considered wearing a pair of All-Stars with slacks. They actually looked good on Larry. Sugar walked in the door, said she was going to make another pitcher of Kool-Aid before she stopped dead in her tracks.

"Gosh Larry, you clean up real nice."

Larry swallowed. "Why thank you."

"Strange how much you look like Jack, must be the clothes," Sugar said as she walked by me.

That's who he looks like, me. This is going to help out considerably. "Larry, you handsome devil, when you get done eating we're going to take a little walk. That ok with you?"

"Yeah, I suppose so, where we goin'?"

"We're going to Cheely's and pick up some spark plugs and a new alternator for my coupe. Then we're going to the Coca Cola plant to see about a job. I know I didn't ask, but would you be interested in a job if I could get you one?"

Blue Note

"A job for me, are you serious? Why I'd do almost anything for a real job. I'll work twelve hours a day if I have to. Good lord this sure is turning out to be a wonderful day. Gosh, thanks Jack."

"I don't think you oughta thank me just yet. This is going to depend on a friend of mine coming thru with a job for me. He doesn't know that the job is really for you. Let's keep our fingers crossed."

"I guess that means I can't have one a them beers that were staring at me in the fridge."

"No, drink your slurpee. You'll have to wait 'til we get back. The beer will taste that much better because you waited."

"Well, if that's the case, then I'm ready to go now. I'll eat the rest of the sandwich and have a beer when we get back. You ready?" he asked.

"I'll be ready in a minute. Why don't you carry the Kool-Aid upstairs for Maid Marian? When you come back down we'll go, ok?"

"Sure thing, wanna show Li'l John my new duds before we leave," he said as he picked up the pitcher.

I took a hundred out of the frozen bag and stuck the cold hard cash in my pocket. I went in my bedroom and opened the hidden compartment of my jewelry box and grabbed some identification. Then I headed out to meet Larry, Cat was waiting for me.

"Ok, come on in. I have something special just for you."

I gave him a small piece of tamale and a saucer of milk. He thanked me with a head-butt.

Larry tapped on the kitchen window. "Jack, I'm ready to go."

I looked at him; it was kind of like looking in a mirror. He had a loopy smile on his clean-shaven face.

9

Larry and I headed north on Broadway, Cheely's auto parts was on the other end of town. I went in and paid for the parts and then asked the old guy behind the counter if I could pick them up later, he nodded yes. The Coke plant was just past the dairy all the way on the edge of town. We had another five-minute walk ahead of us, Larry was following me. I looked back at him a couple of times and couldn't help but notice him noticing himself. He liked being clean cut and well dressed. I looked back at him once more, he'd stopped walking.

"Something wrong?" I asked.

"Maybe, but I'm just not sure. Jack, I have something I've wanted to ask you since we saw that Rat character. Ok if I ask you a personal question?"

"Larry, when a person has a question they want to ask stuck in their head, eventually it's going to work its way out. So you might as well get it over with, what is it?" I asked completely in the dark.

"You sure it's ok?" he hesitantly asked.

"Yes Larry, go ahead and ask."

"I saw your face just before you hit Rat. Was you on the verge of the epo-shit?"

He had caught me off guard. I was not ready for the question or the reminder. I looked around me for a place to sit down. "Larry, let's go on up to the bus stop and have a seat, ok?"

"Sure Jack," he said with that worried look on his face people get when they think I'm ready to come unglued.

Blue Note

The bus stop was only about fifty feet away, but it seemed like miles to me before we actually sat down.

"Larry, before we get started I have to ask you something, is that ok?"

"Sure Jack, go ahead," he said as he slid away from me on the bench.

"Larry when you say epo-shit do you mean epilepsy?"

"Yeah, what'd you think I meant?"

"That's what I thought, just had to be sure. When I was about five, we'd been traveling a lot, that is, Mom and me. Sometimes my aunt tagged along for company. We were on our way to Deer Lodge, Montana when Mom pulled the coupe over so I could use the restroom at a filling station. Don't remember what kind of gas they sold. Anywho, I go in the little office to look at candy and stuff when all of a sudden, I get that first tingle in my head. Then the lights went out, I guess I hit my head pretty hard on the floor. The man running the place held on to me real tight so I wouldn't wreck anything."

"Were you scared?" Larry asked all excited.

"Didn't know to be scared, didn't remember a thing afterwards either. When I was finally able to move, Mom put me in the back of the car and took off like a shot. She didn't know what to think, but I believe she thought it was a one-time deal. It wasn't. The episodes kept happening. So Mom takes me to a doctor, don't remember what state, but I think it was Wyoming. Anyways, he tells Mom, because I can't remember what happens after I have an episode, I have a rare type of epilepsy called T.E.A. In short it stands for amnesia. Sometimes I'd black out without even having an episode. That was ok because I had no clue it happened. But there were times the doctor said I was into the 'tonic'."

"You mean like hair-oil or something?"

"No Larry, it was what you saw in the cave. I guess it's when all the muscles in my body are forcefully contracting. I was told it can be so darn extreme a person can bite their tongue or vomit or sometimes even wet their pants."

Larry looked down at the front of the pants I'd given him. "Hope you didn't have these pants on when you had one of them tonics."

"No I didn't."

"So you been dealing with this ever since you was a little kid?" he asked.

"Well, yes and no. Mom moved around from state to state looking for a doctor that could actually help me. We finally found a doctor in Kansas that had me try some stuff called Lani-something or other. It worked and for the most part the memory loss and the seizures stopped."

"Didn't look like they stopped to me," Larry said with some pizzazz.

"Yes, I guess from where you were it didn't look like they'd stopped. Here's the problem, about six months ago the medicine quit working. That's when the swearing and the tics started up. Remember the snake with hands you told me about."

"How could I forget," he said with a shy grin.

"I was in Egypt with my friend Ivy. We were on what he calls a 'dig'. Anywho, all of a sudden, I have the desire to swear and say awful things at two guys that were just sitting having coffee. I said some dreadful things. I couldn't help myself."

"Yeah, I know," Larry said.

"Well, Ivy was quick to remove me from the scene of the crime, but somehow he knew it was just the beginning. And since that day I get these urges Ivy says are caused by angst and ire."

"What?"

"Angst and ire, it means worry and anger. The episodes, the ticks, and the epo-shit had started. So Ivy takes me to a shrink in Los Angeles. He says I have some rare condition called Tourettes syndrome. And then he tells us there is no cure," I said before I had to stop. I guess saying it out loud had a bigger impact on me than I thought it would. It was kind of like admitting that I'm a sicko.

"Gosh Jack, I'm really sorry to hear that. Jack, why do you say the things you say?"

"I don't know. All I can tell you is it's like doing the exact opposite of what you know is the right thing to do."

"You mean like breaking the law or the rules, just cuz you wanna be foul?" he asked.

"I guess you could say that. It's like being at a funeral, and laughing right out loud in the middle of the service. You know it's wrong, but you just can't help yourself. That's how it is with me. The more disgusting and hurtful the words are, the more I want to say them; the urges are too strong."

"I know. I was there, I heard you. Jack, I have something to say that you might not agree with, but I'm gonna say it anyways. I saw the urge and the look on your face with that Rat guy and then you hit him and the look was gone. Maybe when you feel a tingle, you need to sock someone. Might help, at least it's worth a try. Cuz I gotta tell ya the counting coins shit ain't workin'. And once that medicine you take wears off, you're ready to say some mean-ass stuff. I wouldn't mind it if when you felt a tingle you went ahead and hit me. No kicking or any bullshit like that. Just sock me a good one once or twice," he said with the sincerest look on his face.

"Larry thanks for offering, but I can't go around hitting you or anyone else for that matter. I'd end up behind bars," I said as I stood up. "Larry, we need to get going. Can we leave this behind us for a little while and go get that job we talked about?"

"Sure thing Jack, let's get to it."

When we got to the Coke, plant I went in the office and asked for my friend, Tony Riles. I was told he'd just left on his delivery route. I thanked the young lady in the office and went outside. The look on my face must have read defeated because Larry's smile changed to a faint frown.

"Ain't no job, is there?" Larry softly said as his shoulders drooped.

I started to answer him when the young lady held the front door of the office open and called out, "Sir, are you here about the loading job?"

"Um yes I am, is the job still open?"

"Yes sir, come in and fill out the application. They needed someone yesterday, you ready to work today," she asked with a smile.

"I sure am," I said as I followed her into the office.

Only took me maybe fifteen minutes to fill out the application. She said the road on the side of the office would lead straight back to the warehouse, told me to ask for Duke. I must have had a blank look on my face.

"He's the little fella that intentionally walks like John Wayne, you can't miss him," she said as she giggled and mumbled Duke, to herself of course. "Oh, you'll have to show Duke your birth certificate, and maybe a driver license, so have them ready."

"Yes, ok I will," I said as I ran out to Larry.

I grabbed his arm and pulled him around to the side of the office. "Larry, do you know where the town of Laramie is?"

"Uh, Wyomin'."

"Yes, ok I'm going to make this real short. Larry, as far as this job goes, from this day forth your name is Jack Laramie. Say it back to me." He didn't say a word. "You want a job or not?" He nodded his head yes. "Ok, what's your name?"

"Jack Laramie, was I born in Wyomin'?"

"Yes, in Laramie. Makes it easy to remember that way, doesn't it. He nodded his head yes again. "Ok, Jack, all the information you need is on this birth certificate. You understand. It's easy peazy. Just keep it in your pocket. There's not that much you need to remember. Just take a look now and then and study it. But don't you dare lose it!"

"I won't. You know we had a bonfire burnin' out back of the orphanage one time and a girl said I was too chicken to jump over it. Well, ain't no girl gonna call me chicken, so I jumped. Burned the seat of my pants, but I made it all right. Well, because I'd jumped over the candlestick, for the rest of that night all the kids called me Jack. I liked bein' Jack. The very next day Friar Tuck come and got me outta the orphanage; after Friar Tuck and I left, I was back to bein' plain old Larry."

"Who is Friar Tuck to you?" I asked out of curiosity.

"Well, I don't rightly know. He showed some legal papers to the head-master and said he was a relative." He stopped talking for a moment. "I don't know who he is, but I don't care. I'm just thankful he got me out of that awful place."

"Jack," I said with gusto. I think you better get going. Wait a second," I said as I hustled back in the office. I ran back out. "Jack, you're going to be here 'til ten o'clock tonight. Can you do that?"

"Yes, don't worry 'bout me. I'm fired up and ready to make a real livin.'"

56

"Jack," I said again which still felt weird to me. The new Jack didn't seem to mind at all. "Jack, can you drive a car?"

"A car, hell, I can drive anything. I can drive a car, a truck, a tractor; I'll bet I could drive a tank. Why?"

"Do you have a California driver license?" I asked, hoping he'd say no.

"No, I ain't never had any license, but I've driven lots of ve-hicles."

"Ok good," I said as I handed him a wallet with a Wyoming driver license in it. He immediately opened the wallet.

"Hey, that looks like me," he blurted out.

"Yeah, ok Jack when were you born?"

He looked at me, the confusion and the hurt obvious. "I really don't know when I was born."

"Now you do, look at the license. You were born on December 22, 1941. You ok with that?"

"Sure am, you have no idea how nice it feels to have a real birthday. This year I'm gonna celebrate the 22nd like nobody's business."

"That makes two of us," I said, he didn't hear a word I said.

"Jack, can I keep the wallet?"

"Yes, you can keep the wallet," I said, as he ogled the wallet. I'd bought it in Tijuana, it had a burro and a big red rooster painted on the front.

"Gosh Jack, thank you. I ain't never had a wallet neither. And this one here is pretty damn nice. Thanks again," new Jack said to me.

"Ok look. After I pay my landlord, I'll drive back over here and bring you dinner. Ok?"

"Sure, but what if they won't let me take a break so's I can eat?"

"I'll make 'em."

"Ok Jack, well, I guess I'd better get goin'. This Jack will see ya later. Hey, who do I ask for?"

"Oh right, his name is Duke. The girl inside the office said he tries to walk like John Wayne. Just ask for Duke. Bye," I said as he turned and followed a truck that was heading towards the warehouse.

I couldn't leave it at that. I just had to ask him something. "Jack," I hollered at his back before I ran up to him. He turned his head but kept walking.

"What?" he asked with that loopy smile.

"Are you going to be ok?"

"Yes, I'm gonna be great, bye," he said as we shook hands. He waved before he put his head down and started jogging.

I yelled out, "Jack, when were you born?"

"December 22, nineteen and forty-one, bye."

Blue Note

10

I had a healthy smile on my face when I walked in to pick up my stuff at the auto parts store.

"You sure do look happy, has it been a long time since you had your car running?" the old guy asked.

"Yes, too long. Thanks," I said as I walked out into the blazing afternoon sun.

I knew it was going to be hot while I worked on the coupe. I didn't care. It had been nearly half a year since I'd had the old girl running. Dad bought the car brand spanking new right off the showroom floor. Mom always said he bought the car for her, but I know he bought it for himself. Back in the day it had one of the most powerful flathead V8's money could buy. And in my dad's line of work that wasn't a luxury, it was a necessity. Took me a while to walk back to the apartment, but I didn't care, cuz it seemed like everything was turning up jake.

I walked in my kitchen and Sugar was sitting at the kitchen table, a distressed look on her face.

"Something wrong?" I asked.

"Your landlord came by and asked where you were. Then he asked who I was and who that big guy was up on his roof. He said it sounded like a herd of elephants was up there. Well, he goes up and yells at Li'l John to get off his roof and poor Li'l John is frightened. He's very sensitive. He took off runnin' and I couldn't keep up. I'm worried; he's easily taken advantage of. Your landlord sure is mean."

"He can be, but he can be nice too. I wonder if there's something else going on that I don't know about. Sugar, I trust you so you can watch if you want to, I don't care," I said as I opened the fridge and grabbed my bag of money. "I'll be back right after I take care of some business."

"Jack, do I have to leave?"

"No, this is still my apartment. When I get back, we'll go find Li'l John. He can't have gone too far. Ok?"

"Ok, thank you," she said with a soft smile and a worried mind.

I walked in the rear entrance straight to the bar. The tall, flaxen, bartender, Scout Scoggins, had her back to me but smiled in the mirror. She pointed at the office, the door was open.

"He's expecting you. Jack, come get me if you need help," she said with a firm nod of the head.

"Thanks Scout, don't think I'll need help, but that's mighty stand up of you to offer," I said as I headed into the spider's web.

Hurtwood had his head submerged in his file cabinet. He must have felt my presence cuz he turned around and studied me for a moment.

"Guess you came in early to ask for more time. Well, I have bills to pay. So the answer is no."

"Mr. Hurtwood, can we sit down?"

"Ok but seated or standing my answer will be the same."

I sat down on my side of his curiously cold gray metal desk. I took out a few one hundred-dollar bills and a handful of twenties. Hurtwood's eyes lit up the way a wolf's might when he sees a wild hare or maybe a lamb. "Jack, did you rob a bank?"

"No, I was paid for a job I'll start tomorrow. The reason I wanted to sit down is I'd like to make a deal with you, you up to making a deal?" I asked.

"I suppose, what've you got in mind?" he asked with a keen eye on the money in my hand.

"What do you think the comfort level would be for a landlord if he was paid, oh let's say maybe six months in advance?" I didn't give him time to say one word. I read the look on his face as the wheels of greed burned rubber. "If you'll work with me on this, I could make it happen," I said as I held up a handful of cash.

"Jack, you're a fairly bright person. And you know as well as I do that no matter how you slice it, six months rent is seven hundred and fifty dollars," he said with a grin only a hyena could fashion.

"Ok," I said as I got up and set a hundred and forty dollars on his desk. "You can apply the leftover change to next month's rent."

"He quickly scooped up the money."

"Can I have a receipt?" I asked.

"Ok Jack, what did you have in mind?"

"What I had in mind was seven hundred for six months rent and maybe a hundred more to rent the roof."

"I see. So this is about the giant. Not a good idea if you ask me."

"Mr. Hurtwood, how many times have you had to call the police because a car was broken into or people were fighting in the parking lot. Remember that time you had your license taken away for... what was it three months? Some taps were making money selling beers to underage kids waiting out in the parking lot. I think it's against the law to have liquor out in the parking lot, isn't it?"

"Jack, stop with the threats, you're not very good at it. You're not scaring me."

"Ok, how about the benefits of having a giant looking down over your property, every night?"

"Every night?" he asked.

"Oh, you might give him a night off here and there, but for the most part yeah, every night."

"And you're going to pay me, and not the other way around?" he asked waiting for some kind of catch.

"Yes, I'm going to pay you a hundred dollars every six months."

"Jack, I'm willing to try it, but only him. No others."

"Deal; there will be no others that stay up on the roof all night."

"Jack, don't fool with me. I mean no others, and when the bar closes, so does the roof."

"Fair enough, that's eight hundred dollars," I said as Hurtwood held out his hand. I did the same. "First things first, I'll need a receipt, please."

He stood and opened his file cabinet and took out his big receipt book. He quickly scratched out the receipt and tore it from the book. He leaned over and shoved his face in front of mine. "I'll take the money now, please."

As I was walking out, receipt and a smile in hand, Mr. Hurtwood murmured, "Jack, it's none of my business but I don't think hiding your money in my apartment is a very good idea."

"You're right, it's none of your business," I said as I walked out of his office. I wanted to jump up and holler. I had to be cool as I walked by Scout.

"See ya Scout, why don't you come up and see me sometime?"

She looked at my reflection in the mirror as I passed by. She waved a peace sign and kept right on cleaning the bottle of Jack she held in her hand. I ran up the stairs and told Sugar the good news. I sensed a smile but never saw one. She was too worried about Li'l John to celebrate just yet.

"Ok Sugar, would he go to the cave?"

"No, he wouldn't mope in front of others."

"Ok that leaves the canyon out too. Where's the quietest place the two of you see on your rounds each day?"

Her brow wrinkled as she grabbed her bag of tricks. "Follow me."

"Where are we going?" I asked in good faith.

"We're going to the one place he loves most, Friendly Street."

"What's on Friendly?"

"The library, it's quiet and he loves to look at the pictures in the children's books."

"Can he read?"

"I'm not sure. Sometimes he tells me what signs say, but I think he has memorized what he was told the signs say or something like that. Jack, we have to hurry. Li'l John broke a chair in the library once and he scares some of the kids."

"Did he throw the chair at someone or break it over his knee?"

Blue Note

"No, gosh give him a little credit. He just sat on one of chairs in the children's section. All the people in the library know he's gentle, but some old bitty that brought her granddaughter in complained. Miss Juju, that's Li'l John's favorite person in the library, told him he had to go outside for a while. He was so heartbroken he cried right there in front of all the kids. One of the mean little girls started laughing at him. Didn't take very long before all the kids were laughing at him. I held Li'l John's hand and led him out. There's a bench just outside the library. We went out there and sat down. About ten minutes later the old lady and her granddaughter left. Miss Juju came out and told Li'l John to check with her when he comes to the library, said he could sit in the sorting room with her. She told him she would go get all the books he wanted and bring them to him. I believe that's probably where we'll find him. Let's go," she said as she took off down my stairs.

As I chased after her, I looked over at my old coupe. *When am I going to have the time to get it up and running?*

I walked as fast as my tired feet would go. Remember, I had already walked across town once. I wasn't prepared to do it again. That said Sugar and Li'l John are worth the effort. We walk in the library and were directly met by a woman bent slightly at the waist, her concern and her age hidden in the soft lines of her face. She spied up at me with glasses glued to the tip of her nose. Her hair was piled high over her head like a handsome loaf of German black bread. I wondered if her hair was angry with her for making it stand at attention all day. I suppose being surrounded by row after row of dusty books along with the stifling silence is what made me think of something so screwy. Sugar nodded yes to me.

"Hello, you must be Miss Juju," I said in my upbeat howdy-do voice.

Every person within eyesight stared. I forgot I was in a quiet zone.

Miss Juju put her finger to her mouth before she softly said, "Yes, I'm Miss Juju, and it's nice to finally get to meet you. You must be the Robin Hood I've heard so much about. Please, follow me," she said as she pointed at an open door.

She turned and ever so quietly motioned for us to follow her. She put her finger up to her mouth again as we looked inside the sorting room. Li'l John was sitting Indian style on the floor in the middle of the room. He had a gang of books all around him. He was gyrating and talking up a storm. I think he was talking to someone in the book.

"John, you have visitors," Miss Juju said. He looked up at Sugar and me, and by his reaction I'd say he'd been expecting us.

"Robin, look at us fight," he whispered as a ray of sunshine flew my way. "I beat you. It's ok, you don't always have to win to be a good person," he softly said as he held the book up for inspection.

I looked at the tattered picture in the book. I'd say it was a good likeness, of me that is. At least my fragile ego thought so. In the picture I had my hat squashed in my hand as I climbed out of a river. I think my buddy Li'l John must have put me there.

"Li'l John, did you whack me into the river?"

"Ahh, ha-ha yes, but it was fair fight. This time you lose. Maybe you do better next time," he said. His tooth and eyes sparkled as his great cheeks glowed with happy.

He stood up and patted the top of my head a few times. "Robin, after I put books back we go fix car, ok?"

I immediately looked at Sugar.

"I told him you and Larry went to pick up parts for your car," Sugar said in a matter of fact way.
Li'l John looked at me waiting for an answer.

"Ok, sure. I could use the help. Here, we'll help you take all the books out and put them back where they belong."

"That won't be necessary. Just put the books on this rolling tray," Miss Juju said.

We had the books on the tray within a minute or so. Li'l John smiled.

"We go now, bye Miss Juju. Thank you," he said as he hurried out of the room.

"It was a pleasure meeting you," I said before Sugar hugged Miss Juju. I looked over at a book on her desk. "Can I have a look at that book?"

"Why certainly, are you a Civil War buff?" Miss Juju asked.

"No, not really. There's something I was told a while back that I want to look for."

Blue Note

I opened the book and by the third page I was staring at a young man lying dead on the battlefield at Chancellorsville. His boots were off and strewn on the muddy ground next to him. *Wow, it's true,* I said out loud, to myself. I looked up and both of the ladies gave me strange eyes. I continued until I came to a picture that caused me great harm. It was of a young man, you could even say boy. The caption below said the picture was taken after the Battle of Bull Run. A dead soldier boy's boots had come off or they'd been taken off. Either way there was another young man sitting next to him getting ready to try them on. The very thought made me sick. I asked myself if I would take a dead man's boots off his feet. *No, God no,* I said to myself as I closed the book.

I must have had a deflated look on my face because Miss Juju asked if I was all right.

"Yes ma'am, thank you. I'm ok; it's just that the pictures in that book are a bit disturbing."

"Yes, I think so too. You're not alone, many others have had the exact same reaction you did," Miss Juju said before an uncomfortable period of silence filled the room. Sugar finally broke the ice.

"Miss Juju, was Li'l John sad when he came into the library today?" Sugar asked.

"No, I wouldn't say sad, maybe a tad more timid than usual," Miss Juju said as she put her finger to her temple. "Sugar, you do understand that sad or not John is always welcome in the library?"

"Yes I do, and thank you for making him feel so at ease. We need to get going now; I don't like leaving Li'l John by himself for too long. Bye now, and thanks again," Sugar said with a smile.

Sugar and I raced out of the entrance so we could catch up to Li'l John. He was hiding behind a tree, seemed so odd to me. I don't believe five trees would do the trick.

11

The minute we walked into the parking lot, I went straight for the coupe. I had a truncated broom-stick holding up the hood within a matter of seconds.

"Li'l John, please go over to the porch and get the box with the new alternator in it? Oh and the bag with the spark plugs too. He nodded and took off. I opened the trunk of the car and got my tool box out. I had converted the electrical system to 12 volt; so I knew which tools I'd need. I started to set them out when Li'l John told me he would get each wrench for me when I needed it. Just to test him, I asked for the ½ inch socket; it was in my hand before I could say boo. I don't know how anyone else would feel, but I was more than a little surprised that he knew one size tool from another. I had the alternator out in less than twenty minutes. Took me two hands to hold the darn thing up, it was heavy. I turned to ask Li'l John for the new alternator, he already had the box open and the new alternator in his enormous hand.

Took fifteen minutes more and the job was done. It was hotter than a pistol under the hood of the car. I needed a cold drink so I motioned to Li'l John to come up to the kitchen with me, he shook his head no. I went up and drank a cold glass of Kool Aide. When I went back down, Li'l John had already put all the sockets back in the toolbox and was carrying it to the trunk. I had to stop him.

"Wait, wait a second. I still have to put the new plugs in."

He gave me a one tooth grin as he opened his left hand and showed me all eight of the old plugs.

"New plugs already in," he said with a bright smile. I looked in at the motor and he'd wiped and cleaned the plug wires. The radiator cap was off and sitting on the air cleaner. "Need antifreeze, but some water will do for now," he said and suddenly stopped. "Forgot oil filter, you have roll of toilet paper?"

"Yes, but I think if we're going to change the filter we should go ahead and change the oil."

"No, I checked; oil good color, smell good, and taste good too. Only filter dirty."

I was running the fact that he'd tasted the oil through my head. *Who is this guy? And how does he know so much about cars?* "Wait here, I'll go up and get a roll of toilet paper."

I came back down and watched him work. He not only knew exactly what he was doing, but he was quick too. No wasted movements. He put the battery cables back on before he took the air filter off. I had about a quarter of a can of gas. He poured a little in the carburetor and told me to get in and turn the key. The motor roared for a bit and then died.

He looked around the hood at me. "Pump gas three times."

I did and he yelled, "Turn key."

The motor turned over again, it sputtered a few times and then smoothed out. He smiled at me as he shut the hood. He gave me a thumbs-up and then walked over next to me on the driver's side. I rolled down the window.

"I get Maid Marian and we go for ride."

I thought, *why not*. "Ok," I said with a smile.

Sugar was down the stairs and clapping her hands within seconds. "You boys did a great job."

She got in next to me and told Li'l John there was room for him in the front.

"No, not allowed to ride in front. Always ride in back," he said as he filled up the entire back seat. "Ok, go," he said like an excited child.

It was a hot day, but the wind moving around us felt great. I flew north on the coast highway with no intended destination. As I looked west, there was just enough soup from the waves to give the ocean a nice contrast of blue and white. I've heard people say the water is everything from emerald green to aqua. I really don't give a damn what color it is, I just like it. I counted three puffy clouds on the horizon. One of them rolled in front of the sun as I counted the boats at sea. I looked over at Sugar and she was somewhere else in thought. I mashed the accelerator to the floor and the coupe dropped down into passing gear as the carburetor's secondaries kicked in. Sugar gasped out of fear and Li'l John screamed in unfettered joy. I eased the coupe across the highway and parked in the scenic area overlooking the beach.

Sugar was the first to jump out, she didn't even look back, just took off running for the water. I was close behind her when I waved at Li'l John to follow us. I was halfway across the sand heading for the water when Li'l John passed me. By the time I got down to the water Sugar had her boots off; her blouse was soon to follow. I was a bit stunned when she pulled off her blue jeans. She was wearing a pair of silky black underwear under a white bra that didn't know it would soon be see-thru. Not sure if it was instinct, but I immediately turned to see if there was anyone watching us. There wasn't, we had this small section of the California coast all to ourselves.

I sat down as did Li'l John, difference was I sat on the dry sand and he sat down in the water.   He   splashed   and frolicked like a child as I watched Sugar wade thru the waves. A thousand artist's could paint the picture I was so fortunate to view and still never capture Sugar's grace and beauty. I took off my shoes and socks; the sand was blistering hot. I eased out across the wet sand and thru the ebbing shoreline. When the cool water hit my feet, I felt my heart skip a beat. I just stood in silence and watched the wave's crash against Sugar's body. Her golden mane trailed behind broadcasting her runaway joy.

I walked back and sat down on the part of the beach that was neither hot nor cold; it was however a bit on the wet side. As I was putting my shoes back on, a great shadow surrounded me when Li'l John walked up. He just stood and smiled. I took a close look at his clothes; they were patched together in Frankenstein fashion. I guess it would be tough to find clothes for someone so large in a thrift store.

His t-shirt was sewn together by using the material from at least three. And his overalls, well, I have no idea how they were made, but they worked and he seemed not to care. He sat down next to me and gazed out at the boats cruising along the horizon.

Blue Note

Of course, he hadn't bothered to take off his monster sized boots, didn't seem to bother him in the least. I waited a good half-hour before I stood and waved at Sugar to come in. She blew me a big kiss. I tried not to stare as she wiggled her way back into her clothes.

We walked up to the coupe and headed east on 46 and then south on the 101. I can't tell you how great it felt to be out on the road again. I don't mind walking, but very few things can compare to cruising down the highway with a pretty girl next to you; oh and a giant in the back seat. We were halfway back to Blue Note when Li'l John tapped me on the shoulder.

"Car not charging - need new regulator."

I looked at the gauge and he was right. The car should have been charging like crazy, but it was doing just the opposite. I headed back for town and when I drove up to Cheely's the old guy was locking the front door.

"I need a new voltage regulator, please."

He looked at the coupe and then Sugar and Li'l John and said, "Sure, why not."

Li'l John had the new regulator in the coupe in a matter of minutes, and this time when we drove away, the battery was charging. Cool and happy, we headed back to the Redwood. When I pulled in the parking lot, the bartender named Scout was waiting on the steps leading up to my apartment. She waved and whistled as I drove by.

This sure has been a nice afternoon, wonder what she wants? Maybe she's just here to say hello.

12

I pulled in my parking space and revved the motor a couple times before I turned the old girl off. Have you ever wondered why cars, musical instruments, boats, and most every other toy men have are always referred to as females? I know why, but it's my why. So you'll have to come up with your own.

I walked up to Scout and she gave me a pair of concerned eyes. *Lately, I've had a lot of people giving me those same eyes.*

"I see you got the old girl running, good for you," Scout said as she gave Sugar and Li'l John a short hello wave.

"Yes, she's running great. Scout, you didn't come here to hear just how great my car was running, did you?" I said more than asked.

"That's what I love about you Jack, you're so subtle. I think we'd better go inside," she said as she turned a concerned eye toward my company.

"Give me five minutes, and-"

Before I could say another word, Sugar had my hand in hers. "Jack, please be nice and listen to Scout. She's on your side; she's on all of our sides."

Scout smiled and walked away. I looked over at Li'l John. He stood flashing his front tooth at me through the intense western sun.

"Robin, car is dirty, want me to wash car?"

"Not now Li'l John, it's too hot. We'll wash it when the sun dips down below the roof. Then there will be shade in the back of the bar. Ok?" I asked.

"Ok, but I check tire pressure now, tires look low. I saw gauge and pump in trunk. I get just right before we wash, ok?"

"Ok," I said as I looked at Sugar.

"Jack, you go ahead. I'm going to the store and get something for dinner. What would you like?"

"Well, I'm a sucker for fried chicken. How's that sound?"

Sugar smiled and Li'l John licked his lips.

"I shouldn't be too long," I said before I headed into the tavern.

I cozied up to the bar, Scout was there, but she wasn't alone. Mr. Hurtwood was standing right next to her. Hurtwood looked down the bar and told the other bartender, Andy, to cover for Scout.

"Jack, we'd better talk in the office," he said as he walked away.

I waited for Scout to go in and when I went in, Hurtwood told me to shut the door and sit down. "Jack, I don't feel like wasting any time with small talk. Do you know Mason Cook?"

"The firebug, Mason Cook?" I asked.

"Yes, the very same, he was seen eyeballing your apartment while you were away today." Before I could say a word, Hurtwood confronted me. "Jack, is there a reason he would come to see you?" He asked as he got in my face.

"No none that I can think of at the... oh shit. Well, there could be one."

"And what would that be?" Hurtwood asked with that concerned look I've seen so much of lately.

I went through the entire story about the job I was to start the next day and when I mentioned Rat, both Hurtwood and Scout gave me that look, only this time the look was housed in angst and ire.

"Dang it!" Hurtwood yelled at the top of his lungs. "Jack, do you know who the decoy was while Rat was breaking into cars and stealing money off the bar? Yeah, that's right. It was Mason. I could go on and on about the misery those two have caused in Blue Note, hell, every other town around here too."

"Where does Mason live?" I asked.

"I don't know," Hurtwood said as he peered down at the floor.

I looked at Scout; she backed away, but only for a second. "Jack, I don't like the look in your eyes. Is something wrong?" she asked.

I took my medicine, I mumbled in an absolute panic. "What?" Scout asked. *If I lay down on the floor, maybe I can stop it before it happens.* Scout and Hurtwood gazed at me, their eyes filled with alarm. *"Scout, I'm sorry. If I start shouting or thrashing about, please just keep me from hurting anything, especially you and Mr. Hur!-"* was all I got out before the first nickel exploded into the world.

I heard voices, lots of them, before I actually opened my eyes. Sugar was holding my head in her lap. Scout was sitting next to her. Hurtwood was bent over and pacing the floor as he looked down at me. My eyes rolled across the office before they landed in a corner. Li'l John stood there weeping like a child; crocodile tears ran over his mammoth cheeks. Of all the things that can damage your sense of self, I think seeing a child cry because of something you have done is the worst.

"What happened?" I asked. "Why am I here? Sugar is everything ok? Did I fall?"

"Yes Jack, you fell down. Scout tried her best to catch you. Does your head hurt?" Sugar asked as she brushed my hair back from my face.

I felt a shooting pain just over my right eye. There was a substantial bump that wasn't there only minutes before.

"I'm going to call an ambulance. Jack, you need to see a doctor," Hurtwood insisted.

I looked at Sugar and she knew my eyes said no. "He was just at the doctor's a day ago. The doctor said this was going to happen, but once the medicine he takes works its way into his system, the episodes will stop. I trust the doctor. Jack, do you trust the doctor?" Sugar asked as she looked down at me.

"Yes, thank you for caring but I don't want or need an ambulance. What Sugar just told you is true. It's a mild case of vertigo. Old Doc Henderson says it'll be gone before the next blue moon. Yep, that's exactly what he said." I looked around me and Li'l John was the only one there that I think believed me. He gave me a confused smile.

Blue Note

I stood and dusted myself off before I took a cautious step or two. *I'm ok*, I said; to myself.

"You sure about this?" Hurtwood queried. "Jack, I have to ask, did you mean all those things you said to me?" Hurtwood asked with slits for eyes.

"Sorry about that, no, I just start yelling stuff. I didn't mean any of it. I was just a little tired is all. Think I'll go up and take a nap. See ya, thanks for taking care of me," I said as I looked at Scout.

She nodded. About the time I made it to the door, Hurtwood said, "Jack, what about Mason?"

"Oh yeah, well, Ivy will be here tomorrow evening. I think it would be wise to have him in on the conversation. We'll figure something out then, ok?" I said as I walked out the door.

I didn't realize Sugar was holding my hand as I walked up the stairs to my apartment. When I glanced sideways at her, she smiled. Cat was waiting for us just outside my kitchen window.

"Sugar, can you give Cat a little something to eat? Thanks," I said as I collapsed onto my bed.

I must have been asleep when I hit the pillow because I was startled something fierce when Sugar set the bag of ice on my forehead. I lasted another ten seconds and then I was down for the count.

13

I opened one eye and watched Li'l John watch me. My neck, chest, and the bedding were soaking wet. I sat up and felt cool air being forced my way.

"Li'l John, where did the fan come from?"

"Mr. Hurtwood bring it, he was nice to me."

Sugar came in and sat down right next to me. "You look better, do you feel like eating?"

"Yes, I suppose so. Sugar, how did I get all wet? Was I sweating that much?"

No silly, the ice melted is all. How's your head feel?"

The bump hurt but I wasn't about to let on. "It doesn't feel, and that's a good thing. Listen Sugar, before I eat, I think I'll take a shower."

"Want me to hold you up?" Sugar asked. "No, I'll be ok."

I went in and turned on the shower and the moment I heard the water, I remembered my promise to the new Jack. "Sugar, what time is it?" I yelled.

"It's just after seven, why?"

"Why, because I promised Jack I'd take him something to eat."

"Jack who?" she asked.

"Larry, he's the new Jack." She opened the bathroom door and gave me the strangest look.

"I'll explain after I get dressed."

My self-esteem had plummeted to a new low in the last few hours. I was hoping the shower might get me out this funk.

Blue Note

Truth be told, I knew I was at the end of my rope. I'd just had an episode in front of everyone that made up the little world in which I live. As the water pounded off my sore head and neck I asked myself, *what am I gonna do? I have a job to do and more importantly a life to live. I can't go on like this. Maybe I'll wake up tomorrow and everything will be ok. You're an idiot. At least Sugar had the decency to admit she's a dreamer.*

I turned the water off and when I pulled back the shower curtain, Sugar was standing there. She did her best to smile, but it looked to me like she wanted to cry.

"Jack, I'm sorry. I was just worried. Don't be mad at me," she said as she handed me a towel.

She's such a good, good person. She turned her back while I dried off. I pulled my dirty pants back on and said, "Thanks for caring, I'll be ok.

I had no sooner finished the sentence when she handed me one of my pills. "Please take the pill."

I stood there like a stone for too long. I say too long because I gave her just enough time to start crying.

"Sugar, after I eat I'll take the pill, ok?"

"I'm sorry Jack, thank you," she said as she shuddered just a little bit.

I put on a clean shirt and my rough-out boots. For some reason the boots always make me feel as though I'm in charge of things. Crazy but true. Went back in the bathroom and combed my hair as I looked down at the pill sitting on the sink. I went out and sat at my little kitchen table. There was a plate of cooked carrots; not my favorite, mashed potatoes, one of my favorites, and two drumsticks, my absolute favorite.

Took a bite of the carrots first, just to remove any doubt Sugar may have had. Then the taters, they were real not store bought. I finally got to the chicken legs and they were perfect. I knew I had to drive to the Coke plant, but I couldn't resist and went ahead and had a beer. Two chicken bones lay on the plate when I was done. I smiled at Sugar just to let her know how good the meal was. And right about that time, Cat let out a crazy loud yowl. He looked at me through the kitchen window as if I had betrayed him. Sugar took the plate from me and set it on the floor before she opened the front door and let Cat in. He pounced on the chicken bones. Of course, being the sweetheart that Sugar is, she added a few pieces of chicken for Cat to eat. That was just before she gave me that look I've seen so much of lately.

"Ok, I'll go take the pill. But we'll have to go to the Coke plant immediately or I'll fall asleep at the wheel."

"I can drive," Sugar quipped in a way that made me believe she was just kidding.

"Yeah, ok right," I said for her enjoyment.

"Really, I can," she said in a serious voice.

"Ok, well, that's good to know. If we get in a fix, you can drive." I turned and winked to myself. I guess she didn't feel like pursuing it any further.

I took my pill and then went straight out to the coupe. It was washed and waxed and polished and buffed and shining like a black diamond.

"Jack, you want black wheel cover or baby moons?" Li'l John asked from behind the open trunk.

"Li'l John, now that you asked, I think we'll show the old girl off a little and put the baby moons back on her. I only use the black when I don't want to be seen. Before you put them on, I have to thank you. You have done such a wonderful job. Did you have time to eat?"

"No, I eat with Larry, sorry; new Jack," he said from somewhere in the clouds, a guilty grin shining across his front tooth.

"Sugar already told you about new Jack?"

"Yes, I did," she said from behind me. "I had to tell him for fear he might say Larry. Isn't that what you were afraid of?" she asked.

"How'd you know?" I had to ask.

"It was just the way you said it to me, that's all," Sugar said waiting for an answer. I didn't say a word. "It is isn't it?" she asked again.

"Yes, but how did you know?" I asked in an aggressive way.

"Well, I don't know if this fits, but it seems to me you like to deal from the bottom of the deck," she said with a sideways smile.

76

"I don't have time right now, but later on, you're going to explain why you said that," I said waiting for a sign. She gave me a poker face.

Li'l John held the trunk open so Sugar could put her bag of tricks in. I held the passenger door open for her. She let Li'l John jump in the back and then she got in the front and scooted over right next to the driver, that'd be me. I started to get in but ran upstairs instead. I brought down my old Kodak and both of my passengers hammed it up as I walked around the car snapping pictures. Of course, Sugar just had to take one of me sitting behind the wheel. Ran out of film and then off we went.

Made it to the Coke plant in nothing flat and when I drove down the road to the warehouse, I got my first look at the little red-headed guy named Duke that walks like John Wayne. I parked the car on the side of the warehouse and opened the trunk. I walked around the building and up the concrete stairs that lead to the loading bay; Duke met me before I reached the top step.

"Jackson said you'd be bringing something to eat. It's nice to meet you. I'm Duke."

"Um, I'm Jack," I said as I ran Jackson thru my head. Follow me," Duke said.

We walked by row after row and crate after crate of Coke bottles. We went in a little cafeteria and there sat Jackson, a gilded grin glowing.

"Gosh, I told Duke you'd come, but to tell you the truth, I wasn't sure. Thanks for coming to see me Jack," Jackson said with a wink. He looked at me real close, "Jack, did you bring my...?" he hesitated for a bit hoping I'd say yes.

"Yes, I brought your dinner."

Jackson smiled, "Can't tell you how hungry I am, thanks again."

"Wait here, I'll go get Sugar and... listen, Duke, would it be ok if my girlfriend and another friend come in and sit with Jackson while he eats?"

"No problem. I'm going to be on the phone for a while. Come get me if you need something."

I went out; Sugar and Li'l John were both waiting next to the car.

"Come on you guys, follow me," I said with a wave.

Jack Hawkins

Wasn't 'til we were inside that Sugar noticed Jackson wasn't wearing my clothes. He had on a crisp blue button up shirt with a big Coke patch over the left front pocket. He had on matching blue pants and a pair of boots. I thought *why didn't I notice the clothes?* Right about then zombieville came a calling. Sugar set the food for the guys on the one table in the room.

"Jackson, I sure do like your uniform, where are your clothes?"

"I have a locker in the dressing room. Duke says I'll have a clean uniform to wear each day. All I have to do is get here. Duke said by next week all my uniforms will have my name embroidered on the front, imagine that; Jackson written in fancy letters on my shirts."

I got up and looked around for Duke as the guys dove into their dinner. When I sat back down, I asked old Larry how new Jack became Jackson.

"Well Jack, I thought it might help get rid of confusion. You know, people sayin' 'hey there Jack' and both of us looking up. I mean I like Jack, but I like the name Jackson even more. You don't mind, do you?" Jackson asked.

"No, I don't mind at all. In fact, I think it was a smart move. What do you think?" I said to Sugar.

"Yes, it makes sense and all, but what I want to know is how did you make up a name and a person in the first place? I mean you have to have some kind of identification to prove you're who you say you are. Jack, what if they ask Jackson for some I.D?" Sugar said as she gave me a sideways look.

"What-da-ya mean? I have identification, got a birth certificate and a driver's license. Don't need any more than that," Jackson said as he looked at me for validation.

As he looked at me, Sugar followed suit.

"Sugar, it's a long story, but I'll make it real short. My dad's the one that came up with the idea of having more than one name and one place of birth. And that's all I'm going to tell you right now. Maybe when we have time some other time I'll explain, but not now," I said in a 'don't ask me again' tone.

Sugar could tell it was a touchy subject and backed off. And Jackson, well I don't think he cared much at that point. Sugar got up from the table and filled Li'l John's plate again. Didn't say a word; he just smiled that toothy smile of his. Duke stuck his head in the door and told Jackson the truck would be there in a few minutes so he'd better finish up his dinner. Jackson walked us out and when he saw the coupe, he whistled as he jumped down off the ramp.

"Gosh Jack, she sure is a beauty. I don't remember seeing the car, where'd you have it hidden at?"

"It was in the shade under my porch, it was so dirty it kind of melded into the background."

"What is it, I mean I see it's a Ford, but what year and such is it?"

I started to tell him, but Li'l John did it for me. "Uhh, uhh Jackson, it's a 40 Ford Deluxe Coupe. It has a 49 Lincoln 337 flathead V8 and four speed GM hydromatic transmission. The Muffin Man was here today and told me he seen lots of cars like this in old gangster movies."

The three of us stood there staring. I didn't even know some of the information he'd given us. Sugar walked over to Li'l John and gave him a kiss on the cheek. "You're so smart."

"We go for ride now?" Li'l John asked.

I stopped "Li'l John before he got in the car. "Who is the Muffin Man that came by today?"

"The man with clown eyes, he wears a white sailor hat and has a big muffin for a tummy," he said in a matter of fact way.

When we were walking out to the car, I'd felt the sluggishness that the medicine causes. But after Li'l John described the Muffin Man to me, a colossal explosion erupted behind my eyes. I had to ask him while the iron was hot.

"Li'l John, did this Muffin Man have a matchstick in his mouth?"

"Yes, I told him it was dangerous, he told me not to worry."

"Did he light the match?"

"Yes, while it was in his mouth. How'd he do that?" Li'l John asked in a childlike voice.

He had described the firebug, Mason Cook, to a tee. I told Sugar that we needed to get back to my apartment and the sooner the better.

Jack Hawkins

I said goodbye to Jackson, at least I think I did. I got behind the wheel. Sugar and Li'l John got in, only took her one look at me and she knew.

"Oh Jack, we need to get you home. I don't want you falling asleep at the wheel," she said as she pulled me over to the passenger side. I didn't resist, I guess I didn't because I couldn't. Don't know how much after that it was but I remember watching the lights at the intersections turn colors as we drove by. When Sugar opened the door for me to get out, I tried to walk, but I couldn't. Li'l John carried me up the stairs and put me in bed. Not sure, but I think I saw Cat somewhere along the way.

14

I opened my eyes and there were two unusually dark eyes peering down at me. "Morning Jack, how're you feeling?" Ivy asked.

"I don't know," I said as I looked over Ivy's shoulder at Detective Knox. She had her game face on.

"Ivy, when did the two of you get here? Wait a second, how did I get here?" I said as the detective and I exchanged stares.

"Sugar drove you," Ivy said as if nothing out of the ordinary had taken place.

I slid over and put my feet on the chilly floor. I waited for my head to clear as I wriggled my toes. *Ok Jack, make sure everything you say is crystal clear,* I said to myself.

"Ivy, you're not supposed to be here until this evening. Is something wrong?"

"Jack, last night Scout called me, said you had another episode." He waited for an answer.

"What? Do you want me to lie or make up something? Yes, I had an episode, ok?" Nobody said a word. "Ivy, that doesn't explain her, why is she here?" I asked as I looked Detective Knox in the eye.

"Jack, I'm here because something very bad happened last night," she said in a way that wasn't aggressive, which immediately made me worry.

"Is this about Mason Cook or Rat?" I asked.

"I'd say both. Jack, you left a can of gas out behind the tavern. Do you know what a temptation an accelerant left out in the open is to a firebug?" she said.

"I take it that was a rhetorical question," I said as the smartass in me reared his ugly head.

"Jack you dumb-shit! Mason Cook tried to burn the tavern down! Christ! And you just sit there all smug like you had nothing to do with it," she said with a wicked scowl that shot up through her eyes and across her crinkled brow.

"Ok, yes I left the can of gas out there, but I didn't do it on purpose. I'm sorry; did you catch the son of a bitch?"

Ivy turned to Detective Knox. "You can hurl stones later, Jack is right. You should be out looking for Mason and his accomplice, Mr. Johnson. You just had to throw a little blame around, didn't you?"

If looks were bullets, Ivy and I would've been full of lead. That was a little more aggressive than I had ever seen or heard Ivy. And true to his nature, he immediately apologized.

"Miss Knox, I apologize for what I just said. And if there's anything Jack or I can do to help, please ask," Ivy said in his gentleman voice.

"You can help by staying out of this!" Miss Knox hollered as she marched out of the room.

We heard my front door slam just before she hurled a salvo of mean-ass epo-shit our way.

"Ivy, I don't' think the detective likes you."

He gave me a crazy stare as I stood to go out and have a look at the damage Mason the firebug had caused. I tiptoed down my steps and followed Ivy over to the northeast corner of the tavern. There was a three-foot-wide blackened section that ran up the wall for maybe ten feet.

"Ivy, did the detective or anyone else tell you whether or not they saw Mason do it?"

"A guy was getting in his car to leave when he saw the flames going up the side of the building. He turned on the hose and put the fire out. As far as I know, nobody saw Mason."

"Well, they may not have but someone did," I said.

"What do you mean," Ivy asked.

"Yesterday Li'l John saw Mason here in the parking lot. Mason asked about my car."

"Jack, we need to tell the police. This is very important."

Blue Note

"Yes, it is. And I've already told the police," Mr. Hurtwood said from behind us.

Hurtwood didn't look angry, which confused the heck out of me.

"I'm sorry Mr. Hurtwood," was all I could think to say.

"Jack, stuff like this has been going on since the day I bought the place. And it may sound strange, but I'm glad he did it."

Ivy and I both gave him confused eyes.

"Why would you be glad?" I asked.

"I'm glad because now neither Mason nor Rat will be able to show their faces anywhere near here. Everyone in town will be looking for them, not to mention the entire police force. And I believe that if he really wanted to, he could have burned the place down. No, I think his little fire display was meant to send a message; to you Jack." Hurtwood was right. If Mason wanted to, he'd have burned the place down.

"Mr. Hurtwood, I think you're right," I said.

Hurtwood started to walk away but stopped. "Jack, I think I'd like Li'l John to keep a special eye out for Mason and Rat. Can you tell him I said that, please?"

"I will definitely tell him."

"Thanks," was all he said before he walked away.

I looked at Ivy, "Now what?"

"Now we have an appointment with a doctor. So get yourself dressed."

"What are you talking about?"

"I'm talking about finding a way out of this mess you're in, that's what. Jack, you can't go on like this. You were not put on this earth for a banausic existence." I gave him a pair of dead eyes. "Jack, a nonintellectual, meaningless job would destroy you. You were meant to be challenged." I gave him the same eyes. "Jack, I just paid you a compliment. So don't look at me like that."

"You did?"

"Yes, now go get yourself dressed. We have to find a medication that will allow you to live and do all the things at which you excel."

"Gee Ivy; I didn't know you cared so much."

"All I'm saying is you were not meant to live a utilitarian life."

"Thanks, was that another compliment?"

He shook his head and mumbled to himself, "And to think I took the day off for this," he said out loud. *I may have pushed the smartass button one too many times.*

I got cleaned up and ready to go. I did have one question for Ivy. When I walked into the kitchen, Ivy was meowing at Cat. *And people think he's so level headed.*

"Ivy, I have a question that is killing me, but I have to ask it." He didn't say a word. "Ok, should I take a pill before we go or not?"

"Absolutely not! The specialist wants to see you in your everyday state, whatever that may be. So, stop with the angst and ire and let's go."

I fired up the coupe and by the look on Ivy's face, I'd say he was impressed. That was just before he made me move over to the passenger side. He tooled his way out of the parking lot and when we hit Broadway he laid a patch for at least thirty feet. I had no idea Ivy had that kind of energy and thrill seeker in him. We were about halfway to San Louis Obispo when he asked about the job I'd accepted.

"Ivy, I was hoping to surprise you, how'd you hear about the job?"

"Sugar told me before she and Li'l John took off this morning, sleepy head."

I didn't respond. Actually, I didn't care what he called me, but I wasn't going to let him know.

"Ok Jack, tell me about the job and what it entails."

"It's really pretty simple; we have been paid, and I should add, quite handsomely, to find out who killed that boy we followed the other night. His name is Timmy Allen. That always confuses me, should I say his name is or was?"

"Is, his name still is Timmy Allen. Was would suggest to me that he had changed his name, which reminds me of something Sugar told me about this morning. Jack, who is Jack Laramie? And where did you get identification for this person?"

"It's a long story, too long to tell right now. And it has an emotional edge to it that, at the moment, I don't believe I could handle; unless of course you wouldn't mind seeing me have an episode right here in the car."

Ivy looked over at me, not once but about six times. "You're serious, aren't you?"

"Yes Ivy, very."

He left it at that. We pulled into a section of faculty parking at Cal Poly.

"Ivy, I thought you said we were going to see a doctor. This doesn't look like a hospital to me."

"Doctor Lee is doing research for a privately funded firm. Truth is, there's a U.S. senator that has a daughter that suffers from episodes similar to yours. This senator pushed a few buttons and made all of this happen. It's purely research, but... Jack, I believe you would do almost anything to be episode free. Am I right?"

"Yes, you already know that. Ivy, is episode the right term?" He gave me a strange glance. "What I mean is, shouldn't I be calling them something else, something more clinical?"

"Strange you should ask. If you're looking for a fancy term well, there isn't one. The fact is, the term most doctors use is, 'Rage Attacks'. Would you prefer we call them Rage Attacks?"

"No! Park the car and let's go see Dr. Lee."

Rage Attacks my ass! I'd just as soon call it 'epo-shit'. The nerve, Rage Attacks.

Ivy led the way through a maze of buildings and walkways full of curvy co-eds.

"Ivy, where are all the guys?"

"They're here; you just can't see the forest for the trees."

"That tree thing is so over used. Where is this Dr. Lee?"

"Right here," Ivy said as he began walking down the steps to what looked to me like a basement of some kind.

He opened one of those huge metal doors you might find on a bomb shelter. A pretty co-ed sat behind one small desk, the rest of the room was bare.

"Hello, I'm Doctor Ivy Fin, I'm here to see Doctor Lee."

"Oh yes, he's expecting you," she said as she pointed at the only other door in the room. "You'll find him first door on the right."

"Thank you," Ivy said as we walked away. The young lady stood up and smiled at me in a way that didn't feel good. It felt to me as if she was trying to tell me, 'it'll only hurt for a little while.'

When we reached the door, there was a sign that read: Henry Lee M.D. I did my best to envision the doctor. I pictured a tall, thin, bearded man with huge eyebrows, wearing a tweed jacket.

Ivy opened the door and a small Asian man in a white lab-coat sat reading a journal of some kind.

"Well, hello Ivy. Geez, I thought you'd never get here. What took you so long?" Dr. Lee said as he spied me.

"We ran into a small problem. Hank, this is Jack Hawkins."

The doctor stood and shook my hand. He had a real firm handshake. We both said hello and then he got right to the point.

"Jack, before we do anything, there are some papers you have to sign," Dr. Lee said as I took a step backwards. "Jack, I won't do anything without your prior knowledge and approval. It's just that this is all research," he said as he held up both hands and did the quotation thing. "Jack, there might be a few things I'll do that another doctor might not be willing to try. You understand, don't you?"

I looked at Ivy.

"Jack, do you trust me?"

"Yes."

"Then sign everything and do everything the good doctor asks you to. Ok?" he said waiting for an answer from me.

I looked in both men's eyes; one at a time of course. "Ok, where's the pen and paper?"

Dr. Lee said, "Excuse me," as he walked out of the room.

I looked at Ivy for a second.

"I expected Dr. Lee to have an accent that was hard to understand. He actually speaks pretty good English."

"Jack, profiling in that manner is what makes you and others appear to be full on racists."

"Shit Ivy, I'm not one of them," I said and then stopped. He was right about the profiling, but there was no way I was going to admit to it.

Blue Note

"Jack, for your information Hank grew up in San Francisco. And I can guarantee you Dr. Lee's knowledge of the English language is far superior to yours. Now quit with the squalor and confrontation and give the guy a chance. Ok?"

"Yeah, ok," I said as Dr. Lee walked back in the room.

He pointed to his desk. "Jack, you can sit there. Just initial all the places where you see an X. And sign your name on the last page, please."

I started writing my initials on every X I saw. I didn't have the patience or the wherewithal to read everything. I didn't see the point. I did see a lot of the same damn words over and over again. Consent to this and permission to do that. I figured I needed the help, so to hell with it.

"Jack, do you always ball your fists like that when you're writing?" Dr. Lee asked.

I looked at my left hand and it was squeezed together so hard I could barely get it straightened out. I wiggled my fingers a little and then told the doctor I was ok. He just looked at my right hand, so I did too. My knuckles were white and the fingers were so tight around the pen that my veins were bulging. I set the pen down.

"Jack, did you take your medicine today?" Dr. Lee asked.

"No, Ivy told me not to."

"Good, for now you can leave the form as it is. I trust you to sign the rest before you leave. Ok?"

"Yes, ok. Look doc, I'm sorry I didn't trust you to begin with. Bottom line, I need help."

He walked over and turned off the lights in the room. "Jack, come over here and lie down on this lounge."

I had been so paranoid by the whole thing I hadn't even noticed the psychiatrist couch. At least that's what I would call it. I lay down on the couch and looked up into the young lady's eyes that met us when we first came in. She put a thermometer in my mouth and then wrapped one of those blood pressure thingies around my arm. She sat beside me and when she was done, she said something to the doctor in a low voice; I couldn't hear what she'd said. Then she wrapped a tourniquet tight around my arm and said, "I have to take some blood, you'll feel a little pinch is all. Take a deep breath for me."

"Ouch! Shit that hurt!" I shouted out.

"Jack, I know that some people have what is called the white coat effect, but this is more than just that. Your pulse is quite rapid, 88 beats per minute. Your temperature is slightly elevated to just over 100 degrees. Your blood pressure is an entirely different story and presents a very dangerous picture. Elaine, will you please bring me two 'so and so's', medical terms I didn't understand' and one, 'blah, blah, blah,' another word I didn't understand. Jack, when was the last time you had a checkup?"

Don't know why, I looked over at Ivy for an answer before I said, "When I was in Montana, a few months ago."

"Did the doctor tell you what your blood pressure was?"

I blurted out, "No, why would he?"

"I just told you why. Your blood pressure is dangerously elevated."

The young gal named Elaine came back in and handed Dr. Lee two bottles.

"Jack, as you can see," he said as he put one bottle in front of my face. "No medicine is indicated. The only thing written on the bottle is dosage. Take one of these in the morning when you wake up and one when you go to bed. The other bottle says the exact same thing. Do as instructed. Before you ask, they are both meant to help control your blood pressure. First things first, now tell me where the nickel, dime, quarter came from."

I looked at Ivy again. I guess it was a look of confusion. I felt as if Ivy had sold me out.

"Jack, Ivy had to tell me as much as he could about you before I would even consider bringing you here. Now, where did you hear about the coins, why do you do that?"

"People on different medications can exhibit dangerous behavior. So, during my P.I. training I had to learn to differentiate common outward behavior caused by medications from outright aggression."

"Did you see these first hand or on film?" Dr. Lee asked.

"Only on film, I guess you would call them teaching tools or documentaries."

"So, would it be accurate for me to say your behavior was learned rather than involuntary?"

"I guess so, what are you getting at?"

"Jack, I'm doing nothing but trying to get at the true nature of your disease. And at the same time pinpoint exactly what disease it is. It's as simple as that. Exactly what disease was it that you were told from which you suffer?"

"I thought you already knew that!" He didn't say anything. "I was told I have Tourette's syndrome and that there is no cure."

I was on the verge of getting angry. Why? I don't know. I guess I expected him to know all about my Tourette's and, therefore my problem. He walked away from me and turned the lights back on. He went over to his desk and opened a drawer. He pulled out a small green notebook and brought it over and handed it to me.

"Jack, during the day do you make repetitive movements or unwanted sounds?"

I looked at Ivy, "Ivy, do I do those things?"

"No Jack, you don't."

"Jack, there are many disorders that can copy or mimic Tourette's syndrome. Huntington's disease, OCD, anxiety, and several dissociative disorders can all appear on the surface to be Tourette's. And since you accepted the first diagnosis you were given, you have in essence welcomed Tourette's into your life. Jack, I could be wrong but I'm not totally convinced you have Tourette's syndrome, but I believe you've convinced yourself that you do. So, I want you to keep a log of situations or events that lead to the emotions which cause the episodes, etc. ok?"

"Sure, ok, anything else?" I asked out of confusion.

"Yes, I have some more questions. Is that ok with you?" Dr. Lee asked. Before I could answer him, he said, "I understand you have both twitching and tics. Is that correct?"

"Yes, I think maybe I do all of that."

"So you don't really know what you do."

"Yes, I do!" I said as the anger welled up in me.

"It doesn't sound like you do. What I hear you saying is it's others that tell you after the fact. Would that be a fair assessment?"

"Yeah, whatever."

"Jack, I can't help you unless you decide that you want help. Do you want my help or would you rather go back to the way things were?"

Strange how many times in my life that very same ultimatum has come up.

I looked at Ivy. "Damn it Jack, can't you see Dr. Lee is trying to help you?"

I'd never heard Ivy swear. I took a deep breath and then a tingle hit me like a tsunami.

Dr. Lee looked at me and he knew.

"Jack, do not say the coin thing. Do you hear me? Do not say the coins! That's an order!" Dr. Lee screamed at me.

I retreated inside myself for a minute or two. You have no idea and I could never explain how much I wanted to say the coins. But I didn't.

"Jack, keep your eyes closed. Now I want you to breathe as slow as possible, almost to the point where you think you're not getting enough air."

I slowed my breathing down to almost dead.

"Good, that's very good. Now, I want you to breathe deep thru your nose. Good, good, yes that's better."

Neither Dr. Lee nor Ivy said another word. I think I passed out; at least it felt like I did.

"Ok Jack, you can open your eyes now," Doc Lee said in a real soft voice.

I looked around for only a few seconds. "Did I have an episode?"

"No Jack, you didn't," Ivy affirmed.

"I didn't?"

"No, you didn't," Dr. Lee confirmed.

"Then what happened?" I asked, completely confused.

"Nothing happened," both doctors said at the same time.

"Jack, how do you feel?" Dr. Lee asked.

"You'll have to ask Sugar," I quipped.

"What?" Dr. Lee said.

"Pay no attention to the dullard," Ivy said.

"Jack, I want you to bring in the medicine you've been taking so I can have it analyzed ok?"   "Ok."

"Listen Jack, would you be willing to try an experimental drug?" Dr. Lee asked.

"What do you mean by, experimental?"

"It's experimental in that I will give you one dose today and it may last for a few weeks. At first you may feel a little disjointed or drowsy, but that will wear off within 48 hours or so."

"I have band practice tonight, I can't start now. No, I'll have to come back another time."

"Ok, we can wait a day or two, but I'd start ASAP. Jack, for what it's worth, I believe in this drug. I think it will significantly reduce the chances of a Rage Attack."

I objected to the term he used and quickly put my hand up in the stop position.

"I don't like the term you just used. Can we just say episodes or something along those lines?" I insisted more than asked.

I think Dr. Lee could feel the desperation in my voice. "Sure Jack, episodes will work just fine."

"Doc, should I continue taking the medicine I've been taking?"

"No, from what I've heard and understand, it isn't working. You wouldn't take a pain reliever that gave you a headache would you?"

He didn't give me time to answer.

"No, I don't believe you would. I want you to do what I told you to do. Never say the coins again and when you feel the first tinge of emotion, close your eyes and breathe as slow and as deliberate as you can. If it makes you feel better or maybe I should say safer, lie down. Ok," he said with force.

"Ok," I said.

"Oh Jack, I forgot, keep your personal log going; what I mean is, write down how you feel the moment something bothers you, don't wait. I expect at least one entry each night before you go to bed. Will you do that for me?"

"Sure doc," I said as I looked over at Ivy.

"Yes Jack, we can go. You don't have to stare at the door like that," Ivy said in his scolding voice.

"I wasn't staring."

"Yes you were," Dr. Lee said with a smile.

"Sorry, nothing against you," I said with a grin.

Ivy and I said our goodbyes and thank you's to Dr. Lee and then went out to the young lady named Elaine and did it all over again. That was just before I signed the rest of the papers. I looked inside myself and asked the same question I ask all the time. *Now what?*

15

I let Ivy drive on the way home so I could write in the notebook. I listed the first ten things that ran thru my mind.

"Jack, are you having strong feelings right now?" Ivy asked as we jumped on state highway 1.

"Yes, Dr. Lee told me to write them down, so that's what I'm doing."

"Would you mind giving me an example of what you've written so far?"

"No, I don't mind. Number one: talk to all the employees at the bowling alley. Number two: go talk to Senator Rose. Find out how Timmy Allen got along with others and if the senator knows of any enemies or anyone that may have wanted to hurt him. Number three-"

"Jack, Dr. Lee gave you that notebook so that you could write down what leads up to your episodes. He did not give it to you for investigative purposes. Don't you ever do as you're told?"

"Ivy, relax and drive. I know exactly why he gave this to me. And I'm going to do everything he asked me to do. But that doesn't mean I can't write other stuff too. He may find it interesting, may even come up with an idea or figure out a clue to help us," I said waiting for Ivy to say something negative. He didn't. In fact, he didn't say a word.

"Ivy, are you going to continue to help me in my work. Or are you trying to tell me something by not telling me something?"

"Jack, that was one of those convoluted things you say that somehow make sense. Yes, I'm going to help in this investigation.

The challenge and the hunt are what I live for. But you already know that?" Ivy said as he turned for a second and gave me those dark eyes of his. "Well," he said.

"Yes, I know that, just wanted to hear you say it, is all."

"Jack, keep writing," Ivy said.

We got back just in time for me to take an hour nap before band practice. Ivy had some errands to run, so he left me alone. When I woke up, I felt better than I had in weeks. I went down early so that I could say hey to Whitey; he's the leader of the band. And I wanted to warm up a little on my old black Byrdland guitar. Had to pawn it to Whitey, but now I had enough money to buy it back. I walked in the tavern and hunkered down next to the bar. As usual, Scout had her back to me. She gave me a smile and a peace sign in the mirror.

"Jack, do you want something to drink?" she asked.

"No, just came down to say hey to Whitey and the guys before rehearsal."

"Ay, ay, ain't gon, gon, gon, gonna b, b, be no, no, no re, re, re, rehearse, rehearsal."

I looked in the mirror at a childlike face with a sparse mustache under a pug nose. A brown plastic cowboy hat with the yellow stitching sat high on top of unruly black hair. Stuttering John's lips bounced off one another as he waited for me to acknowledge his presence.

"Hello John, why isn't there going to be a rehearsal?" I asked as I turned around expecting to see strings attached to his shoulders. Tiny brown and yellow boots emerged from faded hi-rise blue jeans that were at least four inches too short. He held on with both hands to a plastic star belt buckle. A bright red shirt with embroidered sparkling saddles on both pockets finished off the ensemble. Yes, I've been told before what color the stuff is.

"Be, b, be-cuz Whi, Whi, Wh-Whitey said so. Th, th, th, that's wh-why!" Stuttering John said as he wrapped a yellow bandana around his neck.

"Are you sure about that?" I asked as the angst and ire inside me began to percolate.

"Y, ye, yeah, I, I, I'm pa, pa, pa, positive. Wh, wh-wh, Whitey se, se, sent me ta f, f, fire yer ah, ah, ah, ass!"

I turned hard to look at Scout. I was thinking, maybe she knew something about what was going on.

"John's right," Hurtwood said.

I didn't have to wonder where he came from. He was probably sitting in his office when he heard me come in.

"John, you've said your piece, now can you take a walk and leave us alone for a bit," Scout said in my defense.

"Sh, sh, sure Scuh, Scuh, Sc-Sc Scout," John stuttered as he grinned at me.

I took a step towards him; he hopped back out of my reach. His lips bounced as if he was going to say something. Scout started walking around the bar and yelled, "John you little prick, you'd better move before I crack your head wide open."

Stuttering John grinned and giggled at me before he ran out the door. I turned to Hurtwood.

"Whitey told Ivy to make sure I showed up tonight for practice. What's going on?" I asked in a huff.

"Jack, the only reason Whitey wanted you to show up was so he could fire you. I guess he didn't have the guts to do it himself," Hurtwood said.

I turned and tried to walk out of the tavern, but my legs wouldn't move. I was paralyzed by the extreme rage running thru me. I knew I couldn't stay; I had to get out of there. I looked down at the floor in front of me and willed my right foot to take a step in the direction of the door. And one foot, one leg at a time, I marched out the door and up the stairs to my apartment. Ivy was sitting at my little table.

"Back so soon," he said just before he yelled, "Jack, don't say nickel!"

I heard him but I couldn't stop myself. And the race was on. Nickel was followed by dime, and so forth.

16

I looked up into worried blue eyes.

"Hi Jackie, I'm here. You don't have to say anything. Just lay still for a little while longer, ok?" Sugar whispered.

I looked past her at Ivy, Li'l John, Scout, and Dr. Lee. I didn't want them to know just how low I was, but a little bitty tear let me down. I felt so small and so... I don't know. *Jack, get a hold of yourself! Stop that!* I yelled from inside my head.

I pushed Sugar away from me and sat up on the kitchen floor. I backed into a corner and stared up at everyone. Then the room started swirling. It turned in small circles and then earth sized orbits. I looked across the room.

"Dr. Lee, please help me!"

"Jack, it's going to take some time, try not to worry."

"What's going to take some time?"

"The experimental drug I administered. You remember the drug we talked about?" he asked.

"I didn't say you could do that," I protested. And as I spun, I looked at the band-aid on my arm.

"Oh, but you did say you would try the drug. You just wanted to wait 'til after band practice. But, it appears there won't be any band practice," he said as Ivy gave him a pair of threatening eyes.

"Dr. Lee that was uncalled for," Ivy scolded.

"I'm sorry; I did not mean it to come out that way. Jack, I'm very sorry," Dr. Lee said as he bowed and then backed away.

"Jack, how do you feel at this very moment?" Ivy asked.

"Dizzy."

"Besides being dizzy how do you feel?"

"Like I'm in a dream, crazy thing is I don't think I want to wake up."

"That's a good answer," Dr. Lee said.

"Dr. Lee, I was supposed to start working on a new job today. When do you think I'll get out of this dream and be able to start work?"

"I see no reason you can't work on whatever it is right now. Even though you're in this dream your speech and cognition are quite clear. What do the rest of you think?" Dr. Lee asked as he looked up at the others. Nobody said a word.

"That does it, Ivy we're going to get started this evening. Can't think of a better time than tonight to hit the bowling alley and see what we can see."

"I agree," Ivy said in a hesitant voice.

"Jack, can I ask what this job is all about?" Dr. Lee asked.

"You can ask, but I can't tell you. I'm sorry but that's just the way it is," I said.

"Jack, if you need help or someone to talk to, come get me," Scout said as she waved goodbye and walked out the door.

I looked at Sugar and she was studying Scout as she walked out. It was pretty obvious to me Sugar didn't want other females horning in on her territory. *You know what; she acted the same way when Detective Knox came to see me. She's jealous,* I said to myself as Sugar turned and gave me two of those concerned eyes I've seen so much of lately.

"Jack, I'm going to go home and put my suit on. It's just after six now, I'll be back within the hour," Ivy said as he headed out the door.

Ivy always wears a coat and tie when we're working. It gives the two of us a professional look or something like that. Heck, it worked for the Suit that hired me.

"Jack, I will be checking in on you for the next week or two. Can I have your phone number, please?" Dr. Lee asked.

I wrote the number down on a corner of the calendar and tore it off and gave it to him. He waved goodbye to everyone as he and Ivy walked out of the apartment together. *Geez, I need to pay the phone bill so I can get my phone working again. I hope he doesn't call tomorrow morning.*

"Jackie, are you gonna be ok?" Sugar asked.

"Sure, I feel better already. Why?" I asked.

"Cuz, Li'l John and I are going to make our evening run."

"What evening run?" I asked.

"We take food from several restaurants and such out to the men in the cave every evening. They depend on us and I don't want to let them down, and I'm late as it is. I'll be back later. Jackie, please be careful. And do like Dr. Lee says; don't say the coins anymore, ok?" she asked.

"No, I won't say the coins or at least I'll try not to."

"Ok, good. Oh, and one other thing. If you need to talk to someone, you can talk to me." she said in a way that said she wasn't asking, she was telling me.

Li'l John flashed his tooth at me, and Sugar gave me a peck on the cheek before the two of them walked out the door. I stood still for an awful long time. I was wondering if the medication Dr. Lee gave me would actually work. A tinge of doubt barged its way into my private thoughts, I kicked it out.

17

I've shown the old girl off during the day, but it was time for the cloaking devices. I took the baby moons off and put the black wheel covers on the coupe just before Ivy parked his car. He motors around in a red, right-hand drive MG-TD. Nice little car, but too slow and too small for our line of work. I started the coupe and sat warming her up. Ivy opened the passenger door and jumped in.

"You ready to do this," he said in a cocksure voice.

I looked over at his suit and just nodded yes. We took off going up Broadway to Easy Street and then headed west for the bowling alley. I parked next to a sea-sprite green 51 Ford Woody. I looked inside; the interior was all original and sweet. We walked on in and started for the manager's office, didn't make it five feet when we were confronted by a young lady sitting on a stool behind the cash register.

"I'd say you're definitely a size twelve."

She was pretty, too much makeup, but pretty. She couldn't have been more than fifteen years old.

"You're darn good at your job. I do wear a size twelve. How 'bout him, what size shoe does he wear?" I asked as I pointed at Ivy.

"Oh, he's definitely a ten, maybe ten and a half. That is, if he's been on his feet all day."

I looked at Ivy; he didn't let on what size shoe he wears. He's real private like that. I looked back at the girl; she had a name tag on her bowling shirt. It read: Welcome to Cabrillo Lanes, but there was no name.

"Aren't you supposed to have your name on the name tag?" I asked.

She stood up off the stool she was on and eyed me. Mister, are you trying to put a move on me? Cuz if you are, I can have my dad here in about five seconds. He owns the bowling alley, and he's right over there in his office.

"No, I'm not trying to do any such thing. I came here to ask you a few questions about the boy that was killed. I was told he worked here."

"Oh, poor Tim, gosh, why didn't you say so in the first place?" she said in a hurry. "What is it you want to know?"

"Well, for starters, how well did you know him?"

"Well enough," she said as she narrowed her eyes at me. "I think I need to see some identification. You don't look like a cop to me."

I took my wallet out of my coat pocket and let it flop open in front of her. I paid a lot of money for a badge that's big, shiny, and impressive.

"How 'bout Suit?" she said as she locked eyes with Ivy. "Does he have a badge?"

Ivy reached inside his King's Road suit coat and much to my surprise pulled out a wallet that looked a lot like mine. And, there was a badge inside the wallet that was bigger and brighter than my badge.

"My dad doesn't allow employees to date. So, if you tell my dad I'll deny it, but Tim and I were sweethearts," she said as a chubby young man with a bad case of acne walked up. "George, can you fill in for me for a while?" she asked.

"Sure sweetie," the boy said.

"George, I told you not to call me sweetie. Do it again and I'm gonna have dad fire your ass."

"Ok, sorry Jill," the boy said as he backed away to let her walk by.

"Follow me," Jill said.

She walked ahead of us. She was pretty and by the way she walked, she knew it. We kept right on going the length of the bowling alley and out a side door. Once out the door she stopped, reached down, and pulled a pack of Tareyton's from her sock. She had the cigarette lit before I'd stopped walking. She looked like the grown women on the T.V. ads with black eyes that say, 'I'd rather fight than switch.'

"Does your dad know you smoke?" I asked.

"Yes, he bought these for me. We have an agreement. I can smoke, but only if I keep my grades up in school. I'm a solid B student. Does your mom know you smoke?" she said out of the corner of her mouth at me.

I actually started to answer her when she cut me off. "I can tell a smoker a mile away. Want one?" she asked.

I looked at Ivy for approval, not sure why. He nodded his head yes before saying, "Go on Jack, it might help you relax."

She took a cigarette out and lit it for me, a very adult thing to do. I thanked her and thought *I might have been wrong about her age*. She looked up at me after handing me the cigarette and her eye liner was beginning to run down one cheek. *Maybe I was right about her age.*

I didn't realize how raucous it was inside the bowling alley 'til we were outside. The quiet was just what the doctor ordered; at least it was for me. I was just starting to relax when she yelled, "Why would anybody wanna kill Tim? He never hurt anyone!" she said before looking away to hide the tears.

"That's why we need your help, everyone has said the same thing about Timmy. I want you to try real hard, go back as far as you need to. There has to be someone that didn't like him."

"That stupid guy inside didn't like Tim, but that's only because he knew he had no chance with me. George was just jealous, is all. But I know for a fact that he didn't hate Tim, he told me so."

"We heard Timmy was seen arguing with a bearded man about an hour before he got off work. Do you know who this person is?" I asked.

"No, I don't. I wasn't here when they argued. I already told that to the police bitch who wears the tight pants. I don't know why, but I don't think she believed me. Is that why you're here?"

"No, we work separate from her. Why do you say she's a bitch?"

"I don't know, maybe it's the way she looked at me?"

Jack Hawkins

"How'd she look at you?" Ivy asked.

"She looked at me the way men do. Like she was undressing me or something, gave me the creeps. I think she was trying to let me know she could do a man's job. She might be pretty and stuff, but I know a bitch when I see one. Do you know her?" Jill asked as she glared at me.

"Yes, we know her. I've had run-ins with her too," I said.

"Oh good, then you think she's a bitch too."

"I wouldn't go that far," Ivy said in Detective Knox's defense. "Listen; would it be ok if I call you Jill?" She nodded yes. "Thank you. Jill, someone told the detective that Timmy Allen was seen arguing with a bearded man. If it wasn't you, then who was it?"

"Billy told the detective. But he has a habit of making things up, he could be lying."

"Billy who?" I asked.

"Billy O'Dea, he tells a lot of lies."

"Why would he lie?" I asked.

"I don't know why, he just does."

"Jill, is Billy here tonight?" I asked.

"Yeah, he's fixing the ball return on number 18. Come on, I'll take you back there," Jill said as she flicked her cigarette butt across the parking lot. Sparks flew in all directions. I dropped my cigarette and stepped on it.

The moment Ivy opened the door for her, it sounded like we'd walked into a construction site.

"This way," she said, just before she made an immediate left turn down the side of what I think was lane 36.

As we walked down the side of the alley, I took a look back. The place was filled with adults, all talking at the same time. There were a few teenagers bowling all the way on the other end of the place. The closer we were to the machines that set up the pins, the louder the noise. She pulled a key ring out of her pocket and opened a door into what I would call the heart and soul of the bowling alley. The sheer volume of noise was disturbing. I grabbed Ivy's arm and closed my eyes for a moment. He stopped me; Jill just kept right on walking.

"Jack, are you ok? I can go get the kid and bring him out here if you want."

Blue Note

I blinked a couple of times and then opened my eyes. The moment Ivy looked at me, he knew I was ok.

"I'm alright, it's just noise. Come on, she's going to wonder where we went," I said as I walked by Ivy.

Jill was standing looking back at us with a confused look on her face. She turned and bent down and a young man jumped up off the floor. He had a set of headphones on and lifted the left one from his ear. They spoke for a moment and then Jill walked back to us and at the top of her lungs yelled, "Sorry, I should have brought him outside in the first place."

She walked past us and walked the exact same route in reverse. The three of us waited outside for the young man. Billy had a cigarette dangling from his mouth when he came thru the doors.

"I told that slinky detective the truth, and I ain't gonna change my story one damn bit!" Billy yelled as he groped his pockets for a light. Jill didn't offer him one.

Billy was a little older than Jill and Timmy. He was a good sized young man. I think he liked getting his hands dirty, and they were.

"Billy, we're not here to doubt you. We just want to hear what you saw that night," I said in my easy-going voice.

"Yeah sure, just as soon as you tell me who the hell you are and why you wanna know," he said just as he found the book of matches he had stuffed in his back pocket.

"Yeah, you guys never told me your names," Jill said in a semi-loud voice.

"I'm Jack Hawkins and this is Dr. Ivy Fin. We were hired by an independent source to find out who killed Timmy Allen. You don't have to believe me, but we're on your side."

The two of them looked us over and as they did, I watched their faces relax. *We're the good guys,* I said to myself.

"Who is this independent source?" Billy asked in a loud voice.

He'd caught me off guard with the question, and he knew it. I had to calm this guy down or we weren't going to get anywhere with him.

"I don't know who the source is," I said as the two of them gave me suspicious eyes. "If I could tell you who it is, I would.

You can doubt me if you want, but it's the truth. All we want to do is find out who killed Timmy, don't you?" I asked.

"Of course we do!" Jill yelled.

The ball was in their court now and I think questioning their desire to find out who killed Timmy
hit the intended target.

Ivy stepped forward. And in a tranquil voice said, "Jack was given a lot of money to do this job. Why? Because he's very good at what he does. Billy, if you were offered a couple thousand dollars to find out the truth about all of this, would you take it?"

"I'd do it for free, but if someone wanted to pay me that kind of money, I'd take it for sure," he said with some attitude.

"Yes, I thought you would. How about you Jill?" she nodded yes. "Now, have we asked either of you anything that would lead you to believe we're against you in any way?"

Billy and Jill looked at each other and at the same time said no.

"Thanks Ivy," I said as I stepped forward. "Billy, I just want to know about this guy with the beard. And then I want to know anything you can tell me about Timmy that others might not know."

Billy took a long drag off his cigarette and looked over at Jill. She nodded her head yes. At that point I thought about telling them that Ivy and I had been there when Timmy was killed. But because it could make them think we did the killing, I stopped myself short of that. And it looked to me as though Billy was about to let go and tell us what he knew.

"Tim and the guy with the beard were all the way down on the other end of the machines, so I couldn't hear a word that was said. But I can tell you the guy sure had his finger in Tim's face."

"Was Timmy arguing back?" I asked.

"Oh yeah, Tim was a real nice guy, but I can tell from fights we got into as kids that he has a breaking point."

"What?" Ivy asked.

"A breaking point, a moment when he knows he ain't gonna take anymore, and if he don't fight back, things are gonna escalate. I used to pick on him and bully him something fierce. Well, one day he decided he'd had just about enough, and he smacked me a good one right across the nose. I bled like a fountain. Oh, he apologized right away, but I knew I deserved it. I was kind of proud of him for fighting back, if you know what I mean."

"Billy, can we go in a different direction for a bit?" Ivy asked.

"Sure, what are you drivin' at?"

"Was there anything about the guy other than the beard that stuck out? I mean anything unusual?" Ivy asked.

"Yeah, now that you mentioned it there was. He had on one of them jumpsuits guys wear that are working around dangerous chemicals."

"Do you remember what color the jumpsuit was?" I asked.

"Uh, geez, you're talking to the wrong guy. I'm color blind. Don't know one color from another, and I really don't care."

"Billy, guess what," I said.

"What?" he asked.

"That makes two of us that are color blind. Can you tell me if the jumpsuit was light or dark in color?"

"Light, are you really color blind?" Billy asked.

"Yep, I sure am. And I don't care either. How about the guy's size? Was he big, small, or in between?"

"He was the same height as Tim but real husky. He was bigger around, but so was everybody else. Tim has always been on the bony side."

"How about his hair and beard, can you tell me if his hair was light or dark?"

"Had his hair cut in a Peter Gunn style, a real fresh cut too. His beard was the same, you know like he trimmed it every day. Oh yeah, light or dark. I'd say it was black, but it could have been brown."

"How about facial features, anything you can remember that stuck out?" Ivy asked.

"No, like I said he was too far away."

"How about his shoes, was he wearing boots or loafers or what?" I asked.

Billy put his finger to his temple for a few seconds. That juicy detective asked me the same darn question."

"Billy, you said you were working. If you got down on the ground and looked across the work area floor do you think it might help you remember?" I asked.

"You know what, I think it might. Come on Jill let's go back inside and I'll lie down. If you want, you can lie down with me," Billy said as he looked at Jill and licked his lips like a pervert. Then he rubbed his hands together as if he was hungry for something.

"Real funny, you big Howard," Jill said as they walked away.

I figure Howard was an inside joke or maybe a term kids around Blue Note use for dirty old men. I knew they'd be gone for a bit, so I went over my notes to make sure I asked everything I could. There was one thing I had not asked. I hadn't asked him whether or not anyone else there saw the guy with the beard. I was just about to go back in and get them when they walked out the door.

"You won't believe this but I had Jill stand where Tim and the guy were, and after I lay down and looked at her, I remembered what shoes the guy had on. His shoes are exactly like my postman wears, except they were an off white. Kind of like the shoes a nurse would wear, only bigger."

"They matched his jumpsuit, that must be why you couldn't remember at first," Jill said.

Makes sense to me, I thought to myself.

"Ok, good to know. Listen Billy; was there anybody else here that saw the guy with the beard?" I asked.

"Nope, shit!" Billy blurted out.

"What's wrong?" I asked.

"I was gonna go down and tell the guy to take a hike when he just turned around and went back out the door. I relaxed for a few seconds and then the damn ball return broke again. Some old guy walked all the way down the gutter and yelled at me while he stood next to the pin setter. Well, by the time I get the damn thing working again, Tim was gone. Never did see him again. Gosh, that haunts me something awful. If only I'd a gone down there and kicked the guy's ass, Tim might still be alive. Fuck! If only I had gone down there!" Billy yelled at himself.

Jill got close to Billy and held his hand.

"Billy what you're going through is a very natural response. You have nothing to feel guilty or otherwise about. And from what I know, this guy and maybe others wanted Timmy dead. I believe he either saw or heard something he shouldn't have. And they knew it. Problem is, we don't know who they are. But I can guarantee you I'm going to find out," I said hoping to alleviate some of the pain Billy and Jill were both going through.

I looked over at Ivy.

"Ivy, do you have any other questions you'd like to ask Jill or Billy?"

Ivy shook his head no. We had caused some pain for these kids, but that's our job. I thanked both of them several times, as did Ivy. We decided not to go back inside, it was just too noisy. The two of us walked around the side of the building headed for the parking lot when we heard Billy yell stop! We did. He and Jill came running up to us.

"You didn't ask if we had any questions," Billy blurted out.

"Sorry, you're right. We didn't," I agreed.

"Well, Jill has a question to ask that might help and then again, it might not," Billy said as he looked at Jill.

She stepped towards us and before she could ask the question, she had to stop and fight back the tears. The three of us waited for her to speak. She finally gained control of herself.

"I just wanted to know if you've talked to Senator Rose. The reason I ask is Tim let on that a lot of weird shit went on at the senator's ranch."

"What kind of weird shit?" I asked.

"I don't know for sure, but nearly every time Tim came back from there, he'd be shaking his head. I guess there's a lot of secret stuff that goes on with politicians and those they're associated with."

Ivy and I both looked at Jill with what must have been confused faces.

"I'm sorry, I can't tell you exactly why it's important but I know it is. Does that make sense?" Jill asked.

"Yes Jill, it makes all the sense in the world. And thanks for caring enough to bring it up," Ivy said in his soft voice. "I give you my word; we're going to find out everything we can about the senator and his associates."

We were about to say goodbye for the second time when a guy with dark wavy hair just like Jill's yelled from the front door across the parking lot. Couldn't tell exactly what he said, but Jill sure did.

"We gotta go, and you better get out of here too. That's my dad. I'll explain to him why we were out here. See you guys later," Jill said as she and Billy bolted for the front door of the bowling alley.

Ivy and I watched them run before we made our way to the coupe. I got in the car and started it. The car was running great but my mind wasn't. I had this overwhelming feeling that I was being watched. I turned to Ivy and told him. He hesitated for a long time, too damn long if you ask me.

"Jack, are you feeling anxious?"

"No Ivy, this is not about any tingles or any of that other shit. This is about feeling like someone is watching us, that's all!"

"Jack, don't go getting yourself all worked up over nothing."

"Damn it Ivy, this is something," I said as I opened my door and stepped outside of the car.

I stood there for maybe ten seconds before I hustled over to the front of the building. I ran up the steps and gazed out over the parking lot. *I knew it!*

I walked back and got in the coupe and drove out of the parking lot. When I was near Broadway, I pulled into a tiny strip mall and parked. Ivy started to ask me something but I told him to be quiet. I hid behind my car and watched the silver XKE drive by. I slunk back in the coupe and pointed the XKE out to Ivy.

"That's the Suit that hired me. Now do you believe we were being watched?" I yelled.

"Yes I do, and I'm sorry I doubted you. Jack, can we go back to the Redwood now?" Ivy asked out of frustration.

I drove in the lot and parked in front of my apartment. Ivy got out and while I was staring up on the roof at Li'l John, Ivy said he'd see me in the morning. I watched him walk away, he was pissed. I waved to Li'l John as I climbed my stairs.

"Hi Li'l John, is everything ok?"

"Yes, all is quiet. Nice night for me. Thank you for asking."

"You're welcome, night," I said.

I walked into my kitchen, which is in reality, my front room, dining room, and kitchen. Hurtwood was sitting at my little table with Sugar.

"Evening Jack, how're you feeling?" he asked.

"I'm fine, hi Sugar."

"Hi Jack, how're you feeling?"

"Sugar, I feel fine. But I'm not going to feel fine if everyone keeps asking me how I feel!"

They both tried to act relaxed but the worry in them was raging, or maybe it was the angst in me that I saw.

"I'm sorry," I said as Cat brushed up against my arm.

I picked him up and sat down at the table. I never do that, but for some reason it felt right.

"Jack, I didn't want to bother you, but there has been a car buzzing the parking lot all evening. Sugar thinks she's seen it before, but she's not sure."

"Was it a silver XKE?"

"Yes, how'd you know?" Hurtwood asked.

"He's the Suit that hired me. I guess he's just checking up on his investment. He did pay me a lot of money. I'd say he's harmless."

"Ok good, I'll see ya later," Hurtwood said to the two of us as he stood up from the table.

"Mr. Hurtwood, thanks for watching out for me and well, for caring. Thanks again."

"You're welcome, bye," he said as he shut the door.

I looked over at Sugar, she was still smiling.

"Ok, just a minute or so ago you were all worried for me and now you're smiling. What's up?"

"Nothing is up. I'm just glad that you feel good."

"Sugar, did you get the food for the guys in the cave?"

"Sure did, and guess what?"

"What?"

"That Duke guy that hired Larry, I mean Jackson. Anyways Duke has a double wide that he's going to let Jackson and Friar Tuck live in. They have to pay rent and all, but it's still great. I've never seen Friar smile so big, not ever."

"Did you see Jackson tonight?"

"No, just Friar Tuck, Jackson was at work."

"That is great, where's the trailer?"

"Jack, it's not a trailer, it's a mobile home. It's in a quiet mobile home park south of town on the Old Creamery Road."

"That's too far to walk. How's Jackson going to get to work each day?"

"He bought a bus pass, for now he and Friar will have to share. But it's still wonderful?"

"It sure is," I said as I opened the refrigerator door. There was a six-pack of Olympia bottles staring at me. I involuntarily grabbed one and opened it.

I turned and smiled at Sugar. "Gosh, you're the greatest. Thank you. You want one?"

"No Jack, I just want to sit here with you."

"Ok say, there's something I'm supposed to do every night, and I think you might be the perfect person to help me. Dr. Lee wants me to write down my thoughts, keep track of my emotions; you know how I felt about stuff that happened that day."

"Is that what that green notebook is for?"

"Yes, how'd you know?" Sugar gave me a funny look. "I guess you know because it's sitting next to my bed." She gave me another funny look. "Ok well, did you take a look inside?" She gave me a pair of daggers for eyes.

"Jack, I'm not that curious, ok maybe I am a little, I think all girls are. But I'm not so curious that I would invade your private space. I hope you know that, you do trust me, don't you?" she asked with sad eyes.

"Yes, implicitly." She gave me a pair of puzzled eyes. "Sugar, can you go get the notebook, please?"

As she walked away, I thought of something Dr. Lee had asked me to do. Sugar came back and sat down next to me and set the notebook on the table.

"Sugar, the next time I go see Dr. Lee can you remind me to take my medicine with me? He wants to do something with it."

"There's no need for a reminder."

"Why not?" I asked, wondering what she knew that I didn't.

"Because the doctor took the medicine with him when he was here."

"Good, one less thing for me to worry about. And while I'm worrying about things, I want to ask you a question." She didn't say a word. "Sugar, you know the Suit paid me a lot of money. And well, I haven't given any to Ivy."

"You told me once that Ivy doesn't want you to pay him because he doesn't need the money. It's a hobby; he does it for 'the thrill of the hunt.' I think that's the way you said it."

"Yes, that's what he told me, but this isn't even close to the same. We're usually tracking down missing persons or hunting for someone that skipped bail. This is totally different."

"Makes it that much more exciting," she said.

"Yes that's a good point, but…"

"Jack, you really do wear me out asking all your crazy questions. Is Ivy coming over tomorrow morning?"

"Yes."

"Then ask him if he wants you to pay him? Not a big deal," she said as she wrapped her warm hands around my balled fists.

We sat like that for a while and my hands did relax, sure felt good. I think Cat liked it too because he stood up and meowed in my face.

"Forgot you were here, want something to eat?"

He ran across the table and leaped onto the kitchen counter. We speak the same language.

18

I woke up the next morning and put my feet on the cold floor. I stretched a couple of times before it hit me. I was rested, relaxed, and my mind was clear. No dream world hovering around my head. I wanted to tell someone, but Sugar was gone. So I walked out to the kitchen, opened the door, and told Cat. He ran in and jumped up on the counter before he head-butted me about six times. I'd say he was happy for me, but he might have been hungry.

I put a pot of water on the stove to boil and gave Cat a saucer of milk. He was happy. I was going to put my beach combers on but when I opened the drawer I keep them in, they were gone. I scratched my head as I stared at a new pair of Levi's. Sugar! I put them on and took a look in the mirror before I slipped on my huaraches. Went straight out to the steps and skipped up to the roof, there was something I wanted to see. As I stared, I said, "I should have known this was going to happen."

I wasn't angry or anything, which was a very good sign. There was a makeshift bed just behind the couch, a pile of books were scattered about next to the pillow. I grabbed the first book I saw and opened it. Sure enough it had property of Blue Note Public Library stamped inside the cover. It was a collection of fairy tales with nice drawings. I put all the books back. *I wonder if Li'l John borrowed the books or... Guess it doesn't really matter.*

Ivy was waiting for me when I opened the door to my kitchen.

"Morning Jack, how are you feeling?"

I gave him a look. "Morning, I feel great!"

"Good Jack, how about we go eat breakfast at Mel's, my treat."

"Sounds good to me, is that why you turned off the burner on the stove?"

"Yeah, go get cleaned up."

I ran in my bathroom and turned the shower on. Then I hurried over to my closet and picked out a clean shirt. I had just jumped under the water when Ivy yelled, "Jack, have you seen the morning paper?"

"No, I haven't. Why?" I yelled back.

"I'll show you after you get dressed," was all he said.

After I was all clean and shiny, I hurried to find out what was so important in the paper. Ivy must not have been in as big a rush as I was, because he told me we could talk about it over a hot cup of Joe. It took all of five minutes to drive over to 3rd Ave. and Mel's diner, my favorite place for breakfast, lunch, and dinner.

We sat in our usual place, the booth in the back corner. I was anxious but there was no way I was going to let on.

"Jack, you're being awfully calm and patient today. And I'm not sure I like it, it bothers me. Will the real Jack please stand up?"

"Sorry about that Ivy, but this is the new me. I know it sounds weird, but I haven't had even the slightest tingle. And the fog that was wrapped around my head has lifted. Aren't you happy for me?" I said in a Boy Scout voice. He just stared at me while June took our orders.

After we ordered, Ivy took the paper he had sitting on the table in front of him and set it on his lap.

"Ok Ivy, read me the damn paper!"

"That's the Jack I know and—"

"Ivy!"

"Jack, I don't need to read it. The paper says that Senator Rose is a person of interest in the death of Timothy Ward Allen. That parasite, Herb Cramer, wrote the piece. Anyway, he said he didn't know all the specifics, but items that belong to Senator Rose were found at the scene of the crime. Now what do you suppose those items could be?" Ivy asked as he stared at me.

"Well, has to be the penlight and the murder weapon... or maybe something we didn't see. Geez Ivy, do you think the Suit that hired me is connected to the senator?"

"That's the first thing that ran across my brain after I read the article. In fact, were I a betting man, that's where my money would land."

"This might complicate things. I've racked my brain trying to come up with a way to get in and talk to the senator. Have any ideas?"

"Yes I do. Tell him the truth about being hired to find out who killed Timmy Allen. If he truly is innocent, he'll gladly help us. If he's guilty, he will probably have us thrown out of his home. Don't mix messages, just be brutally honest. I think you could accomplish that in your sleep," Ivy said as June filled his cup and then mine with black coffee.

I always like to smell the coffee before I take a sip. Truth is, I want to test it and see how hot it is before it touches my tender mouth. I don't handle hot food with much grace. There have been times when I had to spit out the food or drink that had just found its way into my mouth - makes for a messy situation. I was looking down the long narrow counter that runs the length of Mel's diner when a familiar face raced by the front window, our eyes met. I jumped up and ran like a maniac out the door. I looked left then right and watched Rat leap in the waiting open door of a 'gold' Bonneville. I had my idiot boots on, you know the ones that make me feel like I'm in charge. I tried chasing after the car, but it was no use. The getaway car burned rubber for half a block as it sped away. There were too many cars angle parked on my side of the street. I never saw the Bonneville's license plate. The car and Rat were gone before I made it ten feet. I turned to go back in and walked right into Mel.

"Something wrong Jack?"

"Don't know, maybe. Mel, do you know Rat, I mean Bobby Johnson?"

"Yes, I know Rat Johnson, why?"

"I'll tell you in a minute," I said as I headed straight for the coupe. I'd locked it before going into the diner, but where Rat is concerned you can't be too careful. I checked the car inside and out and, on the surface,, everything seemed ok. I walked back.

Blue Note

"Mel, I recently had a problem with Rat. We were up by the Blue Note and I smacked him once or twice."

"Good!" Mel interrupted.

"So when he was what he considered a safe distance away, he threatened me. His voice and body language told me he meant what he said. I hadn't seen since, but he just ran by the diner."

"Jack, Rat and his spooky friend Mason are not welcome here. Is there something you want me to do? I can call the police if you want?"

"Nah, Mel can you do me a favor?" I asked as he wiped his hands on his apron."

"Sure, what can I do for you?"

"I'm going to write my phone number down. If you see them, not just here but anywhere, could you give me a call?"

"Absolutely, I'd be glad to."

The moment he said he'd be glad; panic ran roughshod across my mind. I hadn't paid the damn phone bill. I waited for a tingle, but it didn't happen. We walked back inside and when I sat down, Ivy had a piece of thickly buttered toast stuck in his mouth. He muttered, "Everything ok?"

"Yeah, but before we head over to Creston and Senator Rose I want to go pay my phone bill, which leads me to a question I need to ask you."

Ivy's dark eyes asked the next question.

"Ivy, I told you I was paid a lot of money for this job." He nodded yes. "But I haven't given you any."

"Jack, we went over this, years ago. Why do you think I dig up bones for my research?" I didn't say anything. "Because I live for the hunt. Jack, I've got more money than I need. Now I'm not going to waste anymore time with this, and I'm hungry. So eat your breakfast before it gets cold," he said just before he scooped up a forkful of scrambled eggs and set it on a piece of toast. I think that's a strange thing to do.

As we ate, my mind went into overdrive thinking about Rat, phone bills, the strange absence of tingles, and of course, Senator Rose. Ivy had said breakfast was going to be his treat, but before he could object, I paid the bill. I drove half a block over to the phone company and paid my bill. We were heading east for Creston, a quaint little community dotted by a few thoroughbred stud farms, a country store, and lots of money. I pushed the coupe hard and she responded. I eased off the highway and onto O'Donovan Road. I came around a bend and could see our destination on the right. I made an immediate hard left turn up the driveway of the ranch house directly across the street from the senator's home.

"Jack, what are you doing?" Ivy asked in his nasty step-dad voice.

"Ivy, there's a Blue Note police car parked in the driveway."

"You sure, I didn't see it."

"Yes, I'm positive. I'm going to park behind the garage. We're going to have to find a spot where we can see the front of the senator's house."

Step-dad didn't have anything to say, at least not yet. I parked the coupe behind a very large garage and then we tip-toed out to have a look. An officer I didn't recognize was standing next to the patrol car.

"You know Jack, this actually makes sense. I mean the paper did say the senator was a person of interest." I didn't respond.

"Come on, we need to get over to that bush so we can get a better look at the front of the house."

"Jack, how do you know we'll be able to see the front of the house? And what about the people that live here in this house? What if they decide to call the police on us?" Ivy asked.

"They're not going to call anybody because they're not home, now shut up and follow me," I said as Ivy gave me a look only an angry parent could produce.

I ran the forty yards or so to the bush, making sure to keep an eye on the police officer across the street. When I turned around, Ivy was still standing by the damn garage. I motioned for him to run but he shook his head no. *What a fraidy cat.*

There was a ten-foot hedgerow in front of the senator's house. I moved over to see up the driveway. There was another police car next to the front door. I recognized the car. At that point I knew I didn't want Ivy trying to make it over to the bush. So I motioned several times for him to get back. He did as I asked. I kept one eye on the house and the other on the cop standing out front. I looked at my watch, it was ten past ten. I waited there for five more minutes before Detective Knox walked out and opened the back door of her car. She yelled, "Ok, bring him out."

Sergeant Klavinski walked the senator out of the house and put him in the back seat. I sat down and got small. *This changes everything, now what?* I motioned to Ivy one more time to get down. He did. The sergeant drove and Detective Knox sat on the passenger side looking back at the senator. Couldn't tell if the senator had been cuffed or not, but I guess it didn't really matter. They drove right past me and the other officer followed in his car. I stood up and motioned to Ivy that the coast was clear. He was hunched over as he tip-toed to me.

"Ivy, why are you hunched over like some freaking nut? The cops are gone."

"I don't know why, and what difference does it make? Geez Jack, get off my back."

I think he expected me to say something else, I didn't. I started walking across the street, didn't look back at Ivy. I figured he'd follow me, he didn't. I turned to motion to him to get his ass over to my side of the damn street when at the top of their lungs someone bellowed, "Stop, right where you are!"

I looked back and there was a bearded man standing on the front porch of the senator's house. He had a handgun pointed at me. "Put your hands up and walk over here." I put my hands up and hollered, "Don't shoot; I'm on your side."

"My side, you say. How in God's creation could you possibly know what side I'm on?"

"Just don't shoot me." I said before I put my hands up over my head and started walking towards him. "I don't know what side you're on but I know I'm not against you. And if I'm not against you, then I must be on your side."

He relaxed the gun a bit. When I was ten feet from him, I stopped and asked if I could show him my identification. "No!"

"Ok, then what would you like me to do?"

"Keep your hands up and turn around, yes that's good. Now don't move," he said as he shoved the gun barrel into my lower back. "Where is your identification?"

"It's inside my front left coat pocket."

"He switched the gun to his left hand and reached across my body with his right. He held up my license in front of me and said, "Private Dick, hah?" He backed away. "Turn around." I did.

He was grinning, but the gun wasn't.

"Can you please put that gun down, you're making me nervous."

"Sorry, no can do. Why are you here?"

"I'll tell you right after you give me back my wallet."

He handed my wallet to me and as I put it back inside my coat, I moved about a hundred and eighty degrees to my right. He did just the opposite.

"Look, I was paid to find out who killed Timmy Allen. That's why I'm here. Now, everything I've told you is the truth. Problem is, I have no idea who you are or whose side you're on, so if you're not going to shoot me, then put that damn gun down?"

He didn't budge an inch. The gun was still pointed at my chest when Ivy clubbed the guy with the butt of my gun. The moment the bearded guy hit the concrete his gun went off with a bang.

"Christ Ivy, he could have shot me! Did you have to hit him? And what took you so damn long?"

"I had to be sure he didn't see or hear me. I just might have saved your life and, as usual, you're complaining."

"Thanks Ivy, now shut up," I said as I picked up the gun that had been pointed at me.

The bearded guy started moaning before he moved a little bit. I wasn't about to help him up.

"Ivy, how'd you know where to look for my gun? I had it hidden in a good place."

"You think under your seat is a good place?"

"It is for me, makes it easy to get to."

"Jack, I'm glad the gun was there, but I know you're not supposed to have it anywhere near your person 'til you get your license back."

"Yeah, well I'm glad I brought it with me. And if I got caught, I had a great alibi worked out."

"And what may I ask was your great alibi?"

"I was going to say you brought it."

118

"What!" Ivy yelled as the bearded guy rolled over onto his elbows and looked up at his gun.

"I'll have the two of you arrested before this day is done," he said as he narrowed his eyes at us.

I got down right next to him and shoved the barrel of his gun against his cheek. "You're going to apologize to me right now or when the police get here, I'm going to tell them you pulled the gun on me and we struggled before I shot you, I have a witness. Are you gonna apologize or get shot? Which is it?"

"Wait, don't shoot, ok I'm sorry."

"That's better. Now we're going to start this whole damn thing over again. I told you the truth and now you're going to do the same, understand?"

"Yes, perfectly, can I get up now?"

"No! You can sit up, but don't get up 'til I say to. Ok, sit on your ass and don't you dare move. Now who are you and what are you doing here?"

The guy sat up and started rubbing the back of his head. He looked up at me as he winced. He didn't say a word, but he did give me the look from hell.

"You don't listen very well, do you?" I said as I stuck the gun barrel tight against his forehead. "This is your last chance asshole. One wrong answer or one wrong move and I'm going to put one right between your eyes. Now, who are you!" I screamed.

"I'm Jacob Dowdy, Senator Rose's footman, valet, aide, and butler."

"Good answer, I see your cute little butler outfit, but can you prove it?"

"Yes I can," he said as he glanced at Ivy. "Who's he?"

"He's my footman, valet, aide, and butler."

Ivy glared at me. "I'm Doctor Ivy Fin and at the moment, I'm also a private investigator."

"You're not dressed like a private dick but I'd say you are one," footman Dowdy said just before I slapped the smirk off his face.

I raised my hand again and he flinched. "Ok, you can quit with the Mafioso crap."

I looked over at Ivy. "Ivy, I think we'd better take this guy to the Blue Note police station and tell them he admitted to killing

Timmy Allen. Come on, let's go asshole!" I said as I stuck the gun in his face again.

"Ok stop, I'll behave. What else do you want to know?" he said with a straight face.

"Get up and turn around," I ordered.

He got up and brushed himself off. "Now, what?" he asked.

"Now start walking out of the public eye and around the back of the house. You make one wrong move and one of us will shoot you."

"On that you can rely," Ivy trumped.

The butler and I both looked over at Ivy. I'm positive we were thinking the same thing. The house was much bigger than it appeared from the street. Butler Dowdy kept walking 'til we were in front of what looked to me like granny quarters. He stopped. "This is where I live. If you want to check, there are a few pictures and mementos on my dresser." I kept the gun on him and asked Ivy to go inside and check.

Ivy was gone for all of thirty seconds before coming back out. "Upon further inspection I believe valet Dowdy's declaration is genuine."

Once again, the butler and I gave Ivy a look.

"Ok, where is a good place for us to talk?"

"The kitchen is here in the back of the house. There's a table at which we can sit. Follow me," he said as he slowly made his way towards a rear door. We walked into a massive gleaming kitchen. A fair sized whitewashed country table sat at one end.

"Sit down," I ordered.

Ivy sat down.

"Not you Ivy!"

"Ok, so that I don't have to ask a bunch of questions that run into each other, tell me everything you know about Timmy Allen. He started to open his mouth. "Not yet, first I want to hear what Timmy did for the senator that you couldn't."

"Well, Tim was in charge of the pool, the lawns, and cleaning the stables. And now and then he would go to the market for Senator Rose. That's just about everything. I suppose I could have performed some of those tasks, but I'm already so busy with the everyday workload I wouldn't have had the time."

120

"How did Timmy get the job? And how long has he worked here?"

"I have no idea how Tim acquired this job. He didn't have any special skills of which I'm aware. Senator Rose has a finger in many pies, so I'd say there's an excellent chance Tim was hired during one of the summer employment efforts. Yes, I think that's probably exactly how he gained employment here. As far as how long, my guess would be about a year, give or take."

"How well did you know Timmy?"

"We said hello and goodbye, that's about it. Now and then Tim would sneak up and ask me about something, but for the most part we never spoke."

"What do you mean by sneak?" Ivy asked.

"Oh, I didn't mean it to discredit Tim; it was just a little disconcerting the way he could walk up on you without making a sound. I even asked him once if he were part Indian. He didn't understand the reference. He walked and talked very softly, which is the reason I find the murder to be so baffling. I don't believe Tim had any enemies, none whatsoever."

"Jacob, it says in the paper that something found at the murder site belonged to the senator. Do you know what that is?" I asked.

"I don't think I should, no, I can't tell you."

"Can't or won't?"

"Take your pick. I'm sorry, but I will not divulge that information."

"Jacob, where were you Saturday night when Timmy was murdered?"

"I was on my way home; I had just dropped the senator off at the airport. I guess that's why the detective took the senator in for questioning. She's going to find out the hard way that the senator was a couple thousand feet in the air when Tim was killed."

"If that's the case, then why won't you tell us what was found at the murder site that belonged to the senator?"

"Because I don't want to give the person or persons that killed Tim any information that might help them. I suppose I trust you, but only a little."

Ivy stood up and walked around the kitchen for a few seconds and then he headed for the dining area. He came straight back.

"Come here, I want to show you something," he said as he pointed at Dowdy.

Valet Dowdy did not move until I gave him a hard look. He slowly got up and the two of us walked behind Ivy to an ornate cherry-wood China cabinet. Ivy pointed at the key that was still in the lock.

"Open, the cabinet footman Dowdy!"

"I don't have to," Dowdy protested.

"Oh but you do, if you don't now, you will when you wake up. So what's it going to be?"

"Why don't you open it yourself, the police sergeant did."

"You know what Ivy, he's right. Go ahead and open it. Just don't leave any prints."

Ivy took out his handkerchief and held it to the key as he turned it in the lock. The door opened and Ivy immediately removed a box containing a large serving set from the cabinet. He opened it and all eight butter knives were there. He closed the box and put it back in the China cabinet.

"Jack, stay here with the lackey, I'll be right back."

"Go on back in the kitchen," I ordered.

We went back in the kitchen, butler Dowdy sat down at the table and waited. I heard Ivy walking all through the house. He was gone for quite a while before he strolled back into the kitchen. A tiny yet distinct smile was etched across his face. He gently set his handkerchief on the table in front of Dowdy, there was something hidden underneath it.

"Footman Dowdy, I looked all over Senator Rose's desk for something, but I couldn't find it. So, I took the liberty of going through all the drawers and guess what I found?" Dowdy wiggled in anticipation. "I found the box his letter opener came in, but it's empty. I'll bet it's the letter opener with the fancy R on it that was used to kill Timmy Allen."

"Dowdy leaped to his feet. "How could you possibly know that unless you were there at the…"

He stopped and looked away from us.

"Dowdy, finish what you were going to say!" I yelled.

"Time, I was going to say at the time."

"Sure you were," Ivy mocked.

"Dowdy, you're lying. I'd shoot you right now, but the D. A. is definitely going to need you to testify in court."

"I don't have to talk to you, leave me alone!"

"Dowdy, a man with a beard was seen at the bowling alley an hour before the murder. You wear the exact same beard that the witness described. So, where were you Saturday night before you took the senator to the airport? And don't lie to me!"

"I was here with the senator."

"You're lying!"

"No, I'm not. Wait! The next-door neighbor was here too. His name is James Gosling, go ahead and ask him. You know what; screw both you, I'm not telling you anything else. Go ahead and kill me. You'll spend the rest of your life in a jail cell. I dare you, go ahead!" he screamed.

"Ivy, put the box back," I said. "Be sure to wipe off any prints you may have left."

Ivy took off. "Jacob, how many questions did you answer for the detective?"

"None, Senator Rose told me I didn't have to, so I kept my mouth shut."

"What kind of light fixture is that?"

He looked up; I hit him square on the chin. He slumped over. I carried him out to the little hovel he calls home. I walked out into the yard at about the same time Ivy did.

"Where's the butler?"

"I put him in his stupid little house and told him to stay there 'til he knows we're gone. Come on, I don't want him to see us leave. Let's go."

We ran to the coupe and, within a minute we were back on the road. I'd gone a mile or so when I slammed on the brakes. I flipped a bitch and headed back to the senator's house.

"Jack, what're you doing? We need to get away from here."

"Yes, but first there's something we just have to do."

"What?" Ivy said more than asked.

"Ivy, I want you to go up and ring the next-door neighbor's doorbell. Ask if Steven Gosling lives there."

"What!" Ivy hollered more than asked.

"It'll work, damn it just do it. You know as well as I do that we have to find out if Dowdy was telling us the truth."

Ivy didn't argue. I stopped next to a small cookie-cutter house that stuck out like a sore thumb. The mailbox had Gosling painted on it in stenciled white letters. Ivy ran up to the door. I heard someone yelling just before my door flew open. In jumped Ivy. "Get out of here, now!" Ivy screamed.

"What happened?"

"I asked for Steven Gosling and he says, 'I'm James Gosling, are you responsible for firing that gun?' I backed up off the porch. Then he screams, "You have ten seconds to get off my property or I'm calling the police." I ran like the north wind. It was actually kind of exciting. But it won't be if he calls the police. They'll catch us long before we ever get back on the highway."

I tromped on the accelerator and the coupe responded. When I got back into Blue Note, I drove up Friendly Street by the police station. I had to see if the detective's car was still there, it was.

Blue Note

19

We'd just driven in my parking lot when Ivy turned to me. I could tell by the look on his face a bomb was about to go off.

"What?" I said.

"Jack, you have to tell me the truth right now or I'm going to vacate this job." I didn't say a word. "After you ran over to the bush to spy on the police, I walked around and checked the address of the house you so nonchalantly parked behind. I pay attention to details when necessary. That is the house you were caught breaking into. Why were you trying to get into that house and how'd you know the people were, so conveniently, not home?" Ivy said in a cocky tone. It was as if he had just figured out the combination to the safe holding the Crown Jewels.

"You're going to be disappointed when I tell you."

"I'll be the one who decides whether or not I'm disappointed. Start talking," he demanded.

"Ok, you asked for it. When I was working on my license, I lived in the basement of that house. I didn't know you then. I hadn't found you and your little MG dead on the side of the road yet, had I?"

"No Jack, I hadn't yet had the great pleasure of making your acquaintance. Jack, if that's the truth, then tell me the names of the people that live there?"

"Rita and Jack Laramie live there, does that name ring a bell?" I asked in my smartass voice.

"Is that the same Jack Laramie that Larry has become?"

"Yes, and he wouldn't be Jack Laramie if I hadn't snuck back in and grabbed the identification."

"Wait a second, you stole the guys I.D?"

"No, I didn't. I didn't because it's his son's identification and his son won't be needing it."

"Why not?" Ivy objected.

"Because Jack's son changed his name, that's why!"

"Jack, if you're lying to me, I'll find out. I'm only going to ask you this one time. Are you telling me the truth?"

"Yes, I swear on my mother and all that is sacred. It's the truth, so help me God."

He didn't say another word.

"Ivy, let's go in the bar, I'll buy you a beer." He stared at me. "Come on, it'll do you some good to relax. You look a little uptight."

"Be quiet Jack."

"My, such rude language, what happened to the polite professor I used to know?"

"He met you," Ivy said, before he chuckled at how clever he'd become.

"Come on Ivy, we accomplished a lot today, let's have a beer."

"All right, you go ahead and have a beer. I'm going to have a cocktail."

"Have whatever you like, it's on me," I said as we walked in. I took a long look at Scout's behind.

"You must be exercising Scout."

She turned around. "I saw you staring. Yes, I have to be in shape for the ski season ahead. What can I get for you enlightened rogues?"

"I'll have a Budweiser. Ivy probably wants something a little more sophisticated."

"What'll it be Ivy?" she asked.

"Think I'll have a Manhattan. Jack said he is buying, so make it a double."

Scout eyeballed Ivy. "Ivy, I don't want you drinking and driving."

"Thanks for your professional concern. I'll wait the requisite amount of time before I get behind the wheel. Ok?"

"Sure," Scout muttered.

Scout handed me my beer before she started mixing Ivy's drink. When she was done, she turned to us and asked if we wanted something to eat.

"That's a capital idea. Yes, I believe I'll have the ham on rye. Oh, and some fries too, thank you," Ivy said as he turned to me. "Jack, aren't you going to eat something?"

"No, I think I'm going to take Sugar out for dinner. Yes, that sounds good, just the two of us."

I had a few beers while Ivy ate his sandwich. He only took two sips from his drink, so I finished the rest of it while I ate his fries.

After we had lunch, I decided, without asking Ivy, that we needed to hit the bowling alley again. And in my line of work you can never be too early or too often in your quest for information. I paid Scout and when we walked outside, I watched Ivy twist and turn, stretch and yawn. I think he was worn out from all the excitement.

"Jack, I think I'm going to go home and take a nap, we are done for the day aren't we?" he asked in a real nonchalant way.

"Sorry Ivy, but we still have a lot of work to do," I said in a way that could have been construed as joking.

He turned and rested his dark eyes on me.

"Jack, the drink and the food were great and I want to thank you. Can't you just leave it at that, please? I can take only so much of your juvenile play acting."

"I'm not acting, I'm serious." He stared back at me. I think he thought he could get me to laugh or something like that. When he realized I was serious, his head drooped. "I have an idea, you follow me in your car, that way you can go straight home after we're done, ok?"

"Jack, where are we going?" he asked in a weary voice.

"We're going back to the bowling alley."

"Why?" he asked, wearier still.

"We're going because I have to know right now not tomorrow if butler Jacob Dowdy was the bearded man that spoke to Timmy Allen the night he was murdered. If Billy positively identifies him, we are going straight to Detective Knox."

"Jack, the only way we can do that is to take Billy all the way back out to Creston."

"No, I'm going to do the opposite. I'm going to take valet Dowdy to Billy."

"How in the world are you going to do that?" Ivy asked with wide eyes.

"With these," I said as I reached in my jacket and handed Ivy the pictures I'd borrowed from butler Dowdy.

He stood and went through all four pictures.

"Jack, you could get in trouble for this. He'll probably want these back."

"Ivy, footman Dowdy has a pretty big ego. I'd say he has lots of copies. Now, get in your car and let's go."

"Jack, I'd just as soon ride with you. We are a team you know."

"Yes we are, thanks Ivy," I said as I headed for the coupe.

We had a short drive, but enough time so that I could tell Ivy about Jacob Dowdy's closet. He was a little concerned that I'd gone thru Dowdy's personal property, I didn't give a damn.

"Ivy, try to remember we're talking about a murder, the murder of an innocent boy. So make no mistake, I'm going to do anything and everything I can to find the person or persons responsible. Now, don't you want to know what I was looking for in his closet?"

"Jack, I know exactly what you were looking for." I gave him a glancing gaze. "You were looking for the white jumpsuit the bearded man was wearing when Billy saw him, right."

"Well done, Sherlock," I said with a smile.

"Well, was it there?" Ivy asked in an excited voice.

"Nope, but I knew it was a long shot. I mean if you wore something so easily identified, would you leave it lying around. No, I don't think so. So I hope Billy can identify Dowdy from the pictures," I said as we drove in the bowling alley parking lot. He parked next to the same sea-sprite green Woody I'd seen the last time we were at the bowling alley. When we got to the back of the building, Ivy put his hand up.

"Jack, you've been drinking, it wouldn't be wise to advertise the fact. I have an idea that might work. I'll go in the back door and see if I can find Billy. You wait here, I'll be right back," he said as he opened the door.

Ivy went in and I stood staring into space. Five minutes later he came out, alone.

"Where's Billy?"

"Right here, you naysayer," Billy said as he walked up behind me, a lit cigarette dangling from his mouth. He yanked the cigarette away with one hand and reached out to me with the other. "I'm as curious as you are Jack, so let's see the pictures."

I handed all four to him and he moved over directly under the sun. His face changed little as, one at a time, he studied the pictures. He looked up at me. "This one here taken from the side is exactly the way I remember seeing him."

"So it's him?" I said in my eager voice.

"Naw, he's the wrong guy. This guy here has the same haircut and beard, but he's way too thin. Remember, I told you the guy was real husky."

Billy handed me the pictures and I couldn't help myself and yelled, "Shit," right in his face.

"Jack, you smell like a brewery. How much have you had to drink today?" he asked as his grin turned into a concerned half smile.

"Not enough, shit, I thought for sure we had the right guy. Thanks for your help, listen Billy I'm going to write down my phone number. If you or Jill or anybody else comes up with anything you think is important about this whole thing, can you please give me a call?"

"Sure thing," Billy answered.

I wrote my number on a blank page in the green notebook Dr. Lee had given me and tore it out and handed it to Billy.

"Jack, you ok to drive?" Billy asked with a straight face.

"Yes I am, but I'm going to let Ivy drive. Thanks for your help and concern, bye now."

Ivy and I headed for the coupe. I got in and had the same damn feeling I did the last time we were there. I reasoned that the Suit knows my whereabouts from plain old logical thinking. I didn't even take the time to look for his silver XKE. We made it home in one piece. Ivy parked the coupe; we decided to start the same time the next morning. Neither of us said much more, we were both disappointed. I went up and had myself another beer as I looked over all of my notes. I wrote down a few for Dr. Lee. Sugar and Li'l John rolled in at six o'clock. They looked tired, thirsty, and hungry.

"Hello you two," I said as Sugar smiled and returned the hello.

"Hi Robin," Li'l John said as he vanished up the stairs to the roof.

"Sugar, I was going to ask him if it would be ok if just the two of us went out for dinner." She gave me a pair of concerned eyes. "Sorry, I guess I should have asked you first."

"It's ok Jack, but I think we should stay here tonight. There's still food in the fridge. I'll make us something good, I promise."

"Ok, I'm not the sharpest guy in the world, but I know when something's wrong. Sugar, please tell me what's wrong."

She took the pitcher of grape Kool Aid out of the fridge and poured herself a glass before she sat down at the table.

"Jack, I just talked with Friar Tuck, and–"

I butted in, "I thought he and Jackson were moving into a trailer?"

"It's a mobile home and they can't move in until this weekend." I started to interrupt her again. "Jack, please sit down and listen." I did. "Friar Tuck told me the man from the county that's been hunting for me came by the cave today. He said he's going to ask the local police for help finding me. He's like a bloodhound, he just won't quit."

"Can we talk about this on the roof? I think I want to have a beer while we watch the sun set. Bring the pitcher, ok?"

"Ok, thanks Jack," Sugar said as she smiled.

We sat with Li'l John while he drank from the pitcher of Kool Aid. Then we walked over and sat on the edge of the building and watched the sun fall.

"Nice up here, I like it. You like it Robin?" Li'l John asked as he stretched out on the couch.

"Yes, we love it too," I said for the two of us. The sun was just about ready to dive into the ocean, hard for me to imagine a more beautiful night. I looked south down Broadway, then north. The town was bustling with cars going in all directions. My beer was empty and as Sugar gradually took it from my hand, I stared at the silver XKE as it flew across Marlin Street, heading our way.

"Sugar, stay here please?"

"What's wrong Jack? You look like you just saw a ghost," Sugar proclaimed.

"Just stay here, Li'l John you stay here with Sugar, ok? Don't let anyone come up on the roof."

"Ok Robin, nobody on roof."

I ran down the steps and into the parking lot. The back door of the tavern was open, I hid behind it. Suit drove into the parking lot and when he saw my car, he parked and eased out of his car. I watched him as he ambled over and looked up at my apartment. He crept up the stairs and looked in the kitchen window. Cat was waiting for him and hissed. Cat must have scared the crap out of Suit because he jumped back, nearly fell down the steps.

"You lookin' for me," I said from under my porch. He jumped again. "We sure are jumpy tonight. Hi Suit, what can I do for you?" I asked as I walked up my stairs.

"I came by to check on your progress, have you gained any new and pertinent information about the murder of Mr. Allen?"

"Suit, why have you been tailing me?"

"What makes you believe I was following you?" he said with a straight face, too straight for my liking.

"You know if we're going to get along and work towards finding out the truth, you're going to have to be more forthcoming, and tell the truth while you're at it. Now I'm only going to ask you one more time. Why were you following me?"

"I follow orders, which is the reason I made an attempt to follow you. That said, you have proven to be quite the adversary," Suit said with what could be deemed a smile, I thought of it as a smirk.

"I don't believe adversary is a fitting word for someone that is supposed to be on your side. Do you?" I asked with a real scowl on my face.

"You're right; adversary was an invalid and poor choice of words. I'm sorry. May we go inside now and talk, I can only stay for a short time. I have to report to my employer."

"Ok, but you'd better get right to the point; I have company waiting for me."

I don't think Suit knew that he involuntarily peered up at the roof. I let it slide. We went in the kitchen and I sat, Suit stood. As he looked around, it was hard not to notice the disgust his eyes revealed. I guess he thought I lived in the Hilton.

"How can I help you?"

"I need to know if you've made any headway in your search for the truth."

"Would you like to sit down?"

"I don't believe so, thank you for asking."

"We know much more than we did a day ago. We've made great strides towards the truth."

"When you say we, do you mean you and the police detective or someone else?"

"Suit, listen carefully for a minute, ok?" He didn't say a word. "I've seen you following me and so I know that you know about my partner. For now I'll leave his name out of this. We, as you said, are on the verge of breaking this thing wide open. I make it a habit never to share information, not even with my employer. Loose lips sink ships. You do understand, don't you?"

"Yes, quite. I guess I'll have to take you at your word. My employer will be pleased to hear that you've made great strides," Suit said as he reached in the pocket of his haute couture duds and pulled out an envelope. It was exactly the same as the envelope left in my fridge on Monday. "Good evening," Suit said as he turned and walked out my door.

I wanted to open the envelope, but Sugar was waiting for me. So, I fought the urge and put it in the freezer. *A freezer for a bank, interesting,* I thought to myself.

Before I went back up on the roof, I made a quick trip inside the Redwood, Scout was busy with customers. I waited 'til she had a few seconds.

"Scout there's something very important that I should have told you when I was in here earlier." She stood patiently listening; I guess bartenders have to do that a lot. "Ok, since I have you so captivated, this morning Ivy and I were eating at Mel's and I saw Rat Johnson run by the diner. I took off after him but he jumped in the back of a gold Bonneville before I could catch him. You do know what a Bonneville looks like," she gave me a pair of frustrated eyes.

"Ok then, can you please tell Mr. Hurtwood for me?"

"I will, that's important information, I'll let him know. Jack, I know what you think, but believe it or not there are a few of us little girls that know the difference between one model car and the next," she said with a razor-sharp tongue, pointed at me.

"Yes, I suppose there are. Ok, I guess I'll see ya later Scout," I said before I hurried out the door.

I ran up the stairs, Sugar had a worried look covering her entire being.

"Jack, remember we were going to talk about the guy that's hunting me down."

"Yes, I know. The problem is, you won't tell me what he wants. Sugar, I can't help if you don't at least give me a hint as to why he's looking for you."

"That's the problem, I don't know either."

"You must have an idea why."

"I don't, the only thing I can think is maybe I have a relative looking for me. I don't want anyone looking for me. Either that or he wants me to apply for aide of some kind. I don't want any aide; I don't want anything except to be left alone."

"Ok, I guess you're going to have to stay away from the cave and the bakery for a while. He'll surely keep trying all the old familiar places, that's what I would do. As far as getting the police to help him, I don't know. I know the local police are short handed as it is. And right now, they're busy with this murder. I don't remember when the last time was we had a murder in Blue Note, but I do know it doesn't happen very often. Sugar, is there something you want me to do. I'll do whatever you ask me to."

"I want you to lock your door and if someone knocks, don't answer it. And I want you to hold me at night," she said in a way that actually caused a tingle. I slowed my breathing down and then I thought about Sugar and not me.

We had a relaxing night. We ate dinner up on the roof with Li'l John. I drank too much, maybe way too much. I guess I felt the need to self-medicate.

.

20

Cat woke me the next morning. I guess Sugar let him in when she left. My head hurt a little. I put my feet on the cold floor before I got up and stretched. Then I went out to the kitchen to give Cat a saucer of milk before he woke up the entire neighborhood with his nuclear yowling. Ivy was sitting at my table.

"Geez, you sure did sleep late. Do you know what time it is?" he probed.

"No. What time is it?"

"It's after nine o'clock. You never sleep this late."

"Yeah, you're right. Listen, I'll take a quick shower. I'll be out and ready to go before the clock strikes ten," I said as I rushed in to shave and shower. I rushed back out. "Please give Cat something to eat, before he roars the house down."

"Head hurt?" Ivy asked in the voice he uses when he wants to ridicule me.

"Shut up Ivy."

"Oh my, someone's touchy today," he said just like another smartass I know.

I'd just turned on the shower when Ivy yelled into the bedroom, "Scout wanted me to tell you she saw the Bonneville last night. She ran out to see the plates, but when the driver saw her, he floored it. She got the first two numbers. I'll tell you the rest when you're decent."

As I dressed, the Bonneville was heavy on my mind. I put my shoes on and hurried out to the kitchen.

"Ivy, tell me the rest of what Scout told you about the Bonneville?"

"She said it made at least one pass through the parking lot. I suppose the persons inside wanted to see whether or not you were here." "And," I asked.

"And as it drove by the back door, Scout ran out to have a look. She's not positive, but she thinks the driver was wearing a sailor hat. She is positive Rat was in the back seat, because he looked right at her before ducking down. Scout immediately called the police and gave them the first two numbers on the license plate, the numbers are, 6-6. Oh, and one other thing, the car is tan not gold," Ivy said in a way that felt like he was criticizing me.

"Hey, those colors are close to each other," I said in my defense.

"No, they're not, and how in the world would you know?" he said more than asked.

"Haven't you ever heard of a golden tan?"

"Yes, but… oh what's the use. The car is tan, period!"

"Ivy, can we drive over to see Dr. Lee?"

"Why?" he asked with a confused look.

"Because I think you need some of whatever it is he gave me," I said with a smile.

"Funny, very funny, Jack, neither of us said it was a definite, but are we going to Mel's again?"

"I thought about that last night when I was falling asleep. I think if we keep throwing out a little cheese, we just might catch us a Rat, know what I mean?"

"Yes I do and it makes perfect sense, except for the fact that Rat may in turn be setting a trap for the two of us."

"Yeah, I thought about that too. Either way we need to keep our guard up. I will say the little jerk sure has balls driving in the Redwood parking lot."

"Are you ready?" Ivy asked.

"Let's go," I said as I walked by him and out the door. Cat ran out too, he was ready for the day.

"See ya Cat," we both said at the same time.

Cat said bye with a yowl and a wiggle of his broken tail.

We went straight to Mel's and had a peaceful breakfast with no Rat sightings. I think there's a good chance Rat was playing the game right along with us. Ivy and I went over our notes and decided we needed to go back to Creston and talk to the senator. We had no idea whether he would actually talk to us, but we had to at least try. I really wanted to find out if I was being paid by Senator Rose; made sense to me.

I turned the coupe around and headed for the police station. Ivy just gave me a look.

"Jack, I thought we were going to Creston to talk with Senator Rose?"

"We are, but first I want to talk to Detective Knox. Don't you want to know what she knows?"

"Yes, I suppose so. Jack, you're not going to tell her we're working on this, are you?"

"Absolutely not, but I am curious. If she's half the gumshoe I think she is, she already knows."

"You think so?"

"Yes I do," I said as I looked at Ivy for a little longer than usual. His eyes beckoned me to say something.

"Ivy, there's something I need to tell you."

He zeroed in on me; guess he could hear a small amount of angst in the new timbre of my voice.

"Go ahead Jack, tell me before you have an episode," he said with a fearful look.

"Ivy, you can let your guard down. It's not what you think."

"Damnit, you don't know what I'm thinking so out with it!"

Last night the Suit came by my apartment. Actually, he snuck by. Anyways, he wanted to know how things are going with our investigation. I told him we don't share information." Ivy began to fidget. "Suit gave me another envelope. It's full of cash, two thousand dollars to be exact. You're doing half the work and I'm the one getting rich, doesn't seem fair to me."

"Just put the money in a safe place," he said in an open-ended way.

"Is there something you haven't told me?" I asked as he drifted a mile away - right there in the front seat of my car.

I pulled over and stopped the car.

"We're partners - what is it Ivy?"

Blue Note

He rubbed his well manicured hands together and fought something deep inside his head. I thought about asking him again, but I knew he'd heard me the first time.

"Jack, the university has decided to remove the funding for my study. I will have to go back to teaching full time come the new semester," he said as he stared out the windshield at nothing.

"Who told you?" No response. "When did they tell you?" No response. "You can't stop right in the middle of the story. "Ok, how'd you find out?"

"The head of my department sent me a copy of the letter he received from the President of the University. I guess funding is scarce right now in the state system. I understand that part, it's just that the letter suggested that the findings of my study are and would be of little value to the world at large," he said in a way that suggested he was humiliated by the contents of the letter. Just like everyone else on this planet, Ivy has feelings and an ego.

I wasn't sure what to say and, truth be told, even after going on a "dig" with him, I still had no clue as to what his study was really all about.

"I needed to tell someone, I'm sorry."

"Ivy, no matter what, we're still a team, and a damn good one at that." He didn't say a word so I pulled away from the curb. *No sense in beating this dead horse.*

I pulled into the parking lot that served both the police and the fire department. I was out of the car and halfway to the detective's office. I just happened to look beside me, no Ivy. I stopped.

I did something he hates, I whistled at him in public. He nearly tore the door off the hinges in his haste to get out of the car. I stood and watched as he trudged my way. We entered the building thru a back door. A sign on the door read: not for public use. I nearly ran Detective Jo Knox over.

"Jack, can't you read? What the hell are you doing?" she hissed at me.

"I was coming in to see how you're doing?"

"I'm doing fine, now get out of my way," she said as she pushed me aside.

"But Jo, we never get to talk."

"Talk to this," she said as she held up one of her fingers for me to enjoy.

"Gosh Jack, do you always have to be so…" Ivy started to ask and then stopped.

"So what?" I said as he walked away.

I was a little on the defensive side of angry when I started the coupe. I sat back, eyes closed and breathed slow and easy.

"Jack, are you going to have an episode?" Ivy asked.

"No Ivy, I'm not! Stop asking me that. Just sit there and be quiet!"

He started to say something; I gave him my raging eyes. He turned away from me. It took me a few seconds before I was able to say, *Jack, he's concerned for you,* to myself of course. When I was calm and the need to scream had passed, I put the car in drive and took off barreling west for Broadway. Of course, Ivy immediately asked where I was going.

"I'm going back to the murder site. There's something I have to check."

"Jack, I thought we agreed that this morning we were going to go talk with Senator Rose?"

"We did, and we will, this won't take long."

Ivy sighed in objection as he sat back against the seat. I drove down Broadway and pulled into the alley behind the hobby shop next to the dumpster where he'd found Timmy Allen. I got out of the car; Ivy remained in the passenger seat with a pouty look on his face. I walked around the dumpster and on the third trip I finally found what I was looking for. I walked straight over and motioned for him to roll down his window.

"Ivy do you have your camera in your car?"

He stared at me for a moment. "Yes, I always keep it in my car, why?"

"Because I want to know, that's why. Ok you need to go get your camera."

"Why?"

"Because I said so, that's why. Ivy please just take the car and go get your camera, please?"

He squirmed across the front seat and started the coupe. He gave me one dark glare as he pulled away. I'd say it took him less than ten minutes and he was back. He got out of the coupe with two cameras in his hand.

"We only need one," I said.

"Jack, are you a photographer?" I shook my head no. "Ok, then be quiet." I didn't say a word. "One camera takes high quality pictures that I'll have to develop at home. The other instamatic will give us a picture right on the spot. Isn't that what you want?" Ivy asked in good faith.

"Yes, I guess so," I said as Ivy set both of his cameras on top of the coupe.

"Hey, we're going to need those. Bring them over here," I requested.

"Jack, show me what it is you want a picture of. Then I'll know which camera to start with."

"Follow me," I said as I walked to the exact spot where Timmy Allen had collapsed and died.

I pointed at the asphalt and Ivy looked down.

"What am I supposed to be seeing?"

"You don't see the paint?" I said as I put my index finer right next to the smear of paint.

"Are you talking about this smudge of red paint?" he said as he stared down at the asphalt.

"It's red?" I asked.

"Yes, blood red to be exact," Ivy said as the thought of blood crossed his memory banks. "Jack, what does this have to do with the murder?"

"I wasn't sure 'til we got here and I looked around." Ivy gave me a pair of confused eyes. "Ivy, I was going to wear my boots this morning. I took 'em out of the closet and when I started to put on the left boot, I noticed one little spot of paint or whatever on the toe. I reasoned it had to have come from when I was hiding behind the dumpster. I think if we looked, we'd find traces of paint all around the dumpster."

"Yes, and what would that prove? I mean an awful lot of people milled around here that night, and who knows how many since?" Ivy said.

"Yes, Ivy. And all of them spread the paint around just a little. So, we wouldn't be able to prove anything by finding red paint on someone's shoe, would we?" I asked with a point in mind.

"No, probably not," Ivy answered.

"But what if we could find a complete shoe print in the red paint?"

"Jack, what are you driving at?"

"This," I said as I motioned for Ivy to follow me over to the dumpster. I opened the lid and pointed at the bottom of the dumpster.

Ivy leaned over and peered down at the footprint left on the floor of the dumpster. He stared in disbelief just as I had done.

"So the murderer wasn't waiting behind the dumpster, he waited inside. Jack, how did you know to look inside the dumpster?"

"I didn't until I thought about all the ribbon and yarn and stuff that was outside of the dumpster. Whoever dumps the trash doesn't throw the stuff on the ground; they put it in the dumpster. So, I figured all the cuttings and such came out of the dumpster when the murderer came out," I said as I flipped the lid of the dumpster all the way over with a bang.

I crawled inside the dumpster on the opposite side of the footprint and cleared the area around it. There was actually one full print and the front half of another. Not sure what size the shoe was, but I'd say it was definitely made by the murderer. And in my mind the murderer was the bearded guy Billy saw talking to Timmy at the bowling alley. Ivy cautiously eased down into the dumpster and I handed him each camera as he asked for it. He took at least a dozen pictures from all angles with the better of the two cameras. He took six with the instamatic before he stood up. He looked me straight in the eye.

"Guess what Jack?" he said more than asked.

"What?"

"There are two prints here, but they weren't made with the same shoe."

"What? What are you talking about?" I said in a raised voice.

"They're not the same shoe. The print on the left was made by a right foot. And the print on the right was made by a left foot. And they're distinctly different from one another. See for yourself," he said as he handed me one of the instamatic photos.

Blue Note

He was absolutely right. The half print from the right foot was of a shoe with a more pointed toe. The print made by a left foot was definitely a boot of some kind. I stepped back as the realization of what took place became clear in my head. Two assailants were crouched next to each other waiting for Timmy. They probably had the lid open an inch so they could see and waited in the dark like two stinking vultures. That might be the reason for the penlight.

"Ivy, it's no wonder they made quick work of Timmy. They overpowered him and then one held Timmy while the other killed him or something along those lines."

Ivy and I sat in the car for a long time. Why, because we couldn't make up our minds what we should do with the photos. In the end, we decided to go talk to Senator Rose and then we would give the pictures to Detective Knox. I hauled ass across the highway that connects the towns and communities in the San Luis Obispo area. I made it to Creston in just under thirty-two minutes, in my mind a world record. I was going to park across the street again, but when I drove up, I decided to get up close and personal.

I pulled into the small circle drive and parked right next to the senator's front porch. I was still in the car when I saw the vertical blinds part just before our little friend, valet Dowdy, motioned for me to stay where I was. Ten seconds later the front door opened and out came the butler.

"This way," he said as he motioned for us to follow him around to the back of the house. As we walked, he turned to me. "You didn't have to hit me. You could have just told me to stay put 'til you were gone. And why'd you steal my pictures?"

"I had to make sure you weren't the person that talked to Timmy at the bowling alley."

"Well," he said.

"You weren't identified, if that's what you want to know," I said as we rounded the corner of the house.

Senator Rose was sitting barefoot next to the pool. He was wearing a pair of off-white Hang Ten surf-shorts. He had one of those reflector thingies in front of his face. His eyes were closed when he said, "How can I help you?"

141

He didn't even open his eyes when footman Dowdy introduced us. I looked at the butler a couple of times before he motioned for me to talk, so I did.

"Senator Rose, I'm Jack Hawkins and this is Ivy Fin. I'm sorry to bother you, but it's important that we talk to you." The senator made no attempt to look my way. "I was paid to find out who killed Timmy Allen." Still, not one sign of interest. "My partner and I were there when the boy was killed."

Senator Rose put the reflector thingy down as he slowly turned my way.

His dyed hair was parted just above his right ear and combed over to the left ear. Now and then a puff of wind would lift the hair before he could push it back down. He was sitting but I'd say he was five feet six inches tall, at best. He didn't have an ounce of fat anywhere on him, which probably explains his willingness to wear surf clothes. He stood and walked over to an umbrella-covered table and pulled a white t-shirt over his head. He grabbed a sweating drink off the table and walked back to us.

"Do the police know that you were there at the murder site?"

"Yes, they do," I said in a casual voice.

"If that's the case, then why didn't they tell me there were witnesses?" he asked in what I would call an accusatory tone.

"I don't know who you mean by police. But if you mean Detective Knox, I'd say she didn't tell you because she didn't want you to know what cards she held in her hand."

"That's probably true. Before we continue, I think I'd like to see some identification from both of you," Senator Rose said as he cast an intense eye on his butler. "Jacob, you brought these men to me. Did you take the time to check their credentials?"

"Yes sir, I did. They both have badges that identify them as licensed private investigators in the State of California. I believe the badges are genuine."

Senator Rose walked back to the table and slipped his feet into the flip-flops he'd left there. He walked by us, and when he reached the back door to the kitchen, he motioned for us to follow him in. We sat in the kitchen at the same table as before.

"Ok, tell me everything you know about this murder and then and only then will I answer any of your questions."

Blue Note

When he spoke to us outside he held his chin in the air in a haughty way. I guess he'd come off his high-horse because now he was looking us straight in the eye. I started from the beginning and told him everything I could remember from the night of the murder. When I was finished, he turned to Ivy.

"Mr. Fin, I must say your comportment is not that of a private investigator. Do you have another occupation?"

"Yes I do. I am an anthropologist."

"Then you must hold an advanced degree of some kind."

"My P.H.D was completed at Stanford and my M.D in Psychiatry was completed at Berkley."

"My, my, that is impressive. You look quite familiar. Have you had any of your work published?" the senator asked in a genuine voice.

"Yes, for years now I have worked closely with the University of Chicago Press."

"I knew it," the senator said as he stood and walked away for a few steps. "I'm sorry; stay right there, I'll be back in a jiffy."

I looked at Ivy, he shrugged his shoulders. I looked over at the butler, he did the same. We heard the senator hoot just before he came back into the kitchen.

"I knew I'd read your syllogism on humans and advanced speech. Before I consider answering any questions about Timmy, I insist that you explain what you so eloquently wrote in this article, please?"

I looked at Ivy and he in turn looked at the senator. "Senator Rose, I don't believe this is the time or the place. You do understand I was ridiculed by some of my colleagues," Ivy said with his dark eyes narrowed and brooding.

"It's now or never, what's it going to be?" Senator Rose said as he looked at me.

"Ok, but make it fast," I urged.

"Dr. Fin, please explain to me why you need a forensic scientist. And do so in terms a child would understand." the senator said with an impish grin.

"In the animal world there is no dominant handedness, they're split down the middle fifty-fifty, right and left hand, paw, hoof or whatever. But ninety percent of all humans today are right handed. The question you have to ask is why. The answer is really quite simple; the speech center of the brain is on the left side, which in turn controls the right side of our bodies. As we began putting together more complex sentences the shift from fifty-fifty or right and left handedness was altered. We shifted from the middle all the way to ninety percent right handed people and ten percent left. I believe a team of forensic scientists could study the butchering or cuttings on bones and then determine whether the butcher was right or left handed. In turn we would be able to ascertain when modern or complicated speech first took place. And that in a nutshell is what drives my research."

"That is simply fascinating," Senator Rose said as my eyelids drooped. "Dr. Fin, you believe that when the percentage moved to as low as sixty percent right handed, we were already communicating in organized and fairly complex sentences."

"Most certainly, and as our vocabulary increased, so did right handed dominance," Ivy said as the fire in Senator Roses eyes sparkled.

"Ok, are we done with the Australopithecus afarensis stuff?" I said.

"I am," Senator Rose said with a smile.

"I am too. Jack, where did you hear the term Australopithecus afarensis?" Ivy asked.

"From you," I answered.

"Oh," he whispered to himself.

"My turn," I said. "Senator, did the detective ask you about a letter opener? And if so, what was your response?" I asked across the table.

The senator leered at me as the smile vacated his face. Looked to me like I had thrown a hot potato at him and he was not ready to catch it.

"I don't believe I want to continue playing this game. I have an excellent attorney and he has advised me to say nothing further on the subject. I am going to let the powers that be figure out what caused this horrible event."

"But Senator, you said you'd answer our questions. You can't just renege like that," I vented.

"No, I didn't say that at all. I said I would consider answering questions. And I've considered and decided it's in my best interest not to say another word. So, Dr. Fin, I want to thank you for taking the time to explain your intentions where it concerned your study. That said, I have to ask you both to leave. Jacob, will you please show our guests to the door," Senator Rose said before he turned and walked thru the dining area and out of sight.

I yelled, "Is the Suit working for you! Hey, you didn't offer us any refreshments." He didn't answer me. "Ivy, we've been duped, let's get the hell out of here."

"Serves you right," valet Dowdy said in his snottiest voice. "This way, gentlemen, please don't make me have to call the police."

"I think you're involved in all of this. You've been lying to the senator. You're not going to like it when I catch you at your little game, Jacob," I said as I looked him in the eye.

"Goodbye," he said as he closed the door in my face.

I was livid on the way back to Blue Note. In fact, I was so angry I had to pull over. I got out of the car and walked alongside the road for a bit. *The jerk played us like mice*. I needed to think so I asked Ivy to drive. He tooled along at the speed limit, all the way back to the police station.

21

Ivy parked the car and we went in the same back door we had earlier that day. I peeked in her office hoping Detective Knox was there. She was and, from what she said, I'd say she was waiting for us.

"Jack, you jerk. What took you so long?" Detective Knox said with a scowl on her face.

"Hello Jo, my you look nice today."

"Jack, if you use my first name again, I'm going to have one of these nice policemen throw you in our little jail. I doubt it, but maybe a few hours or a day in jail might remind you to use a little caution when addressing me."

"I beg your pardon; did you say something about undressing you?"

She stood up and glared at me for a second. Her fists were balled up, reminded me of me.

"Jack!" she screamed just before Ivy did the same. "Jack, shut up and sit down!" she ordered.

I peeked over at Ivy; he'd picked up a folding chair from a corner of the room and set it down next to Detective Knox's desk.

"Ivy, you sure are a good boy," I said out of my disgust at how quickly he had cowered down to the detective.

They both gave me eyes that I had not seen since grade school. Suffice it to say, being in trouble at school was an everyday thing for me. I took the big cushioned chair from the opposite corner and drug it across the linoleum floor. Yes, it made a terribly loud and annoying sound. *Take that*, I said to myself.

146

"Jack, one more idiotic word and you're out of here. So state your damn business," the detective fired across her desk at me.

"I came here to help you, but if you're going to be rude, then maybe I'll just leave," I said in my best jerk voice.

"Jack, just this one time would you please be quiet and listen," Ivy asked with that sad little boy face he's so accomplished at.

My instincts told me to crack wise again, but I kept my mouth shut.

"Thank you, Ivy," Detective Knox said. "Now, how were you going to help me?" she asked in what I thought was a sincere voice.

"I, we have some pictures that I think you're going to want to see," I said and then smiled at her.

"Are they like these pictures," she said as she opened an envelope and handed me a picture. I was staring at the picture while Ivy breathed down my neck, for Ivy to be quiet is one thing, but for the two of us to be completely mum is quite another.

I stopped staring at the picture for a moment and looked up at Detective Knox.

"Where did this come from?"

"I wish I knew. The pictures were left on the front desk, addressed to me. Jack, what were the two of you doing in the alley?" she asked with a glance at both of us.

"We were taking pictures," I softly said.

"Yes, I see the cameras, pictures of what?" she asked.

"Before I say anything else, are there more photographs of me or us?" I asked.

"Yes, plenty, someone has been following you all over town. There are pictures here of you and Ivy at the bowling alley, Mel's diner, drinking at the Redwood, at the college with Doctor Lee, there are even a few of me at your apartment, and there are at least a dozen pictures of you at the Senator's home in Creston; taken on different days!" she screamed.

The rage in me was beginning to boil and Ivy knew it. He came to my rescue before tragedy struck.

"Detective Knox, please let me explain," Ivy softly said in his professor voice. He held up the picture we had been staring at.

The picture was an instamatic of Ivy and me standing in the alley next to the dumpster. "Jack, close your eyes and slow your breathing down. Yes, that's right - very good. Now, I want you to relax your shoulders. Thank you, that's excellent. Now when you are totally at ease, you can open your eyes. Just quietly look and listen while I explain everything to the detective." I didn't open my eyes, but I did listen.

Ivy started with the Suit and then explained everything in detailed chronological order. And when he finished, he asked to see the other photos.

"Detective Knox, these photos tell quite a story. Now we told you about the Bonneville and that there was a chance we were being followed. In fact, Jack has caught the man that wears the expensive suits following us; and I should add, more than once. And there can be no doubt that Jack and I initiated the desire to share information when we came by this morning. You do remember, don't you?" Ivy said as Detective Knox quietly said yes. Now all the photos you have are attention-grabbing, but they do little to help with this murder case. On the other hand, the photos you don't have are critical in this homicide," Ivy said and then abruptly stopped.

I think he stopped at exactly the right time, because the detective nearly jumped out of her chair.

"What photos are you talking about?" she asked in what I would call an urgent shout.

I opened my eyes and watched Ivy hand her one of the instamatic photos of the footprints. I'm not positive, but I think she may have had her own kind of episode. She jumped up with the photo and ran out of her office. She was gone for five minutes before she calmly walked back in smoking a cigarette.

"You got an extra?" I asked.

She pulled another long cigarette from the case and lit it for me.

"Which one of you knew to look inside the dumpster?" she asked in a soft voice.

"Jack did, would you like to know why?" Ivy softly asked.

And as she listened with eyes wide open, he explained about the debris outside of the dumpster.

"So let me get this straight Jack, you figured that the yarn and ribbon and stuff came out of the dumpster when the murderer jumped out."

"Yes, but you've missed an important part of this discovery," I said as I winked at Ivy. He didn't like me gloating and glared at me with his dark eyes.

"Jack, you have been quiet and helpful of late so don't blow it. What important part am I missing?" Detective Knox asked.

Ivy rummaged through the photos and found one that clearly showed two different footprints. I'd say it took ten seconds of her staring, but it could have been less before she leaped to her feet and ran out of the room, screaming. She came back about a minute later with Sergeant Klavinski.

"Afternoon gentlemen," was all he said.

He sat down opposite me on the far edge of Detective Knox's desk and listened. For the next thirty minutes all sides shared information. Now and then we did stop to argue a bit about this or that, but in the end we would have been a team except for one minor detail.

"Jack, I can't just turn my head to the fact that your P.I. license has been revoked. If the senator wanted, he could put you in jail for what you tried to do today," Detective Knox clearly said.

"That little shit let us tell him everything we knew and then he turns around and tells his butler to show us out," I said with clinched fists.

"Jack, you're in the presence of a lady. Can you please refrain from using vulgar language? You were doing so well, gosh," Ivy lamented.

"Yeah Jack, watch your damn language," Detective Knox said with a grin.

Ivy softly whimpered, "Oh dear."

The sergeant looked away and chuckled.

"Ivy, we're in a turbulent situation, so letting off a little steam is probably a good thing. I want the two of you to listen for a minute more. The senator is no fool and he played his cards close to the vest and, for now, he is winning. I think if one of us were in his shoes, we might have done the same. The senator has more rivals, enemies, and haters than Jack, and that's saying a lot." I scowled at her. "He has to be careful. If I tell you what I think about the murder, can the two of you keep it a secret?"

Ivy and I looked at each other and in unison nodded our heads yes.

"Ok, plain and simple, I think he was set up. And if not for the emergency trip to Sacramento, he might be sitting in jail. The letter opener was not just his. It also contained a clear set of prints. He was being ambushed, but why and by whom?" she said as she stood up. "Jack, if anyone asks, I'm going to tell them that because you and Ivy were there after the murder, you volunteered all the information you've given me; which in essence is the truth. Now, I think the two of you need to keep two eyes in front of you and two eyes covering your rear ends. Someone is hot to know what you know and, at some point, this person may feel you're no longer needed and want you gone. So be careful. Ivy, can I keep the photos?"

"Yes, that's why we brought them."

"Thank you. Jack, do you have anything else you'd like to share with me?" she asked in a sincere voice.

"The smartass answer would be a bed. But on the serious side, I have no more information to share. Thanks for your help and good luck," I said as I stood and waved goodbye to the detective and the sergeant.

"Jack, you're handsome and all that, but do the world a favor when you leave here and don't talk so much. That way there might be a small chance that people won't find out how dimly lit you really are," Detective Knox said with a smile.

"I think she likes me," I said to Ivy.

I smiled and Ivy nodded as the two of us walked out of her office. When we were outside, I asked Ivy to drive back to my apartment. I had a few unanswered questions running around in my head. When we reached Broadway, I turned to Ivy.

"Ivy, did you notice there wasn't one picture of your car?"

"No, not 'til you just mentioned it."

"Ivy, when you drive in and park my car, I want you to get out and wave goodbye to me. I don't know if anyone will be watching but we can't be too safe. Go in the Redwood and wait ten minutes or so. I'm going up on the roof and look for the silver XKE and the Bonneville. If I don't see them, I'm going to go down and slip into your car. When you walk out, go straight to your car and drive the exact same route you always do to get home. Oh, leave the cameras in my car. Ok, got it?" I asked.

"Got it, see you in ten," Ivy said.

He parked the car and did what I asked as I leisurely walked the stairs up to my apartment. Cat meowed hello, so I gave him a little tuna and milk before I snuck up to the roof. I looked every direction for 360 degrees, several times. I saw nothing. I snuck back down to my apartment and then eased down the stairs to the parking lot and ducked behind cars all the way to Ivy's MG. A few minutes later Ivy jumped in and we were off. He headed straight for his little cottage in San Luis Obispo and when we were a mile out of Blue Note, I told him to turn around.

"We're not done yet. I want you to head over to the old creamery building in Harmony."

"What's there?" he exclaimed.

"Just do it, please?" I said in my nice voice.

22

We pulled up to the front of the building. We looked everywhere, and there wasn't a soul in sight.

"Take that little path and go on around back. You can park there," I said as Ivy frowned.

There was a trailer with a garage attached to one side. I got out of the coupe and walked up to the side door on the trailer and knocked hard.

"Who out there? I have a foty-five pointed at yo mothuh-fuckin' headt!"

"Domino, it's me - Jack Hawkins. Put down your gun and open this damn door before I come in there and whoop your ass."

"Hawk, you play-actin', foolish sum-bitch, you know you cain't whoop my ass. But come ahead on in," he said as he opened the door.

He smiled to beat the band and laughed like a child before he lifted me up and hugged the breath out of me. "How the hell you been, my old friend?" Domino asked.

"I've been doing great. Domino Culpeper, I want you to meet my friend, Ivy Fin."

Domino stuck out his hand as he took a step back. "Ivy, come on up in here and shut the do. I've been in the bidness for a long time and I got mo than my share a mean hombres that would like a piece of my black ass, if you know what I mean. I'm glad to make yo acquaintance," Domino said as he and Ivy shook hands.

I wish I had a picture of the utter confusion and wonder on Ivy's face. That said, Ivy was just as gracious and humble as always as the two of them greeted one another. I took a long look at Domino, his afro had begun to turn gray and his skinny frame was skinnier still, but the pugilist from Watts was still very much alive and kicking.

"You thoisty, I ain't gots a lot ta drink 'round here, but what I gots I'll give to you," Domino said.

I looked Domino in the eye. "Do you have any of that high class liquor you usually keep?"

"Sho do, you can take yo pick between the Olde English 8 hunerdt in the fridge o the Old Crow sittin' over yonder."

I followed his finger as he pointed down at the fifth of Old Crow on the floor next to his recliner.

"I suppose I'll have both," I said as the two of us turned and looked at Ivy.

"Oh, no thank you. I have to drive," Ivy said just as natural as can be.

"What? What's that gotta do with anythin'?" Domino said more than asked.

"Domino, sit down. What would you like me to get you?" I asked.

"I'll have a beer wif you," he said just before he motioned for Ivy to sit down on the couch.

Ivy just smiled as he looked at the old couch.

"Ivy, sit down," I said as I headed over to the yellowed fridge. I took out two cans of Olde English and as I stood next to the kitchen sink, I said in a loud voice, "Domino, you had any work lately?"

"No, so get to what you gonna ax me."

"You feel like making some good money?"

"What kin'a goodt we talkin' 'bout?"

"I'm talking gas money, lodging, if need be, and twenty-five dollars a day good."

"Thirty a day sound a whole lot goodter."

"Ok, thirty it is," I said as I handed him his can of beer.

I explained everything from beginning to end and when I was done, Domino just shook his head.

"Lordy Hawk, it's just amazin' the amount of pure misery you can get yosef into. Now, you say this XKE is probably the car followin' you, but it could be the Bonneville or some unknown car, am I right?"

"Yes exactly. Now for the next few days Ivy and I aren't going to be doing anything that pertains to the murder."

Ivy stopped me at that point.

"What are we going to be doing?"

"We're going to be helping Friar Tuck and Jackson move into their trailer."

"Hawk, excuse me but most folks like to refer to them as mo-biile homes," Domino corrected.

"I know that, so anyways we'll be easy for you to follow," I said to Domino.

"I seen the little red hoopty you drivin', when you pulled up. Whatever happened to that old Ford of yours?"

"She's up and running like a champ, decided to leave her at home. I don't think whoever has been following us is looking for the hoopty."

"Ok, so when do I start?" Domino asked.

"Right now, Ivy's going to drop me off at the 7-Eleven by my apartment. I'll buy a six-pack and then walk home. I see you finally have a phone, does it work?"

"It sho do, I'll write the number down fo you when ya leave."

"Ok, well my phone is working too. I think it would be best if we only communicate by phone. I don't want to take the chance of someone seeing us anywhere near each other, got it?"

"I got it aw'ight, but what I ain't got is no jingle in my pockets," Domino said as he held out his hand.

"Here's sixty to get you started," I said as I started counting the money. After I handed it to him, he kept his hand up and gave me a pair of demanding eyes.

"Ok, we'll make it an even one hundred for now."

"Thank you Hawk, come wif me out to the grage. I think Ivy had ought'a see what old Domino will be followin' you in. Come on," he beckoned.

We went thru a door that Domino had cut in the side of his trailer. His car had a tarp over it. He yanked the tarp off. The paint on his Oldsmobile was just as dull and unremarkable as always.

"What is it?" Ivy asked.

"She's a damn Oldsmobile and she's the best car I ever owned," Domino said as he frowned at Ivy.

"Oh," was all Ivy could say.

"This ol' Rocket 88 ain't much ta look at, but she can get up and go wif the best of 'em. Cain't you girl," Domino said as he patted the hood of the car.

"Ok well, let's go inside and seal the deal with a jigger of that expensive whiskey you got," I said.

After Domino poured our drinks, we decided that we would communicate just one time each night. We decided on ten o'clock. If it was an emergency, we agreed to call at any hour, day or night. Domino went out and started his car to warm it up and came back in.

"Ok, don't either of you dare look over yo shoulduh or anythin' like that. You'll tip off whoevuh followin' you fo sho. I'll be 'round, just act natchal and do what ya gotta do. Got it?" he asked.

"Got it," I said as Ivy nodded.

"Ok then, it was great seein' ya Hawk, and it was a pleasure meetin' ya Ivy," Domino said.

I chugged down my beer before I gulped the rest of my Old Crow. I thanked Domino. Ivy drove me back to the 7-Eleven; there was no waving or goodbyes. He just took off for home.

23

Sugar, Li'l John, Ivy, and I spent the next two days helping Jackson and Friar Tuck get situated in their mobile home. Duke loaned us a pickup truck even though there wasn't much to move. We did make several trips to the second-hand store. Jackson bought each of them a single bed, a dresser for their clothes, and a little black and white T.V. that came with a gigantic antenna. Being the gentleman I am and the least talented when it comes to fixing things, I let Friar Tuck and Li'l John go up on the roof and secure the antennae. The reception was excellent, made me consider buying a T.V. In the end, I decided against it. I had forgotten about Domino, that is 'til he called the second night.

"Hawk, the XKE folluhed you 'til ya got ta the second hand sto. He stopped after that. I guess he got tired a watchin' you move stuff. I ain't seen no Bonneville yet. See ya."

"Thanks, ok see ya," I said.

I woke up the morning after moving the beds and stuff and put my feet on the frigid floor, Sugar was still sleeping. I knew immediately that something was different, but for the life of me I couldn't figure out what that was. I stretched and went out and said hello to Cat, he was looking in at me thru my kitchen window. I gave him some milk and put some water on the stove to boil, thought I'd surprise Sugar with a little instant coffee, ain't I clever. When I sat down, it came to me. I stood up and stretched all over again, I was right. *This is the first day in months that I woke up without any soreness, even after picking up stuff and hauling it from the store to the truck and from the truck to the mobile home.* I hollered, "Yahoo!"

Sugar came running out of the bedroom with a worried look on her sleepy face.

"Jack, why'd you scream like that?"

"Because I woke up and I wasn't sore. This is the first time in… well, I really don't know when, but it's been a long time. This is great!"

She smiled and softly said, "Good for you," as she walked into the bedroom and fell back in bed.

Although it was a bit nippy outside, Cat and I had a good time sitting out on the steps. After a while I decided to sneak up the stairs to the roof and say good morning to Li'l John. He was sawing logs, so I left him alone and went back down to the kitchen. Ivy walked thru the door with a big smile on his face.

"Good morning Jack, this sure is a wonderful day."

"Yes, it is," I agreed. I told him all about not being sore and how great it was before I asked him why he was so happy.

"I'm happy because instead of looking for a murderer we're going to be helping Friar Tuck and Jackson find a recliner and a small couch, should be fun."

"Coffee?" I asked.

"Sure, any word from Domino?"

"Yes, he called last night and said the XKE followed for a bit yesterday, but when he saw what we were doing, he disappeared. I guess he could see that we weren't working on the Timmy Allen case. Ivy, do you think Suit is the one taking the pictures?"

"I don't know, but I believe the next time you see him you should ask. If he nictates or looks away." "Nictates?" I interrupted. "Quickly blinks, before he says he's not the one taking the pictures, he will be lying. I hope I'm there to witness the event."

I handed Ivy a cup of coffee and sat down just as someone knocked on my door.

"Come in," I said thinking it was Li'l John or maybe Mr. Hurtwood. It was Suit.

He looked a bit stunned to see Ivy sitting at my table.

"Um, good morning gentlemen, Jack I've come by this morning because I was told by my boss that your services will no longer be needed," Suit said with a small scowl etched across his face.

"Oh, that is a surprise. Is it because I haven't been working on the case for a day or so?" I asked to see if he'd mention my helping Jackson and the Friar move. He looked out the kitchen window.

"I didn't know you weren't working on the case, but I'd say that is not the reason. My boss feels you've done enough, is all."

"Suit, we visited the police station the other day and an officer there showed us several pictures taken of Ivy and me. Some were taken while we worked on the case and some when we weren't. Did you take the pictures?"

Suit blinked before he gazed at the painting of John Wayne and Maureen O'Hara. Then he turned back and looked me straight in the eye.

"Why of course not, I would have no reason to take pictures of you."

"Ok well, I was just wondering. It's not a big deal."

"Jack, do you know who the murderer is?" he asked in a very direct way.

"That is a strange question and the answer is no, but I think we're getting close. And now you tell me you want me to stop?" I said.

"Yes, my employer would like you to stop all activity on the Timmy Allen case. However, he has decided to pay you for your most recent efforts," Suit said as he laid an envelope on the table.

"Thanks, but I'm a very curious person. So, for my own reasons I'm going to continue working on this case 'til I know for sure exactly who killed the boy, and why."

"Due to the dangers involved and the risk of personal harm I would strongly advise you to cease with this investigation," Suit said in a forceful way.

"Thanks for your concern, but you should know by now that I never stop 'til I get my man."

"Again, I would strongly advise against it. Thank you for your time and effort. I will let myself out. Goodbye," Suit said with a short nod.

Blue Note

Once the door was shut I sat and stared at the envelope. It took maybe ten seconds before I came out of my money trance.

"Ivy, he was lying, wasn't he?" I said more than asked.

"Yes, he was lying about everything. I have to give him credit though. When he looked you in the eye and answered your question he almost had me believing him. He's an experienced liar. That said, I suspect trouble is waiting around the corner. Jack, we need to be extra cautious from here on out. And we must be diligent in our effort not to involve innocent people of which there are many. Sugar and Li'l John for example," Ivy said with a stern eye.

Up until Ivy mentioned them, I hadn't taken three seconds to consider others. I chastised myself before I came out of my little trance. When I looked up, I was shocked, Ivy had opened the envelope.

"Whoever Suit's boss is really wants you to stop. He has thrown in another five hundred dollars, and you and I have done little to earn it."

I heard Sugar stirring and took the envelope and put it in the vegetable tray on the bottom of the fridge. Not sure why, but I think I did it because of the saying, never put all your eggs in one basket. Ivy watched me.

"Jack, I strongly advise you to stop with the troglodyte attitude. What you're doing now is foolish. Put all your money in the bank, it will be safe there. I might add there are those that would do anything to hurt you, which would include stealing your money."

He was right and I knew it.

"You're right, I'm going to make a trip to the bank today and deposit all the money."

"Jack, you promised me you wouldn't put my money in the bank," Sugar said as she walked out into the kitchen.

"No Sugar I won't, I was only talking about my money. We don't want to keep all the money in the same place, do we?" I asked.

"I guess not. Please don't put my money in the bank, please?" she begged.

"Sugar, sit down and have a cup of coffee, I give you my word I will not touch your money or put it in the bank, ok?"

"Ok," she said with a smile.

Not a word was said for at least a couple of minutes before I decided I should tell Sugar that I had been fired from my job. I thought she'd be worried or something along those lines, she was actually happy and said so. I had a question burning a hole in my brain that I had to ask Ivy.

"Ivy, do you think Senator Rose feels he is out of the woods and so he has decided to fire me?"

"I've already asked myself the same question and it makes too much sense to ignore. Yes, I do think he was behind your being hired and fired."

Blue Note

24

Late Saturday we found a recliner for Friar Tuck and a small couch for Jackson at a thrift store over in Atascadero. When we were all done with the moving, I headed home. I was sitting in the kitchen debating on whether or not to go down and have a beer with Scout when the band started playing. I looked over at Sugar and she was smiling, guess she liked the music. I had to admit the band sure did sound good, maybe a little too good.

"Sugar, do you want to go down and listen to the band for a while?"

She gave me a smile the likes of which I had not seen before, at least not from her. She took a little time to clean up before skipping down my steps to the parking lot. I could hear happy feet on the dance floor, and lots of them. The moment I walked in the door I understood why Sugar had smiled so big and why the band sounded so great. In the far corner stood a tall disc-jockey, he was looking thru his 45's.

I immediately looked over at Scout and she had a smile that matched the one Sugar had given me. The song ended at about the same time Sugar and I cozied up to the bar.

"Ok Scout, what is going on?" I asked with a smile of my own.

"I think I should let Mr. Hurtwood explain," she said as she looked over my shoulder.

"Evening Jack, hello Sugar, so what do you think of my new band?" Hurtwood asked with a grin.

"They sound great, what in the world made you change to a disc-jockey?"

"Jack, the truth is I've been losing money for over a year now with the live music. So after Whitey fired you, I decided to fire him."

"Wow that must have been difficult. You and Whitey have been friends for a long time."

"No Jack, you made it very easy for me," he said before he told Scout to give Sugar and me a drink on the house.

I asked for a draft beer and Sugar asked for a Shirley Temple.

"Mr. Hurtwood, how did I make it very easy for you?" I asked just before I took a long drink.

"Jack, I didn't like the way Whitey handled the situation with you. Fact is, he didn't have the guts to come in here and fire you himself, so as you know, he sent poor Stuttering John to do his bidding. I told him how disappointed I was just before I fired him."

"Wait, you fired him because he fired me?"

"Yes, you could say that, that and the fact that I've been losing money," he said as the next song rocked the room.

When the song was finished, I went outside and looked up at the roof. Li'l John was right there looking down at me, his tooth all aglow.

"Hi Robin, do you like the music? I do," he said followed by his signature haaaa ha-ha.

"Yes I do, would you like to come down and sit inside with us?"

"No Robin, I have work to do," he said with a glance over my shoulder.

"John, it's ok, come on down and join us," Hurtwood said from behind me.

"You sure," Li'l John asked.

"Yes, I'm positive. Come down and listen to the music with us," Hurtwood invited.

For a second, I thought Li'l John was going to bound over the edge of the roof, but he ran down the stairs instead. He whisked by me and sat down with his hands in his lap as he watched the people dance; he had a faraway look in his eye. Scout walked around the bar and handed Li'l John a drink, I think it was a Roy

Rogers. He sat on the stool and tapped his foot on the floor as he bobbed to the music. A slow song came on and Sugar got up from her stool and walked by me and asked Li'l John to dance. I thought Li'l John's face might break he smiled so big. Sugar led him out onto the floor and then at arms length she put her right hand under his left and her left on his shoulder and they began a smooth circular stroll. She counted the beats to him and he nodded his head to her. All the people that had been dancing walked off the floor and from a distance watched as Sugar gently guided Li'l John from one end of the dance floor to the other and then back again.

Scout moved down the bar and whispered in my ear, "They look rehearsed, don't they?"

"Yes they do," I said as I marveled at the joy on Sugar and Li'l John's faces.

The moment the song ended the disc-jockey began slowly clapping his hands. He was soon joined by every person in the bar, me included. Sugar took Li'l John by the hand and whispered something in his ear just before she walked him out of the building. A minute later she hurried back in the bar and asked if it would be ok if she took Li'l John's drink up to him.

Scout looked at Mr. Hurtwood and he in turn looked at Sugar. "Young lady, thank you for asking. I should have been taking refreshments up to him long before this evening. Please take his drink up to him."

Sugar wasted no time and was back in the bar in seconds. I was still a bit amazed at what I'd seen and walked by her and out the door. I looked up and was met with a grand smile from Li'l John. I waved and smiled at him before I walked back in the bar and sat down next to Sugar.

"Sugar, I don't really know what to say, so I guess I'll just say thanks, that was fun to watch."

She gave me one of those private smiles that begin inside the person before they show themselves to the world outside. I let her have her moment. She didn't mention the dancing again and neither did I.

25

Sunday afternoon came around and I felt like giving Jackson and Friar Tuck a surprise party. So the gang and I drove to the Coke plant, picked up Duke, and then headed for the nearest grocery store. We bought enough chow for an army and then headed for the trailer park. We took our party into the clubhouse all the people that live in the park share. We ate 'til even Li'l John was full. It was a sunny afternoon but the air was a bit cool. I sat and let my mind drift off into space. Sugar was telling the others about all the new friends Li'l John had made since he started patrolling the roof. Then it hit me in the gut. I looked at Sugar and then Ivy and then my eyes rested on Li'l John.

"Li'l John, Sugar told me the night the boy was killed that you knew a murder had taken place. How did you know that?"

Sugar immediately jumped in the middle of the conversation before it started.

"Jack, you have that look in your eye."

"What look is that?"

"The one that makes people not want you around."

"I didn't know I had that much power," I said in a soft voice.

"Jack, she's right," Ivy said.

"Jack, ask me the questions. I can answer all of them for Li'l John," she said in an obvious attempt to protect him from... something.

"Ok, how did Li'l John know there had been a murder that night?"

164

Sugar looked at Li'l John and then at me. "I guess because he goes to the hospital every night to look for someone that was very important to him. Is that right?" she said as she looked at Li'l John.

"Sugar, I'm not trying to blame you or him or anyone else for anything. Now what you just told me is kinda strange, so I'm not going to ask who he was looking for. All I want to know is how'd he know someone had been murdered?"

Sugar looked at Li'l John for only a second before he said, "Heath told me."

"Heath, who the hell is Heath," I asked.

"Heath Abbey," Sugar said.

"Li'l John, what did Heath tell you?"

"Heath told me that he was going to pick up Tim Allen because he was murdered and dead."

"What does Heath do?" Ivy asked before I could.

"Heath is a paramedic," Sugar said.

"How did a paramedic know his name? The police didn't even know his name!" I yelled.

"Jack, you're yelling," Sugar calmed.

"And I'm going to yell some more if I don't get a straight answer, and right now!" I yelled.

Duke did his John Wayne walk over to me. "Jack, please calm down or I will have to ask you to leave. The people that live in the park are old and your yelling is going to upset them. Ok, so please stop yelling!" Duke yelled.

"Ok, sorry. I won't yell anymore. Li'l John or Sugar or someone, please tell me how Heath knew about the murder."

"Because he also drives an ambulance, he's the one that picked up the boy," Sugar said.

I looked at Li'l John. "Li'l John, did Heath say Timmy Allen's name before he left the hospital?"

"Yes, I ask him if he was going to pick up my mom and dad, but he said it was just some stupid dead boy name Tim Allen."

At that point I blew a fuse; my mind went haywire as I tried to put together the pieces of this broken puzzle. I looked at Ivy; he immediately knew I was heading for disaster.

"Jack, do not say the coins please, whatever you do - do not say the coins!"

I rolled over from the lawn chair I was sitting on to the floor. I turned onto my back and closed my eyes. Each nickel that flew by was chased away.

"Jack, breathe slow, yes that's good. Now try to imagine yourself floating on a cloud. Excellent, ok, listen to each breath you take. Slow and easy, and then again, slow and easy," Ivy said in his soft voice.

I opened my eyes for just a moment. I had to find out if I could handle the world outside with my eyes open. *So far so good,* I said to myself.

I rolled over onto my side and with a gentle push, I sat up. Sugar was holding my head. I think she thought I might crack my noggin wide open.

"Sugar, thanks, but I'm ok. Ivy, I want you to have Li'l John tell you what this Heath fellow looks like.

I sat with my eyes closed as Li'l John told us about the big man with the beard. I felt like yelling but I'd given my word that I wouldn't yell anymore. My first instinct was to find Heath and kill him. The thought had just trampled my brain when Ivy tapped me on the shoulder. I came out of my death trance for a moment and then Ivy got right down next to me and whispered, "Jack, I know you want to kill Heath, but we need him alive so he can lead us to the others."

Ivy was right and I knew it. I felt a little more like myself when I stood up and asked Li'l John what clothes Heath was wearing when he told him about Timmy Allen. Li'l John called it a "keep clean suit."
I've got you now you son of a bitch, I said to myself.

Ivy apologized to Jackson, Friar Tuck, and Duke for all the commotion as he led me out to my car. Ivy drove the gang, Sugar, Li'l John, and me home. Along the way I asked Sugar why Li'l John would go to the hospital to look for his parents. She said she didn't know why but that he checks nearly every night. After that, we rode in complete silence; I think Sugar knew I was angry with her and I wasn't buying her little story.

Domino called me at ten o'clock sharp. He said no one followed us the entire day.

26

Woke up the next morning and reached for Sugar, she wasn't there. I eased out of bed and went to look at my calendar, there was no note. But there was Ivy; he sat wrapped in grim, his eyes dark with injury.

"Sugar left this on the table," he said as he handed me a yellowed newspaper clipping. It read: Legendary NASCAR mechanic, Johnny Plum and wife; Kate Plum, dead at age 42. They're survived by their 22-year-old son, John Jr. and their 7-year-old daughter, Violet. The Plum family was on their way to Chicago when a trucker lost control, crossed the median, and hit them head on. John Jr. was to report to the Chicago Bears. He starred as an All American offensive tackle at USC and had been a first round pick in the NFL draft. When I finished the article, I looked at Ivy; knee-deep in angst he pointed and said, "Jack, look at the date on the article."

It had been written ten years ago. I raced out the door and up the steps to the roof in a panic.

No Li'l John and no Sugar, I was all alone as I screamed to the heavens. I paced for a while before I ran down and asked Ivy if he'd seen Sugar leave. He softly said no. *You just had to keep pushing her. Sugar, I'm so sorry. Lord, what have I done?*

"Ivy, I have to find Sugar. She can't have gone far." He had a distant look in his eyes.

I had never told Ivy about the man from the county that was pursuing Sugar. When I was dressed to go, I decided I should.

"Ivy, you don't know this, but there has been a man from the county pursuing Sugar." He gave me a pair of dreadfully dark eyes.

"I think now I know why." Ivy looked at me with a pair of accusatory eyes.

"And you didn't make the effort or take the time to find out why?" he half yelled.

"Ivy, it's not like that at all. I asked her why he was after her; of course, she said she didn't know. That said, I suppose now we know why. School is mandatory to age eighteen in the State of California. Do you think she's been taking care of Li'l John and out on the streets for the entire ten years?" I said as Ivy sat down again.

"Jack, it's counterproductive for either of us to cast blame. This was Sugar's secret, a secret that she guarded with her very life. Li'l John is Sugar's big brother yet without little sister he would never be able to function in society. But with her help, the two of them have actually done quite well. What a noble sacrifice Sugar has made. She gave up her childhood to protect her older brother," Ivy softly said.

"So let's go find them," I replied.

"Let's, ok Jack, where do we start?"

"We'll start with the hobo cave. Sugar said if I ever needed to find her, I should go there first."

We drove the coupe to the tourist area next to the Blue Note Cave. The first thing I heard when we exited the car was the grommets banging against the flag pole. Down the steps we went through the cave as we listened to the whirring Blue Note. We ran the quarter mile along the cliffs inland to the hobo cave. I told Ivy to wait for me outside. The air had cooled since the last time I ran into the cave. This time there were twice as many men huddled around the fire. Of course, the same man that greeted me the first time stood and held his ground. When he recognized me, he softened his stance a bit.

"Look, I'm sorry to barge in on you men this way, but I have to find Sugar and Li'l John. Have you seen them?"

The grizzled man turned to his fire mates and softly asked if anyone had seen Sugar. A man stood up from the rear of the group and walked over to me. It was as if the cave produced men in duplicate. He had the sullen look of someone that was hungry but not for food.

"Sugar ain't stayed in the cave or even come thru for quite some time now. I believe the man that is after her is the reason for her staying away. Matter of fact, I heard she was staying permanent like with you. Your name is Jack, ain't it?"

"Yes, I'm Jack. And you're right about all of that. How about the canyon behind the bakery? Do you think she'd go there?" I asked.

In unison all the men shook their heads no.

I thanked the men and ran out to Ivy. I shook my head no and then asked him to wait there. I ran back in the cave and emptied my pockets. The thank you's I received were sincere and gratifying.

Ivy and I raced back to the car and although I knew the chances were slim, I drove straight to the bakery. The men in the small canyon gave me the exact same answer as the men in the cave. I went in the bakery and asked the employees. No one had seen Sugar or Li'l John. Our next stop was the thrift store. Sugar had not been there either. I wrote a detailed note to Sugar that said I would help her in any way possible. For the most part I begged her to come back home with me. The woman that took the note said she'd make sure to give it to Sugar when she saw her. I knew she'd read it and know how desperate I was.

From that point we drove up and down every street and alley in Blue Note. The two of them had vanished. At some point, I made the decision to drive over to the Coke plant. Duke and Jackson were there. They had not seen her. There was no phone in the trailer so I had to drive out to the mobile home park to see for myself. Friar Tuck was genuine as can be when he promised to deliver Sugar and Li'l John to me if and when he saw them. The day had gone by in a hurry. When I returned to my apartment, I trudged up the stairs and thru my door hoping to see Sugar sitting at my little table, it wasn't to be. I told Ivy we would try again the next day. Stoop shouldered and haggard, he made his way to his car and went home. I sat at my table for a while with dark thoughts running around my head. Are they ok? Are they angry at me? Will I ever see Sugar and Li'l John again?

I fell asleep at the table with my head tucked in my arms. When the phone rang, I was so startled I nearly knocked the table over. I leaped to my feet and headed for the wall next to the fridge to pick up the phone.

"Hello."

"Hawk, it's me Domino. Was you sleepin' o somepin'?"

"Yeah I was, it's been a long day."

"I know, been followin' yer ass all damn day. What was you lookin' fo?"

I went thru the story from the very beginning to the end, actually did me good to talk about it. He didn't say a word 'til I was done.

"Hawk, you got a damn good reason ta have a worried mind. And what I'm fixin' ta tell you right now ain't gonna hep matters none."

"Why, what's wrong?"

"Hawk, you was followed taday aw'ight, and that ain't so unusual. But what is unusual is that damn XKE let you get completely out of sight several times befo he drove straight to yo ass."

"I don't understand, what do you mean he let me get out of sight?"

"Hawk, he stopped to get a cup of coffee and then he stopped to have lunch. And then he stopped to make a phone call. And every time he stopped, you kept right on a goin'. Then when he would get back in his car, he would drive straight to you. Now I had no idea where you was goin' and neither did he. So how da you think he knew where you was? I'll tell ya how, he put a damn trakin' device on yo car. Don't know when he did it o where, but I know he did."

"That goddamn Rat!" I yelled at the phone.

"Hawk, what Rat you yellin' 'bout?"

"Domino, the day I first saw the Bonneville a guy named Rat Johnson ran by the diner where I was eating. He must have put the device on the car then. Hell, they've known where I was every minute of the day and night. Shit!" I screamed into the phone again.

"Stop hollerin' into the damn phone at me. Hawk, so what you gonna do?"

Blue Note

"Tomorrow morning I'm going to go out and find the bug on my car. Then we'll see what they do. If the XKE still follows me then we'll set up a little trap for him. Shit, no wonder they have pictures of us all over creation. Damn it."

"Hawk, what pictures you talkin' 'bout?"

"Never mind the pictures, they're not that important."

"Hawk, you know it'd be a might easier for us to catch the Suit if you leave the bug on yo car."

Domino, you're right. And it would also be a lot easier to take him on a wild goose chase if I leave the bug where it is. Domino, thanks for doing a good job. I'll talk at you tomorrow night. See ya," I said as I started to hang up.

"Hawk, slow yo damn roll, you need ta slow yo ass down sometimes. You ain't never toldt me to follow the Suit home, but I did. I know where his crib is, I just don't know 'xactly which crib it is."

"What do you mean?"

"He live in one a'them condominimums. You know the ones that's stacked up one on top a th'other. Hell, there must be two hunerdt of 'em in the high rise where he stay."

"Where's this high rise?"

"It's down town Bispo."

"Ok, that's good to know, why didn't I think of that?"

"Cuz you ain't as clever as old Domino, that why," he said as he chuckled into the phone. "So I was thinkin' one a'these times I'mona go there befo him and wait for his ass. He'll never be the wiser, cuz he don't know me from Adam. Yesiree, that's what I'mona do."

"Yes, now that I know he's been sneaking around behind my back, I'd like to know who he is. If you go there, be careful. There could be more than one of him, if you know what I mean."

"I'll coitainly be careful, you can count on that. Ok, Hawk, good luck with yo search and such. I'll talk at you tomorra night," he said as he hung up.

171

27

I was underneath my car, when Ivy drove up the next day.

"Jack, what are you doing under there?"

"Searching for something, what took you so long to get here? It's after ten thirty."

"Last night I was on the phone for a long time. When I got up this morning, I got right back on the phone again."

"Who were you talking to?"

"People, that's who, I found out when Sugar stopped going to school and why. Her attendance was spotty at best but she made it thru the eighth grade at a public school in the heart of Los Angeles. When John was able to walk again, she stole him away from the mental institution in Camarillo. They've been on the run ever since. I was told that just before they were hit by the semi, John wrapped himself around Sugar to protect her. As a result, he suffered some severe physical trauma, mostly to the head."

"Didn't they ask who you were and why you wanted to know all of this information?"

"Yes, I told them I was a researcher with the university and that I was looking for a subject like John to study. They said good luck finding him. The county and the state have been looking for nearly four years now, with no luck at all."

"Well, I don't know why that makes me feel better, but it does. Last night I had myself convinced that Sugar and John have been out here on the streets ever since the accident, but it's actually way less than that. It's still a long time, but…"

Blue Note

"I talked to a matron at Camarillo and she said John still believes his parents are alive and that they will show up some day at the hospital, such a great tragedy. Ok enough of that, Jack what are you looking for?"

"Domino called last night and told me my car has been bugged. He said Suit didn't even have to know where I was. Sometimes he just drove straight to me. I figured that day–"

"That day at the diner when you saw Rat run by, yes, that has to be when the bug was placed under your car. Do you need help?" he asked.

"Nope, cuz I just found it," I said as I slid out from underneath the trunk of the car with the little bug in hand.

I handed it to Ivy while I dusted myself off.

"I believe it works in tandem with an uplink, a downlink, and a transponder," Ivy said as he peered at the device. Jack, I think you might want to leave it where you found it. If needed, we may be able to use it to lead them into a trap," Ivy said.

"I'm way ahead of you. When we get back from the bank, I'll stick it up there next to the rear bumper again. For now, I don't want them thinking about my money or anyone else's for that matter."

"Jack, where are we going after the bank?"

"We're going to make the rounds and see if we can find Sugar and John. Then we're going to go pay our buddy Heath a visit. That damn name of his could cause someone to start up a lisp. 'Heath on hith way' and shit like that," I said thinking I was clever.

"Jack, at times the things you say worry me. Really makes me wonder what goes on in that head of yours."

"Stop worrying and follow me," I said as I headed up to my apartment.

I cleaned up and then we drove straight to my bank and deposited the money. Afterwards Ivy and I made the same rounds as the day before but we didn't see hide nor hair of Sugar or Li'l John. Ivy tried his best to reassure me that in due time she'd come back. Strange how only minutes before I had told Ivy not to worry and here I was doing exactly that. When we got to the hospital, I let Ivy go in and see what he could see while I slunk around to where they keep the ambulances. I was hunkered down behind a tree over maybe half a football field from where some guy was giving an ambulance a bath. He was very young and didn't look to me like he could grow a beard even if he wanted to. I figured he was too young to be one of the paramedics or a driver. He did a decent wash job and when he was done, he whistled for someone to come out and inspect his work. Out walked our man, Heath Abbey.

I guess Heath gave the young man the ok, cuz the kid turned the hose off and then he grabbed the bucket and sponges and walked out of sight. I sat there wondering what I should do next when Heath walked back in the garage area, took off his jumpsuit, and hung it up. He walked down a pathway that led back inside the main lobby of the hospital. I ran over to the parking lot worried that he'd see my car. He never came back out. I sat and sat before Ivy came strolling down the sidewalk towards me.

"Jack hurry, he's going to get away," Ivy said as he jumped in my car. "He's in a blue Stingray convertible. You can't miss him."

I had the car running and heard the Stingray before I saw it go by in my rearview mirror. And the chase was on. I drove in the same lane about ten car lengths behind him. He took the Cabrillo Highway all the way into San Luis Obispo. Then he made a series of left turns before he pulled into the underground parking lot of a high-rise building. I made a hard right and drove a block away and parked.

"Ivy, Domino told me that Suit lives in a high rise just like that one. Could they be connected? What should we do?"

"I think we should let him believe he's safe, for now. We can stay here all evening if need be."

"Do you think it's possible that Suit and this Heath guy are in this together? I mean I'm not sure if this is the same building Domino was talking about, but it could be. Wait, Domino must be around here somewhere. I'm going to drive around the block and come in from behind where we first came in. I'll just bet we find Domino. Let's go see."

I went in a full circle and headed back to the high rise. Domino's car was parked three blocks from where I parked the first time. I pulled over and told Ivy I'd be right back, I eased out and snuck over to Domino's car, he wasn't in it. I turned and waved to Ivy to stay where he was. I started walking towards the entrance to the parking garage when Domino softly yelled my name. He was sitting at a bus stop with a newspaper opened in front of him. He peered around the paper at me and said, "Sit down."

"Domino, how long have you been sitting out here?"

"Long befo you got here. Hawk, Suit has somehow figured us out."

"How do you know that?"

"I snuck into that damn buildin', then I went 'round the back. There's a way out of the parking lot in the back. Was you after that blue Stingray?"

"Yes, how'd you know that?"

"I knowed that cuz I seen you roll by just after the Stingray pulled into the parking garage. You too late, he already drove out the back. He long gone and now they know you know. Stingray must have a device in his car just like Suit does. Any which-way you cut it he knew you was followin' him."

"Domino, that can't be right. I found the bug this morning and took it out. I planned on putting it back but forgot."

"Oh, this ain't good a'tall, no sir. Hawk, they dun outsmarted us and led us here on poipose. We's probably miles and miles from where they really stay. What you gonna do now?"

"Go to the police, that's what I'm gonna do."

"I don't like the po-lice, but sometimes you just have ta ax 'em fo they hep. Ain't no crime in axin'."

I stood up from the bench and was going to leave when Domino stopped me.

"Who the guy in the Stingray?"

"His name is Heath Abbey, he works at the hospital. I believe he's the murderer. Problem is, we know there were at least three people involved. One person chased the kid into the alley while two others waited for him. Yep, it's time to tell Detective Knox the guy's name. She'll go pick him up and with some luck, they'll find the others. I think it's time for me to get out of this whole damn thing. Domino, I still want you to call me every night, at least 'til we figure this thing out, ok?"

"You got it Hawk, you headin' to the po-lice right now?"

"Yes, you go on home. I'll tell you all about it when you call tonight. See ya," I said as I shook his hand.

Ivy and I drove straight to the police station and went in the same back door. Detective Knox was standing in the hallway smoking a cigarette, she had a worried look about her.

"What's wrong?" I asked before Ivy could say hello to the detective.

She nodded at Ivy and then looked hard at me. "I'll tell you what's wrong. Other than the damn pictures you gave me, I am no closer to the murderer than I was a week ago. Now my boss is being pushed by Senator Rose's attorneys to find the murderer. No doubt he was set up, but why and by whom?"

"Detective Knox, I don't know the why, but I have good news where it concerns the who."

She let the cigarette drop from her hand and slowly crushed it as she did the mashed potatoes with her right foot.

"Jack, don't tease me with maybes and stuff like that. Do you have a name for me?"

I decided to just spit it out, "Heath Abbey is your man. Well, he's one of your men."

"Who?"

I repeated the name before I went through the entire story with her. And the more I explained, the clearer the picture became. She remembered the guy with the beard who was driving the ambulance. By the time I finished the story, she was livid. She was a little upset with me for not telling her about the guy when I first heard his name. But she was mostly upset at herself for not connecting the bearded ambulance driver to the murder.

"Jack, I want you to go home and stay there. I'm not asking you, I'm telling you. I'll let you know where this goes, but on my time, not yours. Do you understand me, stay away!"

Before I could say a word, Ivy said it for me.

"Detective Knox, I give you my word as a gentleman that I will not let Jack go anywhere near this again. I know when to quit and when Jack can put his ego aside, he will too," he said as he leered at me.

"Why are you looking at me? Heck, I'm the one that decided to come here. Detective, you better keep your word and let me know what's going on. You can thank me later, let's go Ivy." I ordered.

Sure I was pissed at how ungrateful she was, but I had a feeling she'd need my help again. It was just a matter of when.

Domino called me that night and told me he went back in the high rise. He asked every person behind every desk where Heath Abbey's office was. Not one person had ever heard the name before. We were definitely set up, but why? I reasoned that they were just being careful. If I had just committed a murder, I'd be careful too. In fact, I'd get the hell out of Dodge.

28

I was in the middle of a dour dream when I thought I heard a phone ring. I sat up in bed as did Cat. *I must have been dreaming* I said to myself just before my head fell back down on the pillow. Five minutes later I heard a phone ring again. I walked out of my dream and into the kitchen and picked up my phone.

"Jack! I'm coming by in five minutes. Get up and get dressed!"

"Who is this?"

"Jo Knox, get dressed!"

I got up and threw the same clothes on I had worn the day before. I set a saucer of milk out but Cat decided to stay in bed. I took a look out my kitchen window, it was still dark. I eyed my black cat clock; it was four in the morning. I sat down and at the same moment, the headlights hit the parking lot. I ran down my steps as Detective Knox frantically waved at me to get in. It was a cold morning; I had the feeling it was going to get colder still.

"What's going on?" I asked in a raised voice.

She didn't answer me, so I asked her again, still no answer.

"Ok, where are we going?"

"To San Louie," was all she said.

I ran every reason in the world I could come up with why we would go there. I drew a blank.

"Is it Heath Abbey?" I asked.

"No Jack, it's not. It's worse than that. The sheriff called me about an hour ago and told me he answered a call to a small residence near the college. He found your number on a scrap of paper inside the house with "in an emergency" written next to it. He said he called you. Did your phone ring a while ago?"

"Yes, but I thought it was a dream. What's he want and whose house is it? *Oh no,* I said to myself.

"It's not a house, it's a cottage."

The moment she said cottage I knew.

"Is he ok!" I screamed at her.

"Jack, I don't know. All I was told is there was a break in and Ivy shot the person. I didn't know Ivy owned a gun, did you?"

"Ivy doesn't, uh oh," I accidently said.

"Uh oh what!" she yelled at me.

"Uh oh, the butler or whatever the hell he is pulled a gun on me when Ivy and I went out to see the senator. I took it away from him, I guess Ivy must have kept the gun, good God," were the last words spoken by either of us.

We pulled up to Ivy's country cottage, all the lights were on inside. Two sheriffs' cars sat in the driveway, empty.

I ran in the front and Detective Knox ran up the driveway and around to the backyard. We met in Ivy's bedroom; the sheriff was there on the floor. He had a knife out and was picking at something stuck in the baseboard next to the floor. He looked up at us for a moment. "Hang on, I've almost got it."

The battle hardened, middle age sheriff stood and showed us the flattened slug he held in his hand.

"I figure from the proximity to the door and the angle, Professor Fin shot someone right here. The blood splatter and tissue tells me it must have been a thru and thru. I think someone barged thru the door and he shot them; he may have warned them first, don't really know. I do know the professor put up one hell of a fight."

I looked around Ivy's bedroom; it had been torn to pieces.

"Where's Ivy?" I asked in a desperate voice.

"Where's the gun?" Detective Knox asked at nearly the same time.

"The professor is in surgery as we speak. He was unconscious and in bad shape when I found him. And yes, we recovered the gun, it was under the bed. Only one shot had been fired, is that what you wanted to know detective?"

"Yes, thank you."

I looked at Detective Knox and she was out the door heading for her car. We went directly to the front desk in the hospital and asked about Professor Fin. The young lady we spoke with had a soothing voice; I suppose that's why she was there. We were told to go to the waiting room on the second floor. An hour went by, then two, then three.

Detective Knox shook me from my sleep and I watched the doctor slowly walk away.

"He said Ivy is in a medically induced coma and cannot be disturbed for at least 48 hours. In short, Ivy is clinging to life by a thread. The injuries are too numerous to count and there may be injuries that will go undiscovered for a while. The internal bleeding is most critical, but for now, is in check. The doctor said they've done all they can. And so now we wait.

"We can't even see him?"

"No, not even. Jack, I know you want to do something, I do too. But there is nothing we can do except pray for Ivy to fight.

29

Ivy heard what sounded like leaves rustling across his courtyard. He didn't move at first, but when he heard the noise a second time, he reached under his mattress and grabbed the butler's gun. He was by no means an expert with firearms, but he believed he could shoot straight. He figured a warning would do the trick. He crept out into his kitchen and watched the shadows scurry by before he hurried back into the bedroom, picked up the phone, and dialed. He told the operator there were strangers in his backyard. She convinced him a car would be there soon but to make sure all the doors were locked. He ran to the kitchen, he was too late. As he backed into the bedroom, he warned the first masked man, it did no good. He fired at the intruder's leg hoping he'd retreat, he didn't. The very first glancing blow found Ivy's forehead, he lurched in pain. Somewhere deep in the recesses of his mind he knew he'd been struck by a solid object, probably a bat. The gun flew from his hand.

Once cornered, the assailants, of which there were four, proceeded to batter his arms and legs. One thud after the other shot to his ears before screaming their way to the pain receptors of his mind. He flailed his fists at and kicked whatever and whoever came near him. Hand after hand grabbed him in the dark, they were summarily bitten. With all his strength Ivy wrapped both arms around one of the assailant's neck and squeezed until his fingers went numb. A mighty blow across his shoulders sent Ivy rolling over the nightstand, shards of his tiny Tiffany lamp scattering across the floor.

Ivy was temporarily paralyzed by one sharp blow to his neck, then another and another. When the beating momentarily halted, he thought all was done. That feeling was short lived as the masked men reacquainted themselves. Again and again they kicked what little air he had from his lungs. His torso cried out for the beating to stop, it was not to be. One of the assailants bent down and whispered in his ear. Unconsciousness was his only friend when at last the masked devils quit. With one final blow to the head Ivy was left in a pool of blood to continue the fight.

30

Morose is not strong enough to describe the mood as Detective Knox drove us back to Blue Note. The sun had lifted its dreary head over the clouds east of us. The scenic drive along the pacific coast at times is so stunning it cannot be described, but on this morning, it was gray and sullen. I decided a word or two might help in some odd way.

"Jo, ok if I call you Jo?" she nodded.

"Did you at least grab Heath Abbey?"

She gave me a long uneasy look. "No, he had the whole damn thing planned out. He gave notice to his landlord and the hospital eight weeks ago. Don't worry, we'll catch him and then his planned exit will only strengthen the premeditated murder charge."

"I figured as much."

She gave me a pair of unsettling eyes.

"I didn't mean it like that; I just figured he'd be in the wind. You do still hold a trump card."

"And what card is that?" she asked.

"I don't think Heath and the others finished what they set out to do."

She gave me the same eyes again.

"I think they wanted Senator Rose gone. But he's still here. He was the target and somehow poor Timmy found out. Butler Dowdy said Timmy could walk so quietly you couldn't hear him coming. What if he walked up and accidentally heard a plot to get rid of the senator? If you're one of the people plotting, you have no choice but to get rid of Timmy. I think Heath Abbey went to the bowling alley to try and dissuade Timmy from talking. He failed, so he had to shut Timmy up, permanently. He or they intended to make it look as though the senator had done the deed. The jackals waited in the wings for poor Timmy to get off work, and you know the rest."

She didn't say anything for a few seconds.

"You came up with that all by yourself?" she said but didn't let me answer. "I'd like to dismiss it, but it makes too much sense to deny. So if I believe you, then the question that remains is who would benefit if Senator Rose were gone? He's not a real popular guy; however, he is a real powerful guy."

"Jo, I don't follow politics so I don't know the answer to my next question. Is there someone in his district or area that wants his job? Might even be somebody that he ran against in the last election."

"Jack, once again you're making too much sense to ignore. When we get back, I'm going to look into the last few elections. See who lost. You know something Jack; you're a pretty smart guy. Not all the time, but sometimes."

"Thanks, I guess."

We sat in silence, she was probably thinking on what I'd just run by her. Since I was emptying my brain of pent up information, I decided to go ahead and tell her what had happened with Sugar.

"Jo, you might want to put me in jail but you were right about Sugar." She didn't say a word, but she did turn and give me eyes that said, tell me more.

I started at the beginning with the newspaper clipping. Then I went through the entire tragic story; including Sugar's true age. She didn't say one word. Of course, I told her how lost I was without Sugar and how much I wanted her back, still not a word.

"I'm sorry; I didn't mean to bend your ear. I guess it all comes down to the fact that I like women, young ones too."

"Nothing wrong with that, I like women and young ones too," she said with an aggressive glint in her eye that confused me for a second or two.

"You mean…"

"Yes Jack, that's exactly what I mean."

"So even if I'd wanted to, I would never have had a chance with you?"

"Not a snowball's chance in hell," she said in a masculine voice.

A chill ran down my spine. Boy, did I feel weird for the rest of the ride home. When we drove in the parking lot at the Redwood, I got out of the police car and told her thanks for everything. When I looked in at her, she acted as if nothing had happened.

"Bye Jack, think positive and pray for Ivy. And believe it or not, I hope Sugar comes home to you, and soon. Bye."

"Thanks, bye," I said.

I was in a man-made fog as I trudged up the steps past Cat and into my apartment. I flopped into bed, a Kafkaesque dream just itching to explode.

The phone rang me right out of another dire dream. I picked up the phone.

"Hello Jack, Dr. Lee here."

"Oh hello, I guess you heard?"

"Yes, that's why I called. I feel helpless as I suppose you do. Then I realized that you're not only vulnerable to an attack when you're agitated, you're also vulnerable when you're depressed. Did you feel as though you might have an episode?"

I didn't answer him right away; I had to think for a minute. "Jack, are you ok?"

"Yes, under the circumstances, I'm fine. You know something, I never even felt the slightest tingle. I was going to tell you that I haven't even been sore when I wake up in the morning."

"You get sore after your episodes?" he asked.

"Yes, extremely sore. I don't remember what day it was. But it was the first time in months that I woke up without pain running rampant all across my body. I would have to say that's a very good thing, wouldn't you?"

"Yes I would. Ok, well I just wanted to see how you were handling the situation with Ivy. Try to stay positive, oh and write down your feelings in the notebook, it will help. I plan on using what you write when the study is all over. I'll let you go now, say a prayer for Ivy. Bye Jack."

I said goodbye before I fell back into another incriminating dream. I like returning to good dreams, but these dreams were not what you'd call good.

I woke right at two in the afternoon, actually, Cat woke me. I staggered about as though I'd never been in my apartment before. The depression was so overwhelming I felt as though I was being crushed by some despair laden gravity. Cat must have told me to get some milk at least ten times before I responded. *Dr. Lee said it'd help if I wrote down my feelings, it's worth a try.*

I opened the notebook and stared at the word transponder. I had circled it several times. It was the word Ivy mentioned when I found the bug. And as the realization became clear, extreme rage followed. The guilt surrounding me was overwhelming. Rage and guilt are a sinister combination. The tingle had a hair-trigger this time. I tweaked across the kitchen floor. The spots before my eyes exploded as a series of convulsions erupted. Cat arched and hissed when he heard the calliope of sound my head made as it pounded the cupboard below where he ate. My head ticked at such extreme speed the brow ridge over my right eye split wide open. Time has no relevance when an episode strikes. I never know how strong or long the duration will be. I retched, twitched, ticked, shuddered, and convulsed, as I drooled into eternity. Silence is golden, but it comes at an extreme price.

My eyes were shut tight before they fluttered. The full understanding and realization of what has happened can take minutes, if not hours. I tasted the blood as it trickled down the side of my face and clung with the spittle on the side of my mouth. At first I jerked to sit up but someone held me down.

"Jackie honey, please don't move, I have you now. Everything's going to be ok."

I lay back and felt a tear in the same eye that was covered with blood. Sugar's here now, I knew she'd come back. Ok, I'm going to do as she said and not move, but that doesn't mean I can't open my eyes and have a look. I opened my eyes and desperation filled my world again. There was no one there except Cat, and he looked pissed. I sat up against the wall by the fridge and looked at the blood smeared across the floor. Cat's saucer of milk was broken and lay on the floor, in about twenty pieces. Then the reason for the episode came rushing back home.

Blue Note

Once again I had only worried about Jack and no one else. I should have known they'd put a bug on Ivy's car too. I should have stopped when Suit told me to. Now look at what I've done. Because of me my partner, my best friend is fighting for his life.

I closed my eyes hoping the desperation and pain would also be shut out, it didn't work. I heard my door open and when I peaked up, Mr. Hurtwood was bent over staring into my face. I opened my eyes all the way and he leaped backwards.

"Jesus, I thought for sure you were dead. Criminy sakes alive if you aren't a frickin' mess."

"Call Dr. Lee," I slurred.

"What!" he screamed at me.

"Call Dr. Lee, damnit!" I yelled.

"Ok, ok calm down. Where's the number?"

"I wrote it in the notebook, it's gotta be here somewhere."

"Found it, I'll call him right as soon as you move out of the way." I shuffled on my hands away from the telephone.

"Hello Dr. Lee!" Hurtwood yelled.

I tried to stand but my head began spinning like a top. Nausea is a demanding reminder of how little our brains can do when the gut says, 'whether you like it or not I'm going to purge.' I lay on the floor and swam my way into the bathroom. I made it just in time to put my head in the shower. I was still there when Dr. Lee's nurse lifted my head onto her lap. The only reason I knew who she was is because she told me not to move when she first rushed into the bathroom. Somehow I remembered her voice.

"Jack, I'm very sorry this happened and I feel somewhat responsible. When I was here the last time and administered the drug, I decided to proceed with caution. Jack! Can you hear me?" Dr. Lee yelled.

"Yes! And if you yell again I'm going to get sick. But this time I'm going to direct everything at you, damnit stop yelling at me!"

"Sorry Jack, for legal reasons I just had to be sure you heard me. Jack, I only administered a small amount of the drug last time. This time I am going to double the dosage. You could be in a depressed state for several days before the effects dissipate. Is there someone that can check on you from time to time?"

"I will," Mr. Hurtwood said from somewhere behind the bathroom door.

"Jack, are you agreeable? Is it ok if I inject you with a larger dose this time?"

"Yes! Do it or get out. Depressed state, you have no idea how depressed, depressed can be. So get it over with or get out!"

I heard the needle plunge into the little cork on his bottle. Then the squirt, then the needle as it put a big ass hole in my arm. I felt like yelling, so I did.

I just lay there like some dead cockroach as the nurse washed my face and hands. She was really thorough, even got in those little bends in my ears. She was gentle when she cleaned up the wound over my eye, but the damn doctor wasn't. I watched him as he positioned himself and then shoved the needle in my head, damnit that hurt. I yelled again.

Kept my eyes closed after that, I figured what I can't see won't hurt me. As Dr. Lee sewed away, I heard Mr. Hurtwood ask how many stitches it was going to take to close that gash over my eye. The last thing I needed was an f'n reminder. The nausea had passed and I was able to stand just long enough to get to my bed. I flopped down on Cat. "Sorry buddy."

Suddenly all was quiet, it was just me and Cat left to fend for ourselves. Someone said, "Kitty, kitty." And Cat left me all alone, which in my mind was the most depressing state of all. For the next day or two I stayed in bed; thirst and hunger never dared cross my mind.

I only have scant memories of my dad from when I was a boy. He was too busy vacationing in places surrounded by enormous walls. One thing I do remember quite well is my dad's affinity for a Dutch painter named, Hieronymus Bosch. He liked sharing this Bosch guy's paintings with me. He'd say, "Jack, if you don't fly right, this is where you'll end up."

To me the guy painted the exact same picture over and over. Every darn painting had lots of devils, naked people, fire, ghouls, and great big mouths. I'm not sure if the mouths ate people or they just shouted. Anyways, for two days in my dreams all I saw were those damn paintings, one after the other.

Blue Note

"Jack, sit up for me. Jack, please sit up for me. It's hard to get the water down your throat when you don't sit up. Jack, get up!" Scout yelled.

I slogged around for the requisite amount of time, drooling all the while. "Shit Jack, you've got to wake up. Come on this is getting creepy. Are you still in there, please say something. Come on Jack, I don't like this you. Say something damnit!"

"Something," I croaked.

"That's better; now say something stupid so I know you're in there."

"You might be able to hear a little better if you get in bed with me."

"Good, that's the jerk I love so much. Jack, I want you to listen to me, ok." I gave her no answer.

"Jack, Ivy woke up this morning."

"Scout, don't you dare lie to me!" I barked.

"I wouldn't lie to you," she whispered.

I stumbled out of bed and fell on the floor.

"Scout, I don't care what you think or what you see. Can you please take my clothes off and put me in the shower, please?" I begged.

She held me down with one leg while she took my pajamas off. "Jesus Jack, you smell bad, come on get up," she said as she crinkled her nose.

It had been nearly four days since I had taken a shower. She held me up while the water danced off my shoulders.

"Jack, I have to wash your hair, lean over towards me a little, not that damn far - get your hand off my boob and out of my blouse! Jack you jerk, you do that again and... will you hold still I have to rinse the shampoo off. God you're an idiot," she laughed.

Scout dressed me before she walked out and sat in the kitchen. I slid my boots on and stood up in front of the mirror, *except for the stitches I look ok.*

"Scout, could you drive me to the hospital, please?" I begged as I walked out to her.

"Yes, I'll drive you, but first I have to put a fresh dressing over the stitches. Took the other one off during the shower, did you feel it?"

"No, but I felt something else."

189

"Shut up Jack and hold still. I don't want to get your eyelashes caught in the tape. Close your eye, all done. Put your hat on, it'll cover the bandage. "

I gave the keys to her so she could warm up the coupe. Meanwhile I hunted for the notebook. I wanted to write down a few things as we drove. The ride to San Louie gave me time to think and time to wake up, somewhere along the way my stomach growled. I was hungry. Scout did all the talking once we were in the hospital, I just followed. We took an elevator, and at some point, we walked down a long hallway and into a quiet room. It wasn't dark, but no lights were on. I walked around a curtain and wanted to throw up. Ivy had one bare black and blue leg on the bed; his arms and the other leg were attached to ropes and pulleys that hung over the bed. He had one eye that wasn't covered with bandages. I watched the eye move as I sat down. My gut began crying long before a guilty tear appeared. For some damn reason I started blabbering to Ivy, don't ask me why.

"I'm sorry Ivy; this shouldn't have happened. I'll find them, I promise you. I'm going to find the bastards. You just wait and see," I said as I turned and looked at Scout.

She had both hands covering her mouth, but the sobs found their way to the outside world. I stood up and moved closer to Ivy, the eye followed me.

"Ivy can you hear me?" The eye blinked. "I know it's a crazy thing to say but when you get out of here, I'm going to take care of you." I whispered.

"Jack, what happened to your eye?" Ivy said.

I was startled and, by the huge gasp she let out, I think Scout was too. I looked for a nurse.

"Scout, is he supposed to talk?"

"What happened to your eye?" Ivy asked me again.

I started to answer when a rail-thin redheaded nurse flew into the room. "Hello, I'm Nurse Calhoun. I'm on duty tonight, Ivy you feel like talking?"

"Sure," he softly said.

"It's ok?" Scout asked in an unsure voice.

"Yes, absolutely but it's entirely up to Ivy. If he sounds or appears to be in any pain, push the call button. As you can see, he has lots that can hurt or go wrong. Ok bye Ivy, you let them know

190

if something is hurting you, I have rounds to make," she said as she scurried out of the room.

"Jack, for the last time, please tell me what happened to your eye," Ivy asked.

"Ivy, I had no idea you'd be able to talk, two days ago they made it sound as if you might die."

"Jack, if they'd wanted me dead, I wouldn't be talking to you. They were sending a message; they just got a little carried away is all. Now please tell me about your eye."

"I left here and didn't feel well."

"You had an episode, didn't you?"

I didn't answer him, there was no point.

"Jack, I want you and Scout, hi Scout, to stop worrying about me. It looks a lot worse than it really is. Yes, some of the injuries are going to take a while to heal, but I'd rather have the time to heal than the alternative."

"Ivy, do you want to talk about it?"

"No Jack, I don't. I'm tired of talking about it. Detective Knox and the sheriff, forgot his name, drilled me for an hour before you got here. They have all the info, if you want to know, ask them. For now, I want to know two things, maybe three. First, have you heard from Sugar?"

"No, tomorrow morning I'm going to start all over again."

"Good Jack, finding Sugar and Li'l John is much more important to me than me. Next question, actually it's not a question. Jack, I will tell you this much, there are four of them. And one of them is going to be walking with a limp for a long time. I'm sorry I didn't tell you when I took the gun. You have a badge and a gun; I guess I wanted the same. Sorry for being so petty."

"Sorry, that's ridiculous. I'm glad you shot him. I only wish you had shot all four of 'em."

"Jack, the guy I shot told me they were just going to scare me, but after I shot him, they decided to give me the beating of a lifetime. Ok Jack, did you go see Dr. Lee after the episode?"

"No, he came to see me, gave me a double. I should be good to go for several months, I hope. He also sewed up my eye, geez that hurt like a bitch! Sorry Scout." She didn't respond.

"Predictable effrontery," Ivy mumbled before he apologized to Scout for my dirty mouth.

He stopped talking at that point and the eye blinked several times as his leg squirmed on the bed.

"Is something wrong?" I asked before Scout could.

"Yes Jack, these are not hard casts on my arms, but they take a long time to get off. Could you please scratch my right arm - just above my elbow?"

I leaned over towards him and felt as if I was going to pass out. "Shit!" I cried out.

Scout jumped up. "You ok Jack?"

"Yes, I'm fine, go scratch Ivy's itch."

"Ah, thank you Scout," Ivy cooed. "Jack, you need to take it easy for a few more days."

"Ivy, what do you think I was doing while you were in the coma?"

"I don't know Jack, what were you doing?"

"I was in my own coma."

"Oh yes, I forgot. Listen, I hate to be a party pooper, but at the moment I'm really in a lot of pain. Would one of you please push the button for me?"

A different nurse came in the room. Seemed to me she knew immediately.

"I have to ask you people to leave now, you can come back tomorrow. Mr. Fin has had far too much excitement for one day. Visiting hours start at nine," she said as she stood waiting for us to leave.

"Bye Ivy," Scout and I said as we patted his bruised leg. "I'll see you in the morning," I said.

"Ok, thanks for coming to see me. You can help scratch my itch some more tomorrow," he said before I heard him chuckle then wince in pain.

On the way to the car I made a promise to Ivy and to myself that I was going to get all four of the guys responsible.

"Did you say something?" Scout asked.

"No, I was just talking to myself. I do that a lot lately."

The ride home was sobering at first, but the longer Scout drove, the angrier I became. Ivy made it seem as though he was ok, he's a trooper. In a literal sense the cowards that did this to him were getting away with murder. I couldn't live with the bad guys thinking they had won. When I got home, I fed Cat, and then I called Domino and told him he was going back to work.

31

I woke up the next morning and went down to the coupe and put the bug back where I'd found it. I got myself all duded up, black hat, boots and all. I wasn't going to sneak around anymore. I went out the door and then back in and gave Cat his saucer of milk.

I ate at the diner, sat in the corner like usual. Mel took a short reprieve from the grill and made a special trip over to ask where Ivy was. I was going to make something up, but midsentence I decided to tell him the truth. He gave me the obligatory, "I'm sorry" and the universal, "what is the world coming to?" Of course, I followed suit and agreed that the whole damn planet was going to pot.

I had a timeline and an agenda written down in my notebook, I intended to follow it to the letter. I left the diner and went straight to the hobo cave. No one had seen Sugar or Li'l John. As I drove away, I turned to see if I was being followed, tough to do and still keep your eyes on the road in front of you.

I made the rounds, no Sugar. I decided to go back to the apartment before heading to the hospital. Hurtwood was waiting for me on my steps, he had an envelope in his hand.

"Jack, this came for you last night. I would have given it to you this morning, but you took off before I got here. It was special delivery."

I opened the envelope in front of him and as I read, a grin spread across my face. The letter was from the State of California. My P.I. license had been updated and was now active again. The letter had a slightly apologetic tone. Seems the people that live in the home I had supposedly broken into told the state I was welcome in their home anytime.

"Jack, you're smiling. Must be good news," Hurtwood said as he walked down my steps.

"It's great news and it couldn't have come at a better time," I said as I rushed into my apartment.

I put my holster and gun back on and started for the front door and stopped. I went back in the bedroom and opened the not-so-secret compartment on my jewelry box. I slid my over/under Remington derringer down inside my right boot. I put the letter in my not-so-secret coat pocket and smiled as I took off for the hospital.

Ivy had been in surgery that morning; he wasn't as talkative as he had been the day before. They screwed a metal plate to his right femur and one to the same ankle; needless to say, he was in a whole lot of pain. In the middle of wincing he made it clear he had something important to tell me.

"Jack, I didn't want to say anything in front of Scout."

"Say anything about what?" I asked in one of my desperate and challenging tones.

"About the rest of what the guy I shot said. Jack, he told me that if you don't stop, they're going to kill you. They couldn't get at you or they would have already done the deed. Jack, you have to stop!"

"I'm sorry Ivy, I can't do that. But I'm not telling you anything you didn't already know, am I?"

The eye blinked several times and although he was bandaged from head to toe, I could see his shoulders slump before he softly said, "Be careful."

I stopped at the bowling alley and before I went in, I checked it off my list. Went inside and the gal named Jill that Ivy and I had met the first time eyed me up and down as I walked up to the counter.

"Hi Jill, it's important that I talk to Billy. Is he here?"

"Why hello Jack, how's things? You sure are duded up, is there a rodeo in town?"

I stepped back. "Jill, you remember the guy that was with me last time?"

"The guy in the suit, wasn't his name Ivy?"

195

"Yes, Ivy is in the hospital. The guys that killed Timmy paid Ivy a visit. To be clear and so that you understand, the guys I'm talking about beat the livin' hell out of Ivy." She backed up and put her hands over her mouth. "I'm sorry," she cried.

"Now, it's extremely important that I talk to Billy."

"He's not here today, called in sick. He's got the flu something awful."

"Shit! Sorry, I couldn't help myself."

"It's ok, I've heard worse," Jill whispered.

"Ok thanks, I'll have to come back another day. I'll see ya Jill."

"Wait, maybe I can help," she said. "I get a break in ten minutes. Wait for me out back."

"Jill, you got an extra cigarette?"

"Sure, hang on a second."

Some chubby middle-aged guy walks up and says, "Hey good lookin' how's about a pair of size 12 and a date?"

"How's about a size 44," I said as I opened my coat and showed him my gun.

He sized me up and thought about objecting. I kept my coat open and let him have a long look at the 44, he backed away mumbling to himself.

"Thanks, I think I like you," Jill said with a wiggle and that look young girl's master. "Here's the cigarette, see you in a few," she said with a wink.

I talked to myself all the way out of the building. I bummed a light from a teenager with one shirt sleeve rolled up over his smokes, kept stroking his peach-fuzz mustache. He flicked his cigarette in the air and took off when a young lady yelled out the back door, "Come back in Slick, it's your turn."

It was another cold day and I found myself shivering. Guess I wasn't fully recovered from my sleepathon. Jill snuck up behind me and blew smoke in my ear.

"Wha-da-ya want to know?" she said with her best effort at a Marilyn gaze.

"I want to know if any of the kids you and Timmy and Billy hung out with still live in town. Who were Timmy's closest friends?"

She put her left index finger to her nose.

196

Blue Note

"There was just me, my sister Ruth, Billy, Joe, and of course Sloan, but he's been in prison now for at least two years."

"Sloan who?"

"Sloan Walker, but as I said, he's in prison."

"Prison for what, wait a second I gotta write this stuff down, ok?" I said as a tumbling blue smoke ring washed off my face.

"I think it was armed robbery, but I'm not sure. My dad ordered me to stay away from Sloan and Joe long before the robbery happened," Jill said in a matter of fact way.

"And this all happened a few years ago," I said more than asked.

"Yeah, they were just supposed to steal some booze and cigarettes. It was an initiation the club had the guys do before they let them in the Blue Notes. But Joe and Sloan got carried away and tried to rob the store. Joe was killed by the owner and Sloan got caught a day later."

"What was Joe's last name?"

"Joe Dowdy, he was a nice guy, sometimes."

"Wait a second, was this Joe guy related to Senator Rose's butler, Jacob Dowdy?"

"Of course he was, they're cousins. Does that matter?" Jill asked completely unaware of what the connection could possibly have to do with Timmy's murder. Truth is, I couldn't make a connection either.

"One other question, let's go back to when you were kids. I mean before High School. Did you guys hang out or play games together? What I mean is; what did you guys do for fun and excitement when you were running around town?"

"Oh that's easy to answer. The most fun we all had was stealing shit from the stores. We started out stealing gum and candy and stuff like that. Then we graduated to clothes and jewelry, bats and balls, then one time, Tim actually stole a motorcycle from Holiday Honda. The old mechanic chased after us for at least three blocks before he ran out of steam. The stupid guy was chasing after the rest of us and ran right by Tim. He didn't even know it."

"How could he not know?" I asked.

"Because Tim turned the bike off and hid, in his favorite hiding place, behind the dumpster."

"Are you talking about the same Timmy I think you're talking about?"

"Yeah, nobody called him Timmy, just Tim. The senator, the paper, and people that really didn't know him are the only ones that call him Timmy."

"Good to know, ok so Joe is dead and Sloan is still in prison. Do you know what prison he's in?"

"No, like I said I stopped hanging with them long before the robbery. Those two were just getting too cocky and stupid."

"What about your sister, Ruth?"

"Ruth? Ruth got married to a cowboy three weeks after she graduated from high school. He was stationed here. They live outside a Butte; now she has two fat kids and a lazy-ass cowboy for a husband."

"How about Heath, did he hang out with you guys?"

"Heath who?"

"Heath Abbey, you don't know him?'

"I never heard of him, what a stupid name. Why do parents do shit like that to kids?"

"I don't know why parents do stuff like that," I said as I looked through my notes.

Shit, Joe is dead, Sloan is in prison, Jacob was at the airport, and Ruth is in Butte f'n Montana. I need four guys and so far I have one guy she's never heard of, and he's in the wind. At least I've got that going for me. Shit!"

"Did you say something?" Jill asked.

"No, I was just thinking out loud. Jill, can you give me a physical description of each guy?" She looked at me as if she didn't know what language I was speaking. "Tell me what Joe and Sloan looked like?"

"Like they came out of the same box, all the guys in the Blue Notes club looked and dressed the same - did it on purpose. They all had dark hair and combed it in a waterfall like a greaser. If their hair wasn't dark enough, they dyed it black like Elvis. They were all pretty big guys for their age, except Tim of course. He was skinny and had blonde hair. He never did fit in," she said as she flung her glowing cigarette butt straight up in the air. I leaped out of the way, she got a kick out of seeing me jump.

"Jill, thanks for all the help, tell Billy I hope he's feeling better soon."

"You're leaving already? Why don't you come back later, I get off at ten? I'd love to take a ride in that coupe of yours," she said with that look.

"I'd like to Jill, but I've got a million things to do and there are only so many hours in a day. Ok if I come back another time? I mean I may have some more questions,"

"Yeah sure," she said in a disappointed tone.

I headed for the police station; I had a list of things I needed to go over with Detective Knox. Of course, I went in the back door and down the hall to her office. The door was closed, but I could hear her on the phone. When I heard the phone click back on the receiver, I knocked hard one time on the door.

"There's only one jerk I know that would knock like that. Come in Jack."

"Howdy, I said as I took off my hat. Jo, I have a few things I want to go over with you."

"Before you start, I knew after seeing Ivy you were going to pull some crap like this. Jack, I made it perfectly clear that you are not to go near this murder investigation. I meant it then and I mean it now! I wouldn't have been so pushy about it if you were legally able to investigate, but since you're not, I have no choice, my hands are tied."

"Yeah I'll bet they are. Well, you can untie them because I'm legal again. I told you it would all be cleared up, just took a little time is all."

"Jack, if you're lying, I will never let you in this office again," she said as I took the envelope out of my coat pocket and handed it to her.

Didn't take long before a nasty grin surfaced,
she handed the envelope back to me.

"Jack, who are these people that say you can go in their house anytime of any day?"

"They're such close friends it feels as though maybe we're related. That's who they are. Now, can we get moving forward with the Timmy Allen and Ivy Fin cases, please?"

She didn't budge an inch. "Jo." She frowned.

"Detective Knox," I said as she gave me a half-smile.

Before I could say a word, she put her hand up in the air. "The gun Ivy used to shoot one of the intruders is registered to Senator Rose. He was happy that we found it. He said it was stolen months ago, along with a few other items he keeps in his desk at home. The next question you're going to ask is who the XKE is registered to." How'd you know that?" I asked in my phony surprised voice. "I know you, and I know what's in that notebook of yours, how do I know? I went thru the whole damn thing one day." "What day was that?" "Jack, you have your secrets and I have mine. The car in question is leased to an attorney firm in San Francisco. Since we can't prove the car was used during the commission of a crime, they are refusing to give us any particulars. I have a man working on a photo and profile of each of the attorneys in the firm, but there's every chance it has been outsourced. We may never be able to match the Suit to the car." I was going to make a suggestion. "I don't want to hear any suggestions. So what if the guy took some pictures, there's no law against that."

"It was used to track Ivy's car to his home so they could beat the living tar out of him," I hollered.

"Jack, the sheriff checked Ivy's car, there was no bug or anything else that could be considered suspicious," she said as my shoulders slumped.

She let me calm down a bit. "Jack, we have the blood type of the person that was shot. And we have been checking all the clinics and hospitals to see if a man or woman came in with what looked like a bullet wound. Now is there anything else you want to know?"

"Yeah, who is Sloan Walker?"

I had caught her completely off guard with the name.

"Why do you want to know?" she asked in an unsure tenor.

"See you don't know everything, in fact just about everything you do know came from me. Now I can go elsewhere and find out but I'd rather we work together on this. Who is he?"

"I had just made detective. Sloan and another young man robbed the 7-Eleven by you. He held a 38 in the face of the store clerk. Sloan thought the clerk was alone, she wasn't. The owner came out of a back room and didn't ask questions, he aimed and fired at Sloan. He missed Sloan but hit his accomplice dead center of the chest. The young man died right there on the floor. Sloan ran but was caught the next day. Actually, he turned himself in. I don't remember the name of the young man that died."

"His name was Joe Dowdy, ring a bell?"

"Dowdy, no it doesn't ring a bell," she said in an anxious voice. "Should I know the name?"

"I don't know if you should or not. Anywho, Joe Dowdy is the cousin of Senator Rose's butler, Jacob Dowdy. Now does it ring a bell?"

"That little twerp, damnit he pissed me off when I was there. He had a few choice things to say about women being in law enforcement. So what is the connection?" she asked in an eager voice.

"I don't know, but I intend to find out. That's for damn sure."

"Ok, how about our two idiots, Rat Johnson and Mason Cook, have you seen or heard anything about them or the Bonneville?"

"The Bonneville is registered to an ex-con named J J Turlock. His last known address is a vacant lot. He has not been seen nor heard from in months. Bobby 'Rat' Johnson is, as you know, a low-life thief and a nuisance but, in my opinion, not a great threat. Now his partner, Mason Cook, is an entirely different story. This morning I spoke at length with a deputy warden in McAlester, Oklahoma about our Mr. Cook. Before I say anyting else, what I tell you stays here in this office, is that understood?" she ordered.

"Yeah, sure," I said wondering what could be so important about a firebug like Mason Cook.

She hesitated. "Mason Cook was a troubled child, declared clinically insane at the age of nine. That was after he burned down the family home, with his parents and sister inside. He was then placed in Paul's Valley, a state-run facility. While there he was raped and severely beaten by two older boys. Mason spent two weeks in their infirmary before he returned to his room. A week later while they slept, he set fire to their beds. Of course, after the boys recovered, they returned and retaliated. Mason Cook was beaten unconscious and then emasculated."

"I don't want to hear the rest of the story."

"You have to! Five years later Mason worked the system and was transferred to another facility, named Enid. It just so happens that the two boys that had committed the atrocities against him were there. Mason patiently waited for the opportunity and when it presented itself, he locked a guard and both boys in a wooden storage shed and burned it to the ground. And so at the tender age of fifteen, Mason Cook was sent to prison."

"Wait a second; you can't put a boy in prison with grown men. They would…"

"Yes, they would and they did. Mason made it through ten years of pure hell without lighting even one fire. Then he was sent to a halfway house where he stayed for two years before being released into the general public. Cook migrated west with Turlock and took up residence in Morro Bay. And from there you can finish the story yourself."

"Wow, I want to hate him but at the same time I feel sorry for him. That said, I think we would agree that Mason Cook should be wrapped up in a straight jacket and put behind bars."

I sat in a fog as I tried to understand how a boy could get so screwed up. I came to the realization that where Mason Cook was concerned, the damage was done long before he ever set the first fire. *When a carpenter makes a mistake, he throws the piece of damaged wood in the scrap heap. Is that what we do with humans? I don't think so, I think we try our best to help the person, and every now and again someone actually crawls back out of the scrap heap, which is probably why we keep trying.* I forgot I was in the detective's office, when I looked up she was staring at me.

"Jack, if you promise to keep what we share with each other from others, I'll work with you. But if I think for even a minute you're compromising this investigation, I'll cut you off like an ugly wart."

"An ugly wart, geez that's awful. Does that make me a metaphor or a simile?"

"Shut up Jack, I meant what I said. Now, call me if you have anything new. I'll do the same, bye."

"Wait, how about the plates on the stupid Stingray Heath Abbey was driving?"

"Stolen, but what good would they do us? We know who he is, and we have a damn bolo out on him. Jack, it's just a matter of time. We'll get him, I promise you. Now I have work to do and you didn't help matters bringing another name into this murder. I'm only going to say this once. See that door behind you."

"What about it?" I asked. She stood up and pointed with her finger and her eyes.

I guess Detective Knox was trying to tell me to leave, so I did. I decided to make the rounds again, no sign of Sugar. My damn dogs were tired and my heart was empty when I went home. I sat with Cat on the roof, drank a few beers while I ate a bowl of chili Scout brought up to me. I thanked her for everything she had done; in my book Scout was standup...

32

That night I sat and waited in the kitchen and at ten o'clock sharp my phone rang.

"Hey Domino, what's new?"

"Hello Jack, who in the hell is Domino?" Detective Knox asked in a hostile voice.

"Nobody you would care about, he's just a friend that calls me about this time at night. So why'd you call?"

She didn't say anything in return; I think she was running what I'd told her through the believe it or not part of her brain.

"Jo, I'm not going to go into who Domino is, but maybe I'll introduce him to you sometime in the future. Now, tell me why you called or I'm going to hang up the damn phone."

"Sloan Abbey Walker, sound familiar, was released from the Fred C. Nelles - School for Boys three months ago. He was sent to a transition home in Cambria. I'll be leaving first thing in the morning."

"I wanna go!"

"I knew you were going to say that, so I asked the Chief, he said absolutely not. I'm sorry."

"Shit that's not fair, I give you the name and I can't go with you."

"Jack, over and over you complain about not being involved, I have a solution to that problem. Go through the academy and become a police officer, it's as simple as that. Otherwise, shut up."

Blue Note

"Shut up, hah? Ok, that's what I'm going to do. I'll solve this thing by myself. See ya, bye."

"Jack! Don't you dare hang up the phone."

"Kiss my ass, and don't you ever try to boss me around again!"

"Jack!" she yelled into the phone as I clicked on her.

I immediately dialed Domino.

"Hey Hawk, I called but the line was busy, who you been rappin' wif?"

"Some damn detective that's who, ok you're gonna have to get up early tomorrow. I want you to go to the Blue Note Police Station and follow the female detective."

"Where she goin' to?"

"A transition home in Cambria, and that's all I know."

"Anythin' else," Domino asked.

"What would you say if I said I was going to follow you?"

"I'd say you's a damn fool. Hawk, you ain't followin' me nowhere's. You ain't experienced like me. But if you just gotta ruin the whole damn thing, then go ahead on," he said out of frustration.

"Ok, I'll wait to hear from you. But the first chance you get you make sure you call me. Got it?"

"Got it, I'll talk at you tamarruh, bye," he said as he hung up.

I sat at my kitchen table and went over the notes. Something wasn't right about the whole damn thing. The numbers aren't adding up, three to murder one boy and four to attack one man, *why?* I asked myself before I made a list.

1. Heath Abbey, definite.
2. Sloan Abbey Walker, probably.
3. Joe Dowdy is dead, Jacob Dowdy, maybe.
4. ?

33

I woke in the middle of a macabre nightmare with my weeping forehead stuck to my table. I crawled back to my bedroom and pulled the covers over my head. A few minutes later someone knocked on my front door, and hard. I reached under the other pillow and pulled my 44 from its holster. I peeked out my bedroom door to see who was knocking.

"Jack, get up and right now!" a female voice yelled at me. I hoped it was Sugar.

I opened the door and Detective Knox yelled, "Ok, you get to go! If I have to explain, I'm going to leave without you," she said before she turned and slipped down the stairs. When she was standing next to her car, she yelled, "You have ten minutes!"

I threw on my new Levi's, boots, clean shirt, corduroy coat, and, of course, my hat. I grabbed my guns and then gave Cat a saucer of milk. I raced down the steps and opened the rear passenger door. Sergeant Klavinski was behind the wheel.

"I'll meet you at the street," I said before I shut the door and started walking thru the parking lot.

I hurried out and looked both ways a couple of times before I saw Domino. He was parked next to a dog groomer on the other side of Broadway. I ran towards him as fast as my pointy-toed boots would allow. He started the Olds up and put it in drive and drove straight at me. I put my hands out in front of me, he kept coming. He stopped with the front grill an inch from my knees. I walked around as he rolled down his window.

"Hawk! You dumb sum-bitch, I didn't know who you was; I could'a ran yo ass ovuh. Lord have mercy what's wrong wif you?"

"Domino, I came to tell you to go home. The detective is going to let me ride along with her."

"I know that, what you take me fo? Shit, I knew she wasn't comin' just ta say hello. Ok, ain't no use in us jawin' out here in the street. Go on but be careful, her car right behind yo ass. Later on," he said with a chuckle.

I turned around in the middle of the street and Sergeant Klavinski had driven the detective's car right up to me. I got in the back and said morning to both of them.

"Let me guess. That was Domino and he was going to tail us," Detective Knox blurted out.

"Yeah, so what."

"Ok Jack, you have probably guessed by now that the chief said you could ride along. You get in the way and the sergeant here has orders to put you in the back of the car and leave you there. Do I make myself clear? Stay out of the way."

"You got it; I'll stay out of the way."

She turned around and picked a cup of coffee up from a box on the floorboard in front of her. She handed it to me without a word.

"Thanks, I didn't need any cream or sugar."

Sergeant Klavinski turned just far enough to narrow one eye at me. "Jack, let it go for a bit, ok? Otherwise, I'm going to stop and throw you out right here. Deal?" he said as his eyes slowly moved to the rearview mirror.

I nodded my head, "Deal."

Took us all of ten minutes to get to Cambria, the home we were looking for was on the east side of town. A woman with long braided gray hair, wearing a sweatshirt over blue jeans and sandals answered the door. She didn't look happy when she heard the name Sloan Walker.

"He's gone on a two-day hike with some of the others," she said in a rehearsed manner.

"I called yesterday and was told that Sloan would be here. Was it you I spoke with?" Detective Knox said as she stood up real erect and threw her shoulders back.

"Um, yes it was. I had no idea the hike had already been scheduled."

"Where's his room?" Detective Knox asked.

"Don't you need a warrant signed by a judge to search his room?"

"Lady, you know I don't need a warrant. He is a convicted felon. He lost most of his rights when he decided to use a gun and rob that liquor store. His best friend was killed that day; I'll bet he didn't tell you that part."

"No he didn't, but still…"

"Lady, you have ten seconds to take me to his room. Otherwise, I'm going to put you in the back of our squad car and take you to jail. One, two…"

The lady turned and trudged down a hallway, didn't look back to see if we were following her. We walked past one room and then she turned right into a small bedroom. She didn't say one word, didn't have to. There were several pictures of Sloan Walker on his dresser.

"Which one of these is the most recent?" Detective Knox asked.

The lady pointed at a picture in a plain brown frame. It was Sloan standing next to his dresser on his release day. He wore his dark hair in the exact same Peter Gun style as butler Dowdy. And he had the same black beard, cut and trimmed to a tee.

"You can leave now, thank you," Detective Knox ordered.

The lady walked out and the detective looked at me and whispered, "Follow her."

I followed her into the kitchen. She took a piece of paper out of her pocket and went straight to the phone, picked it up, and dialed. She said hello and asked for Sloan. I walked in the kitchen and she nearly threw the phone back on the receiver.

"What's your name?"

"Mildred Hunter."

"Mildred, you want to protect poor innocent Sloan, but he just got through killing a young man. Would you like me to tell you how he killed him?"

"No, I don't want to know," she said as her voice quivered.

"Follow me," I said.

Blue Note

I walked her out to the front porch.

"Sit down and don't move from that spot. If I see you move, I'm going to send that big cop out here and have him cuff you and put you in the backseat of the car. Do you understand me?"

"Yes," was all she said as she grabbed a ball of yarn that was in a box next to her.

I walked back in the house and stood staring at her through the front window. She peaked around at me once and then went to work on whatever it is women do with yarn. I walked back into the bedroom and went straight to the closet. I had an agenda that had come to me during one of my nightmares. I got right down on the floor and crawled from one end to the other. There were no boots in the closet, but there were three pieces of ribbon stuck to one cuff of a pair of black Dickies work pants. *I got your ass now you stinking buzzard.*

I left the pants and the ribbon and crawled all the way out on the floor to the bed.

"Jack, what are you doing?" Detective Knox asked as she rummaged thru the dresser drawers.

"I'm going to look under the bed for a pair of boots. Heath was wearing the shoes for work. So our buddy Sloan had to be the one wearing the boots. At least that's my take on things."

I got down and looked under the bed, no boots and no shoes. However, there was a stack of girlie magazines. I took one from the pile and opened it up.

"Jack, remember you're not supposed to get in the way," the detective said with slits for eyes.

I put the magazine back and just sat there. *I was sure he was the one with the…oh shit! He's wearing the damn boots right now.* I looked up at the detective and at the same time she looked at me.

"Find anything?" I asked before I realized the sergeant wasn't there in the room. "Hey, where's the sergeant?"

"He's searching through every doggone room in the house. There have been too many times when we go to pick someone up and they hide in a closet or the attic, the basement or anywhere else a person can hide. We've missed a few like that. For now, I have a lot of pictures that we'll have to go thru but nothing else to tie him to the murder. How about you, had any luck?"

"Yes ma'am, but I wouldn't call it luck."

Her eyes opened real wide before she said, "Ok, I don't think I like the ma'am stuff. So will the real Jack please tell me what he found?"

I headed over to the closet as the sergeant walked back in the room. He shook his head no.

"Sergeant, is there a flashlight in the car?"

"Sure is, need it?"

"Yes, thanks," I said as he turned and walked out of the room. "Detective, come have a look," I said as I parted the clothes next to the pants with the ribbon stuck to the cuff. "I hope you kept some of the ribbon that was stuck to Timmy's face, cuz I have no doubt that it will match those pieces of ribbon you see."

She stared in disbelief. "Jesus Jack, I think we've got him. Funny how the bad guys always miss something. I have to get to the phone right now."

"There's a phone in the kitchen, but before you do that, the lady, her name's Mildred. Anyways, she has a piece of paper in her pocket with the phone number where our boy Sloan Walker is hiding out. You might want to call the operator and ask her to give you the address connected to the number."

She gave me sweet eyes. "Jack, maybe you should become a cop. You see things others don't. I'm glad I brought you, thanks."

"You're welcome - Jo." She stopped dead in her tracks and gave me a soft smile. "I told Mildred to stay put; you'll find her on the porch," I said.

She hurried out just before the sergeant came back in with the flashlight. We were careful as we combed through every piece of clothing in the closet. We didn't see anything else that might be connected to Timmy's murder, but maybe someone else will.

I went out to the front room and watched the local sheriff put Mildred in the back of his car. I think they call it aiding and abetting. Detective Knox was standing there next to the sheriff's car. They spoke for a minute or so and then she turned and gave me the palms up version of stay where you are. She came back in the front room.

Blue Note

"Jack, you can't come with us." I started to object. "And before you get all upset, follow me."

She went to the kitchen and pointed out the window at the back of a house across the alley.

"Didn't you wonder where all the young men that stay here were?"

I scratched my head. "Now that you mention it, no, I guess I assumed they were on the hike with Sloan."

"Nope, there was no hike. The operator and then the sheriff told me that's the house connected to the number Miss Hunter called. You can watch from here. The sheriff is going to go in the front and we'll see who comes out the back."

I stood and watched Sergeant Klavinski pull up in the alley behind the garage. If you were in the house, you wouldn't be able to see his car. Seconds later a good-sized guy wearing a black hoodie ran out the back of the house. He looked around for a second or two and then leaped down the stairs and took off towards the alley. Sergeant Klavinski and Detective Knox both raised their weapons and yelled stop; the young man kept right on running. The sergeant flew at the kid and tackled him hard to the ground. He resisted, but it was pointless. He was on his stomach with his hands cuffed tight behind his back. He had a stunned stare in his eyes when Detective Knox sat on his legs and started unlacing his boots.

"Stop it! You dyke-ass pig, get yer stinking hands off me. Hey, stop that you bitch, you can't take my boots."

"Oh, but I can and I will," she said, and as the young man screamed, she pulled the boots off.

I walked out towards them as a deputy sheriff came thru the back of the house. We met at the same time and listened to Sloan Walker scream obscenities at Sergeant Klavinski. Without a word the sergeant pushed the hood of the sweatshirt back and lifted the kid up by the scruff of the neck and the seat of his pants and threw him in the back seat of the car. The sergeant thanked the deputy and got in behind the wheel. Detective Knox pointed at the house.

"We'll meet you in front of the house. The forensic guys are on their way, we have to wait for them," she said as she jumped in the car.

Ten minutes later I watched two odd looking guys get out of a police van. Detective Knox took them in the house. I walked around and looked in at our man, Sloan Walker. He turned his face away, but with the one look, I knew we had the right guy.

Detective Knox sat with Sloan Walker in the back, I was in front with the sergeant when we took off for Blue Note. The kid went through fits of anger and then he would pout for a bit. Appeared to me he wanted to cry but just wouldn't let it happen. I must have looked back at him one too many times because he suddenly yelled, "What the fuck're you lookin' at asshole!"

I peered over at the sergeant and he slowly shook his head no.

"I asked you a question!" he screamed at my back. I didn't respond.

About halfway back I think Detective Knox had had enough of the kid's belligerent whining, so she gave him a little food for thought.

"Your boots still have the red paint on them. You should have been more careful."

He immediately shut up and was noticeably pensive when he whispered, "Red paint?" to himself.

34

I had to wait outside when they took the Sloan into the police station. I sat down next to a freshly planted palm tree. I waited and waited and finally decided to walk home. I'd walked one block when a police car pulled to the curb. I expected the detective to get out; it was the police officer I had seen standing in front of Senator Rose's house. He slowly walked up to me. "Are you Jack?" I nodded yes. "Detective Knox said you'd be waiting outside, how come you took off?"

"I got tired of waiting."

"Well, I was supposed to thank you and tell you the first chance she gets she'll call you at home."

"I'd prefer she call me Jack."

"What?" he said.

"Nothing, ok thanks for letting me know."

"Oh yeah, I'm supposed to give you a ride home, come on jump in."

"Thanks, but no thanks. I'm going to walk. There's someone I'm hoping to see along the way."

"Suit yourself, see ya," he said as he headed for his patrol car.

I walked to the cliffs over the Blue Note cave and stared out at the ocean for a while. It was another cold gray day. I should have felt great about catching one of the bad guys; I didn't. I didn't because Sugar and Li'l John leaving had left a hole where my heart used to be. I stared at nothing for a long time before I went down the steps thru the cave and headed to the hobo cave. No Sugar. I trudged back up the stairs as the wind began to howl. I listened for the Blue Note; all I could hear were the grommets banging against the flag pole.

I went home and sat with Cat, he cuddled up on my lap. I believe he knew I was a little depressed. After an hour of staring into space, I got up and made a tuna sandwich for both of us. I left Cat curled up on my bed. I went down and warmed up the coupe for a minute or two and then made the rounds, no Sugar or Li'l John. I headed south to San Louie to see Ivy. He was in better spirits than the last time I'd visited. Morphine can do wonders. I told him about capturing Sloan Walker, he didn't seem to care. Because of what one of his attackers had said, Ivy still had this notion that I was in danger. He asked me to stop with the murder investigation. I'd made the promise and I was not going to stop. He didn't like hearing that.

Two weeks went by before Ivy was able to stand unaided on the repaired leg. His doctor signed the release form on the condition that I take him to a safe place. There were still three bad guys out there, we weren't taking any chances. I had a safe place for Ivy to stay. He wanted to go home to his cottage.

I stood by his bed trying to convince him to come with me. His doctor listened but didn't say one word. Ivy finally gave in. "Ok, let's go."

"Ivy, we can't just drive out of here in broad daylight, the bad guys could be watching. And I don't want anyone to know where I take you."

After an hour of arguing, Ivy finally gave in. I think he reasoned that leaving the hospital and going somewhere was better than going nowhere. That night I drove the coupe to the cliffs over the Blue Note cave while a taxi picked up Ivy. He was whisked away in secrecy to the safe house. I stayed and listened to the Blue Note for an hour as the stars above me twinkled and then I drove home. At closing time I snuck down and hid in Scout's Jeep. She drove me to the safe house. I waited for Domino to call.

"Hello."

"Hey Hawk, if you wantin' ta know if you and Scout was followed, the answer is no. But when you went to the Blue Note, the XKE was all ovuh yo ass. I thought you said he was outa the picture."

"I thought he was."

"Why is he followin' you again?"

"I don't know, but I aim to find out. Domino, thanks for all the help," I said. I was going to ask him something else when he interrupted me.

"Hawk, thanks is nice, but money is a whole lot nicer. I dun run outa money, if you want me ta keep woikin' you gonna have ta pay the piper."

"Domino, first chance I get I'll run by and pay you. Deal?" I asked.

"Deal, I'll talk at ya later on, bye," he said.

"Bye," I said to a dial tone.

Ivy was chauffeured from the hospital to the house directly across the street from Senator Rose's home in Creston. It was the house I had lived in for a few years. I worked it out with the owners, Rita and Jack Laramie. I stayed that night so I could introduce Ivy. After he was moved to the basement, Rita; Jack; and I made our way downstairs.

Ivy was standing looking out a ground level window at the dark world outside. When we walked in the room, he stumbled as he turned and smiled at the three of us.

"Jack, I asked the taxi driver where we were going but he wouldn't tell me. The further we drove the more familiar the drive became. And when we pulled up behind the house, I knew where I was. This is more like a dream than any amount of morphine can produce. Before I babble on any further, I want to thank you nice people for allowing me to stay in your home."

"After hearing what all you've been through, we're more than happy to help. As a matter of fact, we feel obligated," Mrs. Laramie said to Ivy.

"Yes, we do," Mr. Laramie agreed.

The three of them introduced themselves as they shook hands. Mr. Laramie excused himself and went upstairs. I had promised Detective Knox I'd call her after Ivy got settled in. I sat down at the desk next to the phone.

"It's late, before I go to bed, is there anything I can get you boys?" Mrs. Laramie asked.

"No I'm fine, thanks again," Ivy replied.

"I'm good, thanks," I said before dialing the number Detective Knox had given me.

"Who is this!" she snapped in a hoarse voice.

"It's me, Jack. You said to call, didn't matter what hour. Anyways, we made it and I don't believe anyone followed us."

"Did Domino tell you that?" she asked in a nasty tone.

"Yes, and if you're going to talk to me like I'm some repeat jaywalker, I'm going to hang up the damn phone." The line went silent. "Are you going to come down off your high horse?" I asked in my own crappy voice.

"I'm sorry Jack." I didn't say anything. "No, really I am. Listen, I have what I think is good news for you. The ribbon found on the pant leg is a match, and the boot print and paint match. But best of all, the forensic guys sprayed luminol on Sloan's sweatshirt and there were three small trace amounts of blood. Our district attorney told Sloan's lawyer and he said his client cut himself shaving. We knew he was lying of course, I mean he has a beard. Best of all the blood type came back AB negative," she stopped talking as if I was supposed to be impressed.

"Hang on," I said to her, "Ivy what is so special about the blood type AB negative?"

"It is the rarest of blood types. I believe it only occurs in one percent of all Caucasians."

I thought on it for a little before I decided to sound like a brainiac.

"So the chances of Sloan Walker having that blood type are about 99 to 1 against him."

"Jack, how'd you know that?"

"I asked Ivy, he's sitting right here with me."

"I should have known. Jack you jerk."

"Thank you. So what happens next?"

"Next, they'll try to plea bargain, but because it was premeditated, I don't think there will be any deals on this one. He's going away for life or..."

I didn't say anything; it was hard to think of a guy that young being put to death. Even though the crime was heinous, the thought of cyanide pellets was surreal. Where is he now?" I asked.

"He's in county 'til the trial. That could be a long time out. The district attorney wants to hold off 'till we grab Heath Abbey.

He says we'd save the state a lot of money if we try them both at the same time. Makes sense I guess."

"No, it doesn't make any sense at all!" I said in anger. "There were three men that took part in the murder. And the guy that chased Timmy into the trap is just as guilty as the two that murdered him. And that doesn't include the fourth person that helped attack Ivy. Jo, don't tell me you're going to quit on this."

"Jack, nobody is quitting on anything. But one in the hand is worth two in the bush," she said as I exhaled into the phone. "Jack, maybe Sloan or this Heath guy will tell us who the others are, there won't be any deals without them cooperating," she said as I exhaled again. "Jack, did it ever occur to you that there might be more than four? I mean for all we know there could be fifty. Jack! we have to take what we can get, period."

Silence.

"Jack, the sun will be coming up in a couple of hours. You're tired - go to sleep, bye," she said before the click.

The next night Scout came and picked me up at the safe house. It was a silent ride home. I didn't know where to go in the investigation and from her vibe, I think Scout was tired of hearing about it.

I continued looking for Sugar but with no luck. I figured she had moved on to greener pastures. The process was measured, but I finally came to grips with the fact that Sugar was never coming back. That said, the loneliness that came with the realization was unbearable. To have someone you love by your side one minute and gone the next causes a pain that I wouldn't wish on anyone. Yet each time I felt the ache, I knew my feelings paled in comparison to the crushing sadness Sugar must have experienced when, in the blink of an eye, she lost both of her parents. She was only seven years old.

35

The first day I didn't make the rounds was the day the earth stood still; at least it was for me. I spent most of the day on the roof shivering. It was cold out, but not that cold. Cat came up and sat on the couch with me, he'd never done that. He was lonely too.

I went down and turned on the electric wall heater in my bedroom. I stood in front of it shaking while I drank a beer or two. Between the beer and the sudden warmth, my eyelids felt like sheets of iron. I gave Cat what was left of a can of tuna and a saucer of warm milk before I fell into bed. I was instantly in a turbulent dream. I was standing on the roof looking down Broadway when a car I'd seen before drove by; I jumped off the roof and chased after. The driver had on a black hoodie. He turned in defiance and looked back at me, and although he wore a mask, I felt as if I knew him. I wanted to keep running but when I heard a young girl crying, I stopped.

I lifted my head off the pillow and looked around for a couple seconds, there was no one there. I fell back into the same dream, I had to catch this guy, but when I tried to run, my feet wouldn't move. The frustration yanked me out of my dream. I blinked a few times and the second I closed my eyes, someone shook me. I looked up into Scout's intense gray eyes.

"Jack, wake up, wake up. Jack! Get up!" she yelled before I heard the young girl cry again.

"Sugar!" I screamed at the top of my lungs.

Blue Note

I leaped past Scout and into my kitchen, there was no one there. I flung the front door open and ran halfway down the steps and sat right next to Sugar and wrapped my arms around her. I hugged her and I kissed her. I tried to wipe her tears away, but she put her hand up and stopped me. "Sugar, please talk to me, tell me what's wrong." She continued to cry.

"Ok you don't have to talk, I'll just hold you 'til you're ready to talk to me. I have all the time in the world."

I suppose taking a little pressure off helped because the sobs softened and she actually looked at me. I started to wipe the tears away again, but she did it for me.

"Jack, I'm so sorry, I didn't want to sneak around but we ran out of money. And John was so hungry," she whispered.

I had forgotten about Li'l John and without thinking, I looked up. Of course, I'd forgotten about Scout too. She was standing on my porch between the roof and me. She moved aside, walked down the stairs, and waved bye. Li'l John was smiling down at me, rosy cheeks and all. "Hi Jack," he beamed.

Something inside my brain itched. He had never called me Jack.

"John, come down here. We're going to go get something to eat," I said. I felt Sugar's shoulders relax a little, but only a little.

"Sugar, we're going to get something to eat but there's something else, what is it? Please tell me what's wrong? Please."

"So many things are wrong I don't know where to begin. I lied to you and I'm sorry. I don't want you to hate me any more than you already do."

"Sugar," I softly said. "I could never hate you and I don't think anyone else could either. You did what you had to do to survive and take care of John. Isn't that why you've always done everything to be the best sister you could? Well, you don't have to answer me, but I think you're a hero. Sugar, I don't hate you, I love you more than all the stars, and that's a lot," I said as she sobbed harder still.

John was standing right behind me now; tears cascading down his cheeks. Don't cry Violet, I'll take care of you," he said as he took a giant step over us and sat down in front of Sugar and held her hand. "Remember, we promised each other no more tears."

For him to use the name Violet caused a chill that shook my shoulders. Sugar reached out with her free hand and gently wiped a tear from his face.

"Yes John, you're right. I should have known you'd be the smart one and remember our promise to each other. Ok, no more tears. Would you like to ride in the fun car?" she asked.

"Ahh, hahh, yes, we all go for a ride," he said as he tilted his head towards me.

"John my boy, there is nothing in the world I'd rather do right now than go for a ride. Well, that's not entirely true because before we go for a long ride, I want to get you something to eat. How's that sound to you?"

John smiled and smiled, but not a word was spoken. He turned and walked down to the coupe and got in the back seat and waited.

"Sugar, is there anything you need before we go?" I asked. She shook her head no. "Ok, I'll meet you in the car in one minute."

I ran up and got the keys and put my holster and gun back on. It had become a habit. We took off across town, I was ecstatic and Sugar was still far, far away. Mel was so happy to see us all together again he said the meal was on the house. Of course, John said he liked eating on the roof. Other than John's smile, breakfast was a sober affair. I finally got to the point where I couldn't take any more silence.

"Sugar, I want you to look at me and tell me exactly what could be so wrong." I set my coffee cup down and softly said, "Please."

Still not one word.

"Ok, how 'bout we start with where you have been hiding or staying all this time."

She finally looked at me. "We took the bus back to the clubhouse in the mobile home park where Larry and Jeb live." I immediately stopped her.

"What Larry and Jeb are you talking about?"

"Jack, we decided to stop playing the game and start telling the truth and nothing but the truth. We were all living a great big lie. So they went back to their real names and so did John and I."

"Does that mean you want me to start calling you Violet?"

"No Jack, I like Sugar. I just don't want you or anyone else calling me Maid Marian. That's the make-believe part we're stopping. Understand?" she asked in a more Sugar-esque way.

"Yes, I do. But what about the Coke plant and Jackson, I mean Larry's job?"

"Duke said if Larry keeps coming to work on time and working hard, he doesn't care what name he uses. He did say something about names and taxes, but I don't really understand any of that," she said in an even more Sugar-esque way.

I didn't say anything because I had so much running 'round in my head. Then it hit me.

"Sugar, did Friar, I mean Jeb, know you were in the clubhouse all this time?"

"No, he didn't know. So he didn't lie to you, at least not at first. But remember, we were friends before I ever met you. And friends and hobos have to stick together."

"So what you're saying is he found out you were staying in the clubhouse and then after that, he had to lie to me," I said in a half-hearted angry voice.

"Jack, hobos have a code of honor just like the knights and their round tables. He couldn't tell you I was there, you understand don't you?"

"Yes Sugar, I understand completely."

"And guess what else happened or changed while we were away?" she asked with the first smile I had seen from her in weeks.

"Now I am John," John said from across the table. He smiled and then went back to his pancakes.

"Yes, you are John and you always will be," Sugar said before she looked back at me. "Jeb finally showed Larry the legal paper he used to get him out of the horrible place where he lived when he was a boy," she said waiting for me to ask what the paper was. I didn't catch on.

"I can't wait any longer for you to figure it out. The paper was Larry Ford's birth certificate," she said and then patiently waited for me again.

"Does that mean?"

"Yes, Jeb Ford is Larry's father."

"Oh gosh that's great. No wonder Fr, I mean Jeb always took care of Larry. That's great news."

"Jackie, I'm sorry about your dad. Do you miss him?" Sugar asked.

"Yes, but not… never mind. So Sugar is that what was bothering you so much. I mean Jeb lying to me about where you were?"

Sugar had been smiling and talking with such ease but the moment I mentioned the reason for her angst and ire, she put up another brick wall.

"Please Sugar, we're more than friends, and friends and hobos stick together, remember?"

Her shoulders dipped and her head slumped before she said, "Jack, we were broke and John was eating everything Larry and Jeb had in their fridge. So I snuck by to get my money out of your freezer," she said and stopped and turned away from me.

"Sugar, please tell me. Remember, we're friends." A tear fell to the floor. "Don't forget, I love you more than all the pretty notes in all the beautiful songs that have ever been played, and that's a lot."

She gently touched the scar over my eye.

"Does it hurt?"

"Only when I laugh."

She gazed at me and then I think something in her heart told her to tell me the truth.

"Jack, I snuck in your apartment while you were sleeping, I'm sorry. I was just going to get a little money, but my money is gone. Someone stole my money," she said and then stopped and frowned. "They stole your money too."

I started to tell her that I had put my money in the bank when the realization hit me. *Yes, I put my money in the bank, but not hers. Someone really did steal her money.* The rage inside of me began to boil, it only took one look and Sugar knew. I got up from the table and walked the length of the counter and out the door, Sugar was right behind me. I walked all the way to my car and then stopped. I closed my eyes and put my hands over my ears to make the world go away. I breathed slow and easy and said to myself, *there couldn't have been that much money*. I opened my eyes and did my best to smile.

"Sugar, how much money was there?"

"I had saved a hundred forty-two dollars and eighty-five cents. Why?"

"Remember when you told me not to put your money in the bank?"

"Yes, I remember."

"Well, I decided your money would be safe in the bank with mine, I'm sorry," I said. She looked at me with a pair of very suspicious eyes.

"Really, Ivy went with me, oh God. Did you know about Ivy?" I asked.

"Yes, I was going to ask. Is he ok?"

"Yes, he's much better. Scout will take us there tonight. Would you like to go see him? I think seeing you and John would help lift his spirits."

"Yes, we would love to go see Ivy. He is one of the best people a girl or a great big guy could have for a friend. You're very lucky," she said as she took hold of my hand and pulled me towards the diner.

We finished our breakfast with smiles on our faces. Sugar asked me to take her to see the men in the hobo cave. I gave her all the money I had in my pockets for the guys, wasn't much, but. Afterwards we drove up the coast highway for about ten miles. It felt great to be out with Sugar and John. On the way back I made them promise to never run away again. We all crossed our hearts and hoped to die.

We turned around and headed back. When I drove in the parking lot, Scout was waiting for us.

"Jack, Detective Knox came by, she said it's urgent that you call her."

"Did she say why?" I asked.

"No, so call her," Scout said as she walked back into the Redwood.

Sugar and I went up to the kitchen, but John kept going up to the roof. I dialed and after only one ring, the detective picked up. "Jack, is that you?"

"Yes, what's so urgent?"

"It's great news. Sloan, with the urging of his attorney, has decided to tell us the, who, what, where, when, and why for Timmy Allen's murder. We're going to take his deposition tomorrow morning. And, he promised to tell us where Heath is. Almost sounds too good to be true, doesn't it," she said with a smile I could see through the phone.

"Yes, it does. Remember you said that. I've heard of guys getting cold feet just seconds before they were supposed to spill their guts, has to do with honor among thieves. Sorry, I don't mean to be a downer. Can you give me a call after you talk to him? You're going to record it, aren't you?"

"We sure are," she said, I started to say bye. "Wait, there's more. Scout told me Sugar came back, I'm happy for you."

"Thanks, I'm happy for me too. Ok, I'll talk at you tomorrow, bye."

"Jack stop, there's more. Are you there?"

"Yeah, I'm still here."

"I received permission from the Mayor and the Chief to bring Suit in if we saw him. Well, I'll bet you haven't seen him, have you?" I started to answer her. "No, you couldn't have because we had him here in the station. Guess what he does for a living?"

"I don't know, is he a lawyer?" I asked.

"Yes, but that part's no surprise. Guess who he works for?" "Who?" I asked. "He's a muckraker, or I should say he works for a muckraker group."

"What?"

"Muckrakers, they dig up dirt and gossip on famous people. He was hired to find out if Senator Rose really did kill Timmy Allen. They want him to be guilty; someone wants the senator's job. So Suit, with your help, got too close to the truth. Somebody threatened him with bodily harm if he didn't quit on the whole thing. That's why you were terminated."

"Who did the threatening?" I asked.

"He doesn't know because it came in the form of a note on his car."

"Wait a second, that can't be true. He's still following me."

"Who told you that? Domino!" she said with a whole lot of attitude.

224

"Stop hatin' on Domino, and yes, he told me. Suit can't be too afraid, can he?" I said. "Say, what's Suit's name?"

"His name is Boyd Dunlop and Mr. Dunlop went back to his people and told them he needed protection. He told me he's protected now. So Suit is going to stay on you until he gets the answers his people are looking for. They still think Senator Rose is involved. Do you?" she asked.

"Jo, I really don't know. And at this point, I'm not sure I care. I think the assholes that killed Timmy are the same ones that attacked Ivy. And if you find out tomorrow who that is, I will probably be out of the picture."

"Jack, I don't like hearing that, you've done so much to help me," she said before she stopped and thought on what I'd said. "I'll call as soon as we're done tomorrow. It might be as late as twelve noon, but whenever it is, I promise I'll call. Bye Jack, and thanks for all your help," she said in what I took to be a sincere voice.

"You're welcome, bye," I said as the thought of finding out who attacked Ivy caused a slight tingle.

36

Late that night we tried to stuff John in the back of Scout's Jeep. We got him in, but there was no room for Sugar and me. Hurtwood ended up letting us take his Riviera. Scout drove out of the parking lot all by herself; at least it looked that way 'til the three of us sat up. According to Domino, because there are lights flashing all over the place, it's easier at night to tell if you're being followed. I kept an eye out; there were no cars behind us or anywhere else for that matter. It was after two in the morning and all the roads and highways to Creston were as Domino would declare, 'bare-ass-nekid.'

This time when we drove into the safe house, lights out of course, I asked Scout to come in with us. She balked at first but the chance to see Ivy and his little safe house was too much for her to pass up. Of course, there were a lot of introductions to be made. First off I had to assure Mrs. Laramie that John was harmless. He does make quite a first impression.

After the introductions were made, we started down the stairs to see Ivy. Mrs. Laramie came down with us. I guess Ivy heard the noise coming from up above, he was waiting for us.

I don't remember seeing so many hugs in one place at the same time. John actually lifted Ivy up a foot off the ground and shook him a little. Sugar had to remind him of Ivy's injuries. John apologized and as Ivy straightened out his back, he said, "Jack, I hate to spoil the reunion but Detective Knox called only two minutes before you drove up. She asked for you to call her office when you arrived. She sounded a bit uneasy."

I picked up the phone and dialed while all the others stood and watched.

"Hello Jack!" Detective Knox hollered.

"Yes, it's me, what's wrong?"

"Everything is wrong!" she yelled and then stopped. I hate when people do that.

"What is it, just tell me. I can't stand this, Jo just say what's wrong, say it," I urged.

"During dinner there was a fight in the mess hall at county jail. All the guards were ordered in to break up the fight. Afterwards all the inmates were told to go back to their cells. Sloan Walker was found hanging in his cell, there were no witnesses. He's dead," she said with a sigh.

"Geez, here we go again. Every time we get close we start slip-slidin' away. I guess he decided he wouldn't be able to live with himself if he ratted out his friends."

"Jack, I don't think he had any friends."

"Why do you say that?"

"I said it because it's tough to hang yourself with your hands tied behind your back."

"He was murdered, shit! Now what-da-we- do?"

"They're trying to find out if any guards or inmates witnessed anything. But you know how it is in the joint; everybody is suddenly deaf and dumb. Jack, enough of that, there's more." I waited for the rabbit punch to land. "Suit's XKE was found out on the old creamery road burnt to the ground."

"How about Suit, where's he?"

"In the car," she said, followed by silence.

I set the phone down on my lap and stared out the ground level windows at the dark of night.

"Jack, are you alright?" Mrs. Laramie asked as she hurried to my side. She wrapped her arms ever so tight around me.

"I'm ok Mom," slipped out.

And while the others stared back and forth at my mother and me, I put the phone back to my ear.

"Jo, I have to hang up. I'll talk at you... I don't know when, bye," I said as she yelled stop.

"Jo, make it fast," I said.

"Jack, I think you should move your car to a safe place, and I think you should tell Domino to do the same. I've seen situations like this before. The people that we're getting next to are angry as hell. They're not going to stop now; I think they've only just begun. Jack, maybe you should stay out of sight for a few days, maybe even a week or two. This is not something to ponder. I want you to act now, please," she said in what I'd call a desperate voice.

I hung the phone up, my mom still had a tight hold on my arm. Ivy led the assault.

"Jack, I know something spooked you, and I care about that, we all do. But before we get to that, I want you to explain why you told me your mom and dad were dead?" Ivy said in a raised tone unlike any I had ever heard from him.

Scout's eyes were crossed when I glimpsed her way. Sugar had taken on a stunned appearance, John smiled at me.

"Ivy, I never once told you my mom or dad was dead." He started to object. "I told you that there was a prison riot at the Montana State Prison and that Jack Hawkins Sr. had died. I told you that to protect my dad's new identity and whereabouts." Ivy boldly stopped me at that point.

"Wait a darn second, are you telling me that the man that lives in this house is your father?"

"Yes I am. Ivy, I told you my dad was one of the most wanted bank robbers of his time, or any other time for that matter. Do you know how long and hard the FBI tried to track him down. They were relentless. And that was before he was sent to prison. Once he escaped, we, my mom and I, had to go on as if he were dead. And if you can't get it thru your head how difficult that was, then…" I blurted out before my mom decided I needed help.

"Ivy, Jack has had to live his entire adult life with two fugitives for parents. I guess he could have turned us in for the reward money, but… Ivy what would you have done? What would any of you have done given the situation? I dare say you'd try to keep your parents safe," Mom said in a soft voice.

Scout was the first to sit down and gaze up at my mom; the others were silent in thought. Ivy broke the silence. "I'm sorry but do you think of yourself as Mrs. Hawkins or Mrs. Laramie?"

Blue Note

"Jane Hawkins was a young adventurous girl, I'm Rita Laramie now, have been for a long time and I'd like it to stay that way."

"How did the name Laramie come about?" Ivy asked as the others waited for the answer.

"That part is a little more complicated," she said as she looked at me. "Jack, we've come this far, I think I should tell them the whole story. Is that ok with you?"

"Yes Mom, but now is not the time. This is an emergency and I have to get back to Blue Note, right now! Ivy, I'll see you first chance I get. Sugar, you and John are going to stay here. Scout, let's go," I said as I stood up and gave my mom a kiss on the cheek. I did the same with Sugar. "Come on Scout, we have to hurry," I said as we ran up the stairs.

Scout drove us back to the Redwood to get my car. It was three in the morning and all was very quiet. I went up and called Domino, he didn't answer the phone. I was in a full-on panic at this point. I ran down and jumped in the coupe. I headed out of the parking lot purposely going in the wrong direction. I was not taking any chances. If they wanted me, they were going to have to drive very fast. I took the long way and when I was a couple miles away from my parent's home, I shut the lights off on the coupe. I eased up the drive and past the house. I opened the garage door and put the coupe inside. For now she was safe.

I went inside and hurried down to Ivy's room and dialed the phone. I saw Ivy sit up in bed, didn't say a word. I let the phone ring and ring. Someone with a nasally voice finally said, "Hello."

"Domino, is that you!" I hollered.

"I'm sorry, you've reached the operator," a lady said into the phone. "The number you're trying to reach is no longer in service. Would you like me to dial a different number for you?"

"What! When did this happen?" I yelled.

"Sir, I can't help you if you're going to yell. All I know is the phone is no longer in service."

I hung up and hurried up the stairs and down the hall to my parent's room. I knocked on the door. Someone get out of bed; by the grumbling I heard, I'd say it was my dad. The door opened.

"Jack, is your watch broken?" my dad asked.

"No Dad and I don't have time to explain. A life may depend on me hurrying, I need a car. Can I borrow yours?"

"Sure you could, if it was here, but it's not. Damn foreign cars are always breaking down. You can use the ranch truck if you want. It's out in one of those empty stables. The keys are in the kitchen, so if you gotta go then go, but be careful."

"I will, thanks Dad."

I drove out of the stables with the lights out, kept it that way for at least a mile or so before I turned the lights on and put my foot to the floor. The old truck was used for hauling hay at one time; it was not used for fast getaways or anything close to that. I headed straight for Domino's mobile home. I saw the flashing lights from a long ways away.

I pulled off the road and parked. I walked up as close as I could before a sheriff's deputy told me to stay back. The XKE was still smoldering as it was pulled up onto a tow truck. I asked the deputy what had happened. He just lifted his shoulders and said, "Car got burnt with some poor sucker still in it, that's all I know. I hope you didn't come back to the scene of the crime?"

"No, I was on my way to a friend of mine's trailer, he lives behind the old creamery building."

"Well, I'm sorry to have to tell you, but your friend's trailer is gone too. Burning as we speak, we don't know yet if he's still in it."

I looked past him in a panic before I took off running back to the truck. "Hey, you can't get near the trailer, they've got it all blocked off!" he yelled at my back.

I tore past the tow truck and once I cleared a small hill, I could see the flames and the flashing red or whatever the hell color lights they are. I did the exact same thing I had just done with the XKE, I pulled over and parked the truck. I ran up to the first cop I saw, another deputy.

"Stop right there," he ordered.

I yelled, "Is there anyone inside the trailer!"

"We're not sure yet, do you know the person that lives here?"

"Yes, he's my friend Domino Culpeper. Let me go see, please," I begged.

"Sorry, that's out of the question," he said as he moved towards me and pulled his gun from its holster. "You'd better stay right here. I think the sheriff would like to talk to you. Stay there."

The deputy walked away and a minute later the same sheriff I'd seen at Ivy's cottage walked out from behind one of the fire trucks. Took one look and he recognized me.

"Jesus, you know some folks leave a trail of bread-crumbs. You leave a whole different kind of trail. I suppose you know the person that lives here," he said in the same haggard voice."

"Yes, he's a good friend," was all I said.

"And the foreign jobby down the road?" he asked.

I nodded my head yes.

"Ok, make it fast. Who lives here and how do you know him?" he said in a more aggressive voice.

"His name is Domino Culpeper and he's a friend of mine. He helps me find people."

"That's right, you're a private dick. So, does this have anything to do with that professor that had the tar beat out of him?"

"Yes, the car down the road, the professor, and this trailer are all connected. Before we go any further, is there a car in the garage?"

"What garage?" the sheriff asked.

"I know it might not look like it, but that's a garage connected to the trailer. Domino built it all by himself. Can I please go have a look, please?" I asked in my nice guy voice.

The sheriff lifted the tape and led me over towards the trailer. It was just too damn hot to get close enough to see inside the garage. But from where I was it didn't look like there was a car inside, I hoped. I walked over to a fireman that was standing next to the fire truck.

"Did you see a car in the garage?"

He pointed to his ears.

I yelled the same question to him again.

He shook his head no and I felt some of the angst and ire walk away from me. Once I was pretty sure Domino's car wasn't in the garage, I walked out to the road and started waving my arms like a crazy person. I thought for sure Domino was watching, but I received no response. I figured I had just enough time to get back to my mom and dad's before the sun came up. I took a circuitous route back to Creston, that's what Ivy calls it. And with the truck lights off, I parked it back where I'd found it. I went in the house and down the stairs. Sugar and John were both up and ready for their day. I looked around, no Ivy. I started to ask.

"John carried Ivy up the stairs, he wanted to see the rest of the house," Sugar said.

The three of us went up and into the kitchen, my mom, dad, and Ivy sat at the table. They were smiling when we walked in, the smiles quickly faded when they saw my face.

"Well," my dad said.

"My friend Domino's home was burned to the ground. Did he happen to call here?" I asked everyone in the room. All I got were shakes of the head, no. I walked down the hall and into one of the spare bedrooms. I was followed by two women.

"Jack, this is now Sugar's room. Were you looking for a place to lie down?" my mom asked.

"Yes and this room will do fine," I said.

"No it won't, Sugar is not eighteen and you are not sleeping in her bed, period."

My mom has been strict with me since I was a kid, but this was a bit much, even for her.

"Ok then, I'll use the next bedroom."

"I'm sorry but John has the other bedroom. There's a hide-a-bed in the basement closet," she said as free and easy as all get out.

I didn't say another word, I just sleep-walked past Sugar as she blushed. I went down the stairs and rolled the hide-a-bed out of the closet. I waited about a half an hour and went back up to sneak in Sugar's room; my mom was waiting for me. She made it real clear something bad would happen if I tried sneaking up there again. I walked stoop-shouldered downstairs and was asleep before my head hit the pillow.

37

My mom gently shook me 'til I parted the build up of crust on my eyes. She was talking, but I didn't really hear one word. I finally sat up on an elbow.

"Mom, what'd you say?"

"I said the detective has been calling for a couple of hours now. I think you should return her call, then you could go back to sleep."

"Ok," I said as I sat up and put my feet on the floor. I looked over at Sugar, Ivy, John, and my dad as they watched Soupy Sales point a pea-shooter at some lady. When the pea hit the lady on the rear-end she flipped and turned summersaults while the four of them laughed their silly heads off.

They paid no attention to me as I picked up the phone and called Detective Knox. She answered after a couple of rings.

"Jo, is that you?"

"Yes, are you ok?" she asked.

"I don't know. So far I've had one friend beat like a drum and still another has had his home burned down. So if you're asking about my physical self, yes I'm ok. But the mental me has crossed the river Styx so many times I reek with guilt." She said nothing. "Jo, my mom says you called several times. Please tell me what bad news you have so I can go back to my night-sweats."

"That's one reason I called. Jack, why didn't you ever tell me your mom and dad lived right here in our backyard?"

"That is a question I'm not going to answer. So what is the other reason you called?"

"Jack, I absolutely hate it when you act like some stupid-ass secret agent."

"Next," I said.

"Ok, I talked with the sheriff. He told me you were there. Have you heard from Domino?"

"No, next question."

"Jack, the fire chief went out this morning so he could look for signs as to how the fires were set. Do you know what he found?"

"Yes, I think I do. He found a matchstick next to the XKE and one next to Domino's trailer. Is that what you were going to tell me?"

"Yes, how'd you know?"

"Because, after Mason burned the side of the Redwood he left a matchstick there too. I found it a day later. I guess that's his moniker or calling card or whatever the hell you want to call it. We're dealing with one sick son of a bitch."

"That's exactly what my chief said.

"Jo, so now the question we have to ask is, have Timmy's murderers joined forces with Rat and Mason?"

"I've already asked myself that question and the only answer I come up with is it looks that way, but why?" she posed.

"I don't know why but I do know we have a two-headed monster on our hands. And I plan on chopping off the first head I see."

"Jack, what if the monster sees you first?"

"I won't let that happen," I blustered.

"I'm sure that's what Suit thought too," she said. "Jack, when the fire investigators finally got in the car, they found out Suit had been duct-taped to his seat. He was alive when the car was set on fire. These aren't your garden variety killers. They're organized and willing to kill to keep their purpose a secret."

"Where was this protection Suit was so sure of?" I asked.

"I don't know, I'll bet he asked the same question. Jack, why do you think they killed Suit?"

"I don't know, but it's not a coincidence that Suit was so close to Domino's trailer. And if he found Domino, then the bad

Blue Note

guys did too. In fact, that has to be what happened. I guess they decided to kill two birds with one stone. Dead men tell no tales. You know what Jo; if the bad guys are making a list and checking it twice, then you and I are at the top of the list." I said. She didn't respond. "And everyone we know is probably on that list with us."

"I know," was all she said.

"So where do we go from here?" I asked.

"Nowhere, Jack, stop shaking trees. Let them make the next mistake, please."

"You honestly think they're going to make a mistake?" I said more than asked.

"Yes, they always do. Stay out of sight. And make sure to keep everyone with you out of sight, please," she begged.

"I will."

"Jack, I hope Domino is ok. If you hear from him, let me know immediately. Stay in touch and out of sight, bye," she softly said.

"Jo, you do the same, bye."

The second I hung up I dialed the Redwood. Mr. Hurtwood answered the phone.

"Mr. Hurtwood, it's me Jack."

"Hello Jack, you know it's kind of crazy that you still call me Mr. Hurtwood. Don't you think it's time you used my first name?" he asked.

"Um, ok what's your first name?"

"Wait, I thought you knew. Cotton is my first name."

"Cotton, you say. I like it, Ok Cotton, can you please go up and lock my door, and make sure Cat is not inside the apartment, please?" I asked.

"I take it you won't be back for a while," he said, I didn't answer him. "Ok, I'll lock the door and make sure the cat is not stuck inside. Anything else?" he asked.

"Well, nothing other than the usual. Keep an eye out for that tan Bonneville, Rat and Mason, and anyone else you think looks suspicious. I can't give you this number, but I'll call now and then. Cotton, thanks for all your help, and I mean it."

"Thanks Jack, I know you do. Be safe, bye."

I set the phone down and the moment I did my mom asked if I was hungry.

235

"No, I'm not hungry."

"Well, Sugar and I are going to make dinner a little early today. So maybe you'll be hungry in an hour or so."

I looked at my watch to see what time it was. It was three in the afternoon. I had been sleeping for nearly eight hours and I still felt exhausted. I took a shower and when I came out, everyone had gone upstairs. I got dressed and then looked out the ground level windows for a while. The sun was bright, it was a nice day out and here we were stuck inside. I was just about to head upstairs when a limo pulled up to the senator's house. Butler Dowdy hurried out and held the rear door open for Senator Rose. The limo drove off and the butler disappeared inside the house.

"Jack, your dinner is ready," John hollered down at me.

I went upstairs and everybody was sitting at the table waiting for me.

"Violet, I like when you say the grace prayer, would you do it again, please?" John asked Sugar.

I think that was a first in my parent's home.

"Lord, thank you for this food and a special thank you to Jack's mom and dad for letting us stay here. Please protect all the children in the world and don't let any of them get hurt. Please make it safe for John and me to go out on our rounds. And let there be peace on earth and goodwill towards men. That's all, amen," Sugar said with a smile.

"That was very nice," Mom softly said.

Sugar blushed when John grabbed the bowl of potato salad. He stood up and walked around the table and heaped a big spoonful on everybody's plate. My dad got a kick out of watching him. Sugar did her best to explain that sharing food was the way things were done in the hobo cave. Sugar asked John to sit down and wait for the food to be passed to him. He did as she asked. At first the table was silent and then small talk led to Ivy asking if he could hear the story as to how I'd acquired more than one last name. My mom narrowed her eyes at my dad and then me; we both shrugged our shoulders and nodded ok.

"Excuse me," Ivy interrupted. "Before you begin I want to say that only a fool could have looked at the three of you and not seen the resemblance. Jack, if you melded your mom and dad you would be the exact replica thereof. How did I miss that?" Ivy said as he scratched his head.

My mom slowly scanned the kitchen, "No sense in beating around the bush, Jack's father's father and his father and so on were all moonshiners. My husband was only six years old the first time his father went to jail. When his father returned a year later, he sat my husband, Jack, down and made him promise not to ever get in the moonshine business. He wanted his son to find a respectable occupation. And so Jack did."

"Robbing banks," Ivy butted in.

"No, not robbing banks, driving fast cars. But at some point, Jack came to the realization that there was no money in cars, but there was a lot of money in banks."

"Here, here," Ivy saluted.

My dad looked at Ivy as if he was a nut, and in my mind, he was right. Mom started up again.

"I was pregnant with our son, Jack, when I rode the bus to the prison in Deer Lodge, Montana. That was the first time Jack senior told me how easy it was to give a child more than one name," Mom said just before Ivy interrupted again.

"Why in the world would anybody want or need more than one name?" Ivy questioned.

"Ivy, you didn't raise your hand. And if you interrupt again, I'm going to tell my mom to stop. Do you understand?" I ordered more than asked.

"It's not polite to talk when someone else is talking," John reminded Ivy.

"Yeah, so butt out," I said as I looked at my mom. "Mom if he stops you again, I'm going to have John carry him back downstairs."

"So I got back on the bus, oh I forgot to tell you my sister, Darla, was with me. So we got back on the bus and twenty minutes later my sister delivered Jack. We went in the hospital and Jack Hawkins had a birth certificate. I put Jack under my coat, we took a bus to Laramie and I went in the hospital there and told them I'd just had a baby. They put his little feet on an ink blotter and gave me a birth certificate. My sister and I had fun and decided to keep going. After three days of riding buses we ended up at my sister's home in Memphis, Tennessee."

Ivy raised his hand. My mom just nodded to him. "So are you telling me he has a birth certificate with the name Jack Memphis on it?" Ivy asked as he looked at me.

"Yes, he does," my mom said with a giggle.

"How many names does he have?" Ivy asked.

"There are four altogether; that is there were four 'til his friend Larry took one of the names."

"He's giving the name back," Sugar said.

"Oh good, then there's four," Mom said with a smile.

"Mrs. Laramie, didn't you have to prove that Jack was just born. I mean didn't they clean him up the first time he was born?" Ivy asked.

"Oh of course they did, but we kept some of the gunk and the afterbirth. And when we went in a hospital, we'd put a little of the gunk back on him. To tell you the truth, I don't think they cared. And when you think about it, why would they?"

Ivy raised his hand again as he looked at my dad, "Jack, why would parents want more than one name for a child?"

"I was born and raised in West Virginia and you'd want as many children as you can get there. The more children you had the more state aid your family received. Hell, I know families that had three children, but the state thought they had six. Folks barely got by as it was in them hills; there was stiff competition in the shine business. It all makes sense if you think on it for a bit," my dad said as he drifted off in thought.

"Ok, I understand all that, but how'd you get the last name Laramie? That's one of your son Jack's names," Ivy asked thinking he was pretty smart.

Dad looked at Ivy. "We took Jack and his birth certificate to the county recorder and told them I was the father, but I'd lost my I.D. They gave me a state I.D. and that was that," Dad said and smiled.

"Was that before or after the prison riot Jack told me about?"

"After of course," my dad said as Ivy tapped his fingers on the table.

"There was a riot in the prison started by two inmates. These two held the Warden hostage, ended up killing the Deputy Warden and a prison guard. I didn't want any part of the riot, but I did want out of there. So I changed clothes with the dead guard and walked out of the prison in the middle of the riot. There was utter confusion; nobody paid any attention to me. A hellacious fire had been set and they found my prison uniform on a badly burned body, the state declared Jack Hawkins dead. Once they figured out the body was the guard, I was long gone. That's why I've had to live in secrecy for all these years," Dad said with that bank robber look in his eye.

"Well, you needn't worry about Ivy Fin. Your identity and so forth are safe with me. I will never tell a soul," Ivy said as he and the rest of us looked at Sugar and John.

"Mom, Dad," I said. "I guarantee you that Sugar and John know exactly why your real identity needs to remain a secret."

"Jackie, we know all about that," my mom said as she looked at Sugar and John with the caring gaze only a mother can give.

It was quiet around the house that night, but I could tell Sugar and John were itching to be set free. That night Detective Knox called again.

"Hello Jack, how're things?" she asked in a strange voice.

"We all have cabin fever, why?" I asked.

"No reason, I just thought I'd ask. Listen, the reason I called is the attorneys that own the XKE called and asked about Mr. Dunlop. They said Suit had told them a day ago that he'd made a deal with the enemy and he didn't need the protection anymore. That's why he was left alone. I told them about the car and Suit and they immediately said goodbye. Suit found out the hard way not to make deals with the Devil. Do you think they'll send people here to hunt for the killers?"

"No, they're chicken shits and they'll do all they can to distance themselves from Suit. No, I don't think you'll hear from them again, but that's just the way I see it."

"I think you're right, but somebody is going to have to claim the body or at least what's left of it."

"Thanks a lot Jo. I was going to have some desert, but now you've wrecked my appetite."

"Sorry," she said.

"Is that it?" I asked.

"Yeah, be careful and stay out of sight. I'll talk at you later, bye," she said as she hung up the phone.

Late that night I tried to sneak into Sugar's room again, my mom and dad were waiting for me.

38

Early the next morning, six frickin' o'clock early, Domino called me. He said he was staying with a relative in Compton. He sounded way too relaxed for someone whose home had just been burned down, didn't take long to find out why.

"Mornin' Hawk, so has you been lookin' all over creation fo po ol' Domino?"

"Yes, why didn't you call me? Shit, I thought maybe you were dead. What the hell happened?"

"I noticed a tail two days ago, it was Suit. That cracker son of a bitch had put a bug on my car without me knowin' 'bout it. How he did it I'm not sho. So anyways, I see him follow me home so soon as he drove away, I did the same. I watched him show them two whiteys where I live befo' they broke in; Jack, they drivin' a blue station wagon now."

"What make of car?"

"I don't know, I was too fer away."

"Did you see any whiteys with beards?"

"Hell no, it was just the three of 'em. So they walkin' back to his XKE and the little Rat sum-bitch hit Suit on the back of the head, busted his skull wide open. Then they tied the sum-bitch in his car and set it on fire. Jesus, you should have seen him squirm. I wanted ta shoot 'em when they was breaking in but I was too fer away. And they was hidden behind the damn creamery building, I couldn't get a clean shot. They walked off when they seen I wasn't there. I relaxed a little and then the fools went back and set my

241

home on fire. It went up like dry kindlin'. I think that fat one with the silly sailor hat knows what he's doin' when it comes to fires. He stood right next to the heat and screamed and yelled shit at the fire. He's one crazy sum-bitch, he sho is. And I ain't even lyin'. They took off and I took off after 'em, followed 'em all the way to that old warehouse by the Salt Works. They parked inside, so I slow-roll by and they come flyin' out a side do at me just a yellin' and carryin' on all crazy. Jack, what the hell have you got yosef into?" he said before the line went dead.

"Domino, Domino!" I yelled into the phone. He didn't respond. I set the phone down, a minute later it rang. The operator asked if I would accept a collect call from Domino. Of course, I told her yes.

"Hawk, is you there?" Domino asked.

"Yes, what happened?"

"My damn cousin grabbed the phone out my hand, said he ain't payin' fo no long-distance calls."

"Domino, I have some important questions to ask you. So be quiet for a little bit."

"But," he says.

"But nothing, be quiet!" I yelled.

"Hawk, I'll be so quiet you won't know I'm here. You know how I'll do that?" I didn't answer him. "I'll hang the damn phone up, that's how I'll do it. Hawk, those crazy mothuh-fuckuhs pulled out a damn rifle and pointed it at my ass. Befo' I could get away, they dun put two big holes in the trunk of my godt-damn car. Hawk, I ain't comin' up there no mo. I called my landlord and he says he has in-sho-ince. So I'll be gettin' paid fo all of my shit that was in the mo-biile home. I'll be sittin' pretty in a mont' or so. I don't need this buah-shit, so whatevuh it is you wants ta know, you bettuh ax me now. Go'headt, ax away," he said and then he was quiet.

"Domino, I understand why you're spooked. But I need to know if there were any other guys with them," I asked in a huff.

"I dun toldt you, no, they was by theyselves, wasn't nobody wif 'em at the fires they set. It was just them two crazy crackers," he said and stopped.

"Hawk, hang on fo a second, my cuz tryin' ta tell me somepin'."

I looked at Ivy, he mouthed, *"Who is it?"*

"Ok Hawk, what else you wants ta know?" Domino shouted into the phone.

"If you're sure there was nobody with them, then I guess that's it. Listen Domino, I'm glad you're safe, can you stay there with your cousin for a while?"

"Yeah, we chillin'. Hawk, you owes me two week's pay. But 'til this shit blows ovuh, I will be stayin' as fer from them crazy crackers as I can gets. You unnerstands, don't ya?" he asked.

"Yes, I understand completely. Do you want to give me the number where you are?" I asked.

"No, that's what Cuz just got thu tellin' me. He don't want you or any other whiteys callin' his crib. That's just the way it is in the hood."

"Ok, I just thought of something else. Are you talking about that old garment warehouse?"

"Yeah, the one full of rats and termites and shit, damn thing is ready to fall over."

"Yeah, the city was supposed to demolish it. Ok then, be safe and thanks for all your help. I hope you get rich, if you need something you make sure to call me. I'll talk at you later, bye now."

"Later days," Domino said as he hung up.

"Who was that?" Ivy immediately asked.

"Domino, now don't bother me. I have to call the detective. You can find out what Domino told me by listening, ok?"

"Ok," he answered.

I dialed the detective, but the phone just rang and rang. *Shit, I have to let her know to go check out the old garment warehouse. I'll bet that's where they've been hiding all this time,* I thought out loud.

"Who has been hiding?" Ivy asked.

"Rat Johnson and Mason Cook have been hiding in that old warehouse by the Salt Works."

"What about the guys that attacked me?" Ivy asked with a little attitude.

"They weren't with Rat and Mason, and it doesn't look like there's a connection between them. Shit! I still have to let the police know."

I picked up the phone again and dialed the Blue Note Police Station.

A lady answered, "Blue Note Police, is this an emergency?"

"Yes, it could be. Can you connect me with Sergeant Klavinski, please hurry?"

"Who should I say is calling?" she asked.

"Jack Hawkins, tell him it's important."

"Hang on sir," she said and then silence for a long time. Too long, I thought.

"Sergeant Klavinski here, is that you Jack?" he asked.

"Yes, thank God you answered. Listen, I just heard Rat Johnson and Mason Cook may be hiding out in the old garment warehouse by the Salt Works. We need to get somebody to check it out!" I yelled.

"Jack, I have personally gone there several times in the last two weeks. There's nobody there," he said in a calm voice.

"They were there the day the XKE was set on fire. They might still be there; oh and they're driving a blue station wagon now. Please?" I begged.

"Ok, if you say so I'll go check myself. I'll call back in an hour, bye," he said and hung up.

I paced the floor for an hour or so while Ivy, Sugar, and John watched me. I tried sitting, but it was no use. I was way too restless. I think they may have thought I was going to have an episode. Seemed like an eternity before the phone finally rang. I answered thinking it was the sergeant, it was Detective Knox.

"Jack, I just got word about the warehouse. The sergeant called me, there's nobody there. And no sign that anyone has been there. Who told you, and when did they tell you?" she asked.

"Domino called this morning and…"

I went thru the whole damn story with her. She was patient with me and afterwards said I was right in having them check the warehouse. She asked if Domino was safe and so on. I ended up more anxious than I was before I talked to the sergeant. It was one more dead-end. I hung up the phone and then fell back into bed.

Blue Note

The sun was starting to come in through the ground level windows. The room filled up with light, I couldn't have gone back to sleep even if I'd wanted to.

A day, then two, then three went by without a word from anyone. We were all going stir crazy. That night Sugar talked my parents and me into letting her and John go stay with Larry and Jeb at their trailer park for a few days. After all, they had nothing to do with this mess. Ivy actually walked on his own up the stairs and out to my dad's truck that night. He rode up front with Sugar and me, John was happy to ride in the back.

Ivy and I stayed longer than we'd anticipated. Jeb told us the entire story how Larry ended up in a home for wayward children and how Jeb finally got him out. It was especially nice to hear a story about a father and son reunion. They finally had a phone put in their home and Sugar promised to call me every night. The ride back to my parent's home was dark and lonely. Hours ran into days and so forth without a word from Detective Knox or for that matter, anyone. Ivy was on the mend, I wasn't.

39

Sugar did as she promised and called every night. She and John were back in their routine, or rounds, as they call it. I don't know what night it was, they all seemed to run into each other. Anyways, I took Ivy to the hospital and he had the cast on his leg removed. Although he walked with a noticeable limp, he was in heaven. We drove straight from the hospital to my apartment; I just had to see how Cat was doing. He purred to beat the band when I walked up the stairs to meet him. We went inside and I started to give him a saucer of milk, but the refrigerator was empty. I went down and borrowed a little cream from Scout. Cat sat and slurped up the cream like the vagabond he is. I was happy to be home, and I think Cat was too. As Cat drank, I walked around the apartment and at some point, decided it was time to move back. I mean how long was I supposed to hide from the bad guys. Ivy talked to Hurtwood and Scout for a while and then slowly made his way up the stairs.

"Hello Cat," were the first words out of Ivy's mouth.

Ivy sat down at my little kitchen table with a peaceful look on his face. "Jack, when are you going to move back home?" I started to give him an answer. "Jack, I have decided to go back home to my cottage. I'm sure you understand that I can't stay with your parents forever."

He was right of course.

"Ivy, I was just thinking the same thing. This story has probably run its course. And the truth is, I don't really care anymore." Ivy looked at me with his dark eyes. He looked puzzled.

Blue Note

"I'm sorry Ivy, I know I made a promise to you but it seems lately I'm chasing the wind. Maybe I should just let the police do their job. They might get lucky." We smiled. "Are you disappointed in me?"

"Jack, after I was attacked, I told you to leave the whole thing alone. No, I'm not disappointed, for the first time in weeks I'm content and happy. I think we should go to your parents, thank them, and then get ourselves back home where we belong."

"I think you're right, there are plenty of other people out there for us to find," I said as I watched Cat devour his supper. "I thought about taking Cat out to my parent's house, but now I won't have to."

I opened the door and let Cat out so he could terrorize the neighborhood. I had just locked the door when the phone rang. I looked at Ivy and he shrugged his shoulders. *Maybe it's important*, I said to myself.

I hurried back in and picked up the phone, it was Detective Knox. "Hello Jack, your mom said I might find you there. Everything ok?" she asked.

"Yes, any reason why it wouldn't be?"

"No Jack, I just thought I'd ask. I called to tell you we found the blue station wagon abandoned down in Santa Barbara, turned out it was stolen."

"Anything left in it?" I asked knowing the answer.

"No, clean as a whistle."

"I thought so, you keeping busy?"

"Yes, with the usual B and E and so forth. Jack, you sound worn out or something. Anything I can do?"

"No but worn out is a good way of putting it. Tomorrow I'm moving back to my apartment. Don't see any reason to hide anymore."

"I suppose not, ok, stay in touch. I'll talk at you later, bye," she said in her own tired voice.

"Bye," I said, don't think she heard me.

I hung up the phone and closed the door to my apartment and had just stuck the key in the lock when the phone rang again. *Shit,* I said to myself. I turned and looked at Ivy; he shrugged his shoulders. I rushed back in and picked up the phone.

"Hello Jo?"

"No asshole, it ain't Jo," Rat Johnson said.

I wanted to holler at him, but I kept my big mouth shut.

"What, cat got your tongue? I've been calling every night just to say hello. Where have you been hiding, Jack?"

I couldn't help myself. Ivy must have seen the look on my face. He came back in and frantically waved his arms as he whispered for me to hang up. The curiosity in me said, *don't hang up*.

"Rat, find someone else to call, I'm out of this now."

"Oh, no you're not!" he screamed. "I told you I was going to get you for what you done to me that day at the cliffs. I plan on keeping my word. You ain't out of anything, you fuck!"

"Rat, I'm going to hang up now. Then I'm going to call the phone company and have them trace the call. Go ahead call back again and then we'll all know where you are, you little chicken-shit, punk-ass Nazi!"

He stayed on the phone for a few seconds. I heard a child in the background over and over saying, "Hurt me Mommy, hurt me Mommy." It had to be Mason Cook, but it sounded like a nine-year-old, girl. I heard the phone rustle around as Rat handed Mason the phone. "Hot, hot, hot, it hurts, that's what you're gonna say. Hot then cold, hot then cold."

Rat yelled, "Give me the damn phone. Jack, I forgot to thank you for the money I took out of your fridge. That was just the beginning, make no mistake about it, I'm gonna get you, you miserable asshole!" he hollered into the phone before it clicked.

I dialed the operator and explained what had just happened. She didn't seem that excited to help. I screamed, "I'm talking about a couple of murderer's. Now get busy and find out where the call came from. You hear me!" I shouted before I hung up the phone. I immediately called Detective Knox at the police station. She answered after a couple of rings.

"If this is an emergency, call the dispatcher," she said from a distance into the phone and before I could get a word in, she clicked.

I screamed, "Wait!" at nobody.

I called the operator again, except it wasn't the same operator. I had to explain the whole damn story again, and once again I was met with resistance. So I asked for a supervisor. It took forever before a lady said, "I'm Supervisor Hastings, and you are?"

"I'm Jack Hawkins, this is an emergency. The guy that called–"

"What's the guy's name?" she asked.

"Rat Johnson and he has a sicko with him named Mason Cook, they murdered a man only days ago. Call the Blue Note Police Department, they know all about it!" I hollered.

"Can I give them your name?" she said in a snotty voice.

"Yes, give them my name or any name you like, just call them ok," I said in a more controlled voice. Least I thought it was.

"Mr. Hawkins, I'm going to do as you have asked. If this is a hoax, I will have you arrested, do you understand me?"

"Yes fine, just call the damn police," I said in a controlled yell.

The supervisor clicked off. I sat down and explained to Ivy what had happened. Didn't take a mind reader to see he doubted his decision to move back to the cottage. We waited and waited and then someone knocked on my door. I had my gun out and in two hands ready to fire when Scout yelled, "Jack! Can I come in?"

I let her in. "Jesus Jack, I heard you yelling. What the heck is going on here? It's after two in the morning."

She started to sit down but turned and went out the door. Five minutes later I heard her walking up the stairs. Didn't say a word, she just sat down at the table and handed each of us a bottle of Bud.

I went through the whole damn story again. She sat and sipped on her beer. I had never seen Ivy drink a beer, but he had his bottle empty before mine. He eyed Scout in the middle of an important part of the story and she handed him another beer. I wasn't quite finished with the supervisor part of the story when the phone rang. I jumped at it.

"Hello," I yelled.

"Jack, don't yell at me!" Detective Knox yelled.

"Jo! Why'd you hang the damn phone up on me?" I hollered.

"That was you?" she asked.

"Yes, it was."

"I thought I heard a frantic child on the other end," she said with a chuckle.

I started to yell again.

"Jack, the operator traced the call to a phone booth down in Pismo Beach. You didn't really think Rat would call from wherever it is they're hiding out, did you?"

"Jo, you know what?"

"No, tell me," she said and laughed at me.

I didn't say a word.

"Jack, I've informed the Pismo police. If they see either of the idiots, they'll arrest them on the spot. I'd say Rat was yanking your chain; and it sounds like it worked. Jack, they won't come anywhere near Blue Note, you know that, don't you?" she asked.

"No I don't, he came here and stole... Oh to hell with it. I'm sorry I kept you up this late. Say, how in the world did the operator find you?"

"We have ways, go to bed Jack. I'll talk at you another day, I'll see ya, bye," she said.

I softly said bye, but she was already gone. Ivy polished off three beers as we sat and shot the shit with Scout. I guess the beer had loosened Ivy up because he looked at me and said, "Jack, I'm feeling as ardent and swarthy as my bioanthropological Sami ancestors, what do you think about that?"

"That's great, just great," I said.

"Jack, I think you'd better take Ivy back to your parents and put him in bed," Scout warned.

"No, I'm staying and having another of these fine elixirs," Ivy slurred.

We let Ivy drink one more and then I carried him out to Dad's truck and plopped him inside. He was sound asleep before we made it out of the city. About halfway home he woke up and yelled at me to stop. I let him out and he puked all over the side of the road. I suppose four beers for an inexperienced drinker on an empty stomach was too much.

40

I woke up the next morning, Ivy didn't. I closed the curtains so he could sleep it off. I went upstairs and ate breakfast with my mom and dad. It might have been my imagination but I think they both missed Sugar and John. I say that because Mom complained about having to do the dishes without Sugar. And my dad complained about having to take out the trash all by himself. It had become a Dad and John affair.

After breakfast, I watched the morning news with my dad, it was interesting only because I hadn't had a television for a couple of years. I was up to date with all the world's events when I went down to see if Ivy was up. He had opened the curtains a little, but I think the light was too much for him. He had flopped back into bed. His face was a strange color. I went over to shut the curtains and looked over at the senator's house. I could just barely see the back of the sea-sprite green Woody I'd seen a couple times at the bowling alley. I moved to a better vantage point.

"Jack, will you please close the curtains?" Ivy asked from a prone position. I didn't answer him. "Jack, please," he repeated.

"I can't, not just yet Ivy, I'm looking at the sea-sprite green Woody I saw a couple of times at the bowling alley. The owner must know the senator or butler Dowdy. I don't know who owns the car but I aim to find out."

"Jack, how could you know what color it is? You're color blind," Ivy said as he set his arm over his eyes.

"He knows what color it is because I told him what color it is, and many times," my dad said from behind us as he continued down the stairs.

My dad walked over to me and looked across the street at the car. "Jack, do you know whose car that is?"

"No Dad, I don't."

I waited for a response from my dad but he was up the stairs before I could turn around. He came back down a minute later.

"Jack, can you call the detective and find out who the car belongs to, I have the plate numbers."

"Yes, I suppose so, why?"

"Because I've never seen that car over there and I don't like it. The plates are California, yellow with black numbers," he said as he handed me a piece of paper with the plate number.

"How'd you get this?" I asked.

"I walked out on my own damn front porch, that's how," he said.

I called Detective Knox, she answered with a lazy hello.

"Jo," I screamed into the phone. Can you run a plate for me?" I hollered.

"Why?"

"Because I asked you to, that's why. Please Jo. There's a car parked in the senator's driveway that I saw at the bowling alley a couple of times."

"Jack, give me the numbers or letters, just read me what's on the plate!" she yelled.

I read, "Z78 024," to her.

"Jack, is there a black number up in the right-hand corner?" I asked my dad, he lifted his shoulders.

"My dad couldn't see it."

"Ok, stay by the phone, bye," she said.

I went over to the window and watched with Ivy and my dad. There was nothing to see.

"Jack, explain to me how you know what color that car is," Ivy said.

"Ivy, if I see something a couple of times and I've been told what color it is, then I know what color to say it is. My dad had a car that was the exact same color. He said sea-sprite green was a very popular Ford color, especially in the fifties. Dad, what year is your T-Bird?"

"It's a 57 porthole. Fun car, 'til I blew it up. It's out in the barn.

"What about traffic lights?" Ivy asked.

"Oh, that's easy. If it's on top I stop. Only problem I have is flashing lights at night. I have to go real slow so I can see if it's flashing on the top or in the middle," I said when the phone rang.

"Hello!" I hollered.

"Jack! I told you not to yell into the phone."

"Sorry, is that you Jo?"

"Yes, of course it's me. If you yell again I'm not going to tell you whose car it is. Are you going to yell?" she asked.

"No, I promise. Whose car is it?" I asked in a controlled volume.

"The car is registered to William D. O'Dea," she said before I hollered shit into the phone. "Jack, you said you wouldn't yell!" she yelled.

"I'm sorry, I couldn't help myself. I can't believe this shit. How did I not see it? Jo, they all grew up together, they all went to school together, and they all joined the Blue Notes together. Fuck!"

"Jack, I don't ever want to hear you talk like that again. You hear me!" my dad yelled.

"Sorry Dad."

"What's all the yelling about?" my mom yelled down at us.

"Nothing, we're just telling stories is all," my dad yelled before my mom shut the door.

"Jo, I have to make a call. I'll call you back in a few minutes, bye," I said as she yelled for me not to hang up the phone.

I dialed the operator and asked for the phone number for Cabrillo Lanes. It took all of five seconds before she told me the number. "Can you dial it for me, please?"

She dialed and a young man picked up the phone. "Cabrillo Lanes, George here."

"George, please put Jill on the phone, this is an emergency," I said. He hesitated. "George, put her on the phone, right now!"

"I'm sorry, but Jill isn't here today."

"Shit! Ok George, do you know Billy?"

"Yeah, I know him, but I wish I didn't. Say, are you that Private Investigator guy?"

"Yes, and I need your help."

"I'll do anything if it helps find the guy that killed Tim."

"Ok George, has Billy ever worn a beard?"

"Yeah sure, wasn't long ago when he shaved it off. Of course, all the girls freaked and told him how handsome he was without the stupid beard."

"Is he there today?"

"Billy O'Dea?" he asked.

"Yes, Billy O'Dea, isn't that who we were just talking about?"

"Billy quit work a week or two ago, said he's moving back east somewhere. His paycheck is still here on the boss's desk. He never came to pick it up."

"George, do you know whether Billy was in the Blue Notes?"

"Yeah he was. All those older guys were. If you ask me, they're nothing but a bunch of jerks."

"George, do you have an address for Billy?"

"Yeah, it's gotta be on his employee card. Give me a minute," he said. He was back in a flash. "You ready," he asked.

"Yes, I'm ready."

"He still lives with his parents; the address is 233 Daisy Street. You know what's funny," he asked.

"No, tell me," I said.

"I always thought the initial D in the middle of his name was for dick, but it's for Dowdy and that butler, Jacob Dowdy is a dick. I guess if the shoe fits you gotta wear it," he said and then chuckled at how clever he was. I thought, *they're all related.*

"Ok George, if anyone asks, you never talked to me. Got it," I said waiting for his response.

"Yeah, I got it. But how about Jill, do you want me to tell her you called?" he asked.

"No George, not even Jill. George, nobody can know we spoke, nobody! Do you understand?"

"Yeah, I'll keep my mouth shut."

"Ok thanks George, if this all works out, I'll make it up to you. Remember, nobody. Thanks for your help, bye." I said as I turned to my dad.

"Dad, let's go up on the porch. I want to get a better look at the side of the house."

"Follow me," Dad said.

"Ivy, you stay here and keep an eye on the car," I said as he gave me a pair of bloodshot eyes.

Dad took off without me. That's when I saw Billy's head travel along the top of his car. He limped around the car and opened the tailgate. Ivy screamed, "He's the one I shot! Jack, that's got to be him!"

My blood boiled as the humiliation of not seeing what was right in front of my face hit me. The buildup was a little more than I could handle. I felt a tingle before I lay down and closed my eyes.

"Don't say the coins," Ivy reminded me.

"I won't, I'm fine Ivy," I whispered.

"What're you doing?" Ivy asked as I reached for my gun. *Ivy would only slow me down.*

"I'm going to sneak over and have a look. You keep an eye out for me. If I'm not back in thirty minutes, call Detective Knox."

"Jack, are you sure about this?"

"Yes, I'll be careful. Just keep an eye out for me."

I ran and hid behind the same bush I had the first-time butler Dowdy surprised me with the gun. Billy was nowhere in sight. I ran across the street and ducked down behind the Woody. I heard voices out back. I opened the front door of the house and peeked inside, there was nobody there. I went thru the living room all the way to the kitchen. I looked out a corner of the window at what sheer treachery is all about.

A body was floating face-down in the pool. Jacob Dowdy and a big guy sporting a beard that had to be Heath f'n Abbey were both soaking wet as they argued over who was going in to retrieve the body.

"Jacob you little shit, that water is cold. I'm not going back in there again. And Billy's crippled. So it looks like you're gonna have to go in and fish him out."

Billy limped around the corner carrying the exact same kind of bag Heath had put Timmy in the night he was murdered, made my stomach turn. I felt a tingle and closed my eyes. I had a sudden desire to shoot each one of them in the face.

"Ok you two assholes can stop arguing now and get him out," Billy ordered.

Butler Dowdy slid in the far end of the pool and shivered. He grabbed the comb-over and pulled Senator Rose towards the shallow end. There were bruises on the senator's neck and arms. He must have put up one hell of a fight. Probably took them some time to drown him. The bag was opened and before they put him in, Heath tore the Hang Ten surf-shorts off the senator and turned to Billy and the butler.

"Look at the skinny little asshole, he walked around all tough, ain't so tuff now, are ya?"

"Heath you sicko, stop screwin' around and get him in the damn bag!" Billy hollered.

Once the body was in the bag and zipped up tight, Heath Abbey kicked the senator's lifeless body several times.

"Jesus Heath, why would you do something like that?" butler Dowdy queried.

"Shut up Jacob, I've done it a hundred times. He can't feel it, he's dead," he said as he made a face somewhere between a grin and a grimace.

The three of them sat down with their backs against the butler's little house. I took my gun out of the holster, I figured why wait around. I'm going to surprise them and if one of them moves, he's dead. I crouched and looked around the back door as Billy handed a revolver to Heath and another to the butler.

Shit! I said to myself as I moved back.

I was running my options when I looked up at the phone on the kitchen wall. I decided to call the detective. I pulled the hammer back on my gun and aimed it at the backyard while I reached up with my left to take the phone off the hook. I lifted the phone and when I heard the dial tone, a pain tore thru me as the crack of broken bones whipped across my ears. I turned to shoot when the gun was belted from my hand. The will to survive does not require thought, it's completely reactionary. I grabbed the bat with my right hand as it sailed at me the third time. I held on with all my might and was pulled to my feet. I kicked Rat in the groin two times before he realized I would soon overpower him and have control of the bat. He screamed with every ounce of strength he possessed before all the lights in Creston, California went out.

I'm not sure of anything but I believe I was dragged out to the pool. Don't think I walked there. A discussion was raging as my ears woke up and my battered eye began to see.

"Rat, where'd Jack come from!" Billy yelled.

"I don't know. I was looking thru the drawers in the senator's desk when I heard a noise. I walked real quiet like out to the dining room and saw Jack by the back door. I grabbed the bat and it was on," Rat said as he stuck out his chest.

"Yeah right, if not for us he'd a kicked your ass. Jacob, go out front and see if there's anybody with him. And stay out of sight," Billy ordered.

They all stood staring down at me. There was a pain running rampant that I finally narrowed down to my left arm. The butler came back.

"There's nobody out there. I didn't see a car either; how'd he get here?" the butler asked.

"I don't know but one thing I do know is we gotta get the hell out of here," Billy said to the others.

"Look at that goddamn arm of his. It's in the shape of a backward C. Never seen anything like it," Heath said to Billy and the butler. "I say we get it over with right here and now. Drowning is easy," he posed to the others.

"Bullshit! You're not drowning him. If you want the money I promised you for helping us, you'll leave him alone. Mason and I get him and that's all there is to it!" Rat hollered at the others.

With a matchstick dangling from his mouth Mason screamed in his little girl voice, "Hurt me Mommy, hurt me, hurt me Mommy, hurt me. It's gonna be hot, hot, hot. Hot then cold, hot then cold."

Rat, you better shut that sick fuck up or I'm going to," Billy barked at Rat.

"Mason, go sit in the car, I'll be there in a minute or two. Go on, aha, yes, keep going. Ok, Jack is going in our car and that's that. Trust me; he will never see the sun come up again. Mason is going to take good care of him. Now, we had a deal and I'm not going to let you go back on your word. So one of you help me put him in the car, I mean right now!" Rat yelled as he lifted his gun.

"Hey, there's no need for that, put that gun down!" the butler yelled at Rat.

"No, I will not!" Rat screamed. "I'll pull this trigger right now. And the cops will come running. Now help me get him in the car!"

"Put the gun down," the butler urged as he, Billy, and Heath backed away.

"Not until Jack's in our car, do it now!" Rat hollered again.

"Let 'em have him, we need the money more than we need Jack," Billy said to the others.

"Yeah, and besides we gotta get this silly senator in the ground," Heath added.

"Ok, help me get Jack in the car. I'll pay you tonight, but only after the job is done," Rat said.

My left arm was duct-taped to my side, then my right before I was blindfolded. They grabbed me by the neck and legs and carried me. I was lifted like a sack of shit and thrown in the back seat of a car. I felt the car backing up when someone pounded on the hood. The car jerked to a stop.

"You can't go out the front, somebody might see you," the butler said in a soft yell.

"Ok, then how do we get out?" Rat asked.

"See that maintenance path on the right side of the garage," the butler said. Rat didn't answer him. "Take that, it runs by the stables all the way out to the frontage road. I'm going to clean everything up then lock the doors. We're gonna bury the senator in one of the horse stalls. Then we'll be right behind you," the butler said in a matter of fact way.

The car started moving; the pain in my arm was unbearable. I got very sick. Rat reached back and slapped the crap out of me. The blood over my eye began dripping down my cheek again. He'd pushed the blindfold over just enough so that I could see a sliver of light out of my good eye. I turned my head a little and I was now looking at the back of Mason's head. He had his sailor hat slanted forward. I looked down at a piece of pink bone

258

sticking out of my arm, just above my elbow; I vomited. Somewhere along the way I passed out and when I woke, all was dark. Rat suddenly yelled, "You asshole, puking all over my car, I have to clean that shit up!" Then he reached over the front seat and flashed a driver license at me. "Who the fuck is Jack Laramie?"

"I don't know."

"That's not what Larry told me."

I thought, *how'd he get my license?*

"I'll make you a deal, give me back my gun and I'll tell you who Jack Laramie is."

"Yeah right," he said as he stuffed my license back in his shirt pocket. They got out of the car, and I passed out again. Sometime later Rat pulled me into darkness just far enough so he could pound my legs with the damn bat. I felt like a sack of shit.

"You're not so tough now, are ya asshole. You ought to see that arm of yours; looks like one of them bent macaroni noodles. Can't see your legs, but I know they're broke. Do they want to scream, Jack?" I didn't say anything. "Tough guy hah," he said just before the pounding began again.

Hitting me on the fleshy part of the upper and lower legs hurt, but when he hit the bones on the side of my ankles and knees it took my breath away. The pounding continued, I think he was making sure even if I wanted to, I couldn't run. And as quickly as it had started, it stopped. Rat pulled me out of the car by my boots and my head bounced off concrete. He dragged me for a ways and then stopped and asked Mason if the coast was clear. "Go, go, go," Mason whispered in his little girl voice.

Rat dragged me through a doorway and into a room. I started to look around when a blanket was thrown over my head. The kick to my ribs came as a surprise, it hurt something fierce.

"How'd that feel asshole?" Rat whispered.

With the blanket over me I could not get a handle on where I was. Time is a strange thing when you're not having fun. It passes, but minutes drag by like years. I kept telling myself, *time is on your side*. I was either falling asleep or passing out, I guess they're about the same, when I heard footsteps, and lots of them, come in the room. The blanket was torn off me. I was looking up into Heath Abbey's eyes. He had the same glower his cousin, Sloan Walker, had when he was shouting at me from the backseat of the police car. Heath stared into my good eye for a moment and then spit in my face.

"Don't kick him!" Billy yelled just before his foot found my broken arm. I wanted to scream but the only thing that came out of my mouth was puke.

Billy sat down next to me. "Jack, why'd you have to come looking for us? I told Ivy that if you stayed away nobody would get hurt. Why Jack?"

"Why'd you have to kill Timmy?"

"Jack, that's something you would never be able to understand."

"Try me, I'm listening."

"Shit Jack, he got Joe killed that night at the 7-Eleven. It was all Tim's fault."

"If you guys didn't trust him, then why was he involved in the first place? From what I heard Joe and Sloan are the ones that screwed the whole damn thing up."

"No Jack, Tim was the qui vive."

"The what!" I objected. "Speak English for Christ sakes."

"It's club talk for spotter, Tim was supposed to be the lookout. He came out to the car and told us the owner, Mr. Hill, had left. Said the coast was clear. So Joe and Sloan went in. Tim was supposed to keep a lookout for anybody coming back. But he just stood by the car; he didn't do what he was supposed to do."

"Who was in the car?" I asked.

"I was. I was the getaway driver."

"Why didn't you tell Timmy to get back and be the 'key' whatever? Sounds to me like you're the one that got Joe killed."

Billy slugged me in the face. "Don't you ever say that again!"

"I'll bet the guilt has been running thru your head ever since. Yep, sounds to me like Joe getting killed was as much your fault as it was Timmy's."

"Screw you," Billy said before he threw the blanket back over my head.

I wondered if Billy had ever told the others what he'd just told me, I don't think so.

"Jacob, why'd you have to kill the senator?" Billy asked Jacob, probably to change the subject.

260

"Because he heard us talking on the phone. After I hung up, I turned to go back in the house and he was standing at my door, it was open. Then he hurried in the house. I followed him so he couldn't get on the phone and squeal on us. He went in the bathroom and then I called Heath. And the rest, as they say, is in the bag."

"Squealers, I hate 'em all," Heath softly yelled. "I can't believe Sloan, my own damn cousin, was going to rat us out!" he bellowed.

"Who killed Sloan?" the butler asked.

"None-a-your business!" Heath yelled as he turned to Rat. "The job's done, where's our money!"

"I'm goin' to get it right now, wait here. And keep your voices down, a lot of old people live here. Listen, I want to thank you guys for helping me with them other three," Rat said as he dragged me outside. Then he reached in my pocket for my wallet, took the money out, and chucked my wallet up on the roof.

"Won't need money where you're goin'," he said before he surprised me. He untied my blindfold and took it off. Then he propped me up on my side.

"There's something you just have to see," he said before he walked over to Mason.

"Mason, are the accelerants ready inside?"

"Yes."

"Are you ready?"

"Not yet, I'll put the frosting on after the car is in place. Yes, dead men tell no tales. Hot, hot, hot, it's going to be so hot in there."

Rat drove the car up against the clubhouse door. I heard butler Dowdy yell, "Hey, what's going on, open the damn door!"

"Frosting is going on, frosting is going on," Mason sang as he and Billy doused the outer walls with gasoline.

Billy ran to the only window, raised my gun, and fired inside three times, inviting a back-draft. Then Mason lit the match that had been dangling in his mouth. He spit it at the wall and a titanic 'rumph' blew forth. And as the flames inside and outside the clubhouse exploded, the screaming began.

All three of the young men were pounding and pushing on the door, desperately trying to get it open. There was no way they could move a car. The horrific wailing and the cries for help that saturated the walls were haunting. "Let them out!" I screamed. "Shut the hell up," Rat said before he turned me to make sure I watched and listened to the misery as it unfolded. An arm covered with blood and blackness came crashing thru the window. Rat fired a couple rounds into the window and the arm disappeared. The screaming stopped, all I could hear was coughing.

They'd found a safe place away from the flames. Five minutes of silence went by as the flames and heat mounted and then the screams lit up again.

The intense heat beat my body and the flames licked at my face before Rat dragged me away from the clubhouse. Mason danced about and yelped as he watched Rat heave me up into the car. Rat circled the Bonneville and pulled me by the neck across the seat.

There was a crowd gathering, I only know that because I heard screams coming from outside the clubhouse that matched those inside. We drove thru the darkness of night. I heard sirens in the distance, but they faded as we raced away.

We drove hard but I had no idea where, that is 'til I heard the grommets on the flag pole. I listened for the Blue Note; it was faint but intensely blue. I thought I heard a voice or two but it could have been the wind. Then the grommets stopped clanking. Rat jerked the door open and drug me outside. I was on my side facing the flag pole. I immediately closed my eyes.

"Open your eyes asshole!" Rat yelled.

I kept them closed.

"Ok, you wanna play it that way. I can make you open your damn eyes," he boasted as he walked back to the car. He wrapped my blindfold on the end of the bat, lit it on fire, and marched over to me. He touched it to my face. I rolled away from him as fast as I could. Rat sniggered each time he leaped over me with the burning bandana. He burned my head, neck, and face so many times I thought, *what's the point*. So I stopped rolling and just kept my eyes shut.

"Ok, if fire won't do it, this will." I heard him pull the hammer back on my 44. He pressed the end of the barrel tight to my temple, "Now open your eyes or I'll close 'em permanent like."

Blue Note

I opened my eyes.

Larry was rolled up in a blanket, his head and feet were sticking out the ends. His face was awash with blood, he wasn't moving. I figured him for dead.

His dad, Jeb, was hanging from the flag pole, his feet maybe four feet off the ground. Mason and Rat had duct-taped Jeb's arms to a two by four that ran across his back; it was eerily Christ-like. He didn't move. I hoped he was dead. Mason doused him with a liquid he had in a metal container. He did a dance as they rolled Larry over to the mouth of the man-made stairs that go down thru the Blue Note cave. Mason danced his way back to Jeb and with a click of his front teeth he lit the match and spit it at Jeb's feet. Jeb went up in flames so fast I didn't have time to close my eyes.

Jeb frantically wriggled and screamed that ugly scream I'd heard at the clubhouse. And while he screamed, Mason danced over to Larry, spit, and lit him up. Rat kicked Larry a couple of times and then shoved him down the opening. Flames flickered and bounced off the walls as Larry plunged downward. I closed my eyes but I heard Jeb shudder and twitch to the end. All was silent when the stench of burning flesh invaded my nostrils. I didn't have time for the coins. I gagged, convulsed, and foamed at the mouth. Mason danced around me shrieking like a little girl. I'd say he liked my show. After I'd stopped twitching and drooling, Rat and Mason put me back in the car. And at great speed we raced away. One of the burns on my face had started to bubble around my cheek, made it hard to see. I guess the jostling around broke the skin open. It hurt like the devil when a patch of skin stuck to the seat and tore off.

We wound our way towards what I figured to be a new place of torture when Mason skidded to a sudden stop. Rat barreled out of the car and I heard what sounded like a chain-link fence swinging open. Mason turned and gazed back at me. His eye makeup had run clear down to his chin. His ruby lipstick was smeared across his cheeks. His eyes blinked nonstop as he rattled off his insane, hurt me Mommy, hurt me bullshit. Then without a warning he set his fish eyes on me and bared his teeth. I wanted to kick his teeth down his throat. *Lord, I hope you're listening cuz this guy needs to be dead. Might be wrong of me to ask, but can you please help me kill him.*

"You scare me," abruptly popped out of his match-stick mouth. "You'll be so hot, hot, hot. I can't wait to hear you scream while you shiver and shake. It's not nice to scare Mason," the little girl said.

"Mason, shut up and drive the car in here and get it out of sight. Hurry up!" Rat yelled.

Mason sped in the shape of a crescent around a corner. We wrenched to a stop and his hat flew off. The skin on his head had the patina of melted plastic, at some point he'd been burned hairless. Rat dashed over and yanked the door open, grabbed me by my pant legs, and hurled me to the ground.

"Mason, get his goddamn cross ready," Rat hissed just before he turned and glared down at me. "Jack, I'm going to love watching your face melt."

I think drowning would have been a whole lot better than being hung on a cross and set on fire.

A level of panic ran through me I had never experienced. The panic reached its zenith when Rat lifted a body out of the trunk, it was Sugar.

Before I could get a word or a scream out of my mouth, Mason hit me across the face with a two by four. He giggled so hard the matchstick flew from his mouth. He dragged me into a building and across a planked floor to a moonlit corner directly beneath a pulley, rope, and hangman's noose. I finally realized I was in the dry rotted old garment warehouse. I lay there transfixed on the noose while Mason pounded nail after nail into my makeshift cross. Then Sugar let loose with a blood curdling scream, "Let go of me!"

I wriggled and twisted and grunted so hard my bladder emptied. I tried to stand but my legs gave way. Then Mason dropped the cross right next to me. He pulled me up onto the board that would run the length of my body; he was sizing me up to make sure I'd fit. He retreated into the darkness but I could hear him huffing and puffing as he doused the walls with gasoline. *This is not just going to be a cross burning it's also going to be a damn funeral pyre.* Mason came back, matchstick dangling from his mouth. He'd covered his blue bell-bottomed pants and his Popeye shirt with a silver fireproof suit. He knelt down next to me and took a huge bowie-knife out of a pocket. I tried to squirm away. He pulled me back and cut the duct-tape off my broken left arm. I couldn't help myself, I had to scream. Mason paid no attention as he taped my crooked arm to the cross. I anxiously waited for him to cut my right arm loose, but he got up and walked over to a far wall and lit his match and spit. The same rumph I'd heard at the clubhouse exploded as the walls all around us went up in flames. "Hot, hot, hot, hurt me Mommy, hurt me," he sang as he danced his way back to me.

I was desperately trying to crawl so I could see Sugar. Mason grabbed the cross where my right arm would be taped and dragged me back under the noose. The heat inside the building was instantly overwhelming as the fire quickly spread across the roof over my head. Mason took the knife out again and held it so that the blade reflected the flames all around us. His eyes glowed as he drooled down the front of his suit. He shook his head once and then cut the duct-tape off my right arm. He looked back for the roll of tape so he could secure my arm to the cross. I forced myself to be silent as I struggled to bend at the waist. With all my might I reached down into my boot and pulled the derringer out. I cocked the hammer back with my thumb. I pressed the barrel tight to Mason's neck and squeezed the trigger. The pop was electric as was his response. Mason shot up to his feet as the matchstick plunged to the floor. He peered down in utter shock, his eyes screaming the terror his lips could not. He wrenched his neck from side to side; all the while his clown mouth agape. He sputtered and choked as blood filled his throat. I aimed at his face and pulled the trigger a second time. His great stomach was in the way as the bullet tracked upward entering his fireproof suit. He arched his back and flapped his arms just before he rose up on his toes and scuttled out the flaming doors and into the night.

Relieved, but at the same time confused and frantic, I turned over and began crawling with my right arm. The fire around me was crackling so loud I couldn't think straight. I finally got to a point where I could see Rat in a far corner, on top of Sugar.

Sugar was fighting him with all the strength she had, but Rat was overpowering her. He'd torn her blouse off and had his hands wrapped tight around her neck. My right arm was doing all it could but I had an entire building to cross. I screamed at my arm to work harder, but it would not respond. Flames and smoke filled the air above me, but all was clear next to the floor. I was getting nowhere so I came to a stop and tried to tear the tape off my left arm.

A shadow lumbered towards Rat and Sugar and then a huge knee pressed hard into the middle of Rat's back. Rat reached back in vain. John laced his fingers across Rat's face and as he grunted, he pulled back. Rat's screams exceeded all those I'd heard that night. John continued to pull back before he begged, "Violet crawl out, please move back!"

John pulled harder still as Sugar scooted back on her hands and elbows. John pulled until the skin in the front of Rat's neck split. Rat was clawing up and down John's arms in a frenetic death protest trying to stop him. His screams burst through the crackling fire in an ear-splitting yowl. The bones in his neck finally gave way and broke. His screaming peeked and then came to a sudden and furious end. The back of Rat's head now lay between his shoulder blades; his dead eyes staring straight up at the inferno that had been a ceiling. Sugar eventually squirmed her way out from underneath Rat. As he gazed at Sugar, John lifted his knee off of Rat's body. I think he said something to her; probably asked if she was ok. John picked Sugar up and didn't look back as he carried her out through the flaming doorway. My calls were muted by the roaring fire, they had no idea I was there.

I turned and in a last-ditch, all-out effort, started crawling towards the doorway. I knew I was going to die, but Sugar was safe and I was at peace when the entire red-hot roof groaned and crackled a couple of times and then collapsed on top of me.

I'd given Ivy strict instructions to wait thirty minutes before he called the detective. Ten minutes had passed when he watched the butler move the woody station wagon. He called Detective Knox; she was already on her way. When Sergeant Klavinski and the detective raced up the senator's driveway all was quiet. The house was locked up tight. At that point they put out an APB and then spent the rest of that day and night hurrying from one fire to the next.

41

No one really knew what had taken place that night; how could they. My parents and Ivy spent hour after dark hour trying to find out what had happened to me and where I was. They didn't say it, nobody said it, but deep down inside they all believed I was dead. Two days later my dad took the morning paper down to the basement and read it to Ivy.

"Blue Note Fire Chief, Henry L. Jones, says the badly burned body recovered from the fire in the old garment warehouse has been identified as that of Jack Laramie, a resident of the State of Wyoming. All six bodies recovered after the fires have now been positively identified. Fire Chief Jones says the fires appear to be the work of a 'Satanic Cult'."

Ivy stood up and drifted over to gaze out the window when my dad said to his back. "Ivy, I guess you still don't understand."

"What's to understand?" he said more than asked.

"Was Jack carrying the Jack Laramie I.D. with him?"

"Now that you mentioned it, no, Larry had the identification," Ivy said as his dark eyes boiled in thought.

"And the hobos found Larry badly burned but very much alive on the steps leading down thru the Blue Note Cave. Larry is in the hospital. So who is the body they found inside the garment warehouse?

Ivy, get dressed we have a lot of driving ahead of us," my dad ordered.

Dad drove Mom and Ivy in the coupe to the Redwood Tavern. They went up to my apartment, it was locked and empty. They went down to the bar; Scout was just opening up for the day.

"Hi Scout, have you read the paper today?" Ivy asked as my parents fidgeted.

"No I haven't," Scout said as she turned to my parents. "I'm very sorry for your loss; Jack was a one of a kind. I sure do miss him."

My mother just could not hold back the tears. Dad held Mom tight as he turned to Scout.

"Thank you. Scout, the reason we're here is a body found inside the garment warehouse has been identified as Jack Laramie, but Jack didn't have that identification on him, so we believe that can't be him. Has anyone from the hospital called or come by to check with you or Mr. Hurtwood?"

"Detective Knox and Sergeant Klavinski have been here several times. The detective is terribly upset, but other than them there hasn't been a soul here. Who is it you think should be here and why would they be here?" Scout asked.

"I don't know who, but it seems to me Jack would've had some identification on him. I know it's probably false hope and I don't want to go look at the charred bodies, but now I have to. Strange the people at the morgue haven't contacted us," Dad said as he pondered the puzzle. "Scout, thanks for always being there for our son, stay in touch," Dad said.

They got back in the coupe and Dad asked Ivy where Sugar and John would be.

"Since the clubhouse was burned down, they would either be in Larry's mobile home or down in the hobo cave. We're close now, so I'd say we should go to the hobo cave," Ivy said before he told my dad to drive to the Blue Note.

They parked in the scenic area and walked by the burned remains of the two by four next to the flag pole where Jeb had been hung.

"Wait here, I'll go down and check," Ivy said.

Five minutes later a vacant eyed Sugar and John appeared at the top of the stairs. As you could expect, Sugar was reluctant to talk about what all had happened that night. She did explain how three men along with Rat and Mason came and held her while they beat Larry and Jeb senseless. Then she was tied up, gagged, and stuck in the trunk of the Bonneville everyone had been looking for. She said after Larry and Jeb were tied up; gagged; and blindfolded, they were locked in the trunk with her. She said the three of them heard the screams when the clubhouse was burned down. Then she went on to explain how John saved her from Rat in the burning warehouse. She burst into tears as she said, "We never saw Jack."

"Sugar, how is it that John wasn't there with you at Larry and Jeb's trailer?" Ivy asked.

"We had gone to the hobo cave as we always do and took supper to the men. Then I rode the bus home and John went to the hospital to wait for our parents. Well, of course they weren't there so he went back to the hobo cave and that's when he saw the Bonneville drive away. The men that found Larry yelled at John to chase after the car. John ran to the warehouse and saved me," she said and stopped to kiss John on the cheek. "I did see that strange man Mason run out through the burning doors, but I never saw…" she couldn't finish the sentence.

"Ok, we have no choice but to go see the bodies they have. We know one is Jeb, but who is the…?" my dad couldn't finish the sentence.

They raced to the hospital, hopes on high, but were told they weren't allowed to see the bodies. My mother got on the phone and called Detective Knox. She made it to the morgue in record time. Detective Knox and my parents were led down to see the body Chief Jones had identified as that of Jack Laramie. An assistant to the coroner pulled back the sheet covering Rat's burnt and disfigured remains and they immediately knew it was not me. The other body was a hulking fat man with the charred pieces of a silver fireproof suit still stuck to his skin. Several men from the hobo camp had positively identified Larry's dad, Jeb Ford. My dad asked if there could have been any other burn victims admitted to the Blue Note Hospital and released, he was flatly told no. Detective Knox then asked the receptionist if she would check with the other hospitals in the area.

After the third call, Detective Knox was told that two badly burned men had been admitted to the San Luis Obispo Hospital. The detective told Dad to follow her. She turned on the siren and the flashing lights and sped away in her car. They all ran into the hospital at the same time. They were directed to room 210. They leaped up the stairs and burst through the door into my room. A nurse had just finished putting new dressings on my burns. I saw the crowd fly into the room but due to the fact that both legs were in traction and my left arm was in a cast that covered the arm and upper torso, they couldn't jump on me.

"Damn-it Jack! Why didn't you tell them to call us?" my mom screamed as she wiped the tears from her face.

"Yeah Jack, you big jerk! Why didn't you call somebody?" Detective Knox yelled at me.

"Stop yelling, all of you. I didn't call because I just woke up for the first time this morning," I said to their stunned faces.

"He's been heavily sedated. I'm sorry, but do you know him?" my nurse asked in a sour voice as she stood between the crowd of people and me.

"I'm his mother; now get the hell out of my way!" Mom screamed into the nurse's face.

The nurse moved but stayed next to my bed.

"Jack, how did you get here?" Mom cried.

"I don't know how I got here. I had given up and decided I was going to die in the fire. I saw John pick Sugar up and carry her out of the building and then the roof caved in and the lights went out," I said as Sugar gently held my hand. I looked at the nurse. "Do you know how I got here?"

"No, I wasn't on duty that night. I suppose I could find out how you got here. Hang on, I'll be right back," she said as she started for the door.

"There's no need for you to check, I brought him here," someone said from the other side of the curtain that separated the room.

The nurse pulled the curtain back and we all stared at Domino. He was propped up on his elbow, facing us. Half of his fro had been burned off. He was smiling like a lighthouse beacon. My mother, Sugar, and Jo Knox all hurried over to hug him.

"You can kiss me all you wants to but please don't hugs me. I got burns all ovuh my rear end," he said with a pained smile as all three smothered him.

Blue Note

"Domino, you told me you weren't coming back to Blue Note. What were you doing there?" I asked, totally confused by the moment.

"You owed me money and Cuz was all over my butt to give him somethin' fo rent. So we took off up to see you, that's when I decided to give that old warehouse a second look. Oh how I wanted them two sick mothuh f... that burnt down my mo-biile home. So we roll up and the whole place is on fire. A mess a hobos had that fat sucker wif the silver suit hangin' by his wrists from the top of that chain-link fence; scared the dookie right out of me. They lit his ass on fire and I couldn't believe my eyes. The sicko stared down at his burnin' feets and axshully smiled. Then I sees the big man run out carryin' you," he said as he pointed a finger at Sugar.

"Thank you so much for coming here and saving Jack," Sugar said with a wonderful smile.

"Yes, hah-hah, thank you," John repeated.

"Thank you from all of us," my dad affirmed.

"Then what happened?" the detective asked.

"So when I sees them, I just knowed Hawk had ta be in the area. I looked in and saw him on the flo tied ta that damn cross. Right when I started in, the roof collapsed on my headt. I grabbed a tight holdt on the cross and drug Hawk out. Cuz didn't know where the hospital in Blue Note is, so he brung us here. I dun passed out when the doctor took ta separatin' my shirt from my burnt backside. And that is just about the whole of the story," he said with a proud twinkle in his eye.

"Your cousin drove the 88 here?" Ivy asked.

"Sho did, and fast too," Domino replied.

"So you've been here next to me the whole doggone time?" I asked.

"I reckon so, I just woke up last night fo the first time mysef. Tried ta get ya talkin' but you was in La-La Land."

"Domino, I can never thank you enough for saving my life. But I just have to ask why you would risk your life and run into a burning building?"

We could all tell by the smile on his face and the immediate response that Domino had been itching for someone to ask the question.

Jack Hawkins

"I ran into that fiery hell because I likes my crackers salted but not burned."